On Sunday, 7th June 1981, Is destroyed the Iraqi nuclear installation at El-Tuwaitha. This is the subject and the heart of A. J. Quinnell's spellbinding new thriller. But there are many strands of recent history, of characters real and invented, of violence and vendettas woven into the complex secret aspects of 'the great game' that preceded the raid.

Part of the story began in Vietnam. Among the dozens of professional photographers from the world's newspapers, David Munger was outstanding. When one of their colleagues got killed - quite a common event - it was customary to auction his effects, cameras and their adjuncts, to raise money for dependants. Fancy prices were paid as charity. No such charity attended the auction of Munger's gear. Munger was still alive. Why had he packed up, deserted, vanished? No one knew.

A glorious heroine, Ruth Paget, plays a central and dramatic role. It is a story interspersed with murder and perversion, bribery and economic blackmail, religious and ethnic intolerance and, occasionally, with acts of intense love and courage. It is the story of a great photographer; his descent into a nightmare and his struggle to climb back out with the help and love of a woman.

The raid itself is the climax. The author postulates that something more happened on that fateful day than was ever reported.

A. J. Quinnell is a pseudonym. His first novel, *Man on Fire*, caused a stir on both sides of the Atlantic and was short-listed for a major award. Next came *The Mahdi*. With *Snap Shot* Quinnell takes another great step forward - it is compulsive reading, you have to turn the page.

A. J. Quinnell is the pseudonym of the author of ten novels including ***Man on Fire*** which was made twice into Hollywood Films - most recently directed by Tony Scott for Twentieth Century Fox in 2004, starring Denzel Washington, Christopher Walken and Dakota Fanning. The book sold more than eight million copies in paperback and was translated around the world.

Full list of titles:

Man on Fire
The Mahdi
Snap Shot
Blood Ties
Siege of Silence
In the Name of the Father
The Perfect Kill
The Blue Ring
Message from Hell
Black Horn

SNAP SHOT

SNAP SHOT

A J QUINNELL

First published in Great Britain by Macmillan London Ltd in 1982

Published by 48

ISBN-13: 9781908426994

With profound thanks to 'Multy' and 'Speedy'
for technical assistance with the aerial
and photographic sequences.

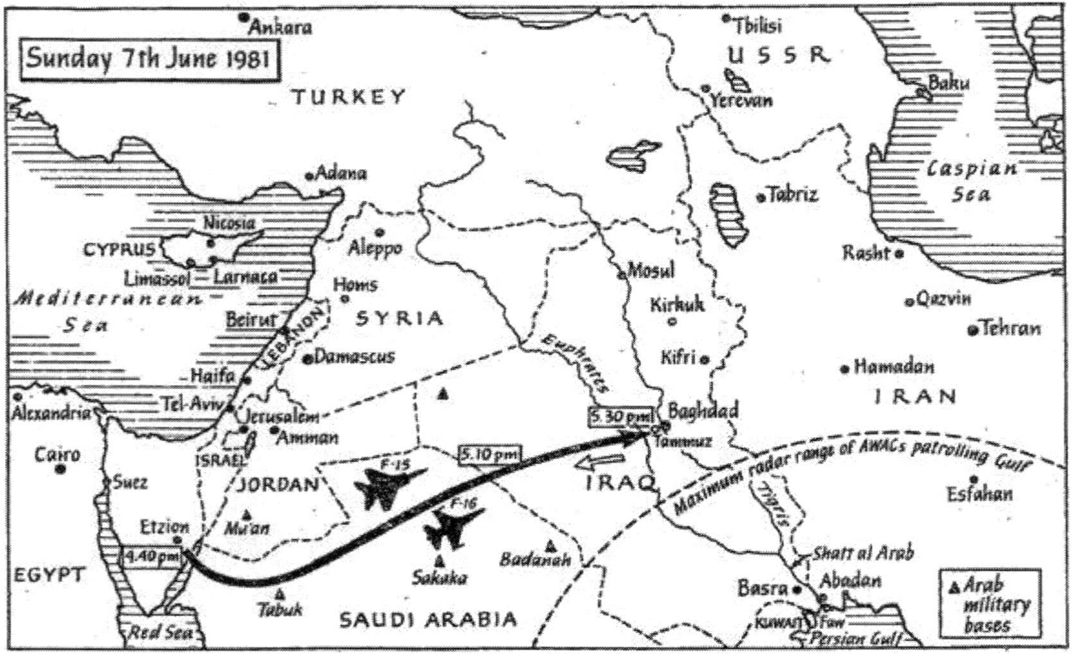
Sunday 7th June 1981
Ankara
TURKEY
Adana
Nicosia
CYPRUS
Limassol
Larnaca
Mediterranean Sea
Beirut
LEBANON
Aleppo
Homs
SYRIA
Damascus
Haifa
Tel-Aviv
Jerusalem
Amman
Alexandria
Cairo
Suez
ISRAEL
JORDAN
Etzion
Mu'an
4.40pm
EGYPT
Red Sea
Tabuk
SAUDI ARABIA
Sakaka
Badanah
F-15
F-16
5.10 pm
5.30 pm
Euphrates
Mosul
Kirkuk
Kifri
Baghdad
Tammuz
IRAQ
Tbilisi
USSR
Yerevan
Baku
Caspian Sea
Tabriz
Rasht
Qazvin
Tehran
Hamadan
IRAN
Maximum radar range of AWACs patrolling Gulf
Esfahan
Tigris
Shatt al Arab
Abadan
Basra
KUWAIT
Faw
Persian Gulf
Arab military bases

CONTENTS

PROLOGUE

At 16.40 hours on Sunday, 7th June, 1981, fourteen aircraft took off from the Israeli Air Force base at Etzion in the Sinai desert. All were advance fighter aircraft: eight F16's and six F15's. But for this mission the F16's had been stripped of their cannon and air-to-air missiles and armed instead with 2000 lb bombs and long range fuel tanks. The F15's were to act as cover and so retained their conventional weapons, although they too carried long range tanks.

The aircraft passed low over the Gulf of Aqaba, the F15's flying slightly higher and bracketing the F16's.

Six minutes after take-off the formation crossed the Saudi Arabian coastline and followed a course which paralleled the Jordanian border.

At 16.52 hours a Jordanian Air Force sergeant technician at the Ma'an base abruptly straightened in his seat as fourteen blips eased onto the radar screen in front of him. Thirty seconds later the Ma'an control tower was asking the aircraft to identify themselves. Their leader did so in fluent Arabic, explaining that they were a Saudi Arabian squadron on exercises from the base at Tabuk. He exchanged the appropriate code words and some pleasantries with the Ma'an control and they proceeded eastward. Three minutes later the fourteen blips slid off the radar screen.

There is no integrated military air control system between Jordan and Saudi Arabia. Consequently Ma'an control did not report the flight either to Tabuk or any other Arab air base.

At 17.00 hours the squadron banked onto a new course taking them East-North-East in a direct line to the Iraqi border.

Approximately 500 miles East-South-East of their position, an American operated A.W.A.C. surveillance plane was flying at 30,000 feet. It was on loan to the Saudi Arabian Government, nervous in the aftermath of the conflict between Iran and Iraq. Its sophisticated antennae were aimed eastwards over the Persian Gulf and the skilled and alert technicians saw nothing of the fourteen intruders who skirted the periphery of their electronic vision.

At 17.10 hours the aircraft passed undetected over the Iraqi border and sixteen minutes later were over their target: the French built Tammuz I nuclear reactor at El-Tuwaitha, ten and a half miles south-west of Baghdad. As the F16's climbed and wheeled to put the lowering sun behind them in the classic bombing manoeuvre, the F15's took up position to intercept any Iraqi fighters which might be scrambled in time to interfere.

At 17.32 hours the first F16 made its low level run and, with devastating precision, dropped its 2000 lb bomb through the reactor's protective dome. The others quickly followed, all performing with equal accuracy. Onboard cameras recorded the complete destruction of the reactor and the total success of the mission.

These facts became known and widely reported throughout the world.

What is not generally known is that of the eight F16's only seven dropped their bombs at El-Tuwaitha. The eighth made a brief diversion seven miles away.

During the raid several senior Israeli Air Force officers in the command room of the Israeli base at Etzion stood in a tense group listening to the radio voice-relays of the F16 pilots. Major-General David Ivri stood to one side. Next to him was a civilian. He was a gross intrusion amid the military atmosphere, for he was short but obscenely fat and dressed in a white linen suit with a dark green tie. Rings sparkled on his fingers.

As the voice of each pilot in turn reported the success of his bombing run, the tension among the officers dissipated to be replaced by rising exultation. Only the fat man retained his anxious expression. Then, after a brief pause, the voice of the eighth pilot crackled through the loudspeaker. It was the voice of a man the fat man knew well, for only a few hours ago he had been in deep conversation with him.

Now the voice came over the airwaves from 500 miles away and reported that he too had dropped his bomb - exactly on target. Slowly the civilian's tightly clenched fingers relaxed and a small smile straightened his over-large lips. One or two of the officers glanced at him curiously for despite his appearance they knew he was privy to secrets far beyond their ken.

The destruction of the Tammuz I reactor at El-Tuwaitha was one of the most controversial air raids in history. The blast created a global shock wave. The Iraqis, backed by the French, claimed that the nuclear installation was strictly for peaceful purposes. The Israelis claimed otherwise. In fact they viewed it as an imminent threat to their very existence. The story of the building of Tammuz I is interspersed with bribery and economic blackmail, murder and perversion, religious and ethnic intolerance, and occasionally with acts of great courage.

This is part of that story - and why one F16 did not drop its bomb on Tammuz I.

It is a work of fiction.

BOOK ONE

CHAPTER ONE

Click . . .

The bastardized Nikon crystallized the image of the black sergeant sprinting across the clearing with a clattering M16 at his hip.

Click . . .

In the next image he was spinning like a marionette, jerked not by strings but a hose of bullets from a hidden machine gun.

Click . . .

He was humped over on the ground. The last convulsive twitch of death, frozen onto film.

A cloud edged under the sun and Munger's fingers adjusted the aperture control. He heard a shouted command and saw the captain break from cover to his left, running in a shuffling crouch, submachine gun slung across his back, a grenade in each hand.

The two Belgians slanted in from the right, spraying the trees ahead with their M16's.

Click . . .

The Nikon recorded the Belgians' moment of supreme bad luck. The hidden machine gunner, faced with a choice, selected them as his first target. He was skilled and experienced. A two-second burst was enough to flop them back like rag dolls.

From opposite sides of the clearing the machine gun barrel and Munger's camera traversed towards the captain. Munger was faster.

Click . . .

The captain, diving forwards and hurling a grenade.

Click . . .

The captain on his belly, trying to squash his body into the earth as bullets scythed over him.

Then the crump of the grenade and a brief silence followed by more gunfire as the rest of the patrol charged across the clearing.

It was soon over and Munger turned away and saw the Vietcong prisoner sitting alone, arms bound behind his back, a noose around his neck tethering him to a tree. For a moment their eyes locked. The Asian's were inscrutable, the Englishman's blank. The camera came up.

Click . . .

It was the last frame on the spool.

They did not bury the dead, theirs or the enemy's. For these men, such a courtesy had long since withered. They marched quickly to get away from the scene and the hostile territory. The Meo scouts were out ahead. The captain had cuffed and kicked them for not spotting the ambush. He cared nothing for the dead members of his command but he cared a great deal for military skill and discipline. The lack of it created his only emotion: anger. It still smouldered long after they had bivouacked for the night.

He sat surly and uncommunicative whilst the others joked and made plans for their imminent R. & R. in Saigon. They would reach Vinh Long by noon the next day, hand over their prisoner and get a chopper ride to the big city.

Occasionally they glanced curiously at the photographer sitting by himself a few yards away. They felt pride at having him on their patrol; also admiration, for they had seen his courage under fire. Their own courage was bolstered by their weapons and they found it hard to understand how a man could face bullets with only a camera, could hold it steady and photograph someone trying to kill him. They discussed this for a while. The Australian thought that maybe he was so engrossed in his work he forgot about the bullets. The Frenchman thought otherwise.

'He has no heart and no soul - so how can he feel anything - even fear?'

The Frenchman was wrong. At that very moment Munger was experiencing fear. Not for his physical being but for his mind. There was something in the recesses of his brain that should not be there. Something trying to force its way forward. He was frightened because although only thirty years old, he had long ago concluded an exercise that gave him precise control over his emotions. He had a cast iron mental discipline, so it frightened him to have something bouncing around back there, out of control. He tried to pin it down, to capture and expunge it. What was bothering him? The horrors he had witnessed during the past ten days? The callous brutality of the men sitting so close? After ten years of such work he was immune both to horror and human brutality, just as he was immune to real affection or intimacy.

Was it something from the more distant past? His mind went back, assessing and cataloguing, but when it reached his boyhood a shutter came down - the shutter that always came down.

He gave up and, perhaps for something to occupy his mind, carried a water bottle over to the prisoner and held it to his lips. The water was gulped thirstily - all of it. Munger should have kept some for himself for the morning, but as he held the bottle to the prisoner's mouth, the prisoner's eyes held his, and he could not move his hand.

Had he thought about that, Munger might have understood what was bouncing around in the back of his brain.

Four nights later he was sitting at an outside table of a restaurant on Rue Catinat. The restaurant was busy, its clientele a mixture of servicemen, correspondents and businessmen.

On a chair just inside the main door sat the owner - a fat Frenchman. He was irritated with Munger for he was taking up a whole table and he had finished his omelette two hours before. Since then he had been drinking a succession of vodka sodas. Had it been anyone else, the owner would have made a comment just rude enough to clear the table, but he knew all about Munger - he was not a man to offend lightly. He watched him curiously and decided that he was ill; his lean face was pinched and his blue eyes sunk deep into their sockets. It could not be the drink for, despite a prodigious capacity for vodka, no one had ever seen Munger truly drunk.

Munger was not ill - at least not physically, He was, however, exhausted, for he had hardly slept for four days and now, even though his body and brain ached from fatigue, he could not get up and go back to his hotel room. He wanted no personal contact but he desperately needed the noise and movement of people around him. He needed something to occupy his mind - to divert it.

A brown, mongrel dog crossed the road, hopping between the cars, motor bikes and trishaws. It was a pathetic sight, small and scrawny and holding one front foot clear of the ground. There was dried blood on the paw; either a casualty of the traffic or some mindless cruelty. It started sniffing among the tables and one of the waiters aimed a kick. As it hopped away the restaurant owner nodded in approval. From his vantage point he could survey the whole restaurant and inside the bar. A minute later he nodded again in approval. Munger had called out to the waiter to bring him a large sirloin steak, very rare. Obviously the omelette had not been enough.

The dog sat out of range and watched with hungry eyes as the waiter put the plate in front of Munger, watched as Munger carefully cut the meat into cubes and then watched with rising disbelief as Munger leaned down, put the plate onto the pavement and beckoned. Slowly it edged forward, its nose twitching, its eyes darting back and forth between the pink meat and the astonished waiter.

The restaurant owner pushed himself to his feet. All the other diners had stopped eating and were watching Munger and the approaching mongrel.

'Monsieur . . .' began the owner indignantly. And then Munger turned and the owner looked into his bleak, blue eyes which had darkened and narrowed.

'It's paid for.'

All eyes, including the mongrel's, watched the confrontation. The Frenchman's mouth opened and closed like a beached fish. Then, with a shrug of disgust, he turned away. Someone laughed and the dog edged up to the plate and started eating. It was no longer nervous, sensing that it was under protection.

At a nearby table two American correspondents watched with interest. One of them said:

'Munger's getting soft in his old age.'

The other laughed, 'I doubt it. He probably did it just to rile old Montague.' They looked at Munger curiously, as he stared down at the dog rapidly clearing the plate.

'He looks ill,' the first one commented, and the other nodded in agreement.

'Maybe it's finally getting to him. He's been covering this war for years with hardly a break. He's hooked on it like a junkie and it's eating him from the inside out.'

'No,' the other disagreed. 'Until the last couple of days I've seen no change in him. Curious. He fiddled his way onto that Special Forces patrol but since he got back he's filed no snaps. None at all.'

The other shrugged. 'So maybe nothing interesting happened.'

'When Munger's around something always happens,' came the reply. 'No, something happened all right, but I can't think what it was that could bother a man like Munger.'

They turned back to their food and started discussing the latest peace initiative.

The dog had finished the steak and was sitting close to Munger's legs. He reached down and scratched the top of its head. Its tail thumped and it licked his hand.

He had not fed it to rile the restaurant owner. He genuinely liked dogs and had an affinity with them. It was the affinity of a lonely man - a man with a character so formed that he could find no way to communicate emotion to other human beings. It was said of him that he was merely a shell; nothing more than a finger on the button of a camera.

But for all that, he liked dogs.

Janine Lesage arrived from Bangkok two nights later. As she drove in a taxi to the city she felt relief and anticipation. She had been three weeks in Bangkok and she hated the place. It was a man's city, with its hundreds of massage parlours, dance halls and brothels. She much preferred Saigon. It also catered for men, but with the war on it had a masculinity which stimulated her. It also had Munger and she was eager to be with him.

It had been too long-over a month. As the taxi threaded through the raucous traffic she wondered yet again what it was that drew her to him and, again, decided that it was purely physical. She was a beautiful woman with an appeal to attract almost any man she wanted, but she was also a woman who craved and demanded sexual satisfaction and in Munger she had known a man who could give her that like no other. In a way it was frightening, for it gave him power over her and she resented that power. She tried to analyse her feelings. Did she love him? She laughed at herself. No. Maybe she hated him. His detachment, his hardness, his independence and his mental isolation. He needed no one. Maybe that was the attraction. She was a naturally dominant woman but found the fruits of domination uninspiring. As soon as she had a man under her spell she lost interest. She had known Munger for over a year and the physical need for him had never abated. She felt again a surge of anticipation. She had met Ram Foster at the airport on his way to Hong Kong and he had told her that Munger had recently returned with the remnants of a Special Forces patrol near Vinh Long. So she knew he would be in Saigon for some time. She was a little puzzled. Foster had also mentioned that as far as he knew Munger had not filed any snaps. He was acting a little strangely and drinking a lot, even for him.

The taxi pulled up at the Continental Hotel. She paid the driver and asked the doorman to collect her bags and, with a wave at a group of familiar faces on the terrace, strode through to Reception. The first thing she did after signing the register was to glance up at the row of room keys. 204 was missing, so Munger was in his room. She did not wait for her bags but went straight to the lift. The Vietnamese receptionist watched her appreciatively. She was wearing a beige shirt dress of Shantung silk - a tall, elegant woman with long, blonde hair coiled high on her head.

At the door of room 204 she paused, reached up behind her and pulled a long silver pin from her hair. It tumbled down, falling almost to the outer curve of her buttocks. She tapped on the door, heard an interrogative grunt, and opened it.

He was lying half-propped up on the bed in the corner wearing just a robe. His cheeks had the stubble of several days' growth. Automatically she said:

'Ça va, Dave?' before the impact of his appearance hit her. 'Are you ill?'

He shook his head.' No. Ça va, Janine.'

She crossed the room, saw the waste paper bin beside the bed and smelled the odour of burnt paper.

'What is it, Dave? What's the matter?' She bent over, kissed him tentatively on the lips and sat down beside him. He did not reply, just shrugged resignedly. She looked into the metal bin and saw the charred ashes of negatives and prints.

'What are they?'

'Some snaps I took.'

'Why did you burn them?'

Again he shrugged.

She reached down and found a print that was only partially burned. In the top corner she could just make out the face of a man. It was contorted, the lips peeled back from the teeth. At first she thought it showed fear or agony, but then, abruptly, she realized it was lust-sadistic lust. She looked up at him.

'You took this on your last assignment? What happened? Who is it?'

He took it from her and glanced at it, then reached for his lighter on the bedside table and put a flame to the charred print and dropped it back into the bin. She watched the smoke curl up.

'Tell me what happened.'

'No, it doesn't matter. Anyway, it's finished. I'm packing up,'

'Packing up what?'

'The whole game.'

Her face showed amazement. 'Your work? You're giving it up? Why?'

'I've had enough.'

'What will you do?'

'Tomorrow I'll go to Hong Kong, leave my camera with Chang to be auctioned and then I'll leave the East and try something else - somewhere else.'

She shook her head as if to clear it from a daze and then studied him closely. There was a haunted look in his eyes. Suddenly she felt she was watching a child - a lost child. First it astonished her and then, being the kind of woman she was, it intrigued her.

'Won't you tell me about it?' she asked persuasively.

He shook his head emphatically. 'There's nothing to tell.'

She did not press it. She stood up and paced the room, getting her thoughts together. On the table she saw the Nikon with its disfiguring attachment. With that camera Munger had become a legend. Why would he give up and sell it? That only happened when a photographer died. She turned to face him.

'OK Dave, we'll talk about it later. You look exhausted.' She glanced at her watch. 'I ate on the plane. Are you hungry?'

'No.'

She smiled. 'Then we'll sleep.'

Her hand moved to the front of her dress and slowly, provocatively, she undid the row of buttons. He watched as her long, tanned body came into view. She laid the dress over the back of a chair. Now only a thin wisp of white silk stretched across her hips. She walked to the edge of the bed and, as she looked at him, her fingers pushed down the silk and revealed the fair triangle exactly matching the colour of her hair. She slid into the bed beside him, loosened his robe and ran her hands down his body.

'It's been too long,' she murmured. 'Far too long. Whatever's on your mind, I will erase it. Believe me.' For the first time a look of animation came into his eyes, followed by hope. He reached for her, pulling her close, burying his head into the curve of her neck.

Ten minutes later she was laughing. It was not a pleasant laugh.

'You can't do it! What the hell's wrong?' She was squatting beside him, his flaccid penis in her hand. The haunted look was back in his eyes.

'What happened to you, Dave?'

Now there was a tone of triumph in her voice. He heard it and shrank away from her. She laughed again and climbed off the bed.

'Dave Munger - impotent!' she taunted, reaching for her dress. Abruptly her laughter stopped and she turned.

'Or is it only with me?' Her face was clouded with anxiety but then it cleared as she saw him turn his head away to the wall.

'No, you must have tried with others.' Again the vicious laugh.

She buttoned herself into the dress, coiled up her hair, took the pin from her handbag and pierced it into place.

'You were only any use to me for one thing,' she said. 'It was good while it lasted. I will buy your camera at the auction. It will remind me of the man you used to be.' With another laugh she strode to the door and went out.

Munger remained lying on the bed, staring at the ceiling. Very slowly his hands came up and covered his face.

Duff Paget was to remember the date very well: October 26th, 1969. The auction was three days before his first wedding anniversary to Ruth and it was the cause of their first full scale stand-up, nose-to-nose row. It was also the incidental cause of much else.

He got the word just after 8 o'clock in the evening. A terse telephone call from Chang the bartender at the Foreign Correspondents' Club. There was to be an auction of photographic gear at 10.30 that night.

'Whose?' Duff had asked.

'Munger's,' Chang had replied in a tense voice. Duff felt his guts twist.

'He's dead?'

'No, Mr Paget. He was here an hour ago. I was just told to put the word out.'

'I'll be there.' Duff hung up and then stood for several minutes looking out of the picture window at the moving lights in Hong Kong harbour below him and the static lights of Kowloon beyond. His first reaction of shock had been replaced by urgent curiosity. An auction of photographic equipment was not an unusual event during that period. He had attended one only a month ago for Hasagawa's gear. The Japanese man had been photographing the Marines on a sweep towards Con Thien when a stray mortar shell (if any shell can truly be termed 'stray') had blown him apart. He had a young wife living in a tiny apartment in Happy Valley and, as he had been freelance and had spent most of his earnings on new equipment, his photographic gear represented the bulk of his assets.

Duff well remembered how the widow sat still and quiet and composed in a corner, her eyes never leaving the long table on which were lined up the rows of cameras and lenses, tripods and filters. They had gleamed black and silver in the noisy auction room. Ruth had visited her in the afternoon and found her cleaning them carefully, dry-eyed, while a six-month-old baby boy had lain asleep in a cot in the corner. It had been Ruth's first exposure to the stoicism of the Eastern mind.

'She showed no emotion,' she told Duff. 'No tears. She made me a cup of tea and talked practically about the baby and the price of airline tickets back to Japan. Then she showed me the camera he'd been using when he was killed. It was all smashed and twisted. She said it was probably no good for the auction and she laughed. She laughed, Duff! I guess it was to hide her feelings - a sort of escape valve.'

Duff had covertly watched her as Bennet, the bluff English insurance agent, who had once been a clerk at Sotheby's, called out the lots and pushed the sympathetic bidding higher. As each piece had been sold and laid aside, her delicate head slumped lower on her fragile neck. Those pieces of precisely machined plastic, metal and glass were her last link with her dead man.

This auction would be different, for Munger was alive, and why should any combat photographer, especially one like Dave Munger, sell the tools of his trade? It was akin to a healthy man donating his eyes to medical research and handing them over immediately.

As he pondered the question, a cruise liner, lit up from stem to stern, moved sedately through the harbour. He could faintly hear a band playing a welcome from the apron of the ocean terminal. Then Ruth's voice cut into his thoughts calling him to dinner.

He watched silently as she laid the dishes, one by one, onto the large 'Lazy Susan' in the centre of the round table. There was chicken in walnut sauce, sweet and sour pork, sliced abalone, a green vegetable of indeterminate type in a brown sauce equally mysterious, deep fried minced crab, pink boiled prawns and in the centre a huge bowl of steaming chow fan. On the periphery were several little dishes containing soy sauce, vinegar, mustard and hot chilli sauce. She finally laid down the bowl of cold thin tea which the Chinese use for washing the fingers after eating. Then she sat opposite him and waited expectantly. He leaned forward and sniffed appreciatively.'

It smells and looks delicious, darling.' He said it with great sincerity. She had, after all, just completed a six-month course in Cantonese cooking at the American Club and this meal, in a sense, was her thesis. Inside he was yearning for a large, thick, juicy steak, singed black on the outside and bloody and succulent in the centre, bracketed by deep fried onion rings and a fat jacketed Idaho potato topped with chives and sour cream.

It had taken him all of six months to admit to himself that he didn't like Chinese food. It had been a difficult admission. His colleagues in the press corps treated it with the reverence of a mystical religion. If sailors have a girl in every port, a foreign correspondent or photographer on the Far Eastern beat has a favourite little Chinese restaurant, be it in Cholon or Vientiane, Penang or Phnom Penh. There seemed to be an axiom that the smaller and dirtier the place the better the food.

'This is where the coolies eat,' Duff had been repeatedly assured as he was pressed into a rickety chair in some fly blown hole in the backstreets of half a dozen Asian cities. He saw it as a contradiction and had often wanted to ask 'Why don't we eat where the rich Chinese go?'

But he was young and green and had tried hard to assimilate the enthusiasm of men whom he often respected and assumed had highly developed and discerning palates.

Now Ruth had thrown herself so enthusiastically into learning Cantonese cooking, he could not bring himself to tell her that he would rather have a steak.

For a moment doubts crossed his mind yet again about the wisdom of marrying just before this assignment. Being honest with himself, he knew the doubts went deeper - into the very essence of marriage. He had discovered much about himself during the past year. He had learned for example that at twenty-seven the restless spirit that had dominated his youth was not going to dissipate with age. On the contrary, the excitement of the past months had highlighted that spirit and in a way shattered the chrysalis and let him fly free. But his marriage had been the culmination of a march of inevitability. He had first met and fallen in love with Ruth during his third year at Cornell University. He had been majoring in political science, she had been studying psychology. It had been an old-fashioned courtship; they were almost oblivious to the young Sixties 'swinging' all around them. Both came from small conservative mid-western towns: his father was a circuit judge, her's a republican mayor of longstanding. The only major difference between their backgrounds was that his family was of Protestant stock from the earliest settlers and her people were second generation Polish Jews.

In spite of a similar conservative upbringing they had sharp differences of personality which only now were beginning to emerge. In simple terms he was a romantic and she was not. In spite of his abhorrence for exotic foods, that antipathy was confined to his taste buds. He could look out from their apartment high in Victoria Peak and see and smell an exciting and mysterious world below. Meanwhile Ruth would be more concerned about organising and running the household. She had taken a part-time job helping out the doctors in the Sandy Bay Childrens' Hospital. It specialised in complicated spinal surgery, and she advised on the mental rehabilitation of the children.

Now as he gingerly fingered the chopsticks, selected various morsels from the spread in front of him and made enthusiastic mouth filled noises of approval, he realised with sudden clarity that the success or failure of their marriage would depend on their ability to accept and compartmentalise their differences and, more importantly, to express that acceptance. He was confident in his own ability to do so. Not so much in genuine acceptance, but in sincere expression, for he knew that he was an accomplished, indeed gifted, liar. It was not an attribute which bothered his conscience. He had long convinced himself that the bulk of his lies, or half-truths, or simple omissions, were a genuine effort to avoid avoidable problems or damaging the sensibilities of others. It was the notion of a romantic, and so he was able to chew on a piece of slippery, rubbery abalone and at the same time mumble 'Delicious, darling,' in tones of gut-felt sincerity.

Ruth on the other hand never told a lie or bisected the truth. He remembered the first time he had brought her home to meet his family. His father had long had a penchant for brewing his own beer. With the enthusiasm of the dedicated amateur he had pressed it on the rest of the family and close friends for years and had been repeatedly assured that it was far superior to anything the commercial breweries turned out. It so happened that Ruth, with some justification, considered herself to be a connoisseur of beers. Her own grandfather had been a brew master in southern Poland before emigrating to the States. In her household beer was drunk, and discussed and criticized at length. On hearing this the old judge had rushed down to his cellar, poured her a glass of his latest brew and watched with anticipation as she took a sip.

Her lovely face had twisted and a second later her lips uttered the never-to-be-forgotten words, 'Yuck! You can't be serious!'

In a way the rest of the family was grateful. Not another drop of beer was ever brewed in the house. Being a judge, of course, the old man had commended his future daughter-in-law on her transparent and forthright honesty; but Duff suspected that thereafter he never truly approved of the match.

As he tried to bite through a piece of long, green vegetable he was half inclined to spit it out and use her own words: 'Yuck! You can't be serious!' But he chewed manfully on, reflecting that it was a pity that Ruth didn't concentrate on the cooking she knew best. From her mother and grandmother she had learned how to make those Jewish dishes renowned in Central Europe. Duff was an addict of such food but Ruth had insisted that if they were going to live abroad then she would learn to cook and enjoy the local cuisines. Anyway, in a few days he would be leaving again for Vietnam and would be away at least a month. There were several excellent French restaurants in Saigon and he could always get good prime steak in any of the U.S. bases he would be visiting. He felt a twinge of guilt at his duplicity but quickly squashed it with the thought that it would be unfair to leave her in an unhappy frame of mind. He truly believed that his love for her justified his attitude. He had first used this rationalisation just after their engagement. He was about to graduate and it had been assumed by Ruth and both their families that he would enter the Foreign Service. He had already been favourably interviewed two months earlier. It was after his second interview that he dropped the bombshell. He had decided, he told her, not to go into government service after all, but to take up photography as a full-time profession. She had been disconcerted. Certainly she knew of his interest in photography. He had been secretary of the university photographic society for two years and had won several prizes in their competitions, once winning with a misty pensive shot of Ruth herself. It was a secret joke between them. The chairman of the awards panel had commented that her expression evoked a sense of transcendental innocence. In fact Duff had depressed the shutter bare seconds after having given her one of the more outstanding orgasms of her young life.

She had assumed though that his interest in the art had been a mere youthful hobby and not the stuff of a serious career. However, he was determined and sent off portfolios to several well-known newspapers and magazines. She had been surprised and truly impressed a few weeks later when a small but influential right wing Eastern weekly had offered him a job as a staff photographer, at what to her appeared a generous salary.

Duff had been curiously complacent about this success. His ambition, he told her, was to be a fully-fledged combat photographer and this was an excellent stepping-stone.

But first he had to upgrade his amateur status and soon after graduating they were separated for the first time when he went to Los Angeles to attend a six-month course in advanced photography.

It had been Duff s first major 'omission' to her. Yes, he was going to be a combat photographer. The omission was that he was still going to be working in the Foreign Service of his government but not exactly in the way she had foreseen.

His time of graduation had coincided with a major policy initiative within the U.S. Intelligence community. Someone had finally realised that it was incompatible for a so-called secret organisation to have a pronounced public image.

It had come about when a senior C.I.A. analyst at Langley had been browsing through a U.S.I.S. hand-out about various U.S. embassies in Europe. Several pages were filled with head and shoulders photographs of embassy staffs ranging from Ambassadors down to secretaries. In each case there were blank spaces, captioned 'photograph not available'. These blank spaces usually coincided with the spaces reserved for Assistant Military Attaches or Cultural Attaches. The analyst hardly needed to reach for the computer to know that every single blank space represented a C.I.A. 'in-house' agent.

It was, of course, a typical bureaucratic fumble but it set into train a whole new spectrum of thought. A four-month study revealed to the nation's senior intelligence officials what everyone else had known all along: the C.I.A. was patently too public, from its 'sore thumb' edifice at Langley to its Brooks Brothers suited agents in all corners of the world.

The recommendation of the report was simple: if the C.I. A. was akin to an inverted iceberg with nine-tenths exposed above the surface, it must simply be tipped back the right way up - and fast.

But here the original analyst came into his own by suggesting that the exposure should, to all intents, remain highly visible. In the meantime a substrata should be created away from the spotlights and deep in the subterranean shadows of the sea. All eyes would be drawn to the gleaming iceberg and the snide comments of competing agencies would continue while an ultra secret section would be set up, using ex-officio agents who had never set foot in Langley or the company's training 'farms'.

So it was that the C.I. A. 'Equine' section came into being.

The original analyst was rewarded by being made its first Director and it was he who had coined its name. He was something of a classicist and a crossword fanatic. Hence equine equals horse equals Trojan. He was rather pleased with it. One of his guiding principles was that all 'Equine' agents must have genuine 'cover', totally divorced from official institutions. A short list was drawn up of likely professions. It included import-export agents, construction and geophysical engineers, travel agents, financial and trade consultants, university lecturers, translators, charity workers, missionaries and so on. In effect, any profession which allowed scope for innocent travel and overseas work assignments. At the top of the list were foreign correspondents and photographers. It was not wildly original. Most European intelligence services had infiltrated agents into the media long before even Marconi was born.

In selecting agents the 'Equine' section dipped into the same reservoir as the other C.I.A. sections: white, right-of-centre, college-educated men and women, preferably of good Protestant stock. There was, however, one additional requirement. Every agent had to have a natural talent - even a vocation for his 'cover' career.

A new and 'virgin' computer was acquired by 'Equine' and set up in its new headquarters which were housed in a company on the outskirts of Gary, Indiana. The assumption being that no self-respecting spy would be seen dead in Gary Indiana. The genuine 'cover' of the company was that it manufactured aerosol cans of insecticide for the do-it-yourself gardener. The analyst-turned-Director, whose name was Ray Sherman, called the company Pterygota Inc., from the Latin name for all species of winged insects. For reasons that would baffle any advertising copy writer, the name caught on among gardeners and from its first year it showed a profit.

The first thing Sherman did was to feed his computer with all the names of promising final year students at good colleges who might have both avocation for a career in a profession contained on his short list and a desire to serve his country. He also fed the computer with the names of the recent applicants to the Foreign Service. The computer was programmed to correlate the two lists and to give priority to any names with bionic categorisation. It programmed the name 'Duff Paget' straight into the first batch. Hence at his second interview in Washington he was deftly led away and confronted with an entirely new selection panel, the chairman of which coyly enquired whether he might like to become a spy. From there on his romantic and restless nature made it all easy. He explained that he was engaged to be married. The panel nodded enthusiastically. They had checked his fiancée's background and found it impeccable; a good and discreet wife after all added to an agent's 'cover'. He pointed out that he was a keen but very amateur photographer. No problem, he was assured. He would be very adequately trained and what is more a job would be 'arranged' for him, as would his future photographic assignments. For the next three days he was put through a variety of mental and physical tests, and passed them all with flying colours. He was particularly gratified by his success in the obligatory lie-detector test.

So he went off to Los Angeles to take an intensive course in photography, but every alternate week was spent in a high security complex near Long Pine in the foothills of the Sierra Nevada. There he was taught the 'trade craft' of his concurrent profession.

Before leaving for California he and Ruth had a long and serious discussion. They decided to get married only after he was settled in his career. They would then wait at least three years before starting a family. Secretly she hoped that by that time he would have changed course again and be headed down a more conventional road. She was patient as well as practical.

However, only eighteen months after starting his job with the magazine they suddenly offered him an overseas assignment. It was to cover South East Asia from a base in Hong Kong. At the time South East Asia meant Vietnam and the convoluted war. So abruptly he was presented with the opportunity of satisfying his desire to be a combat photographer.

He was also abruptly presented with the question of what to do about Ruth. The assignment was for a minimum of two years and she thought such a separation was too long. So inevitably they married. From the practical point of view the marriage was a definite success. She had taken in her stride the culture shock of moving from America to the Orient. Knowing that he would be frequently away she had immersed herself in the expatriate social routine. Apart from her cooking lessons she went to Ikebana classes on Tuesdays and Yoga on Thursdays. Unlike her new friends she decided not to have an amah. The apartment was small and compact, but keeping it clean helped pass the time. She continued to view Duff s assignment as a mere temporary ripple on a smooth and conventional married life.

She looked at him now as he shovelled the last of his chow fan into his mouth and, catching her eye, burped gently and smiled. She knew that after a Chinese meal it was a sign of approval. He was, she decided yet again, the handsomest man in creation. He had a slender, angular face, almost beautiful in its features, large limpid eyes, a straight nose, a wide, mobile mouth but with the lower lip broad and masculine, above a cleft chin. The whole face set off by black, straight, lustrous hair. He was, she knew, very conscious of his looks, sometimes irritated with them, because, like a very beautiful woman, people at first tended not to take him seriously.

'It's why I like photography,' he once told her. 'I will be judged solely by my pictures - not by my looks.' She could understand his feelings for she herself was arrestingly beautiful and they were known among the media-fraternity as the 'Hollywood Duet.'

As she stood up to clear the dishes she noticed that he appeared serious and preoccupied.

'Was the food all right, Duff?' she asked, and then had to repeat her question. He looked up with a start.

'It was perfect. Just perfect. Sorry, my mind was wandering. I'm going to have to go out in an hour-to the F.C.C. There's to be an auction of camera gear.'

Her face turned serious and she put a stack of dishes back on the table and sat down again.

'Whose?'

He noted her expression and smiled and shook his head. 'Don't worry, no one's dead. Apparently Dave Munger is selling his equipment. I can't think why.'

Munger. The name evoked conflicting emotions in her. She had met him once at a farewell party for a Newsweek correspondent, who had been reassigned to the Middle East. It had been a drunken party and Munger had been drunker than most, but less boisterous. He had sat alone and quiet at the bar relentlessly consuming one vodka soda after another. Duff had explained to her that he had been in the war zone for seven months without a break and that he always found it hard to readjust to what people called 'sanity'. She had been surprised by his appearance, seeming small and slight and undistinguished, with untidy fair hair and a pinched look to his narrow face. His eyes were his most distinct feature: wide and deep and a startling clear blue in colour, a blue that changed in intensity with his mood. She had heard the gossip from other wives about his reputation with women. Apparently they were his only other interest apart from what he called his 'snaps'. Also, apparently, they fell at his feet with monotonous regularity. She had not seen it herself at first, could not understand what it was about him that would attract any woman. But later, while she was dancing, she had looked up and seen those eyes watching her - absorbing her image, and in a heartbeat she had felt the shock of physical attraction.

Another aspect was Duff's regard for the man which amounted almost to hero worship. She did not like to see her man so influenced by a third party. Even one whom he hardly knew and only seldom met.

She stood again and picked up the dishes and headed for the door, saying over her shoulder: 'Maybe he finally decided that his work was getting in the way of his drinking and women.'

Duff looked after her and shrugged. He could never explain to her the emotions that Dave Munger evoked in other photographers. In truth she could never understand Duffs own feelings because something had once happened - something which he could never tell her about. It was another of his "omissions'. It had happened two months after Duff had arrived. Two months which had been highly frustrating.

On his arrival in Saigon Duff had first checked in with the local 'Equine' station chief whose cover was Vietnam manager for a U.S. computer company. He was told that for the first year at least his priority was to lay the foundation of his cover 'career'. In essence he was required to build a reputation as a combat photographer.

The secret of good combat photography is to be at the right place at the right time and then to keep a cool head.

Duff had launched himself into it. He criss-crossed the country, 'Cameras at the ready, but his timing and luck were lamentable. He either left a zone just before a fight started or arrived just after it finished. He was reduced to photographing the wounded and the plastic bags containing the dead, and on one occasion a pathetic group of Vietcong prisoners who looked as though they were half-starved truants from school.

At first he took his lack of success lightly. He was, after all, getting to know the country, and making contacts among the military, both American and Vietnamese. But, as the weeks went by, his frustration grew. After each sortie he would return to Saigon, go up to his room in the Continental Hotel and; using the makeshift darkroom he had built in a wardrobe, develop contact prints from his rolls of exposed film. Time after time he would look at those prints and know, with depressing certainty, that they were not interesting enough to be used by his magazine.

Then the others began to rib him about it. 'Got any good snaps lately?' they would call out jocularly in the bar or on the verandah overlooking Tu Do Street. He appeared to take it well, grinning and wisecracking back, but inside acid gnawed at his guts. He even had a note from his editor containing a mild rebuke. They were still having to use wire service photographs he pointed out, and keeping a house photographer on location was an expensive proposition.

After two months it all came to a head. An impromptu party had erupted in the bar of the L'Ange Restaurant. Some correspondents were leaving on R. & R. to Hong Kong and Bangkok, others had just returned. They were a good natured but competitive bunch and again Duff was the butt of some pointed bantering. Dave Munger was one of the group but he remained silent, sitting at the bar, listening and watching and drinking his inevitable vodka sodas.

To Duff it was all damned unfair. Here was a man who was a legend. Instead of having to go out looking for war he merely had to take a stroll and the war came right to him. It was not for nothing that he was known as 'Mohamet'. Of course, Duff knew that there was more to it. Dave Munger was the pure professional.

Over the years he had assiduously built up contacts among the military, not so much with the top brass but among the senior N.C.O.s who really controlled things. Especially those in Transport Commands. It was said that Munger could whistle up a helicopter faster than a three star general. He had done the same at civilian airports. From Saigon's Ton San Nut, to Hong Kong's Kai Tak, to Tokyo's Haneda, Munger knew the station managers of most airlines. Others might flatter and bring gifts for managing directors or flight directors, but Munger knew where the real power lay. While the others would be frantically ringing the home of a director at midnight to try to get onto an overbooked flight, that airline's station manager would be showing Munger to his seat - usually surreptitiously upgraded to first class.

Another aspect of Munger's professionalism was his 'conjuring'. He had taught himself the art of sleight of hand for the single purpose of being able to conceal a roll of film. The recurring nightmare of any combat photographer was to shoot a breath-taking series of 'snaps' only to have the film confiscated or exposed. There had been many policemen, security men and customs officials who had caught Munger either in the act of taking photographs in a 'forbidden' zone or shortly afterwards. They had seen the consternation on his face as the offending film had been appropriated and unrolled in the light. But they had never seen the inner smile-or the original roll secreted on his body while they destroyed his 'decoy'.

Finally there were the steps that Munger had taken to protect his person. Some photographers and correspondents carried weapons on hazardous assignments - a small concealed handgun, a knife or even a can of 'Mace'. Occasionally bodyguards were hired, not so much on combat missions but during sojourns in the seamier cities of the Orient. One famous New York television commentator was known as 'Sinatra' after the phalanx of 'heavies' that accompanied him day and night.

Munger, however, had taken a different track. Very early in his career he had studied most of the Orient's martial arts: Judo, Karate, Tae kwon do, Kung Fu and several of the lesser known varieties. From each he had selected techniques which suited himself and his purpose. So he could, like a cat when cornered, expose and use lethal claws.

As Duff stood, bellied up to the other end of the bar and starting on his third large Scotch, he had faced the daunting prospect of preparing himself to a similar extent. He had been on the job just two months. Munger, although only thirty, had been at it for over ten years. He had covered the troubles in Cyprus and the wars in Biafra, North Borneo, Angola and now Vietnam. With a sunken feeling Duff had also acknowledged that it was not just a question of preparation. There was another intangible requirement. Not a question of being a technically good photographer or even an artistic one. Munger only worked in black and white and his photographs contained no startling or innovative aspects. It was all a question of 'feel' and either you had it or you did not. Again Duff felt a stab of resentment. He had never really had a chance to discover whether he had it, and he was already coming under pressure both from his colleagues and his editor. He thought wryly that he should have been born a limey, like Munger, It was curious how the British dominated the field. Sure, there were good photographers from the States and the Continent - French and German and a brilliant Spaniard. Even the Japanese were well represented by Hasagawa and others, but the British were the cream: the compassionate Larry Burrows, the dispassionate Don McCullin and the young and wild Tim Page. Above all there was Dave Munger, who could photograph the stark features of a young, tired and frightened soldier and stamp the face of war onto a million minds.

As Duff drank more Scotch his despair deepened. The noise and laughter around him seemed to come through a long tunnel. He drained the glass and looked up for the bartender but instead found himself looking at Munger in the mirror behind the bar. For a long moment they stared at each other. It was as though Munger's clear blue eyes were peering right into his head, even into his soul. Seeing everything there - and seeing nothing. He had a half smile on his dark, lean face - a mocking smile? Suddenly Duff cracked. His fingers tightened on the empty glass and, with a cry as if in pain, he hurled it at the image in the mirror.

The splintering crash brought instant silence to the room. Duff stood still, his hands quivering, adrenalin pumping through his veins. He slowly turned, taking in all the eyes watching him, the bemused faces looking as though they had been frozen in a strobe light. Moving with painful deliberation he reached into his back pocket, pulled out a roll of money, blindly ripped off several bills and threw them onto the bar. Then he pushed his way through to the door and passed out into the muggy night air. Behind him the buzz of conversation started again. Someone laughed loudly.

He shook his head trying to clear it, then pounded his forehead with the palm of his hand. A taxi pulled up in front of him, the gap-toothed driver grinning and reaching behind to open the rear door. Duff tumbled in and lay half across the seat as the taxi pulled out into the traffic.

'Where you go?'

With an effort he pulled himself upright and slurred 'Continental'

The driver glanced back at him and his grin widened as he took in his passenger's state. 'You wanna girl, Joe? Sexy - very young.'

With a further effort Duff got control of himself. 'No. Continental Hotel.' The driver shrugged and concentrated on the traffic.

But after five minutes Duff had changed his mind. He had never cheated on Ruth, but in his state of mind he rationalised that he had been a failure at everything else -so why riot as a husband? Besides, it might take his mind off what had happened - and he had never been with an Asian woman.

So the taxi driver took him into Cholon, the Chinese sector of the city, and deposited him at the door of the famous Tai Cheong guest house. It was not how Duff had imagined it. He was shown by an old crone up some rickety, wooden stairs and into a huge, barnlike room. Heavy four-poster beds lined each wall leaving a narrow aisle between. Each bed was draped in a white, wraith-like mosquito net. Some of these shivered gently, either from internal movement or the action of two ceiling fans which stirred the air. In his nostrils Duff could almost feel as well as smell a heavy, sweet aroma.

He had begun to have definite second thoughts, but the old crone took his arm and led him to one of the beds and pulled aside the netting and urged him to climb in. He noted that the sheet and pillow were white and clean - and it was less of an effort than walking back downstairs. As he slumped onto the bed the old woman deftly slipped off his shoes, let the netting fall back into place and padded away.

He lay for several minutes on his back and then, at a slight sound nearby, rolled his head and looked to his left. Through the two layers of white he could dimly make out what appeared to be a single amorphous mass moving to a slow rhythm.

He raised his head slightly and as his eyes adjusted to the gloom he realised it was two forms in the next bed joined in the act of love. He could make out no features, just the shadowy shapes rocking in unison, enveloped in a white mist. That vision in his eyes and the heavy, sweet aroma in his nostrils evoked the most erotic sensation he had ever known. He did not feel like an intruder or a voyeur. He had a sense of being part of it, adding to it. He could have watched for all eternity but he heard a rustle behind him and rolled over and was looking into two dark, almond pools. He focused and the pools clarified as eyes in an oval face.

She climbed up onto the bed and the netting rustled back behind her. Duff pushed himself up onto an elbow. He could see better now. She was kneeling on the sheet, wearing a white Ao Dai, high at the neck, tight over her breasts and waist, then flaring out and split wide to reveal the black silk trousers beneath.

First she undressed him, languorously, somehow with coyness. She giggled shyly as she struggled to pull his underpants down over his erection.

She dropped his clothes somewhere under the bed and then, with unconscious grace, knelt at the foot of the bed and undressed herself. She was slim and almost as white as the netting around them. But her flesh was white shaded and rounded by the low light, and highlighted by the black hair and eyes, high pointed nipples and the dark shadow between her thighs. He felt an urgent impatience but forced himself to lie still. She reached forward and began to massage his feet. Her slender fingers had surprising strength and the pressure she applied was finely balanced between pleasure and pain. From his feet she moved to his calves and then his thighs. She ignored his erection, moving higher to his stomach and then his chest. She was straddling him now, her face above his, her hair falling to the pillow beside him. Finally she worked her fingers into the muscles of his shoulder, fingers that eased away tension. Then she was finished, her face very close, a slight smile on her lips. He could only feel one part of his body, the part she had ignored. It was as though she had isolated it, centred his entire nervous system to the tingling length of his erection.

She lowered her breasts onto his chest and placed her lips against his in a chaste, closed-mouth kiss. Her right hand brushed down past his waist and guided and positioned and rubbed his erection against the moist silkiness at the entrance to her vagina. The sensation became excruciating and with an involuntary jerk he lunged upwards and into her - and in the same instant her lips opened and her tongue slid into his mouth.

Thereafter he hardly moved and in his pleasure-filled mind it seemed to him that she hardly moved either, and yet it felt as though his penis was encased in a tightly packed jar of volatile silk worms.

Perhaps the sensation was too much. A dozen times he felt himself nearing a climax, but each time, only seconds away, it would recede. At first, panting to prolong his pleasure, she deliberately slowed the tempo as she felt him reaching the top, but as time passed she moved faster, urging him on. It was not to be. It began to filter through that he was not going to make it. Being young and with limited experience this had brought anxiety and his erection began to lose its steel. She had felt it and shaken her head and smiled down at him.

'Don't worry,' she whispered. 'You very strong. Relax, you coming soon.'

Then she pulled off from him and slid lower, rubbing her breasts down his chest and belly and onto his thighs. He raised his head and saw her take his now flaccid penis into her small mouth. It was a new sensation - more localised, even sharper, and his erection returned and filled her mouth. Again he climbed rapidly towards a climax but again failed to conquer the peak. It was not for want of trying, his or hers. She reached up her hands and fingered his nipples. His body ached, quivering for the final relief, but it was not to be and she finally realised it and slid up beside him, tucking her head into the crook of his arm, listening to his pounding heart.

'Don't worry,' she murmured. 'Maybe later, maybe next time.' Her words did not soothe him. Again he was a failure, and his testicles ached.

She raised herself onto her elbow and anxiously studied his troubled face. Then she patted him on the shoulder, lifted the mosquito netting and slipped out of the bed.

He guessed that he would not see her again, but ten minutes later she appeared carrying a red lacquered tray, which she placed on the bed, before climbing in beside him. On it was a small oil lamp, a long pipe and a curious shallow bowl, a pair of tweezers, a box of matches and a square of silver paper. On the paper was a tiny brown lump which glistened wetly in the dim light. Duff realised that he was looking at a ball of opium and the means of smoking it. His upbringing should have provoked a shocked response, but by this time his feelings were numb. He watched in silence as the girl lit the lamp, picked up the ball in the tweezers and held it over the flame, turning it deftly with slim fingers. After a few minutes she leaned forward and wafted it under her nostrils, then she nodded, smiled at Duff, and dropped it into the bowl of the pipe. As she offered him the pipe, held on her flat palms, he felt a moment of panic, but then with a mental shrug, he accepted it.

At first he was clumsy, trying to smoke it as he would tobacco. But she showed him how to draw the smoke in carefully and slowly and hold it in his lungs for as long as possible.

It was his first encounter with any form of drugs. He had never even smoked marijuana. He waited for the effects with a mixture of excitement and trepidation. After a few minutes he felt a surge of relief. There had been no sudden warping of his mind or senses. Nothing except an acrid dryness in his throat. He was mildly disappointed. After all, if he was going to be truly wicked he may as well get some taste from the forbidden fruit.

She sat cross-legged on the bed watching him, her naked body still glistening with the perspiration of her recent effort. He decided that she was incredibly beautiful. Not just physically or externally, but with an inner glow. She was like an oil painting - a portrait that at first glance appears merely colourful and well formed, but on closer examination reveals a depth of colours, fading and blending without delineation, giving the face perspective and character. It was happening now. He could see the ivory hue of her skin as though lights were moving under it. Her hair deepened from being merely black to the sheerest ebony. She was sitting away from him but he could feel her skin: the nubs of her nipples, the satin of her inner thigh, the curve and shape of her neck.

Dimly he realised that the opium had after all invaded his senses; heightened and softened them. He laughed but heard no sound, saw her smile and move towards him, felt her press him back onto the pillow. All his anxieties floated away with the smoke that wreathed up and lay in a mist above him.

The morning had brought reality, and a turning point in his life.

It was late when he awoke. Fingers were gently squeezing the lobe of his left ear. He grunted and came slowly into consciousness, feeling immediately the dull ache spreading from the back of his head. Memory followed and he turned and saw the girl bending over him. She was dressed, again in an Ao Dai, and her hair was piled high on her head. The mosquito netting had been lifted onto the wooden frame above, as had all the others. All the mystery had now left the room. It looked like the sleeping quarters of an army barracks.

He pushed himself into a sitting position. He and the girl were the only ones in the vast room. She picked up a bowl from a table beside the bed and handed it to him together with a tiny glass phial. The bowl contained hot tea, the phial was filled with what looked like hundreds of minute brown seeds.

'Swallow them,' she said. 'Good for your head.'

He pulled out the cork with his teeth, tipped back his head and poured the contents into his mouth, then washed them down with a gulp of tea. They had a bitter, musky taste.

'Good Chinese medicine;' She said it approvingly as though talking to a small boy.

'You are Chinese?' he asked.

'Half Chinese, half Vietnamese.'

She turned back to the table and passed him his clothes. They had been washed and ironed. He drained the bowl of tea, swung his legs off the bed and began to dress. She knelt and pulled his socks onto his feet. Now he really did feel like a boy. It was a curious, helpless feeling, and compounded by the variety of emotions he felt about the night before: guilt, excitement and finally trepidation.

The incident in the bar had probably finished both of his embryonic careers. The 'Equine' station head would certainly get to hear of it. An agent losing control was no sort of an agent at all, and his efforts so far as a combat photographer had been abysmal. On top of that he had cheated on his wife and smoked opium - it had been an inglorious night.

Now the girl was easing on his shoes and as he looked down at her lustrous black hair another contrary thought tumbled out. So what! So he had blown his two jobs and maybe his marriage - but it had been a hell of a night and a hell of an experience for a small-town Yankee boy.

'What's your name?' he asked as she straightened up.

'Wei Fong, and you?'

'Duff.'

'Duff?' She repeated it with uncertainty and he forced a smile,

'Yes. Useless Duff.' He glanced at his watch and swore to himself. To her he said: 'I'd better get back to Armageddon.'

She looked at him uncomprehendingly and he reached out his hands and cupped her face and kissed her lips.

'Thanks, Wei Fong. You just might be the last pleasant thing to happen to me in a hell of a long while.'

Her smile was winsome. 'I see you again?'

He shrugged. 'Maybe? If you do I'll bring my camera. I can't capture a war, but I may get the opposite on film.'

She led him downstairs and he paid the old crone and found the same gap-toothed taxi driver waiting outside. Saigon taxi drivers were a breed who, if allowed, would have chained themselves to a good customer. On the ride back to the hotel, total depression finally set in. He watched the teeming crowds: the ever-present soldiers and over-uniformed policemen; the women, some in brightly coloured Western dress, others in the flowing Ao Dai; and here and there the contrast of a patch of saffron as a Buddhist monk passed along. The Chinese medicine had worked and his headache was receding, but it could have no effect on the ache in his heart.

He was a failure and his ambitions were dreams. He wouldn't wait though. As the taxi pulled into Tu Do Street and up to the hotel he resolved to contact the 'Equine' station head immediately. He would also telex his resignation to the magazine. Then he would take the first flight out to Hong Kong and confront Ruth with the whole sad stupid story.

He paid the driver and hurried up the steps to the lobby, so intent on his own thoughts that he failed to see the man coming down, and almost crashed into him.

'Duff! Where the hell have you been?'

It was Greg Harris, a big, easy-going Australian who reported the war for the Melbourne Star. He was just a little older than Duff and relatively new to Vietnam, and so they had a kind of bond between them. Duff looked at him blankly and noted the barely suppressed excitement on his face. The Australian grabbed his arm.

'I've been looking for you all over,' he said. 'Haven't you heard?'

'Heard what?'

'The first Cav. They're having another go at Ah Shau. They went in at dawn. There was a news blackout. The word only got through an hour ago. The others are long gone. I was down at the Delta-just got back. Come on man. Grab your gear, they'll be shuttling out the wounded any time now. We'll get a ride back in.'

Duff could still not comprehend and in his impatience Greg literally shook him and screamed.

'Get moving man. It's the biggest Op. for years.'

The penny clanged. It was a chance - a last chance. Greg was now shouting at Duff's taxi driver to wait. He turned back to Duff.

'You coming? What's with you?'

Duff grinned. 'I'm coming-thirty seconds!'

He raced to reception, ignored the startled clerk, reached past him and grabbed his key. The lift was, notoriously slow so he pounded up the two flights of stairs to his room. The door was open, a maid cleaning the floor. She looked on with amusement as he darted about the room. She had seen it all before. First he kicked off his shoes, then frantically pulled on dark green jungle boots. A flak jacket followed and he scooped up a helmet and his equipment bag on the run. Her high-pitched shout stopped him at the door. She was by the bedside table holding up the plastic press tag without which he would not even get near to a chopper. He dashed over, kissed her on both cheeks, grabbed the tag and was gone, followed by her delighted laughter.

They got a ride in a Medivac Huey with three other correspondents who had missed the first wave. There had been little conversation.

As they lifted off one of the pilots had said tersely: 'It's carnage in there. We have to go in, but it sure beats hell out of me why you guys bother.'

They went in low and fast, the chopper tilting forward over the dense foliage. First they flew through smoke. Then came a sudden metallic clatter like nails being rattled in a giant tin can inside an echo chamber.

'Fuckers!' the pilot spat out. 'Small arms. They're damn close to the landing zone.' He scrutinized the instruments while his passengers glanced at each other and tried not to look as frightened as they felt.

One of the correspondents took off his helmet, raised his backside and pushed it under him. Duff was about to do the same when the pilot called over his shoulder 'Ready to go!' and the chopper banked to the left over a clearing. Smoking canisters delineated the landing zone. There were four choppers on the ground: two Hueys with rotors whirling, a third lying on its side and smoking, and a burnt out Cobra. A group of men linked in pairs by stretchers was running out to the waiting Hueys.

Duff eased the strap of the Nikon round his neck and fingered the lens. But for the noise of the engine he was sure the others would have heard the pounding of his heart.

Then they were down, and leaping out and running for the trees.

For the next few minutes he felt as though he was watching a speeded-up film. From the edge of the landing zone he turned and started photographing. First the burnt out Cobra, then the swarm of medics loading the stretchers. It was all happening too fast, so he flicked on the drive motor and the Nikon hummed and clicked as it sliced images from the movement. His companions had moved further through the trees towards the thump and crackle of gunfire. He would get the Hueys lifting off and then follow. The Nikon's motor stopped, having driven the film through. Quickly he rewound it, flipped open the back of the camera, clicked out the exposed film and unzipped the side pouch of his bag for a new one. He did it fast and expertly - he had practised for many hours. Then his fingers froze and so did his heart - the pouch was empty.

Slowly he rocked back onto his buttocks. The open camera hung loose from his neck as he clasped his arms round his knees and buried his head. He laughed - a painful, hysterical sound. It was the last humiliation.

Only yesterday he had decided to change from using 400 ASA to 800 ASA film. He had heard someone remark that Munger used it. So he had gone out and bought a dozen boxes. Last night, after the impromptu party, he was going to unpack them and make sure each individual container was loose and ready for unloading. It was at least an hour's job and he had cleaned out his pouch ready to take them. Then had come the mirror, the girl and the opium.

That night found him lying flat on his back on the bed in his room. He had lain there for hours, staring up at the ceiling and the slowly turning fan. Back at the landing zone he had considered three options: try to borrow film from another photographer; go back on the next chopper; kill himself.

He had ended up going back on the next chopper. He was not about to ask anyone to lend him film. They would do it for sure, and then grin and remind him to take off the lens cover. As for killing himself, he doubted that he had the courage.

He had to wait an hour to be evacuated. It was the same crew who had flown him in. He sat in the back among the plastic bags containing the dead, half wishing he was one of them. The pilots had said nothing - just looked at his face. It did not happen often but they had seen other correspondents and photographers who could not face the reality of war.

So it was over, his last chance represented by the rolls of unused film in a nearby drawer. He had not bothered developing the single roll. With the heaviest engagement for months going on half a mile away, all he had shot was a couple of burnt-out choppers.

It was over and he felt a stab of irritation at the soft tap on the door.

'Who is it?' he called.

'Letter for you,' came the muffled answer.

'Push it under the door.'

Another hour passed while he contemplated the fan. Then he swung his feet off the bed and headed for the bathroom and saw the yellow envelope on the floor. He picked it up and ripped it open. Small strips of contact prints and negatives fell out onto the carpet, and a single sheet of paper. He squatted down and read the handwritten words:

I don't know how you did today but I got more snaps than I need. Use the enclosed if you wish. It will be between you, me and the gatepost.

If you're looking for a reason, the fact that you attacked the mirror instead of me is good enough.

DM.

He held the piece of paper for a long time then dropped it to the carpet and picked up the prints. There were ten of them in two strips. The first strip was a sequence showing two black-clad Vietcong charging the camera, Kalashnikovs at their hips. By the third print one of them was twisting away, his Kalashnikov spinning out of his hands. In the fourth the other was very close, his face contorted with effort and hatred. In the fifth he was on his knees, his face a mask of blood.

The second strip depicted a G.I. firing a light machine gun. It was a close-up of his face peering through the sights. Eyes narrowed under the helmet. Chin unshaven and thrust forward. On the helmet were chalked the words 'Hell Rider'. The fifth print showed him lying on his back, arched over his gun. His eyes were wide open and staring sightlessly. The helmet lay inverted in the dirt beside him.

Duff drew a deep breath. The snaps were gems. Clear, sharp and screaming in their immediacy. Slowly he laid them down beside the paper, straightened up, walked into the bathroom and urinated into the toilet bowl. Then he lowered the seat and sat down and stayed there for a long time. He always did his best thinking sitting on the toilet.

After an eternity he reached his decision - and he pulled the chain.

There was no way that he could explain that decision to Ruth. Or even explain anything about the twenty-four hours that had marked a crossroads in his life.

He listened now at the clatter of dishes through the open door as she cleaned up in the kitchen. No, she would never understand. Not about the mirror, nor Wei Fong, nor the opium, but above all how he could have left his room that night, gone down and wired someone else's photographs under his byline. Curiously it had never troubled him. He had not tried to rationalise it even by the thought that his actions had been justified by helping to establish his 'cover' as a spy. He had only seen Munger once since that night. It was in the crowded bar of the Ton San Nut airport. They had been separated by a dozen people and it was several minutes before Duff had caught his eye in the mirror behind. He had merely nodded and Munger had nodded back and the message had been sent and received.

It had been the turning point; His editor had sent an ecstatic cable of congratulations. Two days later Duff had gone out with a Marine patrol in the Delta and his photographs had later been described as among the most electric of the entire war. He had also been slightly but honourably wounded in the leg by a piece of shrapnel. The jokes and the bantering had terminated. He had taken Munger's advice and never tried to find a reason for his generosity. But now there was a link between them. He desperately wanted to know why Munger was selling off his gear and if there was anything at all Munger needed.

He pushed back his chair and stood and stretched and went into the kitchen. Ruth was at the sink wearing long, pink, rubber gloves as she washed the dishes. He moved in close behind and kissed the back of her neck and patted her bottom.

'I'm off.'

She turned and kissed him on the mouth and asked:

'Will you be late?'

'No more than a couple of hours. When you've finished, why don't you ring the Mandarin and book that table for Thursday night?'

She smiled at the reminder of their coming anniversary. 'I'll do that - and tell them to have plenty of champagne on ice.'

He shook his head in mock exasperation. 'It's the greatest myth ever put about that two can live as cheaply as one!'

She grinned at him and kissed the tip of his nose and turned back to the dishes. As she heard the door close she wondered if he had bought the bracelet yet. It was supposed to be a surprise, of course, but they both knew. Twice in the past week she had steered him past the jewellery window in Lane Crawfords and just ever so casually drawn his attention to the jade and gold bracelet. She knew that it cost seven thousand Hong Kong dollars and that it was extravagant but she also knew that he had just received his first bonus and they had that much and just a bit more in the bank.

CHAPTER TWO

Walter Blum watched them coming. He had been sitting at his usual table in the corner for the past hour, and as usual a silver ice bucket lay on the table in front of him. It contained a now half empty bottle of Montrachet. He liked watching people. It was both his profession and his sport. Certainly he was unsuited for anything more active, for he weighed something over three hundred pounds and he was not a tall man. His appearance was a parody of the very rich, very fat man with vulgar tastes. He wore a shiny, light grey mohair suit and a maroon tie fastened to a light blue silk shirt by a diamond-studded gold tie pin. Over-large rings glittered on pudgy fingers as he raised and puffed at his fat cigar. The caricature was completed by a monocle hanging from his neck by a thin, black silk cord. No one had ever seen him use it. He came into the Foreign Correspondents' Club almost every night at 7.30, having been deposited at the entrance to Sutherland House by his white Rolls Royce. Even the slight exertion of walking the twenty paces to the lifts would leave him panting and perspiring slightly as he stepped out into the air conditioned foyer on the fourteenth floor. He would make his way to his table nodding benignly to staff and acquaintances. The chilled bottle of wine and four glasses would already, be waiting; Three of the glasses were there in case he invited anyone to join him. Such invitations were eagerly awaited, for even at Club prices a good bottle of Montrachet cost a fortune. He would rise at 9.45 and on his way to the foyer would stop at the bar and exchange a few words with Chang the bartender. By 10 o'clock he would be at his comer table in the Grill Room of the Mandarin Hotel. He preferred to dine alone - it was a serious business.

He had been following this routine for many years. No one knew why he enjoyed the F.C.C. It was not a rich man's club and lacked the opulence that would have more suited his appearance. But the reason was simple. He liked to observe people - a broad spectrum of people and of all the clubs of Hong Kong the F.C.C. was the prime place to do that.

The venerable Hong Kong Club attracted merely the British business and government community, with just a sprinkling of outsiders who had been allowed to join so as to discourage anticolonial criticism. The American Club was . . . well, too American, and the Country Club at Deep Water Bay the preserve of the nouveau riche. Despite his appearance Walter Blum would have shuddered to hear himself so described.

In essence the F.C.C. was cosmopolitan. Only a fraction of its members were genuine correspondents, but it attracted a diverse cross section of the community. There were, of course, the representatives of the local media: editors and reporters from the British and Chinese press, cameramen and commentators from the local television stations, even disc jockeys from the radio station. As they were 'local' and media 'professionals', they tended to adopt a slightly superior attitude to lesser members, such as advertising account executives, commercial artists, insurance brokers and the like. They were only subdued in the presence of the 'aristocracy' - those members for whom the Club had been created: the bureau chiefs, correspondents and photographers who disseminated the region's happenings to the world's media.

Walter Blum had no trouble in differentiating between them. The aristocracy were few. They spent much of their time travelling on the job. They did not dress to a pattern and they tended to talk quietly.

The second strata - the local media men - usually wore the 'uniform'. This was an all-purpose epauletted safari suit overburdened with pockets and special slots for ballpoints. Several Indian tailors in Nathan Road had prospered beyond their dreams in churning them out.

The third strata - the insurance and ship brokers, the travel agents and traders - seemed to be in perpetual expectation of an exciting or scandalous event. They were often rewarded for the mélange of members could, at times, have an explosive effect.

Tonight there was already an air of great expectancy. No morbid curiosity such as would have been normal before an auction, but a rippling of excitement. The prelude to the unexpected. The place was packed for the word had been quickly passed. From the vantage point of his corner table Walter Blum could see the whole of the restaurant, most of the oval bar, and the foyer with the lifts beyond. Once in a while he would nod his head in acknowledgement to one who rated an acknowledgement. There was a group of four at the end of the bar which he found interesting. It comprised Howard Talbot, a First Secretary of the U.S. Consulate; the beautiful Janine Lesage, Far East correspondent of L'Universe; Sami Asaf of the Middle East News Bureau of Beirut, and Klaus Kinkel, the local head of the Goethe Institute. Yes, they were a most interesting group, for Walter Blum knew that among others in that crowded room they were, apart from their obvious credentials, also intelligence agents or, as he much preferred to call them: spies.

Talbot was number two of the local C.I.A. station. Lesage worked for Service de Documentation Exterieure et de Contre Espionage, or in short the French S.D.E.C.E. Asaf was the sole representative and therefore head of the Iraqi Mukhabarat in the Far East, and Kinkel was a rising star in the B.N.D. - Bundesnachrichtendienst, of West Germany. According to Walter's information, he was here on a six-month posting to obtain Far East experience prior to a major promotion. He wondered if any of them knew that the others were spies, or indeed that Chang the bartender, who was polishing glasses and listening to their conversation, worked both for the communist Chinese Secret Service and that of the Kuomintang. The thought amused Walter and he took a sip of his Montrachet and brushed cigar ash from the lapel of his mohair suit. Then his attention was drawn to the lift. Duff Paget emerged wearing light blue slacks, a cream shirt, and an expression of suppressed curiosity. Before entering the main room he stopped, as everyone always did, at the curved panel that separated the foyer from the bar. On it was pasted a variety of photographs taken by the more eminent of the F.C.C.'s members. They ranged from candid portraits of various heads of state to; combat shots that had received worldwide acclaim. No one could study that panel for a few minutes without being affected. There was Eddie Adam's shot of the Saigon Police Chief in the act of blowing the brains out of a defenceless Vietcong prisoner; a young Buddhist Nun sitting cross-legged and frozen in flame as she ritually burned herself to death in front of the Presidential Palace; Larry Burrow's moving shot of a black sergeant holding and comforting a frightened white G.I.: the face of a shell-shocked Marine photographed by Don McCullin, a face that told more of the war than ten million words. Then the face of Richard Nixon grinning inanely at the camera.

But Walter knew that Duff Paget's attention would be drawn to the two photographs that had only recently been added. One showed a U.S. Army Chaplain, incongruous in uniform and dog collar, looking at a passing G.I. on the back of whose flak jacket was chalked the now hackneyed phrase:

'Yea though I walk through the Valley of the Shadow of Death I shall fear no evil, because I'm the meanest motherfucker in the valley!'

The Chaplain's expression spoke volumes. The other photograph showed, in close-up, a girl with almond eyes in an oval face and ebony hair piled high and contrasting vividly with the background of what appeared to be white netting. It was a face of transcendental innocence.

Walter knew that Paget would concentrate on those two because he had taken them, and the fact that the Committee had included them on the panel was his passport to the Club's aristocracy.

Paget paused for a long moment and then passed into the bar and joined the group of spies at the end. Walter wondered about that. Was he also one of them? His interest was more than passing curiosity, for this gaudy, vulgar glutton was himself a spy, and one with an enviable reputation in his own service.

He had come to it late in his life and by a curious channel. He was a Jewish white Russian, whose family had fled to Shanghai after the Revolution. His father had begun importing and then manufacturing textiles for the vast Chinese market. The company was named Walen Trading, an amalgamation of the names of his two children Walter and Ellen. The latter had died of pleurisy shortly after the family's resettlement and so Walter had become the sole heir.

Over the years Walen Trading had prospered and Walter's father had opened branches and warehouses throughout the country, always managed by white Russian Jews. During the war and the Japanese occupation this prosperity had accelerated mainly because his major rivals, the British and French, had been interned. However, in spite of his commercial advantage, Walter's father had been an honourable and courageous man and had used his freedom and his wealth to help the internees to the utmost of his ability, even bribing high Japanese officials to allow extra medicines and food into the camps and taking great personal risks. So, when the war ended, he had both enormous wealth and the eternal gratitude of his previous competitors and the British Government. He was even awarded an honorary M.B.E. and had planned to travel to London to receive it from the hand of King George VI himself. Unfortunately he had died of a massive coronary shortly before the ship was due to sail. As a result Walter, at the age of twenty, had suddenly found himself the owner of a thriving and widespread trading and manufacturing group. It was a lonely task, for his mother had died several years earlier and he had few close friends as he was already a fat and unattractive young man. He discovered, however, that he had not only a great talent for commerce, but also for gauging the political wind. As the Communists and Nationalists fought for control of China he estimated long before most that the Communists would be victorious. He began converting the holdings of Walen Trading into cash and moving that cash out of the country to invest elsewhere in a unique way. He had learned from his father that in trading the most valuable asset, apart from cash, was people. His father had been a superb judge of character and Walter had inherited this attribute and developed an almost unerring instinct for finding the right man for the right job. So he gathered to Shanghai all the senior management of Walen Trading and explained to them the new policy. Each would be resettled in a new country. Each would receive a capital of half a million U.S. dollars and a bank line of credit of one million. In 1948 that was a very comfortable amount. Each of the managers would own 25 per cent of companies they operated. He himself would relocate to Hong Kong, which would become the new base for the head office of Walen Trading.

So, like a handful of seeds scattered on fertile ground, Walter had flung his managers and his wealth around the world. In those days of rigid foreign exchange controls there had been great difficulty in transferring money out of China but Walter had circumvented the problem with ingenuity. The order of Benedictine monks was widespread and influential in pre-war China. Unlike Walter they foresaw an eventual Nationalist victory and were determined to be prepared for it. Most of their wealth was collected and invested in the U.S.A. and Walter had offered them a profitable deal. He would make money available to the order in China and they would credit his account in New York - less 10 per cent. This arrangement had continued right up to the Communist victory, and even beyond, for although the monks' political and military prognosis had proved wrong, the Communists had, at first, encouraged them and many commercial firms to stay on.

Walter had been about to make his final departure when the hammer fell. Apart from sharing a financial transaction with the Benedictine Abbot, he had also shared his mistress: a white Russian lady of volatile temperament. She had been instrumental in bringing Walter and the Abbot together and had acted as a go-between during their transactions. Naturally, before his departure, Walter settled on her what he thought was a generous amount of money. Unfortunately the lady had a different scale of values and, in a rage, had gone to the authorities and laid before them the facts of Walter's exchange control violations. He and the Abbot had been thrown into jail.

It was, Walter knew, only a temporary ripple. The Communists were pragmatic. They wanted money. The only question was how much. His main worry was that his loyal managers now overseas would offer too much. From jail he could not communicate with them, so he feigned appendicitis and demanded to be examined by his own doctor, who was also a white Russian and a trusted family friend. In due course he was summoned and during the examination Walter managed to convey the vital message. The Communists were suspicious however. If Walter were truly ill, something must be done. Hence Walter lost his entirely blameless appendix on the sacrificial altar of commercial expediency,

In due course his New York company transferred the two million dollars he had suggested and after six more months of niggling argument he was released and allowed to leave for Hong Kong. He quickly replaced the weight he had lost during confinement but he had been left with two permanent legacies of that period. One was a scar on his fish-white belly and the other was a total knowledge of every word of Shakespeare's 'Hamlet'. It had been the only book he managed to borrow from the meagre prison library and over the months he had absorbed every line of every page. In this play he made what to him were earth shattering discoveries and in its language he found the expression for everything he had ever wanted to say but could not for lack of vocabulary or verbal lucidity.

Since then his conversation had been liberally sprinkled with quotations from 'Hamlet'. His friends and acquaintances found it disconcerting and his managers scattered around the globe found it necessary to keep a copy always to hand. It became normal for them to receive a telex with a terse epigram reading, for example:

'Act 1, Scene 2, line 192.'

On looking it up the manager would read 'Season your admiration for a while', and the manager would know that Walter was not entirely convinced about a joint venture he had just proposed.

He had found on his arrival in Hong Kong that the seeds of his scattered empire had already begun to germinate. He now had offices as far apart as Rio de Janeiro and Sydney, London and Johannesburg. In the East he was established throughout Japan and South East Asia. Each office was developing according to its location and the temperament and skills of its manager. In Rio they traded in steel and specialised metals. In Japan in the newly emerging fields of cameras and electronics. The manager there had even leased a tuna fishing fleet and its catches were being sold in Europe through the Paris office.

Twice a year Walter would make a grand tour, both commercial and gastronomic. He would visit his managers and the best restaurants in the cities in which they lived. On his 1953 tour he had dined in the Savoy Grill in London and afterwards seen Richard Burton as Hamlet at the Old Vic. He had sat in the front row of the stalls and mouthed every line until at the end of Act II his voice had become unconsciously audible. During the interval a note was delivered to him in the bar. It read:

'My thanks, kind Sir, but I am acquainted with the lines.

R.B.'

He treasured that note as much as any of the paintings by great masters he subsequently acquired.

By the middle fifties he had emerged as one of the richest men in Asia. The Korean War and its aftermath had spurred enormous commercial growth in Japan and throughout the region and Walen Trading had been on the crest of the long wave. Walter had offices and factories in over forty countries and each grand tour now took up to three months. He should have been vastly satisfied and, to the extent of his commercial success, he was. However, there was a missing element. Due to his skill in selection of personnel, and his policy in allowing his managers great freedom, he had little to do with the day-to-day operations of his empire. It was loose-knit and diverse and unlike the structure of a great multinational, too much control from the centre would have stifled its entrepreneurial spirit. In short, he became bored and, in his boredom, began to look for new horizons.

The event which proved to be the catalyst was the 1956 Middle East War. After Israel's success in occupying the Sinai the Israeli Government did what they always do after every war. They sent well-known generals and statesmen around the world to solicit money from world Jewry to fill up the war chest. Moshe Dayan, the hero of the war, was sent to Australia. After receiving pledges of over forty million dollars he stopped off in Hong Kong on his way home.

There were less than three hundred Jews in Hong Kong but they included some vastly rich individuals and Dayan spent several days giving lectures about the war, the state of Israel's finances and the terrible dangers that lay ahead. For Walter he had reserved a whole evening and they had dinner alone in Walter's villa on the peak.

Dayan well knew of the extent of Walter's wealth and had hoped for a pledge of at least a million dollars. However, he found his host curiously tight-fisted. Walter explained that he had an aversion to giving money to governments, either in taxes or any other way. Of course he supported Israel. He was not a mean man and had already given large sums both for the planting of new forests and in grants to Tel Aviv University. His own office in Tel Aviv, which had introduced diamond cutting to the country, had also made its own generous contributions. Dayan had been both blunt and persuasive but Walter had stressed that he would prefer to offer his services in other ways.

'What other ways?' Dayan had asked and Walter had shrugged and pointed out that he had a network of offices all round the world managed entirely at the top level by enterprising Jews. Perhaps he could help Israel in promoting its trade? Dayan had pondered on that for a while and then a gleam had come into one good eye. He spent the rest of the evening and far into the night questing deep into Walter's character and background and found that in spite of the man's appearance and apparent vulgarity he had a subtle mind and an incisive grasp of human nature.

As Walter had shown him out, Dayan remarked that perhaps there was a way that he could make an important contribution. He would have discussions in Israel and someone would be in touch.

At the car Walter thanked him for coming, reached into his breast pocket, and handed him a cheque for one million dollars. He had smiled at the General's look of surprise.

Then Dayan had in turn astonished and delighted his host. During their talks he had noted that Walter's speech had been sprinkled with quotations from 'Hamlet'. He got into the car, wound down the window and as it pulled away called out:

'Act II, Scene 2, line 286.'

Walter beamed after the departing car. The line had sprung instantly to his mind.

'Beggar that I am, I am ever poor in thanks.'

Six weeks later during one of his periodic visits to his office in Israel, Walter had been in turn invited to dinner at Dayan's home. There had been another guest: a small, fidgety man called Isser Harel. After dinner Dayan had left his two guests alone with coffee and a bottle of Cognac. Isser Harel was the then legendary head of the Israeli Secret Service, Mossad. As the level of the Cognac gradually receded he talked long and eloquently about how Walter could be of assistance to Israel. Finally Walter had burst out with some astonishment:

'You want me to be a spy!'

Harel had demurred, preferring to use other less dramatic nomenclature, but Walter was entranced by the prospect and brushed aside the attempts at semantic evasion. He immediately saw the beauty of it. With his network of offices, his commercial communications set-up, his army of loyal Jewish managers, and above all, his great wealth, he instantly saw himself with a magical role to play.

Now Harel was silent as Walter gave scope to his imagination. He quickly ran through the names of those managers who would best be suited to such a role. In the meantime Walen Trading could take existing Mossad agents onto its payroll. New offices could be opened in sensitive areas. He revelled in the whole idea.

Again Harel had demurred. They should move slowly, people must be trained, including Walter himself. Such a network as Walter envisaged would take years to construct. Walter's enthusiasm had not been blunted.

'A spy,' he mused, and then his fat lips had stretched into a smile. 'A Master Spy - I'll be a Master Spy!'

Harel suppressed a smile and later his report to the Cabinet suggested that although Walter Blum and his Walen Trading might be of some use, particularly in communications and as a conduit for covert financial transactions, he doubted that any valuable intelligence would accrue, apart from perhaps industrial secrets.

But Harel had badly underestimated Walter's energy, organisational genius and his inborn flair for the subtleties of espionage. Within six months he was being badgered for training facilities for dozens of Walter's people. As each man was vetted Harel came to recognise Walter's skill in personnel selection. Only one had to be rejected on the grounds that he had immediate family still in Russia and was therefore vulnerable to pressure from that direction. Walter himself made several trips to Tel Aviv, ostensibly to expand his office there but in reality to receive his own training. Within a year information was flooding into Mossad headquarters and the analysts determined that it was of the highest quality.

Way ahead of his original schedule, Isser Harel began drafting his own Mossad agents into Walen Trading and it changed from being merely a passive gatherer of information to a more active role. Harel was wise enough not to undercut Walter's position in any way. He remained the boss of his own network and the dividends began to roll in.

When Israel was striving to produce its own nuclear bomb in the early sixties, it was Walter's network that first provided vital technical information along with certain 'unobtainable' components. Later the New York branch of his organisation was instrumental in 'gathering' quantities of weapons-grade plutonium from the U.S. nuclear installations and then arranging its onward shipment to Israel. In the period leading up to the '67 war Walter had opened trading offices throughout the Middle East, all owned by front companies registered in such countries as Liechtenstein, Panama and Monaco. His trade connections remained excellent in the Arab world and through a mixture of subterfuge and simple commercial bargaining had done much to circumvent the Arab black list of all firms dealing with Israel. After the '67 war he had done a great deal to nullify the embargo of arms instituted by France and other countries. It had been his network which smuggled out the two gunboats from under the noses of the French Navy in Cherbourg after De Gaulle had vetoed their delivery.

By 1969, therefore, Walter Blum could claim with every justification the sobriquet 'Master Spy\ His network was given the code name ORANGE. Walter himself was known as ORANGE ONE and the various elements of the network were designated by other numbers. In spite of the close co-operation between Mossad and the C.I.A. neither they, nor any other intelligence organisation, had learned of its existence.

He had continued to maintain his base in Hong Kong because he felt an affinity for the Orient. However, he had lately been coming under increasing pressure to centre himself nearer to the Middle East. Isser Harel had retired in 1962 and been replaced by Meir Amit until 1968. From then Walter had worked under Zui Zamir.

At their first meeting he had stressed to Walter that in the coming decade Israel faced its greatest danger and his services would be in increasing demand. Would he not move closer to the arena? Walter had promised to give it thought and in the meantime had been beefing up the activities of Walen Trading on the island of Cyprus, which would be a perfect base if he ever moved further west.

There had been some movement at the bar. He noted that Duff Paget had left his group and moved further down. His handsome face was marred by an angry expression. Again Walter's curiosity about the man was aroused. He knew that he represented a magazine whose owner had strong connections with the Washington establishment. A couple of months ago Walter had sent a grade one enquiry about him to Mossad headquarters. This had proved negative and, as Mossad had long ago penetrated to the higher levels of the C.I. A., the conclusion must be that Paget was 'clean'. Nevertheless Walter retained a niggling suspicion. He glanced now at his watch and noted that there was still half an hour before the auction, so he crooked a finger to summon a waiter and sent over an invitation for Paget to join him for a drink.

They made a study in contrasts sitting side by side at the corner table: the one short, ugly and grossly fat; the other tall, slender and impossibly handsome.

When Duff was settled with a glass of wine in his hand Walter opened the conversation.

'I wish to congratulate you on your recent work. It's first class. People are talking of you as a new "Munger".'

Duff shook his head vigorously, although he was flattered by the remarks from a man whom he knew closely followed the media coverage coming out of Vietnam.

'No way,' he said firmly. 'I'm still a novice. Munger's in a class of his own.'

'Apparently that's in the past tense,' Walter said, closely watching the young man's face. 'What's this auction all about?'

Duff shrugged. 'It's a total mystery. He just spent a few days on operations with the Special Forces near Vinh Long. He came out to Saigon, filed no snaps and went on a week's drinking session. He flew into Hong Kong this morning, announced that he was selling off his gear, left it with Chang and then took off for the airport. Apparently he caught the first flight to Europe.'

Walter refilled their glasses and remarked: 'Very curious. What's to happen to the proceeds?'

Duff grinned wryly. 'Apparently they're to go to the R.S.P.C. A. - the local dogs' home!'

Walter's great belly rumbled with laughter. 'Yes, Munger never did much like people - but tell me, can't the beautiful Miss Lesage throw light on the subject? After all, she's been his girl-friend on and off for the past few months.' He saw Duffs face darken again as he looked at the tall, blonde, French woman sitting at the bar.

'No,' Duff said, his voice tight. 'She was with him in Saigon but the extent of her information is obscene in every way.' Anger flowed out of him as he glared at her.

'Do tell me,' Walter urged gently.

Duff took a deep breath.

'She just said that after leaving Vinh Long he couldn't fuck anymore! He tried but he couldn't do it.'

Walter's eyebrows shot up and he blew cigar smoke across the table. 'Not a pleasant thing to say about any man - especially one like Munger and especially in a bar like this.'

Duff grunted in angry agreement as Walter studied the woman. She was long and slender, almost rangy. Walter had once heard her described as being built like a racing snake. Apparently she had venom as well. Her long, corn-coloured hair was twisted into a coil and pinned up on her head. Walter had also heard that she could pull out one pin, shake her head, and it would tumble down to below her waist. He would like to see that - he had a thing for long-haired women.

There was a rustle in the crowded room as two waiters carried out a long table and Bennet, dressed as usual in a pinstripe suit and waistcoat, detached himself from the bar.

The table was placed at the end of the room and most of those at the bar stood up for a better view.

Walter was surprised at how little equipment there was. At past auctions he had seen the table piled high with a great variety of cameras and accessories. This time there was only a battered, metal suitcase opened to reveal a neatly packed selection of items for developing contact prints - three concertina plastic bottles, two developing trays, a timer, a thermometer, a water filter and several reels. Next to it was a small version of die same case, opened to show five lenses, a row of slotted filters and a space filled with boxes of film. Finally, resting on a canvas bag, was one camera. The bag had a drawstring and a dark stain on one side. All eyes in the room were on the camera. It had a curious metal attachment on one side, disfiguring the balance of the body. Walter had never seen one like it. He glanced at Duff and saw his gaze locked into it.

'That's a strange looking camera,' Walter said. 'Would you explain it to me?'

Duff drew a deep breath and, without shifting his gaze, began to intone as though speaking a liturgy.

'It's a Nikon FTN, made out of nickel. Very light weight - very durable. It first came on the market in '65 but Munger had that one at least a year earlier. The factory gave it to him for field testing. After six months he took it to Tokyo and had them rivet on that bracket. It's aluminium and designed so that he could put his hand through it and hold and point the camera with his wrist. That leaves the fingers of the same hand free to work the aperture and shutter speed controls. The bracket swivels so that he can also work on the top of the camera body and change films - all with one hand.'

'It's very elaborate,' Walter said. 'Is it necessary?'

Duff motioned with his chin. 'Look at the canvas bag which he carried it in. That stain is blood. It came from a wound in his left shoulder. He got it at the beginning of the Tet offensive. His left arm was useless, but for the next two days he got some of the best snaps of the whole war.'

Walter was impressed. 'So why don't Nikon make all their cameras like that?'

Duff shrugged. 'They thought it was ugly and it doesn't fit a normal case - it was a one-off. Other combat photographers could fit their own brackets . . . but they don't.'

'Why not?'

Duff glanced at him and his lips twitched into a half smile. 'I guess because they're individualists, and they don't like to be thought unoriginal-' He looked back at the table. Bennet had moved behind it and he clapped his hands for silence. In a loud plum-in-the-mouth voice he called out:

'Auction of camera and developing equipment on the instructions of Mr David Munger . . . all proceeds to go to the R.S.P.C. A.'

There was a ripple of excited laughter and then without further preliminaries Bennet started the auction. He knew that the main interest would be for the camera itself so he left that to the end. The cases of developing equipment and the lenses were quickly disposed of, going for only slightly more than replacement value.

Then Bennet paused dramatically and gestured to Chang who brought him a large glass of Scotch. He drained half of it, put the glass on the table and pulled the canvas bag and the camera to the centre.

'Lot number three,' he announced. 'One Nikon FTN, slightly amended.'

The price of a new FTN was 800 Hong Kong dollars and that was the figure Bennet started with. Within a minute he had raised the bidding to $3,000 and all eyes in the room were swivelling back and forth between the three bidders. There was 'Ram' Foster, bureau chief for Newsweek, who had used much of Munger's work; George Hardy, a photographer who worked for the New

York Times; and Janine Lesage. While the first two indicated their bids with a raised finger, she spoke hers, raising each time in a low, flat, determined voice.

'She wants it badly,' Walter observed, but Duff was not listening. His narrowed eyes were moving constantly between the camera and the bidders. George Hardy dropped out at $3,500 and the bidding slowed. Walter thought that Foster might be bidding for his head office but he too dropped out at $4,000. Bennet called out:

'Going once. Going at four thousand dollars.' His eyes swept the room. So did those of Janine Lesage. Piercing, predatory eyes.

'Going twice!' Bennet s hand was held flat down to slap the table.

'Four and a half!'

All eyes swung onto the corner table and the figure of Duff Paget. He appeared startled at the sound of his own voice. Walter Blum was looking amused. He poured more wine into their glasses. The French woman's voice cracked out.

'Five thousand!'

Now the room buzzed and Bennet took another swig of Scotch, pulled a handkerchief from his top pocket and mopped his face.

'Five and a half!'

Duff was leaning forward, his face rigid. There was a long pause. All eyes swung back to Janine Lesage. Her face showed a mixture of anger and frustration.

'Going once at five and a half thousand,' Bennet intoned, looking at the woman. She sat rigid on her bar stool, a glass clamped in the fingers of her right hand.

'Going twice."

'Six thousand!" she called, and Duff's voice followed in an instant.

'Seven!"

It was over and Bennet knew it. He saw her slump lower on her stool. 'Going once. Going twice.' A pause, a swift survey of the room, then his hand slapped down on the table.

'Gone at seven thousand to Duff Paget - and the dogs thank you, sir!"

He laughed loudly at his wit but he was the only one. Janine Lesage was the centre of attention. She had stood up and was looking at Duff with hatred. There was complete silence. Then she spat the words across the room.

'Va te faire enculer.'

She banged her glass onto the bar and strode out. There was a general exhalation of breath and some nervous laughter and then the talk began as everyone crowded to the bar.

'Do you speak French?" Walter asked Duff, who appeared to be in a daze. He looked up and shook his head. Walter smiled.

'Then allow me to translate. The lady associated you with sodomy . . . not very original for one whose profession demands a wide use of vocabulary. However she did get her message across which was, in essence, that you've gained both a camera and an enemy.'

Duffs eyes remained on the camera. He shrugged and said:

'It would have been wrong. She had no right to it.'

'You will use it?'

Duff shook his head emphatically. 'Never! No one will use it. If he ever wants it again it will be waiting for him.' He sighed and then smiled grimly. 'Lesage isn't the only one who's going to be mad with me.'

'Oh?"

'No, that money was going towards a gold and jade bracelet for my wife. It's our wedding anniversary on Thursday.'

Walter clucked sympathetically. 'And she won't understand?' he asked.

Duff shook his head sadly. 'No, she won't understand.'

Walter reached forward and patted him paternally on the shoulder. 'Well young man, at least you won't have to worry about Miss Lesage. I understand that she is being reassigned to the Middle East in a few days.' He glanced at his watch and heaved himself to his feet.

'Thank you for your company and entertainment. I wish you well with your wife. Remember the words of Hamlet:

"Rightly to be great,
Is not to stir without great argument."'

He waddled ponderously across the room, followed by Duffs puzzled gaze.

So on October 29th, two events took place. Duff Paget presented his wife with a bunch of long-stemmed roses and had a terrible row; and thousands of miles away and by the purest coincidence, the Government of Iraq ratified the Nuclear Non-proliferation Treaty.

BOOK TWO

CHAPTER THREE

1 OF 5
IRAQI NUCLEAR PROGRAMME
Report No. IIA.: 14th July 1975

To: General Yitzhak Hofti, Director General
From: Shimon Saguy, Research and Analysis Director
Sources: Head of Station, Paris
ORANGE4
ORANGE7
Circulation: nil

I am fed up. There are just too many people blundering about; sending contradictory information and taking up an inordinate amount of my department's time. During the past 45 days we have processed reports and prepared analysis for:

Milint 2
Foreign Ministry
Cabinet Secretariat
Cabinet Scientific Advisory Panel
Prime Minister's Office
Chief of Staff's Office
U.N. Ambassador's Office (Why?!)
- and yourself (five times)

I did not join Mossad to become a post office sorter. My staff and I have now repeated ourselves, in various reports, more than a dozen times. I will re-cap on the relevant information we possess and will then make a recommendation:

2 OF 5

1. Various states, which can be classified as enemies (or potential enemies) of Israel are currently engaged in attempting to produce nuclear weapons. Those states posing the most serious threat are: Egypt, Libya, Pakistan and Iraq.
2. There is no doubt that the greatest danger is represented by Iraq because, unlike Libya or Egypt which are under tight control by their respective patrons, i.e.: the U.S.S.R. and the U.S.A., Iraq has sufficiently distanced itself from the U.S.S.R. to proceed on an independent (and therefore unsupervised) course. Pakistan is trailing because it lacks both the financial and scientific resources. In any event its nuclear programme is designed primarily to counter that of India. The threat to Israel is a by-product of the Islamic connection.
3. Iraq's sponsor is France: perhaps the most mercenary of all the developed states.

   Note:

   A. More than 50 per cent of French oil imports are supplied by Iraq.
   B. As part of the commercial nuclear 'package', Iraq has agreed to purchase in excess of six billion dollars worth of French-manufactured products, including arms. We estimate that between the years 1977 to 1981 this 'package' will ensure the employment of over one million French workers.
   C. There is currently a marked anti-Israel (you might say anti-Semitic) trend within the French Government.

These factors, combined with Iraq's oil wealth, and Saddam Hussein's ambitions to lead the Arab world, create, in my view, the most serious threat that Israel has ever faced.

3 OF 5

4. The current situation is:

   Three months ago an agreement was signed whereby France would construct for Iraq a 70 M W nuclear reactor for research and training purposes. It would be supported by a minireactor of 800 KW. We discovered (primarily through the efforts of ORANGE 4) that the contract contained several secret clauses, two of which are particularly relevant:

   i. No information could be given about the size of the complex by either side for a period of 25 years.
   ii. The French will not employ anyone of Jewish origin to work on the contract.

It is significant that the planned reactor is at least twice as large as those normally used by industrial nations for research purposes.

A consortium has been formed of five French firms headed by the government agency Technicatom, to build and install the reactor.

Weapons Capability:

As Iraq has signed the Nuclear Non-proliferation Treaty, it will come under the inspection of the International Atomic Energy Agency (I.A.E.A.) Also there will be French scientists and technicians on the spot for the foreseeable future. So under normal circumstances it would not be possible for the Iraqis either to produce weapons-grade uranium or Pu239. However, once they have a nucleus of their own trained people, they could expel the French and the I.A.E. A. inspectors. They could also steal some Pu239- we did.

4 OF 5

At the present time the Iraqis are also negotiating with Italy to buy four 'hot cell' laboratories. Our information is that the deal will shortly be concluded. These laboratories could be used to extract small quantities of Pu239 from spent reactor fuel.

Iraq already has a small Soviet-supplied research reactor which became operational in 1968. However, the Soviets are far stricter in their supervision than many Western states and we do not consider that facility to present a threat.

The crux is that once all these facilities are 'on stream' the Iraqis will be able to train up to 1000 technicians at a time. If any further proof was needed that the Iraqis are planning to produce nuclear weapons it was provided by reports from the ORANGE network that during the past six months the Iraqis have been attempting to purchase (from various sources) large quantities of uranium oxide (yellowcake). They are actively negotiating with Brazil, Niger, China, Libya and Portugal for large quantities of yellowcake. Note that the reactor which the French have agreed to supply is of a type which cannot use refined yellowcake as a fuel. However, by packing it around the reactor core in a 'blanket' they could produce up to 12 kilograms of Pu239 a year. Enough to make two atomic bombs similar in size to the one dropped on Nagasaki.

5 OF 5

Conclusion:
The Iraqis are determined to produce nuclear weapons and the reactor being supplied by the French will give them the capability.

Timescale:
If the contract proceeds on schedule and if, as I believe, the Iraqis subsequently expel the French technicians and the I.A.E.A. inspectors, they will possess nuclear weapons by 1979/80. They already possess the aircraft to give them delivery capability.

Recommendations:

1. Everybody concerned should re-read 'G.M. Memo Three'.
2. That a single entity within Mossad be set up with the sole purpose of counteracting this threat; and that it should have priority over everything else. END IT.

Walter Blum tossed the report on to the desk and blew cigar smoke over it. Across the desk General Hofti coughed and beat the air with his hands. They were sitting in his office and a sign on the desk proclaimed 'No Smoking'!

Walter Blum was the only one who ever broke the rule, explaining on the first occasion that the smoke would distress the good General far less by its presence than Walter by its absence.

General Yitzhak Hofti had taken over as head of Mossad in 1973 when Zui Zamir had been a bureaucratic casualty of the Yom Kippur War. He was a dour man with just a hint of suppressed humour. Walter liked him and enjoyed teasing him.

'What,' he enquired, 'is the "G.M. Memo Three"?'

Hofti pushed his chair back, moved over to the window and, in spite of the air conditioning, opened it. A gust of hot air swept into the room and he inhaled gratefully. He tried to decide which he disliked the most: the smell of cigar smoke or the cologne in which Walter obviously bathed every morning. In fact Walter assailed all his senses, for the General was a sparse, abstemious man, and Walter represented the apex of over-indulgence. But Hofti had abounding respect for his intellect and his ability to 'deliver'. So he took a deep breath, closed the window and turned back to his desk.

'It's the third of three memos that Golda Meir prepared on her retirement.' He sat down and looked at Walter solemnly.

'She considered them to be her legacy to Israel. The first deals with immigration. The second with internal politics and the third with the security of the state. Naturally it has very limited circulation. I will arrange that a copy will be made available to you. In the meantime I can give you a precise of it as it relates to this report.'

He gestured at the folder on his desk and there were a few moments of silence while he collected his thoughts. Then he talked in a low, precise, voice.

'You know that we produced our first nuclear warhead in 1967. In fact your help was invaluable.'

He was referring to the fact that in 1965 Walter's ORANGE network had been instrumental in stealing 206 pounds of enriched uranium from the Nuclear Materials and Equipment Company in Pennsylvania.

'Since then,' Hofti continued, 'we have built up a stockpile of twenty-three bombs.'

He smiled slightly. 'What you don't know is that in '73, during the Yom Kippur war, we prepared thirteen of them for immediate use.'

His smile widened as he saw the look on Walter's face.

'We would have used them?' Walter asked.

The General shrugged. 'That would have been Golda's decision. Frankly, I doubt it. They were prepared for the purpose of frightening the Americans. You will recall that they'd been very tardy in airlifting military supplies to us in the first few days. Kissinger no doubt thought that if the Egyptians were to take and hold a sizeable portion of the Sinai, we would be more tractable when it came to overall peace negotiations.

'Anyway, Golda gave them a seventy-two hour ultimatum. Either the supplies started to flow or we would use our nuclear arsenal on Egypt. You can imagine their reaction!'

Walter was shaking his head in awe. 'And they believed her?'

'At first, no. But after twenty-four hours we started to prepare the bombs. They're at Dimona and the C.I.A. have an agent in there.' Again Hofti smiled at Walter's look of incredulity.

'Of course, we have known about him for years. They slipped him in when they were helping us, back in the fifties. We left him alone in the expectation that one day he would be useful. Well, that day came. Naturally we let him see the bombs being readied and very soon the Americans began to take Golda's threat seriously. As a result we got our supplies and in short order the Egyptian Second Army was surrounded. Now you see the implications?'

Walter was nodding, deep in thought.

'Obviously, if the Egyptians also had the bomb,' he said, 'Golda's threat would have been idle in the extreme. "This bodes some strange eruption to our state".'

"Precisely,' the General agreed. 'In her memo number three Golda spelled it out, not perhaps with as much erudition as Shakespeare, but certainly in simple, unequivocal terms. We cannot allow any potential enemy of Israel to have nuclear weapons until such time as there is a comprehensive peace settlement which gives Israel secure borders, recognised by all parties and guaranteed by the great powers. The fact that only Israel has the bomb is our ultimate security until we have that peace settlement.'

'That could be a long time.'

Hofti shook his head. 'Not as long as some think. There are already strange vibrations coming out of Egypt. I myself give it ten years. But Walter, the point is that if any other Middle East country obtains or builds nuclear weapons then that estimate could be very protracted . . . and we would finally have to settle for something less than adequate. The Egyptians have already shown they are capable of fighting a determined conventional war. We are facing odds of hundreds to one and eventually we would lose a conventional war. With that scenario we must work for peace and our continued exclusivity in the nuclear field is our only trump card. We cannot lose it.' Again he gestured at the folder.

'Therefore, I've decided to follow Shimon's recommendations. A single entity within Mossad will now be made responsible to ensure that Iraq, or any other enemy, does not obtain, by any means, nuclear weapons.'

He looked hard at Walter who took a deep draw on his cigar.

'I want you personally to be that entity. Of course, you will use the network and any other agency you require, but from this moment your sole mission is to stop the Iraqis getting that bomb . . . your sole mission, Walter.'

With a grunt Walter pushed himself to his feet and started to pace the floor. He was wearing a dark blue sharkskin suit and alligator leather shoes, one of which squeaked rhythmically under his bulk. After waddling back and forth several times he stopped abruptly, looked at Hofti with annoyance and said: 'It's just not true!"

'What?'

'That shoes only squeak if they haven't been paid for.'

Hofti snorted both in amusement and exasperation.

'You make jokes while I talk of a threat to Israel's very existence.'

Walter shook his head, it's no joke. The damned thing cost me four hundred dollars in New York.' He pointed his cigar accusingly at the General.

'And I bought them from a Jew.' His fat lips twitched into a smile. 'Maybe he never paid the alligator.'

He noted the General's expression, moved back to his chair and sank ponderously into it. Hofti was yet again recalling the setbacks in having an agent wealthy enough to buy half of Israel. But he kept his tongue still and waited for Walter to come back to the subject.

'I could of course talk of the great weight of responsibility you're putting on my shoulders,' Walter said, 'but I hate alluding to weight in any form. Have you any suggestions as to how I undertake this mission?'

'Several,' Hofti answered. 'The first one is that you finally move your base to Cyprus. You must be closer to the arena.'

Walter nodded in agreement.

'And also closer to France, because that is where I'm going to start.'

'How?'

Walter held up three fingers. 'There are three stages. First: to try to stop the French by using diplomatic methods. Second: sabotage the deal using any methods; and third: assuming that the reactor is delivered, to render it inoperable.' He thought for a minute and then said:

'I'll consider all the aspects and give you a report in seven days. Meanwhile I'm going to need every single scrap of information available.' He reached forward and patted the folder.

'Your friend Shimon is going to be fed up again - he's going to see a great deal of me.' He smiled benignly at the General and added: 'Let's hope he enjoys a good cigar.'

CHAPTER FOUR

His emergence was caused by a dog and even then it took three long years before he finally crept out into the light.

The dog was a mélange of breeds and it belonged to Androulla Papadopoulos, who was eight years old at the time and an obedient girl. She lived with her parents in a small farmhouse two miles from the village of Phini, high in the Troödos mountains of Cyprus. Her mother often sent her into Phini to do the shopping.

Almost half way to the village was another farmhouse, set back from the dirt road and surrounded by a low, stone wall. Androulla had been told never to go near that farmhouse for a strange foreigner lived in it. A foreigner who hardly ever went out and, on the rare occasion that he did, spoke to no one except the old woman who ran the little general store - and then only to order his supplies.

There had been much gossip about him when he first arrived, for the village was very introverted and would have been suspicious of even a Cypriot settling from another part of the island. But there was little they could find out. He had bought the half-ruined farmhouse and a few acres of land and spent his time repairing it and growing vegetables and keeping a few chickens. The old woman at the store reported that he spoke passable Greek and that the most regular item he purchased was vodka.

A hermit is always the centre of speculation and suspicion and the people of Phini resented his silent intrusion and decided he was a bad man. The village children were told to stay away from him and for over a year Androulla had obeyed her parents and kept well away. She had not even seen him on his rare trips to the village. When she passed his farmhouse she felt nervous and always quickened her step, glad to have the company of her dog. One day, however, a squirrel had run across the road and the dog had set off after it. The squirrel had sought refuge over the low wall surrounding the farmhouse and, in one bound, the dog had followed. As Androulla stood frightened on the road she heard the dog give a howl and then several more. There came a silence and she was about to run for her father when the foreigner's head appeared above the wall.

'Is this your dog?' he called.

Fright had robbed her of speech but she nodded vigorously.

'Well, you'd better come. He's hurt himself.'

The head disappeared and she stood undecided for a while. But she loved her dog and so she had finally walked up the track to the open gate and peered in. The foreigner was near the wall bending over the dog. It lay still and in a sudden panic Androulla ran up.

'Is he dead?'

The foreigner shook his head and then she saw that the dog's eyes were open and his tail thumped gently as he saw her.

'He cut his paw when he landed,'

The man pointed to the blades of a small rotavator lying beside the wall. He was binding a piece of cloth around the paw and Androulla was surprised that the dog lay so quiescent under his hands for it was a fierce dog and not friendly with strangers.

'Is it bad?'

'No, but he'll be walking on three legs for a few days. Make sure he doesn't tear this covering off.'

He finished and straightened, and the dog struggled up, holding the bound paw in the air. He reached forward with his head and licked the man's hand and then looked quizzically at Androulla. There was a heavy silence before the man said:

'You'd better be on your way.'

She looked up at him. His hair was long and he had a beard so she could not see much of his face. She noted that his eyes were very blue and his skin dark and weather-beaten. She was puzzled because he did not look like a bad man, and she knew her dog would never show affection for a bad man. All her fear had now dissipated and was replaced by curiosity. Being only eight years old her question when it came was straight to the point.

'Why do people say you're a bad man?'

She thought she saw a faint smile twitch under the beard but his voice was severe.

'They're probably right. Now off with you and don't let him chase squirrels.'

He turned away to the house and she took the dog by the collar and led him hopping to the gate. The man was just about to go through the door when she called out 'Thank you.'

He turned and nodded in acknowledgement and stood watching as she walked down the track to the road. He stood there for a long time, even after she had disappeared from view.

When Androulla got home and reported to her mother she received a scolding. She should never have gone in there, but come home immediately. He was a bad man.

Androulla was unconvinced and she was stubborn.

'Why is he a bad man? What has he done?'

Her mother told her not to ask questions. She was too young to know about such things. She was not to go there again, not to talk to him again, and not to ask questions.

When she continued to argue her father intervened, sending her to her room and threatening to beat her if she disobeyed her mother.

So she went to bed and the dog jumped up beside her and licked her face in commiseration and then gnawed at the cloth on his paw. She slapped him on the backside, venting some of her frustration. He did not complain. He seemed to understand.

The weeks and months passed and Androulla obeyed her mother and never saw the foreigner. The dog, however, was under no restriction and whenever they passed the farmhouse it would break away and go through the gate. She would walk on and the dog would catch up a few minutes later, his tail wagging.

It might have gone on like that for years had it not been for the invasion of Cyprus by the Turkish Army in February 1973 and the subsequent occupation of the north-east part of the island.

Part of the invasion plans involved the firebombing of the forests of the Troödos mountains as a diversion to keep the Cypriot army occupied.

So one night scores of bombers swept in from the North and within hours the mountains were covered in flames. The area around the village of Phini escaped lightly, for most of the bombing was on the Northern slopes. However, one bomber, perhaps due to poor navigation, strayed from its path and unloaded its incendiaries in a line less than a hundred metres from the Papadopoulos farmhouse. Androulla and her parents had to fight the fire alone for the villagers were guarding their own homes against the expected Turkish hordes. They were fortunate, for the wind was from the north, driving the fire down the slopes and away from the homestead. The only danger lay in a row of four pine trees close to the house. If they caught fire the house would be threatened. So while Androulla helped her mother to carry buckets of water and douse the surrounding scrub, her father took an axe and set to chopping down the pines. He was half way through the last one when the accident happened. Maybe it was exhaustion, but he missed the open wedge, the axe head glanced off the trunk and bit deep into his calf, laying it open to the bone.

Aridroulla's mother was a stoical woman but her heart almost stopped when she saw the wound.

'The village!' she screamed to Androulla. 'Go to the village - get help!'

So Androulla ran off into the dark with the dog bounding beside her. But she did not go to the village.

Her mother managed to drag him into the house and had the sense to twist a cloth around his thigh as a tourniquet. She calculated it would be an hour before help arrived and so, twenty minutes later, she looked up in surprise as the door opened and a man stood there clutching a khaki satchel in his hand.

It was the foreigner. He had run on ahead of the girl.

At first the woman had been uncertain, in a way protecting her man from the unknown. Her peasant instincts made her crouch over him like a lioness defending her young.

The foreigner took in the situation at a glance. When he spoke his voice was quiet and gentle.

'Let me look. I won't hurt him.'

He laid the satchel onto the stone floor and opened the straps. She could see bottles and metal cases and, on the side, the faded white lettering 'U.S.A.M.C.' She could not understand the words and foreigner edged forward, dragging the satchel behind. First he checked the tourniquet and gave her a nod of approval. Then he examined the wound as Androulla came panting through the door.

Looking back on that night Androulla's mother was to remember how completely he had imposed his authority and how he convinced her of what must be done.

First he had assured her that the wound was not as bad as it looked. Although there was a lot of blood, no arteries had been severed. However; it needed extensive stitching. She had an alternative. Either he could bind it up and they would try to get him to the nearest doctor who was in Platres, ten miles away over the mountain roads, or he would do it himself. He was not a doctor but he had experience in such things. There were other considerations.

The roads might be blocked. Turkish troops could be about and even if they got to Platres the doctors there could be busy for days with more serious cases. He told her that according to his radio there was a full-scale war being fought to the North. She had looked at her husband's face, eyes narrowed and teeth clenched in pain, and then at the foreigner - into his blue, steady eyes.

'Do it,' she told him.' Please!'

Androulla had boiled some water and her mother helped the foreigner. First he injected novocaine around the gash, then swabbed it out with disinfectant. He quietly explained everything that he did: the first row of stitches, closing the inner flesh - the sutures would dissolve in a matter of days. Then antibiotic powder and finally closing the outer flesh with more neat stitches. Then more powder, a gauze covering and a precisely bound bandage. By the time he had finished the woman was at ease. Everything he had done and said had carried the stamp of confidence and experience. He had helped her carry her husband to bed and left some pills to ease the pain and then, brushing aside her thanks, he had left, refusing even the offer of a cup of coffee. His confidence and composure had seemed to leave him once the activity of his work ended. As he reached the door she had called out to him:

'At least tell us your name.'

He had mumbled something and left. The woman looked at her daughter and asked' What did he say?'

The girl shrugged. 'He said it doesn't matter.'

They left word at the village and two days later an army doctor drove up and examined the wound and pronounced the stitching to be highly professional. He gave the farmer an anti-tetanus shot and promised to return a week later to take out the stitches.

The brief and bloody war ended when the Turkish army had occupied that portion of the island marked out for partition. All Greek Cypriots were uprooted and, with only what they could carry, expelled to the Greek sector. Apart from the firebombing of the forests, the villages in the Troödos mountains were relatively untouched and life quickly returned to normal. However, Vassos and Helena Papadopoulos and their daughter Androulla faced a continuous problem.

The foreigner had rendered them a service and in their simple and straightforward view of life they owed a debt and wanted to repay it. As soon as Vassos could walk again he visited the foreigner to offer his thanks and an invitation to dinner. The thanks were accepted with a shrug and the invitation turned down. He preferred to keep to himself. A few days later Vassos was sitting outside the village taverna, drinking with his friends, when the foreigner passed by on his way to the store. Vassos called out and invited him to join them, but again he was rebuffed.

Vassos was prepared to withdraw his antennae of friendship but Helena was determined and, being a farmer's wife and a sensible woman, finally came up with the crowbar to lever open the foreigner's shell.

One day she baked a *kleftiko*, a Cypriot speciality comprising baby lamb, vegetables and an intriguing mixture of herbs. She was justly famous for her *kleftiko* and on this one she lavished special care. All day it simmered slowly in the oven then, just before sunset, she ladled it steaming into an earthenware pot and despatched it with Androulla down the road. 'If he refuses that,' she said to Vassos, 'then he's no man!' Androulla approached the farmhouse with some trepidation. Gingerly she laid the pot on the doorstep and tapped hesitantly on the door. Her dog stood watching with interest. The door opened and she looked up at his face and saw the impatience m his eyes. 'Yes?'

'My mother sent this.' She pointed at the pot. 'What is it?'

'*Kleftiko.*'

'Take it back. Thank your mother but I don't want it. I want just to be left alone.'

'If I take it back she'll beat me'

His voice took on an edge of exasperation. 'Of course she won't.' Androulla was at her wits end, for she had sensed that this was the last chance. Then she had an idea. She reached down and lifted the lid off the pot. The steam and the aroma spilled out and up. The dog edged closer, its nose twitching. Androulla looked up; later she swore to her mother that the foreigner's nose was also twitching. She saw the struggle on his face. Then he said gruffly: 'Well, all right. I wouldn't want you to get a beating.' Before he could change his mind Androulla slipped away, calling over her shoulder that she would collect the pot in the morning.

It was the watershed. A few days later Vassos was again outside the taverna when the foreigner passed. This time he accepted the offer of a drink and talked about farming and a little of the invasion and what an exceptional cook Helena was. After that it became a routine. Every week he would go into the village for supplies and afterwards have a drink with Vassos and his friends. They discovered that he knew much about the world and although he was never loquacious, he became a sort of oracle and arbiter of opinion. One step followed another. He accepted an invitation to dinner on Androulla's birthday and bought her a blue cardigan as a present. Later, during the feast day of the village, he joined in the celebrations, even dancing with the men to the *Bouzouki* music and surprising the villagers by his expertise. He had to explain that he had been in Cyprus before, during the earlier troubles; but he never explained what he had been doing then or why he lived there now, almost as a hermit. The villagers did not probe. They now respected his reticence and observed with satisfaction the way he slowly emerged from his shell and became part of the community. It was a slow, almost painful, process, like a man with paralysis gradually regaining the use of his limbs. It took three years before he raised his eyes beyond the confines of the village and decided to spend a weekend in Platres and eat different food and maybe talk a little in his own language.

The waiter threaded his way through the crowded tables, placed the huge salver in front of the guest and, with a brief pause to heighten the effect, slowly lifted off the cover. Walter looked down with satisfaction and anticipation. Other guests at nearby tables craned their necks for a better view of what had become a morning ritual. Carefully Walter checked that everything was there as ordered: four fried eggs with the yolks lightly basted; three tomatoes halved, sprinkled with cheese and grilled; four lamb chops garnished with mushrooms; six slices of sauted liver and a side order of hashed brown potatoes. Another waiter approached and placed on the table a rack of toast, a tub of ice-cold unsalted butter, a jar of Cooper's marmalade and a jug of chilled, freshly-squeezed orange juice. Walter completed his inventory and beamed up at the two waiters.

'Perfect,' he said. 'And the coffee to follow in precisely twenty minutes.'

They moved away, shaking their heads in awe and Walter settled down to what he liked to call his 'international' breakfast;

He was sitting on the terrace of the Forest Park Hotel in Platres and it was, he decided, one of the most perfect places in the world to enjoy a good breakfast. Leafy trees shaded the tables from the morning sun. The vista spread out down the pine-covered hills to the plain and the coast far below. Out of sight he could just hear the piping voices of children as they splashed about in the swimming pool. It was early summer and up there, high in the Troödos mountains, it was deliciously cool after the heat and dust of Limassol. With the mountains, Walter decided,

Cyprus was just bearable in summer. True, his villa in Limassol was air conditioned, as was his office and his Mercedes 600, but it was nice to breathe fresh air and have the aroma of pine cones in his nostrils. He had been based in Cyprus for two years and was a regular visitor to Platres. He had .considered buying a mountain villa but he liked the Hotel with its old-world architecture and charm. In the beginning he had found the kitchen to be barely adequate but his office had arranged that certain delicacies always preceded him up the winding road, and a chef had been brought over from Paris to impart a month's training. Things had definitely improved.

Another reason for his visits was that Ruth and Duff Paget had a home nearby on the road to Spilia and since that auction nearly seven years ago a friendship had grown up between them and Walter. Duff had been transferred to the Middle East theatre in 1972 and was now one of the most respected photographers in the business. As Walter carved into a thick lamb chop he chuckled to himself about Duff Paget.

He had always retained a slight suspicion about him and, three years before, that edge of doubt had suddenly been resoundingly justified. One of Walter's agents had rented an apartment in West Beirut in a block close to the PLO headquarters. His mission was to keep surveillance on the comings and goings of the PLO hierarchy and their visitors. By the merest coincidence the apartment below had been rented by a Canadian who worked as manager for a freight forwarding company. Naturally, Walter's agent checked out all his neighbours and Mossad headquarters reported that this Canadian was suspected of having links with the CIA. Consequently Walter's agent photographed his visitors as well as those of the PLO. Walter was intrigued to discover that Duff Paget was a frequent visitor, often staying overnight, although he had a permanent suite at the Commodore Hotel. So Walter mounted an operation and, by using a fire in the lift well of the building as a diversion, his people managed to plant a bug in the Canadian's flat. So it was that Mossad finally learned of the existence of the CIA 'Equine' network and Duffs membership of it. Thereafter, whenever he was in Cyprus, Walter always visited the Pagets and his own villa in Limassol was always open to them. It was not just a matter of snooping: he genuinely liked the young couple and much appreciated Ruth's talent at cooking Jewish food.

Their relationship though had puzzled him. He could easily identify the disparity in their characters and personalities, and through his agent's surveillance of Duff he knew that he often had casual affairs while on assignments. It had puzzled Walter, for to him Ruth represented the epitome of feminine beauty and grace. He also admired her determination. After the Turkish invasion an orphanage had been opened in Platres for children of the Greek casualties. Ruth had offered her services and with her training in psychology these had been eagerly accepted. She had thrown herself into the work, even studying for several hours a day to improve her already good Greek. Walter had concluded that perhaps Duff was not keeping her physically satisfied and this conclusion was strengthened a year later when she paid a visit to Israel.

Duff had been on an extended assignment to photograph the Kurdish resistance to both Iraq and Iran and Ruth decided to take a holiday and see the Holy Land. Naturally Walter had put the services of his Tel Aviv office at her disposal, and also the apartment he maintained there. He also had her discreetly watched for he did not know whether she was party to Duff's clandestine activities. The report that landed on his desk a few days later evidenced that from the day of her arrival she was discreetly meeting a certain Gideon Galili who, it turned out, was a captain in the Israeli Air Force. Alarm bells immediately rang, but further investigation revealed that the relationship had nothing to do with intelligence. It was, the report stated, primarily carnal. It appeared that she had met Galili while he was on leave a few months before in Cyprus. They had met in the Forest Park Hotel of all places, during a dinner dance. Duff had been away and Ruth had gone to the dance with friends. There had been an immediate attraction and the agent who finally questioned Galili was of the opinion that they were genuinely in love. She had discussed leaving her husband for Galili but it was a decision she was not yet ready to take. In the first place, she did in a way still love Duff. Secondly, Galili was four years her junior and she was not sure whether his attachment for her would last. Since then she had made another trip to Israel and he had once more visited Cyprus. Walter guessed that the time was fast approaching when she would have to make up her mind.

He forked the last morsel of liver into his mouth and, right on cue, the waiter appeared with a large pot of coffee. After the serious business of eating it was Walter's habit to sit for half an hour over his coffee and survey the scene and the people around him. On this morning however, there was no one of real interest on the terrace not even an attractive woman to admire. So Walter's thoughts turned back to Ruth and Duff. She had surprised him six months ago by coming straight out and asking his advice. It was during one of her shopping trips to Limassol and Walter had taken her to lunch at the Amathus. He had felt a curious pleasure walking into the place with a beautiful woman on his arm who, by her bearing and demeanour, had obviously not been paid for.

She had been subdued during lunch and then suddenly asked if he minded whether she asked his advice. Like her he was Jewish, maybe he would understand. She had opened up and poured out her troubles. It took an effort for him not to show that he already knew about Gideon Galili. His first priority though was to ascertain whether she was aware of Duffs intelligence work. He probed gently, saying that maybe the rigours of his job made him difficult to live with. It soon became obvious that to her his sole 'job' was being a combat photographer. Walter had felt relief that whatever advice he might offer would be free from intelligence considerations. She had decided that she would leave Duff. Yes, in a way she loved him, but strangely more as a child than a husband. He was such a romantic, and definitely naive. He was brilliant at his job but too much of his life centred on it. She felt no guilt about her affair with Gideon. Long before that started she had learned of Duffs infidelities. She hardly blamed him - it was part of his nature, just like his frequent lies. Finally it boiled down to his weakness. Maybe Walter could not see it, but Duff was a weak man. Hence the lies and the numerous affairs. He loved her, but he was too weak to translate that love into something positive and lasting and inviolate. Somehow he always found it hard to say no.

Walter did not want to get in the middle. He liked them both. Nevertheless, he found it significant that Duff had never told her that he was a spy. With such a secret to hold how could his love flower? How could he confide and share in only one aspect of his life?

He asked her instead about Gideon. Was she sure of his feelings? She was. She was positive that he loved her. In a way the strength and intensity of it frightened her. He was a man with enormous energy and an almost obsessive single-mindedness. Up to now his energy and purpose had been directed solely towards his career. He told her that he had never been in love before. Had hardly considered the possibility. He had explained it in simple terms. It was like a man, deaf all his life who suddenly and clearly hears a Chopin sonata. She herself thought it more akin to an atheist discovering a new and exotic religion. Gideon had the fervour of a convert and it was disquieting; He wanted her to divorce Duff and marry him. It was her own feelings that confused her. He was everything that Duff was not: honest, forthright and very protective and practical. But in her life she had learned well of the power physical beauty has to bend a man's mind. Gideon was still young and in spite of his practicality he was impressionable. She did not want to go through the same problems again with someone else.

'What about children?' Walter had asked and she had shrugged resignedly. She and Duff had wanted children; soon after they arrived in Cyprus she had stopped taking the pill. After a year with no result she had gone for a check-up and been assured that physically there was no reason why she could not conceive. She had asked Duff to go for a check-up but he had refused. She did not push it. She was a psychologist and could guess that in a way he felt his manhood threatened. That was like Duff, she explained. In his weakness he preferred not to have to face up to it. She had mentioned it to Gideon and immediately he himself had gone for a check-up and told her that there was no reason that they could not have children. It was another factor in the equation.

Walter had been in a quandary. He would have liked to offer advice. To let Ruth lean on his shoulder, take strength from him, but two factors were against it. Firstly: he genuinely did not wish to interpose himself between two friends or take sides in any way at all. Secondly: his feelings for Ruth were more than platonic. Of course, he never seriously entertained the idea that she might feel for him anything more than affection. He had, from an early age, learned that his appearance was not attractive to young and beautiful women. His purely physical pleasures had always been satisfied by a series of highly-paid mistresses. Nevertheless he could dream, and one of his fantasies was that one day a minor miracle might occur and Ruth would see and come to love his virtues of mind and character and be blind to the fact that he was a gross, fat glutton. It was only a dream but it precluded him from advising her to leave her husband and go off with a young, handsome, dashing fighter pilot. So he merely suggested that she give it more time and certainly not do anything precipitous.

She had obviously decided to wait, for she had not mentioned the problem since. Tonight he would have the opportunity to observe the state of their relationship for Duff was home for a few days and Walter was invited for dinner. Ruth was going to cook duck braised in red cabbage and, in spite of his recent breakfast, Walter's mouth watered at the prospect. He decided he would only have a moderate lunch: perhaps a small chicken and just half of one of the lemon pies the chef made so well.

Then his thoughts turned again to his own problems. It had been two years since that momentous meeting with General Hofti. Already the first phase of Walter's operation was completed. Unfortunately completed and unsuccessful. During the whole of 1976 and the first months of 1977 Walter had orchestrated a campaign to persuade the French Government not to supply the nuclear research reactor to the Iraqis. It had been done on two levels. The strongest possible diplomatic pressure had been allied with a huge effort to persuade French public opinion against the deal. The Elyseé Palace had been presented with a thick dossier showing that the Iraqis would try to use the reactor to produce nuclear weapons. It contained dozens of quotations from Saddam Hussein and other Iraqi leaders to the effect that they would proceed. At one time Giscard d'Estaing appeared to weaken, publicly proclaiming that he had not been given full details of the deal. The Iraqis, however, had moved swiftly, threatening to cancel billions of dollars of associated orders and even hinting at an oil embargo, not only by them but joined by other Arab states. So the commercial facts of life prevailed and the contract was to be honoured. The campaign to arouse French public opinion was also a failure. France has never had a very active anti-nuclear movement and all of Walter's efforts failed to create one. Even now he knew that the construction of the reactor was on schedule. His one major success had been in planting an agent in the factory at La Seyne-sur-Mer near Toulon. Three days earlier that agent had reported that all things being equal the reactor would be ready for shipment within sixteen to twenty months. Walter intended that all things would not be equal.

For Walter the end justified the means only when the end could be equated with the survival of the Jewish people - and ultimately that meant the Jewish, state. Walter could envisage just such a situation developing over the coming two years. He knew that if the reactor was shipped and installed any methods he adopted would be justified, but this knowledge was disquieting for Walter was facing a severe problem in the forthcoming theatre of operations. In simple terms he had few agents on the ground in Iraq and the surrounding countries.

During the sixties Mossad had achieved incredible successes in penetrating the Arab states. Successes which had laid the groundwork for the Six Day War. Eli Cohen in Syria had almost been made Defence Minister before being unluckily caught. In Egypt, Wolfgang Lotz had become the confidante of the entire Egyptian General Staff and was only finally discovered in a routine check-up of West Germans before the visit to Cairo of Walter Ulbricht in 1965. Since those heady days, however, the hard-line Arab states had improved their counter intelligence with the aid of the KGB.

Mossad found it increasingly difficult to build up viable networks. In Iraq Walter had only one good agent. He was a member of the Special Intelligence Office - the Mukhabarat - albeit in a lowly position. However, he worked at Kasr al Nihayathe 'Palace of the end', which was once a residence of the royal family. It was now the Mukhabarat's centre for detention and interrogation. He was able to report on the in-fighting among the Ba'ath party but he was not senior enough to have access to those who planned and executed policy. He was also disinclined to take the risk of building up his own network. He had originally been recruited because he was appalled at the regime's treatment of the Kurds.

He was a Shia Moslem himself and already antagonistic towards the dominant Sunnis in Iraq. He was also an intellectual and a humanist and as he witnessed the torture of various Kurdish rebels in the 'Palace of the end' his spirit had revolted. His answer had been to turn to the enemy who could strike the hardest blow at what he conceived to be the devils now running his country, but, try as they could, Mossad had never been able to persuade him to build up a network. He would remain with the Mukhabarat, he told them, distasteful as that might be, and report what he heard and saw. He would do no more. It was enough to satisfy his conscience. To Walter it was infinitely frustrating. He knew that in time he would need a strong presence in Iraq and that time was not far off.

It was the classic frustration of the thinker, unable to realise his schemes and aspirations. It was one of the few occasions when he deeply regretted his own physique and appearance. He would love to work in the field; to be in on the nuts and bolts of operations. It was ludicrous of course. An agent had to be unobtrusive; able to melt into shadows; to be a master of stealth and capable of being just another head in a crowd. Walter was nothing if not wildly visible. The thought irritated him intensely. Made him feel like a man with no limbs, just a fat torso and a brain. He reviewed the options he had for creating a network in Iraq. A network that would allow him, if necessary, to attack the reactor if and when it was installed. The options were bleak. He had on call dozens of skilled and dedicated agents, but getting them into Iraq and in a position to be effective created insurmountable problems. Ever since 1966, when Mossad had persuaded an Iraqi Air Force officer to defect along with his MIG21, the Mukhabarat had been on the alert to prevent something similar. Walter could not see any of his present agents being able to penetrate their defences.

He sighed and drained the last of his coffee, his good mood dissipated by his latest thoughts. With a grunt he pushed himself away from the table and stood up. Behind a row of pines another man was having breakfast. As he lumbered past, Walter caught a glimpse of him - an impression: a beard, long hair, very blue eyes. He moved into the lounge heading towards reception but the impression lingered and there was something else: a startled look in those blue eyes. Walter came to a quivering halt, his mind racing, his memory cataloguing. Then he swung on his heel and headed back to the terrace. The man was preparing to leave, though there was still an egg and some bacon left on his plate. He looked up as Walter reappeared - a resigned expression came into his eyes.

'It is,' Walter said, nodding in satisfaction. 'Somewhat more hirsute but definitely . . . it's Dave Munger!'

He chose to wait until after dinner. He did not want anything to divert attention from the food. As expected it was delicious, the duck preceded by goose liver made perfect by the accompanying pureed potatoes. Walter had sent up a case of Chateau Latour '59 the week before. Duff, although professing a knowledge and love of wine, would certainly have chosen something more obvious and less compatible. The last time Walter had been invited to dinner, an Italian Barolo had been served with salt beef and latkas. This time Walter had taken no chances. He was a good enough friend for the gesture to be appreciated without the hint causing offence.

During dinner Duff had talked at length about the situation in Lebanon and whether President Elias Sarkis would be able to control the leftists. Walter listened with half an ear, occasionally grunting in agreement with some of Duffs points. His senses were primarily occupied with the food, the wine and Ruth. She had lost weight, he decided, although this had not detracted from her beauty. She wore her black hair pulled back into a chignon. The style accentuated her high cheekbones and olive skin. It was a sad face, made more melancholy by the fine lines, gently narrowed cheeks and full lips. Walter found it inexplicable that Duff could or would not direct all his energy into making her happy.

They were sitting in a dining room furnished in formal style. It was adjacent to a lounge a couple of steps below. Beyond that, French windows were open onto a patio surrounded by trees and shrubs which were gently illuminated by discreet spotlights. The lounge had bookcases against two walls, a grouping of comfortable leather chairs around a low coffee table and a wall unit holding a number of framed photographs and various souvenirs Duff had picked up on his travels. In one corner, at the apex of the bookcases, was another small but tall table. Almost a pedestal. There was only one object on it, covered by a glass dome. It was Munger's camera the Nikon FTN. Somehow it dominated the room. Walter knew that no one was ever allowed to touch it. Even the maid was forbidden to dust it. Every month Duff would take it down, dismantle it and lovingly clean it. Very occasionally he would show close friends how it worked and how it had been used, but they were never allowed to touch it. Walter savoured the coming moment when he dropped his bombshell. In the meantime he decided that he had listened enough to the outlines of US foreign policy as it applied to the Lebanon so he asked Ruth how she was getting along at the orphanage. Immediately a spark came into her eyes and she talked about the children and their progress. Now even the youngest were of an age when they could be placed in foster homes. Of course, there were difficult cases and her work was concentrated on these. It had been nearly three years since the war but some of the children retained deep mental scars. There was one boy of six who had seen his parents casually shot. Ruth was determined that the boy would lead a normal existence. Walter listened attentively but Duff's face showed signs of impatience. He had heard it all before and in his work had seen enough similar cases to have become inured. Walter sensed his impatience and, as the maid cleared the dishes, decided it was time.

'By the way,' he said, with the utmost casualness. 'I saw Dave Munger this morning.'

Duff's jaw literally dropped and the fingers of his hands closed up into fists. There was a silence until the maid left. Ruth was looking curiously at her husband. The question, when it came, was one choked word:

'Where?'

Walter smiled and pushed himself to his feet. Of Ruth he asked: 'Are we taking coffee in the lounge?'

She nodded and smiled tentatively and started to get up.

'Where? Dammit!'

Duffs voice was harsh, demanding. Walter looked down at him benignly.

'Here in Platres, at the Forest Park Hotel. Come Duff, I'll tell you over coffee.'

They moved to the lounge and Walter settled himself comfortably while the maid poured coffee and put a large plate of peppermint chocolates next to him. Duff stood in the centre of the room, legs apart, his face a mirror of impatience, his eyes darting between Walter and the camera. Finally, after Walter had taken a sip of his coffee and consumed three chocolates, he smiled again at Duff and told him the story.

It seemed that Munger had been living in the area for some years. Details were sparse but apparently he had a small farm somewhere near Phini. Walter got the impression that Munger was not overjoyed to see him - in fact the opposite. Getting even the barest information had been akin to squeezing a dry sponge. Walter had invited him for a meal, even suggesting that he come along tonight. He assured him he would be welcome. As encouragement he told him that Duff had his camera. Told him the story of the auction. But Munger had refused. Talked lamely about being very busy - some other time perhaps.

Finally Walter had given him his card and asked him to call him sometime. It was obvious that Munger had been made acutely uncomfortable by the contact,

Of course, Duff was totally unsatisfied by all this. When had he come to Cyprus? And from where? What was he doing? How did he look?

Walter could only answer the last of his enquiries. Obviously he looked older, but then Walter had not seen him for over eight years. That would put him in his late thirties. He was bearded and very tanned and his hands were calloused – so maybe he was a farmer. He talked in a curious, stilted way as though unused to conversation, at least in English. Walter's description was full and accurate for he was a skilled and trained observer. Duff immediately wanted to go out and find Munger but Walter deterred him. The last thing Munger had said was that he did not want to be bothered - by anyone. He had Walter's card and if he felt like getting in touch he would call him.

Still Duff remained agitated and unconvinced. The thought of Munger living so close for several years was almost too much to bear. Surely they could find him; at least drop by and tell him he was always welcome to visit.

Walter shook his head. There was something strange. Munger was not at the Hotel for lunch and when Walter enquired at reception they told him that he had checked out immediately after breakfast. They were surprised for he had arrived only the night before and had booked for three days. The register showed his address as being merely Thini, Cyprus'. A check of the register for the past five years showed that he had not been a guest during that time.

Now Ruth interjected. From all that Walter had said it appeared that Munger had been about to emerge from a long period of seclusion. Being suddenly confronted with Walter had probably been a shock. She smiled at Walter to take away a hint that had it been anyone else the shock might have been less.

Finally Duff agreed that it could be counterproductive to go chasing off looking for him. Anyway, he was leaving in two days and would be away at least a month. One thing was sure though. When he got back he was going to locate him and see if he needed anything. He looked again at the camera, solitary and glistening under its glass dome. The least he could do was offer it back to him.

For the rest of the evening Duff reminisced about Munger. Told again the legion of stories about him, extolled his genius as a combat photographer. No one had ever matched him. No one ever would.

Walter and Ruth listened in silence. As ever she was puzzled and slightly resentful. This one man had captured her husband's mind like none other. It had to be more than just his talent. Duff himself was recognised as one of the most brilliant men in his field. There had already been several international exhibitions of his work, and a recent book of his photographs had been a best-seller. No, there was more to it than just respect for talent. She sighed - it was another of the ever-widening voids between them.

Walter listened with interest. He had known Munger reasonably well during his time in Asia and had always been puzzled by him. He was one of the few men that Walter had never been able to understand and categorise. It was as though he lived in a vacuum, totally independent of those around him. Walter was a manipulator of people, of their fears, hopes and emotions, and a man who was immune to him was infinitely fascinating. He listened as Duff described yet again Munger's uncanny ability to be in the right spot when something was about to happen. His skill in getting the 'snaps' he wanted and then extricating himself from the surrounding dangers. He had been like a wraith, like a shadow moving over the ground and through cordons and walls, padlocks and red tape. There had never been anyone like him. And the final days. What had happened on that last patrol to make him quit? To walk away from the only life he had ever known?

Finally Walter had become sleepy. He had drunk a lot of wine and three Cognacs afterwards and even the presence of Ruth and Duff's interesting stories could not keep him awake. So he pulled himself up, kissed Ruth on the cheek and told her that whatever else she did in life her ability to cook duck in red cabbage would ensure her a place in heaven. She laughed and promised to have lunch with him in Limassol next week. At the car he shook Spiro awake and squeezed himself into the back seat, wound down the window and said to Duff:

'Be careful in Beirut, The last I heard it's due for another eruption.'

Duff grinned. 'Don't worry. Didn't Hamlet say that "discretion is the better part of valour"?'

Walter shook his head. 'Wrong play. Falstaff said it, and he was a man who ate and drank to excess.' He winked. 'Never follow the advice of a man like that!'

After Walter had left, Duff took a bottle of Cognac out onto the patio. His mind was too full of Walter's news to allow him to sleep. Ruth sensed his mood and his wish to be alone. She kissed him goodnight and went through into the bedroom. It had been a long day and she was tired. But strangely, sleep eluded her also. She lay in the large double bed listening to the faint ticking of the bedside clock and the occasional muted passage of a car on the road behind the villa. The talk of Munger over dinner had also unsettled her. Not so much the man himself but the memories he evoked: the early days of her marriage in Hong Kong; the slow realisation that it was not following the perfect pattern that she had mentally projected; her own growing up in an alien environment; the discovery of aspects and facets of her character. She remembered the night when Duff had come home from the auction with Munger's camera and her outrage when she learned that because of it he was no longer able to buy her the anniversary bracelet. Now she smiled to herself at the reaction. That was a time when her upbringing and education had tuned her to material things. When love and affection could and should be measured by the value of a gift. When marital fulfilment was a beautiful apartment or a new wardrobe of designer dresses. It was to be expected. Her parents had always rewarded her progress in a material way: a holiday in California when she graduated high school; an M.G. sportscar on her twenty first birthday. She had viewed her position and status as she would view paintings on her walls. That one meant security, that one a good marriage, that one a settled social life.

It had taken some time for her to see that the paintings were vague, given form only by the frames. At first she thought it might have been the transitory and temporary nature of their lives. After two years in Hong Kong they had relocated to Singapore for a year and then to Bangkok. It was only after they moved to Cyprus and bought the villa and furnished it with their collected pieces that she began to feel a sense of permanence and continuity. It was then that she recognized the emptiness in her life. All her pictures were in place and yet there was something missing. She had already learned of Duffs infidelities. Within the media community there were many so-called 'friends' eager to pass on confidential 'snippets'.

She had surprised herself in two ways. First, she had not been outraged and second, she had not confronted Duff on the subject. Perhaps her years in the East had conditioned her to see marriage in a more diffused light than her contemporaries. But still, during all those years she had been faithful to him. Fidelity had been another painting on the wall. A painting that was now a blank canvas.

She rolled over in the bed and pounded the pillow into a more receptive shape. How many nights had she slept alone while Duff was away on assignments? More than half her married life. But that was not a measure of her emptiness. It went far deeper. It went into the core of love itself. She wanted to be needed - completely needed. She wanted to be the centre of someone's existence. In retrospect she realized that only two things could give her that: children of her own or the total, undivided love of a man. Children had proved impossible - at least with Duff - so it had been almost inevitable that when the second option clearly presented itself in the shape of Gideon she had moved into the affair with studied purpose. She was simply seeking fulfilment. In the beginning she was wary of the cloak of infatuation. She was well aware of her beauty and allure; over the years she had discouraged scores of advances. It was only after her trip to Israel and Gideon's second visit to Cyprus that she abandoned her caution and basked in the certainty that he truly loved her. He was strong, accomplished and confident - and he needed her.

Again she smiled to herself, but this time ruefully. Having sought out such an involvement, its very intensity created unease. What, after all, if she could not match it? Surely there must be a balance?

She tried to analyse the emotion of love, but quickly gave up. She may as well try to slice a rainbow. Anyway love was organic. Sometimes it grew and, of course, sometimes it withered. Her love for Gideon would grow in intensity to match his. Especially if there were children. They would fertilize the common ground. It only remained for her to take that decision. To tell Duff and finally parade his infidelities in front of him. She could not clearly understand why she found that decision hard to take. Obviously in spite of everything a part of her still loved him. Maybe it was at the fainter edge of the rainbow's spectrum. Again she pounded the pillow and settled herself and drifted into a shallow sleep.

Walter had fallen asleep only seconds after he touched the pillow but it was not a good sleep. He tossed and turned in the oversized bed until three o'clock in the morning. Then, with a grunt of irritation, he reached out and switched on the bedside light. It was unusual for him, for normally he slept soundly with only the occasional dream. He lay for many minutes looking up at the slowly turning ceiling fan. Then he rolled over, swung his legs to the floor and shuffled his feet into a pair of slippers. He walked through into the lounge of the suite and poured himself a glass of Perrier water, then moved onto the balcony. It was a dark, moonless night, only a distant glow of light showed the location of Limassol far below. He knew that his subconscious had been working. Something was bothering his subconscious and until it was resolved he was going to have to stay awake. He was a methodical thinker and he reasoned that, as he had slept well the night before, his subconscious was being bothered by events of the previous day. He recapped on all that had occurred and, as so often happens in the hours before dawn, his mind was lucid and uncluttered and ideas that in daylight are shrouded and complex become stark and clear.

It was Munger. He was going to need him. The morning meeting was providential. Wide awake, he turned, went back into the lounge and sat down at the writing table. For half an hour he composed a signal to be sent in the morning to Shimon Saguy at Mossad headquarters.

As a matter of utmost urgency he wanted an in-depth report on one David Munger, sometime combat photographer. The report was to exclude nothing. Walter Blum wanted to know every single thing about him from the day he issued forth from his mother's womb. He wanted details of his childhood, his parents, his relatives, his education, friends, enemies, likes, dislikes, medical history, political opinions, his favourite colour, food and drink. He also wanted a copy of every single photograph that

Munger had ever taken. Finally he asked for a priority investigation to establish what might have happened during Munger's last days in Vietnam. He thought back, straining his memory, correlating dates. Then he advised that Munger had gone on an operation near Vinh Long with a Special Forces patrol sometime during the month of October 1969. Mossad agents in the USA were to try to track down any surviving members of that patrol and find out what events had taken place. Similarly agents within the US Army were to try to locate and copy any reports relating to that time.

He finished the draft, locked it into his briefcase and looked at his watch. Then he picked up the phone and told the night porter to call him at 6.30 a.m.

This time he slept soundly, if only for two hours, but within a minute of waking he remembered some words that Duff had spoken the night before.

'Munger was like a wraith; like a shadow.'

CHAPTER FIVE

Her orgasm had been above average and Janine Lesage reached down and patted Sami Asaf's black hair. He raised his head and looked up at her face across the undulations of her belly. He was panting slightly and his moustache glistened with her juices.

'You are so good Sami,' she murmured.

His teeth showed in a smile and he started to slide up her long body. She felt his erection rasping up her left leg and mentally sighed. It had been a long time now since she could achieve an orgasm in the conventional way. It may have been a matter of over-indulgence or merely a vivid imagination, but she needed more subtle stimulation than an engorged penis pumping in and out of her. In any event she would have to take care of Sami's needs. He had laboured long and hard and would now have to be rewarded. He settled over her, wriggled into position and slid deep. She felt almost no sensation but she made appropriate noises into his ear. It would, she knew, take quite a long time for Sami Asaf was one of those men who equated sexual prowess with coital longevity. While she lay under him, stroking his back and rhythmically twitching her buttocks, Janine's mind was elsewhere.

She had deliberately seduced Sami a month before, shortly after being given the assignment of working as liaison between her own service, SDECE and the Iraqi Mukhabarat. The job had been a direct result of the nuclear reactor deal. She remembered the briefing at SDECE headquarters in Paris. It had been conducted by the Director himself, Alexandre de Marenches.

The Mossad would be unrelenting, he had told her, in its attempts to thwart the deal. They had been very active in France during the past two years and once the reactor was shipped they would concentrate their efforts in Iraq. They would most likely use Beirut as a base of operations. As Janine had been working in that area for six years she was the ideal candidate both to co-ordinate the SDECE counter-offensive and to liaise with the Iraqi Mukhabarat. It was fortunate that she was acquainted with Sami Asaf from the Far East days, because he was now a Deputy Director of the Mukhabarat and the man responsible for the protection of the, reactor and the French personnel working on it.

Now Janine smiled to herself as she lay under the grunting Iraqi. 'Acquainted' was no longer an adequate description of their relationship.

De Marenches had gone on to quantify the opposition. Although Mossad were not believed to be in Iraq in strength they were well entrenched in Beirut. Recent reports had indicated that a special section had been set up within Mossad to concentrate on the reactor. It was vital to France, he told her, that the reactor came on stream without interruption. Certain major commercial and arms deals would only be confirmed on that date.

'Have the Israelis genuine reason to be suspicious about the reactor's ultimate purpose?' she had asked.

De Marenches had given her an enigmatic look and a very Gallic shrug. 'They are always suspicious,' he had said. 'Anyway the Iraqis have signed the Nuclear Non Proliferation Treaty. Something the Israelis have never done.'

She had smiled at him cynically and answered 'Of course, then that makes everything all right.'

Finally de Marenches had briefed her about the role of the CIA. She must assume that because of President Carter's paranoia about nuclear proliferation they would be intensely curious about the whole project. The State Department had already brought great pressure to bear, on the French Government to cancel the deal. It was due partly, of course, to the Jewish lobby in Congress.

So apart from watching out for Mossad she must also keep an eye on the CIA. There were two prime factors in her favour. Firstly, the CIA and Mossad were no longer co-operating. In fact since the early severities the opposite was true. Secondly, de Marenches told her with a bleak smile, SDECE agents in Washington had recently infiltrated a hitherto unknown section of the CIA. It was known as 'Equine' and it was believed to be particularly active in the Middle East. He had passed her a sheet of paper listing the known or suspected 'Equine' agents in her area. There were seven names. The top one was Duff Paget.

De Marenches had seen her smile-a combination of delight and malice.

'You know any of them?' he had asked. 'Yes, I know three of them. One in particular.'

He had warned her to be circumspect when dealing with the Americans and she had nodded dutifully.

Sami was beginning to increase his tempo and Janine felt a certain vaginal dryness. Another two minutes, she decided, and then I'll pop him off, whether he's ready or not. Sami Asaf was, of course, vital to her schemes both personal and official. It was one of the reasons she had seduced him a month before. She always liked to be in full control of an operation and she had learned long ago that there were two prime ways to control a man - money and sex. Her experience had shown that of the two, sex was by far the more potent.

She was definitely in control. She ran her left arm up his back to the top of his bobbing head, turned her wrist and glanced at her Cartier watch. It was getting late and she had things to discuss with Sami.

She knew what to do. After a month of frequent sex she understood exactly the fine edge separating Sami's sadism and masochism. First she raised her feet and locked them round his ankles. Then she gripped his hair tightly with her left hand. The fingernails of her right hand dug deep into his left buttock. He gasped at the pain and she pulled his head up and fastened her teeth to the underside of his chin, close to his throat. He began pounding into her, their hips slapping together wetly. Any second now, she thought, and tightened her grip with teeth and fingers. Then he was spurting into her and crying out in a mixture of agony and ecstasy.

One day, she thought, I'm going to kill a man like that. Instead of his chin it will be his throat. She had read somewhere that when a man died in the act of sex he gets an enormous erection which remains after death. That would be something to see - and feel.

Sami lay panting on top of her and, after a decent pause and several whispered endearments, she rolled him onto his side and left the bed. He lay watching as she padded towards the bathroom. She was long and lithe and curved, her hair swinging behind her like a blonde cape .

Who was it, Sami thought, who all those years ago described her as being built like a racing snake?

He heard the water running into the bidet and the sound conjured up an association with prostitution. His first experience with a woman had taken place in Paris and afterwards she had douched herself vigorously; he had been embarrassed and a little angry, thinking that she must have thought him unclean.

He supposed that in a way Janine was prostituting herself. He had no illusions that she loved him and he guessed that once the operation was complete she would nicely but positively drop him. No matter. That was at least two years away and in the meantime he would have constant access to her body. A body which he could not get enough of. It was amazing how in only one month she had discovered exactly his sexual preferences. At the same time he realised he was spending too much time in Beirut on these so-called liaison missions. He had justified them to himself and his director by pointing to the fact that the Mossad threat would originate in the Lebanon and it was vital for the Mukhabarat to strengthen its own network there. But he knew it was the taut body of Janine Lesage and not duty that brought him constantly to the city.

Janine came out of the bathroom, moved to the window and stood looking out. She wore only a towel knotted at her waist. They were in her apartment situated on the top floor of a building in Ras Beirut. It commanded spectacular views of the city and the on-going civil war. Even at that moment he could hear the distant crackle of small arms fire from the direction of the Nabaa district.

Sami glanced at his watch and then sat up and reached for his clothes which had been discarded an hour before in a flood of rising passion. There was a Press Conference at PLO headquarters in half an hour and, as he still maintained his cover as a correspondent for the Middle East News Bureau, he should be there.

Janine turned and watched as he pulled his socks, then said in her harsh contralto:

'Duff Paget.'

'What about him?'

'I want you to kill him.'

Sami looked up in shock.

'He's CIA,' Janine continued before he could say anything. 'And he's starting to meddle in our affairs.'

Sami's look of surprise was comical. 'Duff - CIA?'

She smiled. 'Yes, Sami. Don't look so shocked. He's been an agent for at least eight years. Ever since Vietnam.'

'Are you sure?'

Sami was disconcerted. He was not unused to hearing that acquaintances or even colleagues worked in intelligence but it usually did not take so long for him to find out. Only yesterday he had been having a drink with a group of correspondents in the Commodore Hotel; Duff Paget had been among them and they had spent half an hour chatting about old times.

'Of course I'm sure,' she said impatiently. 'He works for a special section codenamed "Equine". We cracked it a few months ago. We also discovered that one of its primary missions is to counter the threat of nuclear proliferation.' She said it easily. Skilfully blending truth with half-truth. Sami's face showed uncertainty, then she saw a hard look come into his eyes.

'You're not making it up? You always hated him - ever since that auction.'

She shook her head, her long hair swinging behind her. 'Don't be stupid Sami. Yes, I hate him, but I wouldn't let that influence me.'

She started to walk slowly towards the bed.

'Of course it doesn't matter if your plans for the reactor are what you say they are. But if not, and if Paget finds out anything, then my Government is going to come under enormous pressure. We can handle the Israelis but the United States are something else. Giscard d'Estaing may decide to cancel the deal - oil sanctions or not.'

She had reached the bed and Sami looked up at her.

'I don't like the idea of the CIA prying,' he said. 'Even though we have nothing to hide.'

'Of course,' she answered with a narrow smile. 'Anyway, Paget is a threat. You'll be doing less than your duty if you leave him alive.'

Sami sighed. He liked Duff Paget.

'It's a big decision,' he said. 'Killing a CIA agent can set off a whole string of fireworks.'

She shrugged. 'Sami, be realistic. How many journalists and cameraman have been killed in Beirut during the last two years? A dozen? Maybe more. Besides, your people won't do it. Talk to your friends in the PLO. Matter of fact, Paget's present assignment is to spy on them. I have all the details. He's working right under their noses.'

There was a long silence, then Sami said 'I'll think about it.'

She smiled, knowing she had won. Her arms reached out and she pulled his head against her breasts, rubbing them against his face.

'When it happens,' she murmured, 'I want to be there. I want to see it.'

Walter Blum and Professor Chaim Nardi walked leisurely across the broad campus of Tel Aviv University. Walter was dressed in a beige suit and a pink tie. The Professor, a small, bird-like man, wore slacks and a white short-sleeved shirt. He was comfortable. Walter was sweating.

Nardi was intrigued by his visitor. A week earlier he had received a phone call from General Hofti, whom he knew to be the head of Mossad. Hofti informed him that he was sending, by special messenger, a top secret dossier. It contained very complete details of a man. It would be appreciated if the Professor would study the dossier carefully and then discuss it with a certain Walter Blum. The name was familiar to Nardi, but before he could pin it down in his memory Hofti said that it was the same Walter Blum who had been a generous financial benefactor to the University and to Israel in general.

So Nardi had studied the dossier with diligence and interest and, after obtaining clearance from Hofti, had even discussed it with two of his colleagues in the psychiatric department of the faculty.

Walter had duly arrived, and after consuming a prodigious lunch hosted by the Dean, he and Nardi took a stroll.

'It's a fascinating case,' Nardi said. 'You have read my report. What else can I add?'

Walter looked down at him, thinking that he resembled a sparrow rather than the foremost brain in Israel in the fields of psychology and psychiatry.

'I want to know how to manipulate him.'

The Professor winced. He had, of course, realised that Walter was not merely a very successful businessman;

'"Manipulate" is an unpleasant word in such a context,' he remarked primly.

'I'm in an unpleasant situation,' Walter retorted. 'This man could be important. I need him. So does Israel.'

The Professor thought for a moment, then shrugged.

'Well, it's obvious that he's in a trauma. I won't bother you with technical terminology. To be of any use to you or anyone else he has to be brought out of that trauma. He would have to talk about it and, from what I understand, that seems unlikely. It's a great pity that you couldn't find out what happened on that last patrol.'

Walter grimaced. 'We're still trying. But it doesn't look encouraging. It was a mixed patrol of US Special Forces men and mercenaries. We can't find anyone still alive. Also, all records and any reports that were filed at the time have been destroyed.'

Nardi spread his hands in a negative gesture. 'So we remain in the dark.'

Walter stopped walking and the Professor turned to look at him. 'You're saying that he'll be useless unless he's completely cured of the trauma?'

'Not exactly. I don't know what you want him for. Obviously he has all his faculties. He's not insane, it's just that whatever happened has turned him completely in on himself. He's dropped out, so to speak. The only encouraging aspect is that he might be preparing to re-emerge. It's taken a long time, but the mind, like the body, has enormous powers of self-healing. You would have to be careful, though, in anything you attempt-it could have the opposite effect to what you desire.'

Walter started walking again and the Professor trotted along beside him.

'How would you go about it?' Walter asked.

The Professor's voice assumed a slightly lecturing tone. 'Let's examine his history. He was born in April 1941. His father was a minor official in the British War Office. He had failed to qualify for active service due to a weak heart. He was an undistinguished man from a moderately wealthy northern family. The report indicates that he was somewhat boring. Munger's mother, on the other hand, was not. In an age long before the partial liberation of women she had, by her own efforts, won a scholarship to university and gone on to become a doctor. It appears that she may have married partly to finance her continuing studies. She was a vivacious, attractive, strong-willed woman - and she was Jewish, although she didn't proclaim it or practise the faith. She had no apparent interest in Zionism.'

He glanced at Walter either to see his reaction to a Jew who had no interest in Zionism or merely to check that he was being attentive. He was.

'The child adored her,' Nardi continued. 'You could say she was the centre of his life. Apart from his mother he was a lonely boy - as many were during the war. Because his parents worked in London he spent most of his time with his paternal grandparents in Bradford. They were a dour couple and incapable of showing him affection. Hence the weekly visits from his mother were truly the high points in his life. By the time the war ended he was a very introverted child.'

Nardi shrugged. 'Of course, I am having to base this diagnosis on hearsay. However, the dossier was very detailed.'

'It was,' Walter grunted. 'A dozen agents spent weeks compiling it. Go on, Professor.'

'Well, under normal circumstances the end of the war should have brought the end of Munger's mental isolation. He was reunited with his parents and I assume the flower of his mind was opening under his mother's sunlight. Then came the first of two events which were to shape his life. His mother had specialised in treatment for malnutrition. There was a surprising amount of it in Britain during the war, particularly between 1942 and '43. Only two months after the war, and two months after being reunited with her son, she was asked to go to Germany to help with the survivors of the concentration camps.'

'I know all this,' Walter interjected. 'I've read the damn dossier.'

The Professor was not used to having his lectures interrupted and he gave Walter a severe look before continuing.

'She was supposed to stay only one month, but what she saw affected her deeply. One can imagine the difference between a survivor of Auschwitz and an English schoolboy who has been deprived of certain vitamins for a couple of years. Anyway, she spent a year on the job. A year during which she only saw her son about once a month. In the meantime her husband had returned to Bradford with the boy and was working in the family business and living in the family home. During that year the boy started going to junior school which he hated. He was a complete loner and hence disliked by the other boys. After his mother returned from Germany there were two years of relative calm. Again under the influence of his mother's love and personality the boy began to come out of his shell. Then came the final event which was to shape his character for the rest of his life.'

'The 1948 war which established Israel as a state,' Walter said impatiently.

'Exactly.' The Professor's voice took on a musing tone. 'Such is destiny. The future character traits of a seven-year-old child can be moulded in an instant by an event of which he had no knowledge and which took place thousands of miles away.' He took note of Walter's expression and his voice quickened.

'All right, you know all that. His mother gave up her way of life, her practice, her husband - and her son. She came to Israel to fight. She was Jewish, she accepted it, embraced it. Nothing would divert her. Not even the son she loved. She abandoned him.'

'She may have gone back.'

Nardi shook his head, 'I doubt it, Mr Blum. It was a conscious rejection of her past. Anyway, let's assume that the boy realised that she would not come back. Certainly his father would have encouraged that. After all, only a month after she left he sued for divorce on the grounds of desertion.' He shook his head again.

'No, the boy would have understood and the effect was profound. It is well documented in the dossier. His school days, his lack of friends, his introspection - above all his lack of emotion when told that she was dead.'

Walter nodded, his face pensive. 'She died for Israel, abused and killed in the battle for Jerusalem. She was a heroine.'

Nardi spread his hands eloquently.

'For him she was nothing - like everything else he cut her out of his mind. She had deserted him. From that moment a chain-link fence went up around his emotions. He refused either to give or accept affection. Oh yes, when he grew up he became a great womaniser; held a fascinating attraction for them. It's not unusual: women are often drawn to such men. Anyway, he appears to have felt nothing for anyone. When his father's heart finally gave out and he died, the boy showed no emotion. He was ten years old and he didn't shed a tear at the funeral.'

'But his photographs - how could a man without emotion, without feelings - take such photographs?'

Now the Professor stopped walking and as Walter turned he saw that the small man had a look of intense interest on his face. He said: 'I've analysed that, Mr Blum. Studied them, and I will tell you something fascinating. Out of the thousands you sent me only a few, no more than a hundred, were of subjects other than war. They hold the key. There was a series he took while on holiday in Bali. He was with a woman and maybe she bored him, so he took pictures of the scenery and the people. Bali is one of the most exquisite places on earth, Mr Blum. I've been there, have you?'

Walter nodded.

'Well, then you know of its beauty. Yet when I looked at Munger's photographs I saw a different place than I remembered. He photographed the masks of the dancers, managed to isolate them, make them more forbidding or grotesque than they really were. He photographed a tree. A tall, lush, tropical tree, but in his picture there was a thunderstorm behind it, the branches enlarged and made looming by the black clouds. He photographed the surf. I saw it was beautiful and symmetric as it rolled in across the coral reef. He captured it as menacing white spray pounding the still water. Did you see it, Mr Blum? Did you see what I saw or what he saw?'

Walter looked at him quizzically then took his arm and started walking again. This time towards his distant, waiting car.

'What you're saying is that Munger is incapable of photographing anything but a war.'

'More than that. What I'm saying is that the war is inside him. The camera is his eyes. Do you read poetry?'

'Rarely,' Walter answered, a little disconcerted. 'I've read a bit of Shakespeare though.'

'Well, the poet Wordsworth talked of something called "The vision splendid". It allowed him to see what other mortals were unaware of. A particular light falling on a leaf. The colour of a flower. The hue of green on a distant hill. Some poets have it, and they can translate it into words. Munger has the opposite. His eyes are his camera and it translates what he sees onto paper and, Mr Blum, it's all black and grey and just a little white.'

They had reached the door. The driver was holding open the rear door.

'It's why he worked so hard at it,' the Professor said. 'Why he taught himself and trained himself. Just like a poet must learn how to assemble and articulate his "vision splendid". It's all he had-that dark vision of his own.'

Walter nodded, his face sombre. 'It's what made him such a superb combat photographer.'

'Yes,' agreed the Professor. 'And it's what made him only half a man.'

Walter sighed, then held out his hand. 'Thank you, Professor Nardi. You have made it plain that the key to Munger lies in his dead mother. Perhaps shock treatment is the best way. I must think on it.'

Nardi took the proffered hand and shook it, then he said with severity in his voice: 'I know your work is important, but half a man or not, he is a human being. In the wrong hands psychology can be very dangerous and destructive. Is there any further way that I or my colleagues can help?'

Walter shook his head. 'No. Under the circumstances I'll have to work alone.' His voice took on an edge.

'Besides, a lot of people got destroyed in this business. They have no option. The fact is that whether he wants to acknowledge it or not, Munger had a Jewish mother. She died for Israel. He might not relish the idea but he's going to be given the same opportunity.'

Walter climbed into the car, but before it pulled away Nardi said:

'That last patrol.'

'What about it?'

'After he came back he was impotent - or so the dossier said.'

'So?'

'So there's probably a sexual ingredient to his trauma. You should bear it in mind.'

'I intend to,' Walter answered. He signalled the driver and the car moved away.

CHAPTER SIX

They were framed in the viewfinder: four of them - even their facial features were clear - brought close by the telescopic lens.

'The usual bunch,' Duff Paget said and straightened up, rubbing his back. He glanced at his watch.

'They'll be going for lunch. We may as well do the same. There won't be any action now for at least a couple of hours.'

Jerry Kimber nodded. He was looking through the window at the entrance of the building diagonally across the road. He saw the four men climbing into a black Ford. On each side of the doorway men stood holding Skorpion sub-machine guns at the ready, their eyes scanning the street and the sparse traffic.

He turned to look at Duff, who had taken the telephoto lens off the camera and replaced it with an all-purpose zoom. He unscrewed the assembly from the tripod, slipped it into its carrying case and slung it over his shoulder, the lens exposed. As always he was ready, in an instant, to photograph any happening in a city replete with happenings.

'What do you feel like eating?' Jerry asked.

Duff grimaced. 'Anything as long as it's not mutton. Let's take the car and go down to The Smugglers and get a steak.'

Jerry grinned. 'For a world traveller you sure are a cautious eater. Or are you hoping to run into Gina Mansutti?'

'You never know your luck,' Duff smiled. 'She's convinced I can get her an interview with Yassir Arafat. Imagine being that naive. Any time now she is going to drop these elegant designer jeans and really try to persuade me. Come on, let's go.'

Outside on the landing Duff pressed the button to call the lift while Jerry turned the keys in the triple lock.

In the flat above Misha Wigoda, alias Melim Jaheen, had also concluded that his surveillance of PLO headquarters could take a couple of hours hiatus and, like the Canadian and American below, had also decided to get some lunch, although he would eat a Iamb stew at his usual table in the corner restaurant. It so happened that he had punched the lift button a few seconds before Duff and so the lift came to him first. He stepped in and pressed the ground floor button, but it stopped on the floor below. As the doors opened he heard the Canadian saying:

'Just one more fucking month, then I'm transferred to...'

The words dried as he noticed the lift was occupied. They got in and nodded pleasantly to Misha and the lift descended. Misha noted Duff s every-ready camera. He had seen many of the American's photographs in the international press and he admired him greatly. In fact Misha felt a sneaking envy. He was himself highly competent with a camera and skilled in all the intelligence aspects of photography, but he recognised in Duffs work the extra element which separates the artist from the technician. 'One day,' he thought, 'I'll be free to roam with a camera and capture events as they happen, instead of being confined to shooting an endless series of faces of which only one in a thousand is ever in use.' He felt also another kind of envy, for Misha was short and balding with a face that his mother had described as 'full of character' - in essence ugly - while Duff Paget was tall and jarringly handsome.

The lift reached the ground floor and he gestured politely and Duff and Jerry preceded him out into the lobby and through the open doors into the searing afternoon sun. He stood at the top of the steps watching as they walked towards Jerry's battered green

Mercedes parked on the corner. The Canadian was talking again. From the bug that had been planted in his apartment Misha knew that he talked a lot. Not a good trait in an intelligence agent. Duff was listening but his right hand was casually resting on his camera, the fingers curled around the lens casing. A real pro, Misha thought, and was about to turn away in the opposite direction when it happened.

A grey Simca came around the corner at speed, its tyres screaming on the hot asphalt. He saw the two black gun barrels protruding from the windows and his instinct took over, flinging him to the pavement, his right hand reaching under his jacket for the butt of the MAB pistol in its armpit holster. He never pulled the gun. As he rolled onto his side he saw that he was not the target. The gun barrels were now spitting flame and they were pointed at Duff Paget and the Canadian. Misha watched as they were smashed off their feet as though plucked by an unseen hand. The air was filled with the coughing rattle of gunfire. Misba's trained ear instantly recognised the source and he cursed under his breath.

'Uzis, the bastards are using our Uzis.'

The grey car had slowed and it was only a three-second burst but Misha knew that in those seconds the two Uzis between them had spewed over seventy bullets at the two men. Then the car was accelerating away. He saw two faces looking back from the rear seat. Christ! One was a woman - a white face surrounded by black curly hair. He looked back to the two men.

The Canadian was lying against a wall, his body still and hunched, but Paget was moving, a contorted, grotesque movement. His legs were twisted under him, his left arm smashed and bloody, the lower part of his face was shot away. Misha could see the white of his jaw bone protruding from a red maw. But he was moving. Dragging himself like a red rag down the pavement. And in his right hand Misha saw the black camera pointed at the retreating car. Misha felt the breath sucked out of him. The

Mishuganah was shooting film! He was dead. He had to be - but he was shooting film!

Misha came to his feet, started running, his mind in an exalted fury. Duff was motionless now, had rolled onto his back. He was clutching the camera to his guts, trying to stop them spilling out. Misha bent over him, felt repulsion at the sight of his smashed face. Only the eyes were untouched and in them was a last flicker of life. At least one bullet had smashed into the mouth, angling down into the jaw - stumps of broken teeth and bubbling blood. But there were sounds. Not just moans of agony. He was trying to say something. Misha lowered his head. There were other noises now in the street: people shouting, running footsteps, a siren in the distance. He bent lower, his ear almost touching the red flesh. Then he heard it. A word repeated even fainter. It sounded like 'hilm . . . hilm . . . , hilm . . .' Abruptly Misha understood. It was a word from deep in the throat, without teeth or mouth the dying man could not form the letter 'f. He was trying to say 'film'. Misha's eyes flicked to the camera in the tentacle of Duff's right hand.

Now Misha steadied himself. Began to operate again as a skilled agent. He looked up across the street. The guards outside the PLO building were watching impassively, but their guns were held ready. A group of onlookers had gathered at a safe distance.

Under the pretext of helping the dying man Misha lifted his body, pulling it over on its side so his back faced the street. He knew he only had seconds. Now Duff was truly moaning in agony. A horrible, bubbling, choking sound. Misha reached down and twisted the camera free and then almost vomited as intestines spilled out onto the pavement. He panted as he worked and cursed as his fingers slipped on the wet camera. Then he had it quickly rewound and open and the roll of film out and into his trouser pocket. He snapped the camera shut and tucked it back against the body. There were no more moans. The American was dead.

Carefully Misha straightened, looked again at the guards across the street. They were watching him intently. He made a series of graphic gestures with his hands: the first, a chopping motion to show that the man was dead; then a shrug and hands held out wide and flat. He was not involved. Slowly he backed off, edging for the corner. The siren was close now, no more than a block away. One of the guards raised his Skorpion and Misha froze, but he was only hefting it, easing the weight. Misha moved again and then, as the first police truck appeared at the end of the street, he was at the corner and turning and sprinting away, his heart pounding, his right hand under his jacket; ready now to shoot his way out.

Walter Blum sat behind his mahogany desk looking down at its uncluttered, polished surface. It was ridiculously large but he reasoned that by its size it made him look correspondingly smaller. His mood over the past hour had progressed from being sad to pensive. He had been thinking about Duff Paget and his death. The sadness had been for the passing of a friend. The pensiveness was now concern about the future. He had sent a note of condolence up the mountains to Ruth two days ago on first hearing the news. He would have gone himself immediately but a signal had come in that Misha Wigoda had related information and a roll of film. Walter had ordered him to Cyprus to report in person. He had arrived an hour before and told Walter graphically of the manner of Duffs death. The film was now being processed and the enlargements would soon be ready. That evening Walter would drive up and see Ruth. In the meantime he had put a cover watch on the house and knew that just before noon the CIA station chief at Nicosia had paid her a visit. He was wondering about that visit when his intercom buzzed and a voice informed him that the prints were ready.

He eased his chair back on its oiled castors and pushed himself to his feet. Lining the wall behind him was a bookcase replete with leather-bound tomes. He walked over and, with a fat forefinger, pushed the spine of 'David Copperfield' just below the 'D' of Charles Dickens. There was a click and a hum and a section of the bookcase swung backwards, revealing a panelled corridor just wide enough to allow his passage. As he walked towards the felt-lined door at the end he rebuked himself yet again for this piece of melodramatic architecture. He could just as well have housed his ORANGE headquarters in a perfectly normal office building with a standard cover. But still, if he was going to be a master spy, he may as well have some of the more glamorous perks and gadgets.

He opened the felt-lined door and stepped into a large, functional, windowless room. It was the penthouse of the adjoining building and housed six resident agents, a communications network, a records centre and a conference room. He nodded to a shirt-sleeved young man who sat with headphones at a bank of wireless equipment, then moved through into the conference room.

Two men sat at an oval table. One was Isaac Shapiro, nominal Deputy Managing Director of Walen Trading (Cyprus), but in reality head of ORANGE 7. The other was Misha Wigoda. Four 8 x 10 black and white prints lay on the table in front of them. Without a word Walter eased his bulk between their chairs and looked down at the photographs. Two were badly blurred images of the side of a car. There were spots of white at the windows. Wigoda reached out and indicated the spots.

'Muzzle flashes. It must have been reflexive. He was shooting film as they were shooting him.'

Walter looked at the third photograph. It showed the back of the car taken from a low angle. There were two faces peering through the rear window. One was a man: his hair loosely covered in the mottled head cloth so favoured by the PLO 'Fedayeen'. The other was a woman with curly black hair.

Misha pushed the fourth print directly under Walter's gaze. It was an enlarged section of the third. It showed the woman's face almost life size but indistinct in its graininess. Walter looked at the face for a very long time. The other two men looked up at him curiously. Then Shapiro said:

'We've checked against all the photos of PLO female operatives we have on file. Negative.'

Walter shook his head, then leaned forward and turned the other three prints over so that their white backs were facing up. He arranged them around the face, blocking out the curly black hair.

'She's no Palestinian,' he said. 'That's a wig. Without it she has very long, blonde hair.' His voice took on a growl. 'She likes to wear it up. Held in place by a single pin. When she takes the pin out, it tumbles down, it's like a trademark.'

Shapiro was puzzled by his barely controlled anger. He had never seen his boss except in a sardonic or bantering mood.

'Who is she?'

'Janine Lesage. She works for L'Universe - and SDECE.'

Wigoda interjected. 'So what's she doing with the PLO and why was she in on that killing?'

Walter sighed. 'As to the first, we must make it apriority to find out. As to the second, let's just say that hell hath no fury like a woman outbid in an auction.'

He reached forward, picked up the photograph and walked out. Shapiro and Wigoda looked at each other blankly. Then Wigoda asked:

'Was that Shakespeare?'

Shapiro nodded! 'Yes, with a little help from Walter Blum.'

Walter sat in the back of the air-conditioned Mercedes 600 as it wound up the mountain road to Platres. Usually on such a journey he would have chatted to Spiro, his Cypriot chauffeur, about local politics, soccer, the weather or his family. Spiro had five sons and four daughters and they were a diverse and fascinating brood. He had worked for Walter for two years and during the first few months had regaled Walter with stories of their exploits. Two of his sons were in politics, a third ran a large winery outside Limassol, a fourth was a reporter for a local newspaper and the fifth and youngest was a soccer star. Of the daughters the two eldest were happy and settled housewives, the third was a tempestuous *Bouzouki* singer whose love life was the scandal of the island, and the youngest was a member of the Cypriot Communist Party and in constant conflict with her two brothers who were at the opposite end of the political spectrum. She was also the apple of her father's eye. At first, Walter had assumed that the old man was either fantasising or, at best, ' wildly exaggerating. However, after a few months, he had been invited to attend the wedding of the youngest daughter and curiosity had prompted him to go. They were exactly as described: a sprawling, multi-talented, vociferous and friendly family. Walter had been astonished, particularly as several of the children were obviously very wealthy and he only paid their father fifty Cypriot pounds a week. He had broached the subject the next day and Spiro had smiled and explained that he simply enjoyed driving, especially such a car as Walter owned. Besides, he would never allow himself to be supported by any of his children. He treasured his independence and his ability still to act as a stern and impartial father.

So Walter liked him immensely and enjoyed talking to him and occasionally picking his brains about the island's politics and culture.

On this day, however, he needed to think and so he had pressed the button which raised the glass partition and sat back, ignoring even the spectacular scenery. He gave his mind over to his problems.

Walter was soon to have what his instinct told him were two momentous meetings. One with Ruth and the other with Munger. He had no idea how Ruth was taking Duffs death. He knew her to be a strong woman but he guessed that the visit of the CIA man from Nicosia might have had a profound effect on her equanimity. He decided he would make his approach from head on. The last thing she would appreciate would be more lies or half-truths. The only question was whether or not to tell her about Janine Lesage. It could be a motivating point in his strategy. On the other hand it might best be used at a later date.

He had no qualms about manipulating his friends. He liked to think of himself as a prime mover in the 'great game' and by definition his friends were either there to be used in that 'game' for what he saw to be the ultimate good, or they were not truly his friends: In that case, he reasoned, he need have no qualms about using them. It was a satisfying philosophy and one that did not lead to sleepless nights.

However, he was distinctly nervous, as an agent always is when he has to expose himself as such. They call it 'dropping the trousers' and there is no other way to recruit another agent who is not motivated by greed. In Ruth's case his instinct told him that only complete honesty would give him the chance to recruit her. In any event, she was Jewish and he knew she felt deeply about the future of Israel. Munger, though, was a different matter.

His eyes dropped to the seat beside him and the briefcase containing the thick dossier and the report of Professor Chaim Nardi. He wondered if Ruth would agree with his own interpretation and whether she would approve of his tactics. He felt an uncharacteristic stab of fear as he contemplated his meeting with Munger. There were so many imponderables and the man himself was unpredictable. Walter was wary of the unpredictable. Usually his wealth, his intellect and his position gave him more than adequate protection, but in this case he was going to be truly exposed. There was no other way. He wanted Mungar, even if the recruitment entailed a measure of risk. Since that first meeting, he had arranged for Munger's farmhouse to be watched.

His agents had reported that he continued to live the life of a virtual recluse. Once a week he went into Phini to buy supplies. On those occasions he would visit the taverna and take a drink and a coffee with the locals. Very occasionally he would go down the road for dinner with his nearest neighbours. Discreet enquiries in the village had ascertained that he was respected, even popular. It had been difficult to get information. The villagers were curiously protective about him.

Walter thought again of the little Professor's warning about amateur psychology. Anyway, after Ruth had read the dossier he would have a second opinion. Not so eminent, of course, but perhaps more practical.

The car was passing through Mandria and to take his mind off the problem Walter reached forward and opened the small fridge. Inside was a plate holding smoked salmon, breast of chicken and pate. Also a bottle of Montrachet. He pulled up and adjusted the tray beside his seat and settled down to the business of eating. It might be late before he finished with Ruth and he needed a full stomach for the tasks ahead.

Ruth was in the garden, pruning the rose bushes, when he arrived. There had been a little rain the night before and she was wearing bright yellow rubber boots over her jeans. Her hair was tied back into a casual pony tail and, as he stood on the patio looking down at her, Walter decided that whatever emotional impact she had suffered she was no less beautiful.

'Get yourself a drink,' she called, 'I'll be right with you.'

'I've been drinking Montrachet,' he answered, it's a pity to spoil it.'

She smiled and he felt a surge of relief, for it lit her face and expelled any doubts about her state of mind.

'There's a bottle in the fridge, Walter. From the last batch you sent. Don't drink it all - I'll join you.'

He went through into the kitchen and uncorked the wine, collected two glasses and carried them through into the lounge. She was on the patio pulling off her boots.

'Let's drink out here,' she said, 'and watch the sunset.'

He moved out and put the bottle and glasses onto the small wicker table and sank into a wicker chair. It creaked and groaned. Ruth slipped her feet into leather sandals and sat down opposite him. He poured the wine and they both sipped and looked at each other.

'I'm sorry Ruth.'

'I know, you liked each other.'

There was an enigmatic silence. He felt she was having difficulty controlling herself.

'Are you all right? Is there anything you need?'

Her laugh was high-pitched. Bitter. 'No, Walter. All my material needs are adequately catered for. There's the insurance. Royalties on his book . . . and then the pension from the US Government.'

He raised an eyebrow and she laughed again. It was not an attractive sound. She took a gulp of her wine and said:

'He was a spy, Walter! Had been from before we were married.' She looked up at him for a reaction and, seeing none, plunged on.

'A nice little man came out from the Embassy. He was politely surprised that Duff had never told me. At first I didn't believe him. It was monstrous. How can you be married to a man for nearly ten years and not know about something like that? It's obscene.' Again she waited for a reaction but Walter merely sipped his wine and looked at her steadily.

'It's obscene!' She hissed. 'I thought maybe it was regulations. Maybe that wives weren't allowed to know. But the man said it was a matter of choice. Duff chose not to tell me.' She looked away, out over the endless vista.

'I grieved for him, Walter. I forgot about all his weaknesses, his lies, his infidelities. I remembered only the good. I even believed after those first hours that he had truly loved me - only me. I saw him, in my mind, lying dead in that dirty street. Shot down for doing only what he was paid to do. Only what he was brilliant at. Then that man came up here and in his precise, bureaucratic language told me that Duff was a spy. A very senior agent with half a dozen commendations. He gave me papers to sign. Told me I would be receiving a letter from the Director of the CIA. Duff had been killed in the line of duty. He was a hero - a great patriot.'

She turned her head and looked at Walter. 'The body has been flown back to the States. There's going to be an important funeral. Colleagues and friends. Even the Director. I'm not going, Walter. He was theirs when he was alive. They can have him now he's dead.'

Walter reached forward, filled her class and asked:

'So what will you do now?'

She looked at him curiously. 'You're not surprised,' she said. 'You're not shocked.'

He shook his head. 'No Ruth, I've known for several years that Duff was a spy.'

She straightened in her chair, her lips parting in surprise.

'He told you? Duff told you – and not me!'

'He never told me.'

'Then how?'

'Because I'm also a spy. Have been for over twenty years.'

Her expression now was almost comical. She shook her head.

'You Walter? You work for the CIA?'

He smiled. 'No, I work for the Israelis – Mossad.'

She put her glass on the table with a thump; some wine spilled out. Then she pushed her chair back, stood up and walked to the edge of the patio. Several minutes passed while she stood with her back to him. Then she turned and smiled. It was a nice smile, without rancour or irony.

'So you tell me. But he never did. There must be a moral there somewhere.'

'The moral, Ruth, is that in a way I think more of you than Duff did.'

She cocked her head to one side and gave him a quizzical look.

'Are you saying you love me?'

He gave a short laugh and nodded. 'Of course I love you. It's ridiculous and we won't talk of it any more. I won't ever embarrass you with it and I hope you won't even make me look foolish because of it. But that's not why I just told you I was a spy. Now answer my question. What are you plans?'

She came back to the table and sat down and suddenly burst out laughing. A high, tinkling sound.

'Oh, Walter! You a spy! Of course I know you love me. A woman always knows – and you'll never look foolish. But a spy – it's incredible. Now I can see it in Duff. It so perfectly fitted him: his nature. God – even his looks. But you, Walter, I mean . . . you're the last person . . . '

He smiled complacently.

'I'm glad to hear it. After all, no spy wants to looks like one. Besides, I don't creep around in the middle of the night. I don't go dashing about following people or stealing secret papers or planting bombs. I run a network.'

She smiled again at the mental image of Walter creeping around in a dark cloak with a round, smoking bomb in his hand. Then she said very seriously:

'Then tell me about it, Walter. Tell me who you are and what you do. If you're going to tell me then make it everything. I'm so tired of being told bits and pieces or nothing at all.'

So he told her. Right from the early days. He told her something of General Dayan and Isser Harel and General Hofti. He told her a little about his network and what it had done. He talked for over an hour and she was so engrossed that she did not see the sun going down and the sky shading from blue to red to black. Only when it was almost dark did she get up and switch on the lights and fetch another bottle of wine. He had finished his story and as she filled his glass she said:

'It's fascinating, and it sort of completes your character. It gives you a different dimension. I mean, I always looked on you as rich and extravagant. Oh, a good friend and generous, but only interested really in making more and more money, but now I see you in a different way. It's wonderful what you are doing. It gives your character meaning.' A thought struck her.

'If you were married, would you have told your wife?', 'Of course, she would have to be part of it. Share the hopes and disappointments. Believe in it as I do.'

She nodded, watching his face.

'Exactly. I could have done that with Duff. It would have made such a difference. It could have brought us together.'

Walter tried to ease her feelings. 'Maybe he worried that you wouldn't approve.'

She shook her head. 'No. In the beginning maybe. I can imagine his early reticence. I was looking for a settled life: a family, security. But later I accepted a life without that. After all, his cover job was dangerous enough, I had accepted that kind of life; No, Walter. It was the fact of the secret that he enjoyed - it was his nature.'

There was a silence and then she asked: 'So what do you want of me?'

'First answer my question. What are your plans? What about Gideon?'

'He phoned and wanted to come immediately. He was going to apply for compassionate leave.' She gave him a wry look. 'Compassionate leave on the grounds of Duff's death! I told him to wait. Anyway, I'd planned to go to the States for the funeral. I told him I needed time to think.'

'Will you marry him?'

She shrugged. 'It's what he wants and maybe what I want - and need. But I'll wait a year at least. I'm a bit old-fashioned like that.' Walter kept his face impassive but inside he was massively relieved.

'And in the meantime?'

She paused her hands in a throw-away gesture. 'I'll stay here. I have friends, I have my work at the orphanage and,' she smiled weakly, 'I'm financially independent.'

'Good.' Walter pushed himself to his feet, went into the lounge and reappeared with his briefcase. He put it on the table, opened it, took out the two yellow files and placed them in front of her.

'I would like your opinion on something. Would you please read those. The thick one first. I shall go back to the Forest Park. I'll send the car for you at 8.30. I'd like you to join me for dinner. We can discuss it then.'

She had opened the top file and was looking down at the single name typed on the otherwise blank front page.

'David Munger,' she said softly. 'Is he also a spy?'

'No, but with a little help he's going to be.'

They shared a very large Chateaubriand. Walter had four-fifths of it and Ruth the remainder. They sat at a corner table in the half empty restaurant and did not talk much until they had cleared their plates. Walter was wearing a green sports coat and a tie over a pale yellow shirt into which he had tucked his green napkin. Ruth wore a plain black dress cut square over her breasts. Her hair was up and she wore a thin gold necklace with a small Star of David. Two of her acquaintances – retired, formidable English women - sat at a table across the room and eyed her disapprovingly. First it was rumoured that she was not even going to attend her dead husband's funeral and here she was dining out before the body was hardly cold. Furthermore she was in the company of a man known to consort with loose women and one whose profligate ways were scandalous. They clucked and whispered to each other in an orgy of self-righteousness.

'Dessert?' Walter asked after he swallowed the last of his steak. Ruth smiled. 'No thanks. You go ahead while I give you my opinion.'

Walter cocked a finger and a primed waiter wheeled over the dessert trolley and, without waiting for instructions, served Walter with a large wedge of lemon pie. When he had left, Ruth started talking.

She agreed with Professor Nardi's analysis. She said it diffidently. After all, she pointed out, he was one of the world's foremost experts. On the other hand she had the advantage of having met and observed Munger. With the benefit of hindsight many of his character traits now fell into place. She agreed that his mother and her abandonment of Munger as a child had been the pivotal influence on his life. As to the reason for his total withdrawal, that could only be understood with knowledge of what had happened on that last patrol. She then asked what Walter had in mind.

He finished the lemon pie, eyed the trolley again, then sighed and shook his head at the watching waiter. He then proceeded to tell Ruth all about his current mission and the difficulties he was facing in getting agents into Iraq. She listened carefully and made one or two incisive points, both about the dangers of nuclear proliferation in general and to Israel in particular. She was intelligent, well-travelled and observant and Walter found himself unloading onto her many of his doubts and anxieties. More than once she found herself thinking with great sadness that if only Duff had done the same, things might have been so different.

Finally Walter talked of Munger and how he was convinced that this one man might be crucial to his plans. It was no accident that Duff had been recruited by the CIA. A combat photographer was a perfect cover. Munger, although he had not worked in years, had an unassailable reputation. He was known to be non-political and his contacts must still be widespread.

'How will you try to convince him?' Ruth asked.

'Through his dead mother. She was a Jew. That means Munger is Jewish even if he doesn't want to acknowledge it.

He went on to describe the approach he would make when he visited Munger the following afternoon and the words and expressions he would use. Ruth listened attentively, then shook her head.

'It's so risky, Walter. You're going to use shock treatment and it could go either way. You might drive him deeper into the hole he's dug for himself.'

He spread his hands. 'What else can I do? He's got a skin like a rhino hide. Since his mother, no one has ever got close to him. Evoked any deep emotion. He's never let his guard down. Never made a friend unless it was to obtain help for his work.' Ruth held up her hand and then reached for her evening bag. 'That's not strictly true. I don't really understand it but I came across something very curious yesterday.' She took a small piece of paper from her bag. It was old and brown crease lines showed where it had been long folded.

'I was going through Duffs things. He had a briefcase containing his very private papers. It was understood between us that I would never look in it. We had the same arrangement about some of my things. Well, obviously, I had to open it. At first I thought I would have to cut it open; it had a combination lock. But then I tried the numbers of his birthday and it opened.' She smiled wanly. 'Not very professional for a spy. Anyway, there were various letters from girlfriends past and present; a copy of an old will; some other papers that I gave to the man from the Embassy - and this.'

She passed it to Walter and then suppressed a smile as he took it carefully between the fingers of one hand and, with the other, screwed his monocle into his left eye socket: It was the first time she had ever seen him use it and he looked hilarious. Walter read the note.

I don't know how you did today but I got more snaps than I need. Use the enclosed if you wish. It will be between you, me and the gatepost.

If you're looking for a reason, the fact that you attacked the mirror instead of me is good enough.

DM.

Walter carefully laid the paper onto the table, contorted his face and the monocle dropped down and dangled on its black silk thread. 'What do you make of it?' he asked.

Ruth reached forward, turned the paper and read the words again.

'I think I know about the incident with the mirror. I heard the story from the wife of a journalist who had been there. It seems that Duff had been under great pressure. He'd only been in Vietnam a couple of months and hadn't come up with any spectacular photographs. I know it was weighing heavily on him. Apparently there was a party in a bar in Saigon and he sort of cracked and threw a glass at the mirror. That's all I know. I asked him about it later but he shrugged it off as a drunken incident.'

She looked up at Walter's face and said solemnly: 'But I've worked out the timing. It was only a couple of days later that Duff filed the first of his really great Vietnam snaps.'

Walter was nodding his huge head in understanding. 'You're saying that they were Munger's work?'

For an answer she gestured at the note.

'Duff would have done that?' Walter asked incredulously.

She was silent for a moment, then said: 'At the time I would never have believed it, but after all these years I'm sure he would have, and rationalised it to himself very convincingly. Oh, I guess it was just that once. I know just about every snap he ever took in that war and they were his own. I imagine he needed help to get started.' She paused to give weight to what was coming.

'The fact is that Munger helped him. Not the action of a totally selfish or uncaring man.'

Walter looked down again at the paper, then stroked his pudgy fingers over it as if to iron out the brown creases and persuade it to yield more information.

'It would explain,' he said, 'why Duff was obsessed with the camera. Why he bid for it at the auction.'

'Yes,' Ruth agreed and smiled at the memory. 'I used to hate that camera. It cost me a gold and jade bracelet. I was going to throw it out but somehow I couldn't. Yesterday, after I found that note, I even took it down and cleaned it. Don't ask me why.'

Walter stopped stroking the paper. He picked it up and carefully folded it along the original crease lines.

'Can I borrow it?' he asked. 'I'll let you have it back.'

'Of course. Keep it. You'll show it to Munger?'

'I might. It depends how things go. Now let's have a coffee and a liqueur. I want to tell you how you can help - if I'm successful tomorrow.'

So they moved into the lounge under the disapproving gaze of the two old women. For the next hour Walter explained what he wanted her to do. She listened, at first merely bemused, then indignant, then angry. Walter was blatantly manipulating her. How could he profess to love her and a few hours later try to use her in such a way?

Walter was unrepentant. He had a job to do. The future of Israel was at stake. That fact transcended all personal considerations. She was Jewish and coincidentally was now free to help him in his task. She would become one of his agents.

It was an incredible dialogue. Half the time she felt she was in a dream. The events of the past few days had left her punch drunk. And now here was this garishly dressed mound of blubber blatantly recruiting her as an agent and spelling out the details of a bizarre assignment. And yet it was all so matter of fact as to be reassuring. As though such things and what she was being asked to do were commonplace. Her anger dissipated but she was unable to give him a coherent answer. There was just too much on her mind. Apart from anything else there was Gideon Galili to think of. It was possible that she loved him and would want to make a future with him.

Walter was sanguine. Why not? She herself had decided to wait at least a year before committing herself. Within that year she would render a great service to Israel. She would lose nothing. Galili would wait. She knew that.

She agreed that it was possible but what Walter was asking her to do was dishonest and bad. She would have to think hard about it. Anyway, it was premature. He still had to see Munger.

CHAPTER SEVEN

The farmhouse shuddered as Walter Blum's great body hit the floor. He was not unconscious, though he pretended to be. There was a sharp pain in his right buttock where he had first made contact with the ground. His stomach and jaw were numb from the two lightning blows. He lay very still with his eyes closed, his mind a kaleidoscope of impressions and pain. He could hear Munger breathing: short gasps, not of effort but of anger. It was the first time in his life that anyone had ever hit Walter and he did not like it. His predominant emotion though was fear. In the split second before Munger hit him, Walter had seen the blood lust in his eyes. They had literally filmed over red.

His head began to clear. He knew he was very close to death. A short, birdlike man kept entering his brain, warning him of the dangers of amateur psychology.

He lay still for a long time, willing his body not to move. He heard Munger's breathing begin to slacken and the scrape of a shoe as he moved. A second later Walter's eyes opened in shock and his head jerked upright. Munger was standing by the table holding a jug. The contents had been emptied over Walter.

'Get up.'

Walter was not about to get up. He scrabbled backwards into a corner, wincing with pain.

'Get up and get out or I'll kill you.' Munger's voice was flat and unemotional and all the more sinister for it.

Walter braced himself against the wall and pushed himself upright. He almost collapsed as his right leg took some of the weight. With a massive effort he stayed on his feet. Then he lurched forward and got both hands on the wooden table. Munger stood aside watching with narrowed eyes. Walter gauged the distance to the open door, then with a grunt he tottered over to it and out into the twilight. Spiro was waiting beside the car on the road. He saw Walter swaying on the track and ran up. He was old but strong and he got an arm halfway around his body and helped him hobble to the car and somehow got him stretched out on the back seat. He wanted immediately to go down to Limassol and get some 'friends' and mete out vengeance, but Walter curtly ordered him to drive to the house of Mrs Paget.

Two hours later he lay on the couch in her lounge sipping from a large goblet of cognac. A doctor had been summoned and pronounced that Walter was badly bruised but nothing had been broken. It was fortunate, the doctor had remarked, that ample flesh had cushioned the various impacts. Walter had glared balefully at him. With the doctor's prognosis and departure Ruth's air of concern had been replaced by barely stifled amusement. She had pulled a chair close up to the couch and sat watching her unexpected guest.

With a wince he put his glass on the coffee table and said: 'You're far too generous and intelligent to utter such inanities as "I told you so".'

She smiled. 'So tell me what happened.'

He told her. At first the meeting went well. Munger had been surprised and not at all happy to see him but he had reluctantly invited him in. Walter had explained that he had been in Platres, had heard of Duffs death and dropped by to give Munger the news. Munger had nodded and mumbled something about it being a pity. Duff had been a good photographer. He had then stood up and indicated that the visit was over. Walter had remained sitting and asked whether Munger ever intended to work again. Munger had shrugged and said that was his business. Walter had been perversely encouraged and at that point had revealed himself as being an Israeli agent. He would like Munger to consider working for him, using his photographic work as a cover.

Munger had been startled into silence and for ten minutes Walter had used that silence to make his pitch. He had explained the situation *vis-à-vis* Iraq and its nuclear programme. Pointed out how difficult it was for him to get agents into Iraq. He talked of Duff and how he had been killed and why. Very casually he had taken out the slip of paper and put it in front of Munger and watched as he read the words he had written so many years ago in Saigon. There had been a flicker of expression in his eyes. Walter then talked a little about Ruth and how she still had Munger's camera. He could pick it up any time.

Munger had slowly raised his head, looked at Walter and asked what it had to do with him. Walter had paused and then said: 'You can help. The fate of Israel is at stake. The fate of all the Jews.'

'Fuck the Jews.' Munger had said it flatly and Walter leaned forward and asked:

'Does that include your mother?'

'And that's when he hit me,' he said to Ruth.

'I'm not surprised.'

Walter sniffed. 'I had no opportunity to develop my theme. He threatened to kill me if I didn't get out. He meant it.' He sat up, raised his glass and drained it.

'Incidentally,' she said. 'I hardly slept last night. I thought about what you had told me and what you wanted me to do. Munger's reaction has let me off the hook. I decided I wasn't going to do it. I hate to lie, Walter. It's not in my character. Sometimes I wish it was. It would make things easier . . .

The glanced at her and sighed. 'So I've had a very unproductive trip. Instead of recruiting two agents I got none.'

She smiled in sympathy. 'What will you do now?' He sighed again, inflating his great bulk. She watched him closely, feeling sorry for him. He was looking down at the carpet and his round face had literally slumped, the fleshy cheeks hanging. His fat lips were pursed. He sat like that for over a minute, then she saw his expression change. He raised his head and his lips tightened in determination.

'I'll go back to the hotel,' he said, 'and try to get a good night's sleep. In the morning I'm going back to see Munger.'

'You're what?'

'Yes.' He snarled and stood up. 'Either he's going to kill me or listen to me.' He looked down at her, his face showing his anger. 'Fuck the Jews, Munger said. OK – I'm a fucking Jew. So is he.'

He swayed around the coffee table and moved towards the door, shouting over his shoulder:

'And so are fucking you!'

Long after he had gone Ruth sat straight in her chair, then she slumped back and gurgled with laughter. For once Walter had not needed Shakespeare to express his feelings.

Like embers smothered with coal overnight, Walter's anger smouldered and glowed. With the dawn it was white hot and it made him do something totally alien to a lifetime's habit: he forsook breakfast.

Instead he summoned Spiro and drove straight to Phini. He sat in the back of the Mercedes and during the twenty minute drive wrestled to clamp steel hoops round his expanding fury. He told Spiro to stop the car a few hundred yards from the farmhouse. As he started to walk down the road the old man called after him, begging to be allowed to come along. Walter snarled at him to wait.

In spite of his bulk he was, like an elephant, light on his feet and he hardly made a sound as he crept up the track to the open door, briefcase in hand.

For all his efforts, his anger was out of control and as he filled the door and his gaze alighted on the sitting form of Munger, the words spewed out.

'You! You're a fucking Jew! So was your fucking mother! Now kill me if you can!'

Then it was all pandemonium. A dog was snarling and barking. A young girl clung to its collar, her face a mask of fear as she stared up at the colossus in the doorway. Walter, his eyes centred on Munger, had not seen them. A coffee pot crashed to its side as Munger jumped up. Instinctively he grabbed for it, knocking it to the floor. The hot coffee splashed onto the girl's legs and she yelped in pain arid let go of the dog. In one leap it crossed the room and sank its jaws into Walter's calf. He screamed, dropped his briefcase, grabbed the dog by the neck and flung it out of the door. It bounced onto its side, scrabbled to its feet, turned and started to come back. Then came the crack of a gun. Dust spurted up in front of the dog and it veered away and disappeared in a slithering run. Spiro stood on the track, fumbling another cartridge into the breech of a long-barrelled, old-fashioned shotgun.

It was the girl's searing concern for her dog that restored order. She broke away from Munger with a wail and dashed for the door. Walter scooped her up under his arm, shouting at Spiro to put down the gun. The old man stood there quivering with uncertainty. Munger's head appeared over Walter's shoulder.

'Who is he?'

'My driver. He thinks you're going to kill me.'

'I might - but it can wait. Tell him to put it down.'

Walter handed him the writhing girl. "Her dog's all right. He missed.'

Again he called out to put the gun down. To go back to the car. He was all right. His voice was heavy with authority and slowly the old man lowered the gun.

He would wait at the gate, he shouted. Walter should call out if he needed him.

So order was restored. Androulla was calmed down and sent off home. Walter hobbled to a chair and slumped into it and then examined his calf. His trousers were torn and blood-soaked. He looked up at Munger standing by the door.

'I've had more violent abuse in the past twenty-four hours than in the whole of my life! Is the dog rabid?'

'Unfortunately not.'

Munger bent down and picked up the coffee pot. He turned, looked at Walter for a moment, then carried the pot over to the sink, filled it with water and put it on the stove.

'Take your trousers off,' he said.

Twenty minutes later Walter sat trouserless with his right calf neatly bandaged and a mug of coffee in front of him. Munger sat opposite.

'You have ten minutes,' he said. 'Then I'd like you to get out of my life - and stay out.' It was the last thing he said.

Walter spent a minute of his time thinking. Then he opened his briefcase and took out two files and a photograph which he put face down on the table. He placed one of the files in front of Munger and said:

'I explained about the Iraqi nuclear programme. That file contains all the proof that they're planning to build nuclear weapons which will be aimed at Israel. It's my responsibility to see that they don't succeed.'

He picked up the photograph, turned it over and slid it across. 'Duff Paget took that seconds before he died. It's an enlargement of a face looking out of the rear window of a car. He was shot dead from that car.'

He paused as Munger studied the photograph; saw Munger's hands come up and block out the curly black hair surrounding the woman's face.

'Yes,' Walter said. 'Janine Lesage. Your ex-lover. She works for SDECE. Right now she is probably co-operating with the Iraqi Mukhabarat against us. She hated Duff. He outbid her for your camera. At the time he was killed he was operating against the PLO. She almost certainly arranged his death.'

He waited for a reaction but there was none. Munger sat looking down at the photograph.

Walter picked up the second file, placed it in front of him and opened it. Clipped to the inside cover was a large photograph of a woman in her early thirties. She had an attractive but severe face, made more so by the sepia colours of the print. Walter spoke quietly but with tension in his voice.

'Rita Helen Munger, née Rothstein. Born July 20th, 1914. Daughter of Benjamin and Rachel Rothstein. Wife of William Munger. Died June 14th, 1948, in Jerusalem.'

The silence was heavy in the room. Walter's throat was dry. He desperately wanted to pick up his mug and drink some coffee but he kept perfectly still. Munger sat looking down at the old photograph. Walter could read no expression on his face. He took a deep breath and continued.

'In that file are the details of the work your mother did for Israel. The lives she saved; the hardships she endured. I don't think you know how she died. It's time you did. She was captured by elements of the Jordanian Arab legion. They cut her throat, but before that they raped her . . . more than twenty of them.'

Now Munger's head came up. He took a breath, appeared about to say something but then his mouth closed. Walter could see the rigid control being reimposed. With a mounting fear of failure he plunged on.

'All right, so she abandoned you. But she did it from a belief: from a certainty that she was needed to help create a Jewish state and so save the Jewish people after the depredations of the holocaust. You may never understand that, but there are millions of Jews that do. I do.'

Another silence. Munger's gaze never left Walter's face.

'There are things not in the file,' Walter continued. 'No one can judge what she suffered in leaving her only child. I believe she did it to make a commitment. She recognised what she was. Her work helping the inmates of the German concentration camps must have brought it about. It must have been a terrible struggle of conscience. A terrible decision. Her child, or the future of the Jewish people. She made her decision. She died for it.'

He did not care now. He picked up his mug and took a gulp of coffee. He felt a deep despair. He was not getting through. He reached again into his briefcase and flipped his card across the table.

'You may have lost the last one - or thrown it away. If you decide to help, reach me there. Ask for ORANGE ONE. Wherever I am, they'll find me.'

He shut his briefcase, picked up his trousers from the chair beside him and stood up. He knew he presented a ridiculous sight but he did not care. For once in his life he believed that the dignity he felt was reflected in his appearance. He hobbled to the door and turned.

'On every Sabbath,' he said, 'since June 1948, children go to the place where your mother is buried. They put flowers on her grave and they pray for her soul. That will happen always . . . or for as long as the State of Israel exists.'

He turned and went through the door.

CHAPTER EIGHT

Summer turned to autumn and in the Troödos mountains cones fell from the pines. The garden of Ruth's home was littered with them. One Sunday some children came from the orphanage to help her rake them into a pile. There was much laughter and gaiety. She had prepared some fruit juices and plates of snacks and tried without much success to arrange things so that the cones were actually piled and not redistributed. Finally, in desperation, she organised the children into two teams. She would make a race of it. A contest. She would end up with two piles of cones but no matter. She put Miriam, a ten-year-old girl with a sensible disposition, in charge of one team. For the other team she chose Stavros, her problem child. It was an attempt to concentrate his mind. To give him a sense of purpose and importance. The contest had just begun when the maid called to her from the patio. Someone had arrived.

She shouted encouragement to Miriam and Stavros and walked briskly to the house. She was wearing jeans, a blue mohair sweater and a scarf around her hair. Uninvited visitors were rare and she wondered who it could be.

After the bright sunshine it took a moment for her eyes to adjust to the dimmer light inside. Then she saw him standing by the high table in the corner. The glass dome had been lifted off and he was holding the camera in his hand. Anger flooded over her, washing away her high spirits.

'Put it down! You're not to touch it!'

He turned and she started to move forward.

'Who are you?'

But now her eyes had completely readjusted. She saw a man dressed in beige corduroy trousers and a blue jacket. He had a beard and long hair and very blue eyes. He held the camera easily. His' right hand was through the metal attachment on the side, the fingers resting on the lens case.

She came to a halt and drew a deep breath. They stood looking at each other. The laughter of the children tinkled in through the open window. Very softly she asked:

'Do you still know how to use it?'

He turned to the shelf next to him. There were half a dozen boxes of film that she had left there since Duffs death a few months ago. He reached out and picked one up. Weighed it in his hand, then looked at the specifications on the side. When he moved again it was sudden; one action flowing into the other in a rhythmic sequence. The empty box dropped to the carpet. There was a snap as the camera back opened and then another, seconds later, as it closed. He was moving away to the side and the camera came up and she heard the click of the shutter and the ratchet sound of the film being driven through. She stood absolutely still as he moved in front of her. The autumn sun shafted in through the window, highlighting the contours of her face and glistening on the tears that had inexplicably coursed down her cheeks.

CHAPTER NINE

Walter chaired the meeting, even though General Hofti had made a clandestine visit to Cyprus to attend. They sat at each end of the oval table. On Walter's left was Isaac Shapira and Misha Wigoda who, in the intervening months, had been promoted to head the Beirut section of the ORANGE network and was now designated ORANGE 14.

On Walter's right sat Efim Zimmerman, ORANGE 4 from Paris. A pedestal fan had been exactly placed so that it blew a stream of air directly in front of General Hofti's face, thereby diverting Walter's cigar smoke away from his nostrils. The General had thanked Walter for this courtesy in a way that he knew would much please him. In an effort to communicate better with his star agent, Hofti had been reading Hamlet.

'For this relief much thanks,' he said.

Walter grinned. 'I would wish you free of "a foul and pestilent congregation of vapours".'

So the meeting got off to a light-hearted start, but it soon turned serious. It had been called to review progress made against the Tammuz I reactor and to plan future strategy. Efim Zimmerman spoke first.

He was a huge bear of a man with snowy hair. A white Russian who had worked for Walter's father in Shanghai since before the war. Although in his late sixties, he refused to retire. He had told Walter that if it were only a question of making more money for himself and Walen Trading he would have gone out to pasture years ago. But ever since the ORANGE network was set up he had been one of its most effective agents. He loved the work and was brilliant at it. His section had penetrated deep into the French Civil Service, police, intelligence branches and industry. As he spoke the other men listened respectfully.

He made three recommendations. The first concerned the reactor itself. It was scheduled to be completed in June '79. Eight months away. He had now succeeded in infiltrating two agents into the work force in the factor at La Seyne-sur-Mer. One was a Jew - part of his own network. Zimmerman planned to plant a bomb in the factory shortly before the reactor was due to be shipped. It would be impossible to destroy it, but serious damage could be done with a resultant delay of months or even years.

Secondly he proposed a terror campaign against those French scientists who were working on the project.

Thirdly, he had discovered that the man in charge of the Iraqi nuclear programme was an Egyptian scientist called Yahia el Mashad. He made frequent trips to Paris to consult with French officials. Zimmerman proposed that on one of those trips the Egyptian be assassinated.

For the next hour the meeting debated these three proposals. It was quickly agreed that Zimmerman should go ahead with his plans to sabotage the reactor. General Hofti vetoed the terror campaign against the French scientists. It would only serve to isolate Israel still further. Besides, there was another factor: it had been learned recently that President Sadat of Egypt was seriously considering offering a separate peace to Israel. Some moves were expected any day. Nothing must be done to weaken Israel's international reputation in the light of that possibility.

As to Zimmerman's third recommendation, Hofti was in favour. After all, Yahia el Mashad was acting against his own government's wishes. The last thing Sadat wanted was for

Iraq's Saddam Hussein to obtain nuclear weapons and thereby strengthen his claim to leadership of the Arab world.

At this point Misha Wigoda interjected. He had been informed a month ago by a Lebanese scientist, to whom he paid a retainer, that two of Iraq's top nuclear scientists working on the Tammuz project had recently been arrested by the Mukhabarat. Their names were Jabar Mohammed and Saddam Azzawi and apparently in the volatile machinations of the Iraqs Ba'ath party they had come under suspicion of disloyalty.

Now Isaac Shapiro added his voice. Their agent in the Iraqi Mukhabarat, Hammad Shihab, had reported only a few days ago that both scientists had been interrogated in the 'Palace of the end' in Baghdad. Shihab had not personally been involved but he had heard of it. Subsequently they had been transferred to an unknown destination. The agent thought they may have been eliminated.

'It's curious,' Walter said, 'that the Iraqis would dispose of two of their top nuclear scientists shortly before taking delivery of the Tammuz I reactor. You'd think such men were immune to purges. To the Iraqis they're worth their weight in gold - or at least in enriched uranium

Hofti smiled but disagreed. 'You know how paranoid they are. The more important a man is to the regime, the more he had to proclaim and display his loyalty. No-one in that country is safe from a purge.'

'And they're both Shi'ite moslems,' Misha added, alluding to the fact that Saddam Hussein and most of the Iraqi hierarchy belonged to the minority Sunni sect.

Walter was not totally convinced but he kept his counsel while Hofti went on to point out that the information added to the importance of the Egyptian scientist Yahia el Mashad.

Next Misha Wigoda made his report. He advised that since the murder of Duff Paget a close watch had been kept on Janine

Lesage. It had revealed that she was seeing a lot of Sami Asaf - in fact was his lover. It was a reasonable conclusion that SDECE and the Mukhabarat were co-operating closely to protect Tammuz I from Mossad and that this co-operation was personified by the Lesage-Asaf relationship. What should be done about it?

Misha Wigoda was quite confident that in the prevailing anarchy of Beirut he could easily arrange for the lovers to meet a timely death.

Both Walter and Hofti were against it though. The French and the Iraqis would quickly replace them. Better to have known devils than otherwise. In the meantime Misha should do his best to 'bug' her apartment and car.

'Don't worry,' Walter said to Misha. 'In the course of time I'll take care of that lady.'

Finally the meeting discussed the situation inside Iraq. Walter felt uncomfortable. For several weeks he had resisted suggestions to try to set up a new network in Baghdad. He wouldn't explain why but he had been simply waiting. His discomfort now stemmed from the acknowledgement that he had made a mistake. His judgement had been at fault. In spite of expert advice he had followed a personal hunch. He was made more uncomfortable by the fact that most of the men around the table were being solicitous about his mistake. They knew he had delayed, but they did not know exactly why. As they discussed the problem only Efim Zimmerman allowed a note of criticism to creep into his voice. An operation should have been carefully planned months ago, he pointed out. All the actions to be taken in France would only delay delivery of the reactor. In time they would have to act in Iraq itself. Walter accepted the implied criticism. Efim Zimmerman had bounced him on his knee as a boy and had been a witness at his Bar Mitzvah. He was one of the few men who could talk to Walter exactly as he chose. So Walter sat with his eyes lowered and listened in silence while the others discussed future strategy and talked of possible agents within Mossad who might, against the odds, be able to establish themselves in Baghdad. Walter was not feeling very penitent. Many times in the past he had successfully followed his instincts. Espionage was not a cut and dried business. People were its vital element.

Walter would rather have one man in whom he had complete personal faith than a score of skilled agents who, for him, lacked the spark of charisma.

As he listened to the discussion he knew that none of the schemes being promulgated contained a real chance of success. They were merely going through the motions. The knowledge did not lighten his mood or serve to justify his mistake. He sensed that the void in Iraq would prove crucial. It was his responsibility.

General Hofti, perhaps sensing Walter's despair, had just suggested that they adjourn for half an hour, when the yellow phone in front of Isaac Shapiro buzzed.

Five pairs of eyes swivelled to look at it. With a nervous glance at Walter and then at Hofti, Isaac picked it up.

'Shapiro.'

He listened for a moment then said: 'I'll tell him.'

Looking puzzled he cradled the phone. To Walter he said:

There's a man at Walen reception asking for you. He gave your code name ORANGE ONE. Says his name is Munger.'

The others all looked at Walter and saw a beatific smile light his face.

BOOK THREE

CHAPTER TEN

REUTERS: BEIRUT, JANUARY 10th, 1979. 19.33. FLASH . . . David Munger, renowned British combat photographer who disappeared from Hong Kong in 1969 after auctioning his equipment, reappeared today in Beirut. Munger, who covered wars in Biafra, Angola, Cyprus, Borneo and Vietnam, announced his intention to cover Middle East area as freelance photographer. He refused to comment on his whereabouts or activities during past nine years. Stop.

Gordon Frazer, Bureau Chief of Reuters, Beirut, looked over the girl's shoulder as she tapped out the news flash. He sighed as it ended. He would dearly have loved to have been able to add more.

The girl turned and looked up at him, a puzzled smile on her lips. She was a Maronite Arab, educated at the American university, and she was darkly beautiful. She had worked in the Bureau office for only three months and since then Gordon Frazer had divided his energies between gathering news and lusting after her. So far it had been unrequited lust, but he was an optimistic man.

'Why,' she asked, 'does the reappearance of one photographer rate a special flash?'

He smiled down at her, admiring the lovely curve of her neck and the outer sweep of her breasts. His fingers tingled.

'Because he's a very special photographer,' he mumbled and looked up as one of the machines across the room began to clatter.

'That'll be UPI putting out the same flash. Ed Makin must have moved like a scalded cat!' He grinned at the thought of beating one of his arch rivals even by a few seconds. He gestured at the machines.

'Pretty soon the other agencies will pick it up and all over Europe and the States photographic editors will be grabbing their phones, trying to get Munger on contract.'

'He's that good?' the girl asked.

'The best - or he was.'

He unlocked his gaze from her cleavage and walked across to the row of machines. UPI had reported in much the same terms, with the additional information that Munger was now thirty-nine years old and appeared to be in good health.

Then the AFP machine started up. Frazer did not read French but "he saw the name 'Munger' and called the girl over and she stood and translated for him while he peered over her shoulder and gently pressed his front against her buttocks. She stood still and he felt a thrill of anticipation; a week ago she would have moved away from the pressure.

A few more days, he promised himself, and staff intercourse would progress from being merely social to positively sexual.

The AFP report was a rehash of his own. He wished it was longer for the girl now moved back to her chair. She was still curious, for in three months she had never known the agencies to report on any of their own media people.

'What's he like?' she asked. 'And where has he been all these years?'

Frazer shrugged. 'He won't say.'

He glanced at his watch. Her replacement would arrive in a few minutes. He was about to invite her down to the Commodore Hotel for a drink. Munger would still be there and a party would surely develop - but he abruptly checked himself as he remembered

Munger's way with women. Frazer decided he would keep this one well away.

She was looking at him curiously so he told her a little of Munger's past, then suggested that they have dinner one evening and he would tell her more. She agreed readily and he felt another tingle of anticipation, slightly marred by the thought that her easy acceptance might be more out of curiosity than his own charm.

During the short walk back to the Commodore his thoughts turned once more to Munger and the shock when he had strolled into the bar. Frazer and Ed Makin had been alone drinking Martinis. As usual Makin had been complaining in his nasal Bronx accent. He had just returned from a visit both to his head office and his wife in New York.

'My troubles always come in threes,' he had said. 'My boss complained about my expense account. My dentist told me my new bridge work is gonna cost three thousand bucks . . . and my wife whined that with the long separations she ain't gettin' enough sex.' He had sighed, taken a gulp from his glass and looked morosely up at the tall red-headed Scotsman.

'What would you do, Gordon?'

Frazer had shrugged. He liked the small, bald, chubby American and he respected his professional skill, but his perpetual pessimism could be mildly boring.

'It's very simple,' he had answered. 'Move out of your suite and into a normal room like everyone else. Have all your rotten teeth pulled out and get a good set of dentures. Buy your wife some new batteries for her vibrator. Stop complaining . . . and get some more drinks in - it's your turn.'

Makin had grunted in exasperation but looked up for the bartender. He had seen something in the mirror behind the bar and his morose expression had changed to astonishment. Slowly he had swivelled on the bar stool, a curious Frazer did the same, and they had gawped at the figure of Dave Munger standing at the door with a slight smile on his lips.

'So nothing changes,' he had said, moving forward. 'There's a war going on outside and Makin and Frazer are propping up the bar.' He had shaken hands with both of them but they were still speechless. He looked down at their empty glasses.

'Let me guess what will be on the wires tonight: "flash from Beirut: average temperature of Dry Martinis in bar of Commodore Hotel raised by three degrees. This causes major media riot outside Ministry of Information. Government reshuffle expected momentarily".'

He grinned, held up three fingers to the bartender and indicated the empty glasses. Makin had been the first to find his voice.

'Where in hell have you been? We'd given you up for dead.'

'Here and there,' Munger answered, easing himself onto a bar stool.

'Where? What happened?' Frazer demanded. 'What are you doing here?'

Munger held up a hand to ward off the questions. He watched as the bartender finished mixing the drinks and pushed the glasses in front of the three men. Munger picked his up, took a sip and nodded in satisfaction.

'The temperature's perfect. I guess there'll be no riot.' He turned to Makin and Frazer and examined them critically.

'Ed, you've got fatter, shorter and balder. Gordon, apart from a few more freckles you look about the same as when I last saw you in Saigon. That's bad, because then you were cynical and debauched. You should have mellowed with the years.'

The two Bureau Chiefs ignored the bantering. They in turn had carefully examined Munger. He was clean-shaven but the pallor of his chin contrasted with the deep tan on his forehead and arms, indicating that he had recently shaved off a beard. Frazer noted that his fingers were calloused from manual labour.

So he had not been working as a photographer. He appeared not to have aged much, but even nine years ago he had looked older than his years. The lines across the forehead, around the vivid blue eyes and at the corners of his mouth, had deepened a little. It was the sort of face that appeared poised on the verge of middle age without ever sliding over.

In spite of his quizzical smile there was a strange dullness in his eyes. He had never shown much expression but both men had known him well and remembered that if you could read him at all it was through his eyes. When relaxed they appeared wider and the blue of the irises lighter. When angry or tense they darkened and narrowed. They were truly like lens apertures adjusting to the controls of his mood. Now there was an opaqueness, a misting as though a filter had been clipped over them.

'So give!' Makin had finally said. 'What have you been up to?'

Munger had shaken his head. 'The past is gone, Ed. I don't want to talk about it.' His voice was flat and definite and Makin shrugged in acceptance.

'You're going to work?' Frazer had asked and when Munger had nodded Makin immediately asked.

'For whom?'

'I'll freelance for a while. See what turns up. I'll cover the area from here.'

At that Frazer had casually stood up and headed for the door, calling over his shoulder that he'd be right back. Munger had started to question Makin about local conditions and the American had been sketching in the problems faced by the media in Beirut when suddenly he had stopped and jumped up.

'That son of a bitch! Of course, it's news itself. He's filing the story!' He rustled to the door on his short legs, shouting: 'Don't go away Dave!'

Makin's office was in the Hotel itself but Frazer still beat him by a few seconds.

He had only been gone twenty minutes but the word had already started to spread. There were half a dozen men in the bar now, surrounding Munger. It was to be expected. The great phalanx of photographers and correspondents who had covered Vietnam and the Far East in the sixties and early seventies had moved on to the Middle East. It had become the world's perpetual hot spot and so provided the bread and butter for several hundred of the world's leading media men and women.

Frazer pushed through the group around Munger and claimed his original stool from George Blake, a photographer from the 'Toronto Star'. Ed Makin was also back with a glass in his hand. He gave Frazer a baleful glare and muttered 'Bastard!'

Munger was standing with his back to the bar. He had switched from Martinis to his usual vodka and soda. As Frazer settled himself and ordered a drink he heard Munger parrying questions from the newcomers and asking some of his own. He was relaxed and smiling but his eyes were still mirrors reflecting nothing.

So the bar filled up, the level of noise rising. Many of the people knew Munger from earlier years. Others, the younger ones, had come out of curiosity to see a reincarnated legend. War correspondents are drawn to a spontaneous party the way bees swarm to a hive. The more dangerous the place, the more fervent is the atmosphere.

During a lull in the conversation Frazer said to Munger: 'You'll be getting any number of calls tonight offering contracts.'

'They already started,' Munger answered. 'I told the switchboard just to take messages.' He took a sip of his drink and gave Frazer a quizzical look.

'What's the opposition like these days?'

Frazer thought for a moment then held up his left hand with the fingers spread. 'In the top league there's only four.' He indicated the Canadian. 'There's George, and Ray Morris, whom you know. Don McCullin works out here occasionally and there's a young Frenchman called Latière who freelances. He's good.' He shrugged. 'Duff Paget's death left a gap. You heard about that?' He watched as Munger nodded, then asked: 'You knew he bought your camera at that auction?'

Again Munger nodded and for the first time Frazer saw an expression deep in his eyes. 'Yes, I picked it up from his widow in Cyprus a few months ago.'

Frazer's curiosity was pricked. 'How was she taking his death?'

'She was all right,' Munger answered, then abruptly changed the subject. 'Is Janine Lesage in town?'

Now Frazer's curiosity was definitely aroused. From the corner of his eye he could see Ed Makin, who was listening to George Blake, but had an ear cocked to their conversation.

'Yes, she's around,' Frazer replied. 'No doubt she'll be along as soon as she hears.' He paused. 'She's having an affair with Sami Asaf. Remember him?'

'Sure.' Now there was a different expression in Munger's eyes. They had narrowed, grown darker.

'She's still a damned beautiful woman,' Frazer said, watching him closely. A slight smile twitched at the corners of Munger's mouth.

'Gordon, you should have used your first adjective in isolation.'

Frazer laughed and glanced at Ed Makin who was now ignoring Blake. He started to say something but was interrupted by more arrivals who pushed through to pump Munger's hand and ask questions which all began with. 'Where in hell . . .?' Munger parried them easily but firmly. The noise level built up. The manager had drafted in two extra bartenders. He recognised all the signs and was- well pleased! Hotel business in Beirut was very patchy and the media men and women represented his best customers. He stood at the end of the bar, a small, dapper

Lebanese in his late forties. During the Vietnam War he had worked in several hotels in the Far East and he knew Munger well. He too had been astonished when he had walked in a couple of hours ago with four large cases and asked for one of the biggest suites on a permanent basis. Perhaps remembering that, he beckoned to one of the bartenders and whispered in his ear. A few minutes later the noise was interrupted by the popping of champagne corks. Someone shouted 'Hallelujah' and the tempo in the bar moved up a notch. It was now truly crowded and at first the woman who appeared at the door was not noticed. Then slowly, in concentric waves, a silence emanated from her direction and all eyes turned towards her. It was Janine Lesage, dressed in a black and gold Pucci jump suit, a sequinned bag held in one hand and a cigarette in a long ivory holder in the other. Her golden hair was twisted up onto her head and as she looked over the mass of heads to Munger at the bar her lips formed a tender smile.

Feet shuffled on the carpet and a narrow lane opened in. front of her, giving a clear view of Munger. Many in the room had known of her previous relationship with him. Many had heard her comments after his disappearance. Several had been present at that auction.

Very slowly, with her long, sinuous stride, she moved down the lane towards him. He watched her coming without a trace of expression on his face.

A few yards away she paused, her right hand placed the cigarette holder between her teeth, then continued up to the back of her head. A moment later her hair tumbled down as she pulled out the single retaining pin.

It should have been a melodramatic, even laughable, gesture but from this woman it caused only a general exhalation of breath. She moved forward again through the silence until she stood in front of Munger. She was as tall as he was and for a long time they looked into each other's eyes before she said in her husky voice: 'Ça va, Dave?'

She leaned forward and kissed him on the lips, then cocked her head to one side and, together with all the others in the room, waited for his reaction. For several seconds his eyes examined her, then they narrowed and darkened.

'Ça va, Janine. You should cut your hair. It only suited you like that when you were young.'

She recoiled as though from a slap. A low murmur rumbled around the room - a sound of collective approval. 'No one in the bar that night had ever before seen Janine Lesage anything but totally possessed. Many had been the butt of her sharp tongue and cynical wit. Always her beauty and her use of it had protected her from retaliation. So in her humiliation she had no ally and she knew it. She stumbled back as the lane behind her widened. Her face was ugly as it worked in frustration and fury; her eyes were cobra's eyes as they glared at Munger. But she was a cobra backing away from a mongoose. Finally she twisted on her heel and tried to stalk out with dignity. It was a failure. For once the long sweep of her hair was not a curtain of grace but a focus of her indignity. She had the instinct not to toss it in her usual exit style.

She left a silence as all eyes turned back to the bar, then the same voice once again yelled 'Hallelujah!' and the party restarted with the tempo notched still higher.

It was after midnight when Munger finally escaped to the tranquillity of his suite. It was one of the largest in the Hotel and had two bathrooms, which was why Munger had chosen it. Unlike Ed Makin he had no worries about his expense account. Walter had assured him that the funds available were virtually unlimited. He had backed this up by giving him a chamois leather belt to be worn next to his skin. Concealed in it were fifty thousand US dollars in thousand-dollar bills and fifteen pure blue flawless

D colour diamonds, each weighing one carat. So the belt had a total value of close on half a million US dollars - not counting the leather.

Even without Walter's financial support Munger would have had no qualms about paying for the suite. On his way up he had stopped at reception and collected twelve telephone messages. They were from news agencies and magazines in the USA, Europe and Japan and they all begged for an urgent return call. He would get on the phone in the morning and by noon would tie up all the retainers he needed.

On entering the suite he went first to the larger of the two bathrooms. It was to become his darkroom and he nodded in satisfaction as he saw the two narrow tables he had requested, and the extension wires with additional power sockets. Next he went into the bedroom, stripped off his clothes and hung the money belt over a hook on the back of the door. He never considered concealing it for he had long ago decided that the best security for such an item lay in its innocuous appearance.

Before leaving the bedroom he switched on the radio, found some easy music and turned the volume up so that with the doors open he could hear it throughout the suite.

The smaller bathroom, which itself was as large as many hotel rooms, had a shower stall as well as a tub. Ever since spending time in Japan he had developed an aversion to washing himself in a European-type bath. 'You soak in your own dirt,' a Japanese friend had pointed out. So he went into the shower stall, soaped himself and, for fifteen minutes, let the stream of hot water wash away the smell, taste and stickiness of the journey and the sojourn in the packed bar. During those minute he planned in his mind the layout of the darkroom. He had brought with him a lot of equipment, some of which was new to him. There had been significant developments in photographic printing since he had last worked. Also he had never devoted very much time to that aspect of photography, being content to let others do it for him. The impact of his snaps had come from the subject matter rather than the techniques of processing. Now it might be different.

He turned off the shower, dried himself, slipped on a white terry towel robe, moved to the sink and vigorously brushed his teeth. At last the acrid taste of the plane journey was gone.

The mirror behind the wash basin had misted up. With a towel he wiped a clear circle and, for about a minute, stood looking at his reflected face. Had Gordon Frazer seen that image he would have noted the change from half an hour earlier. In the bar there had been some animation as Munger had talked and listened and observed. Now the face was merely a collection of features that made no statement. Identified no feeling.

He turned away from his image and walked through into the lounge. Two large, steel cases lay by the door. He bent down and worked the combination locks and lifted the lids. One contained his original camera, a second camera - a Hasselblad, a great variety of lenses, tripods, boxes of film and several small items for the darkroom. In the other case were the bigger pieces of equipment: an enlarger, paper dryer, paper trimmer, developing tanks, an angle-poise lamp and concertina bottles containing chemicals and fixers.

He dragged the cases across the carpet close to the door of the larger bathroom, then transferred and placed the equipment into position. It only took half an hour because the layout was clear in his mind. He checked it all, then returned to the living room. He arranged his Nikon, the tripods and the lenses and boxes of film on the table, leaving the Hasselblad in the case. Then he crossed to another table on which a bar had been set up. He filled a tumbler with ice cubes and poured Stolichnaya vodka over them. His hand reached out for the soda syphon but he checked himself and took a sip of the neat vodka. It was a clean, sharp taste arid the melting ice would soon dilute it. He stood for several minutes, gently swirling the ice in the glass and occasionally raising it to his lips. He could faintly hear the music from the bedroom: The Commodores were singing 'Three Times a Lady'. His mind switched to Janine Lesage and the incident in the bar. His reaction had been provoked only by the memory of Duff Paget's last snap. He had not heard of her comments in Hong Kong all those years ago. He knew of them now for Gordon Frazer had told him after her departure. In spite of his anger he decided that his comment had been true. Her metre of hair no longer suited her. It served only to accentuate the bones of her face that, with the passing years, had become sharper, giving her a predatory look. Perhaps others couldn't see it. Perhaps others saw her beauty as more refined.

His thoughts were interrupted by a high-pitched buzzing. He turned his wrist and glanced down at his new Seiko alarm watch. It showed 12.55 am. He depressed the button to stop the noise, drained the last of the vodka, walked across to the open case and lifted out the Hasselblad. From a side pocket he took a coiled length of very thin wire. At one end was a flashlight plug attachment. The other end had a round rubber sucker. He fitted the flash attachment into the Hasselblad, carried it through to the bedroom, switched off the radio and put the camera on the bed. Then, uncoiling the wire behind him, he crossed to the window and opened it. He was looking south over the city. He lifted the rubber sucker to his mouth, wet it with his tongue, leaned out of the window and stuck it to the outside aluminium frame. He moved back to the bed, sat down, picked up the camera and set the exposure to 1.7. There was a faint click which would have been absent in a normal Hasselblad. He held the camera in his left hand, turned his wrist and looked at his watch again. He gazed at the dial for forty seconds until the liquid crystals reformed to show 1.00 am then, with his right hand, he worked the film advance lever three times. Two minutes later he repeated the action.

A hundred miles away in a bunker on the Golan Heights a Mossad radio operator lifted his earphones from his head and picked up the telephone which connected him with Mossad headquarters.

Ten minutes later in spite of the hour, a fat and torpid ORANGE ONE was awakened in his villa in Limassol by the buzzing of a bulky green phone on the bedside table. He reached out, switched on a light and pushed himself into a sitting position. He always slept naked and, had there been an observer, his pink, bloated rolls of flesh would have presented a ludicrous sight. With a glance at an ornate gold clock on the wall and a grunt of irritation he picked up the phone. His scowl immediately softened to a smile as he heard the duty officer in ORANGE headquarters inform him that ORANGE BLUE had carried out his first radio check.

Walter cradled the phone, switched off the light, slid down into the bed and tried to recapture his interrupted dream which had involved a mountain of delicious food surrounded by an army of voluptuous women.

At about that time in Beirut Munger was having a nightmare: the same nightmare he had suffered repeatedly for nine years.

It had taken him only a minute to wind up his aerial and put away the camera/radio. The journey, the party and setting up the darkroom had combined to exhaust him physically and within minutes he was asleep. The curtains over the window had not been closed and a nearly full moon cast a soft light into the room. Like Walter, he too slept naked with the sheet to his waist. An observer though would have seen a very different sight. His body was slim and taut and dark from the sun. A wide scar on his left shoulder showed up paler. It was a wound badly stitched after a Vietcong with a Kalashnikov had shown scant respect for famous photographers.

At first he lay on his back, completely still, his head propped high on two pillows. After a few minutes his legs began to twitch and his fingers to clench. He started to breathe heavily and beads of sweat broke out on his forehead.

It lasted for only ten seconds and then his eyes opened wide and he moaned deep in his throat and sat up and, with his hands, wiped the sweat from his face and then held them over his eyes while his body shook in spasms and his chest heaved.

Gradually the trembling lessened and his breathing slowed. He dropped his hands and looked at the square of uncurtained window. Now at last his facial features showed something: they projected an emotion of total despair.

It had been four months since he had last suffered that nightmare. During those months he had prayed to any deity that might exist that it would be the last time. As the weeks had passed he had dared to hope that the devil in his subconscious had been exorcised. Now his face reflected the burial of hope.

He rolled off the bed and staggered to the window and opened it. Heat and the faint murmur of city noise wafted into the room. He leaned out and looked down at the street twelve floors below. Only one vehicle was moving - a jeep of the Lebanese Army - patrolling the recently imposed night curfew.

For five terrible seconds Munger contemplated the release of suicide. He was outside himself, looking at his own body spread-eagled and broken on the street below. Then his head jerked up and with a sob he twisted away and went into the bathroom and ran the shower cold and held his head under it.

The nightmares had always been the same. They started with a face: a wide, high-cheekboned, oriental face. The face of a girl. It should have been beautiful and by its form it was. But the eyes gave it the antithesis of beauty - they too by their curve and slant should have been lovely, but their content was the nightmare. A mixture of pain, despair and utter contempt. The pain and despair were self-centred. The contempt was directed at Munger - directed like a searchlight.

Wherever he turned he saw the eyes. He could not blank them out, could not close his own. In the nightmare he would run; try to escape, but they were omnipresent until finally they filled his own sockets, looking in. The pain and despair entered his head - the contempt became a knife in his heart.

He turned off the shower, turbaned his head with a towel and went into the sitting room. He knew that sleep was now impossible. Those eyes were waiting in the shadows of his brain. He filled a glass with ice and Stolichnaya and sat down and turned his mind to reality. For him reality was events: things that had already happened - not things that might be, or might have been. Walter Blum was reality. Munger's thoughts went back four months to the day he had walked into the office of Walen Trading. It had been the nightmare that prompted it. The nightmare combined with distant memories of a woman with a serene look - a woman who had shifted in and out of his young life, bringing light with her presence and darkness with her absence. It had been crude of Walter Blum to use the memory of his mother, but it was the crudity of a crowbar and it had prised open a chink of emotion. Day by day Munger had fought to close that chink and he might have succeeded if the nightmare had not come and kept him perpetually awake and sapped his mental strength until only the thought of physical activity offered a reprieve.

So he had collected his camera and the moment he picked it up and slipped it onto his hand like a glove he knew that it represented his only chance.

The weeks that followed reinforced that belief. There had hardly been a moment for a morbid thought. Within days he was in a Mossad training establishment on the outskirts of Tel Aviv and for the next ten weeks he was a sponge absorbing new knowledge and techniques. He had been amazed by the changes that had taken place during his years of Isolation. One of the instructors pointed out that they had been the years when space technology had come back to earth from the cosmos. They taught him to use radios that could fit into cameras. Bombs that could be contained in a roll of film; listening devices no bigger than a shirt button. They were clever. They built this technology into equipment that he was familiar with and that he could genuinely claim as his working tools.

Misha Wigoda had instructed him on the latest photographic and printing techniques; shown him the new telephoto lenses that could make a car number plate readable from a mile away. Much of it was still commercially unavailable but the Mossad technicians had packaged it into well-known name brands. So Munger's Nikon lenses would pass any inspection outside the Nikon factory itself.

During those weeks he had learned the spy's tradecraft from the profession's acknowledged masters. In turn he had provided some surprises himself. The unarmed combat instructor had quickly concluded there was little he could teach him. Those skills had not changed in nine years.

Similarly he proved to have an inborn ability to follow a man without-being sensed or detected and conversely to 'feel' a tail when he was the subject.

'David Munger', the chief instructor stated in his final reports, 'is perfect mental and physical material for a field agent.'

Walter Blum had read the words over General Hofti's shoulder and smiled complacently.

Munger's initial mission was simple and explicit: to re-establish himself as a foremost photographer working in the Middle East arena. He was to reforge old links, establish new ones, and by the success of his work and the spreading of his reputation make smooth his movements throughout the area. Nothing more would be expected of him for at least a year and maybe longer.

During that year the Mossad network would be attacking the reactor and the people connected with it in France itself. It was only if and when the reactor was actually shipped to Iraq that Munger would be called into play. By that time he must be able to move in and out of Iraq at will.

The period of training had also imparted a sense of belonging. Munger had never really thought of himself as Jewish. He knew that the Jewish faith was considered to pass through the maternal line, but until her abrupt mental conversion his mother had never practised the faith. He had never studied it or taken part in the rituals or ceremonies. He had never even been inside a synagogue.

During those months in Israel he had been treated simply as a Jew. The instructors had not been disconcerted by his lack of knowledge of the faith. To them it was immaterial. He was a Jew. The fact was enough. At first he thought they might be working to orders, a kind of subtle brainwashing, but he soon dismissed the idea. They were totally natural, assuming that the work he was training for, the risks he would take, could only be accepted by a Jew. By a man motivated by love for Israel and the Jewish people. So he absorbed their attitudes and their motives and began to think of himself as Jewish. He could never accept the religious mantle but then neither could many in the training camp. He saw only a race of people with whom he could finally identify.

On his last day in Israel he had gone to the grave of his mother. It had been in the early morning and the cemetery was deserted. It was one grave among thousands and there were flowers on it. There were flowers on many of them but that didn't diffuse the impact - rather strengthened it. He had stood for an hour at the grave as light rain fell. His thoughts had been a turmoil but as he turned away he knew that, like his mother, he had made a commitment.

It was ironic, though, that as he sat in his luxury suite with a cold glass in his hand, the commitment was threatened by a pair of eyes that had no substance but could well destroy his mind.

He knew the dangers. Understood the thickness of the dividing line between sanity and madness. During those five seconds as he had looked down to the street below, that thickness had become a transparent membrane. The thought sent the cold from the glass to his heart.

To divert his mind he stood up and started sorting through the equipment on the nearby table. He checked his camera, then he sorted through the boxes of film, separating them into different speed numbers.

It was then that he saw it and for a moment was puzzled. Among the boxes was a round, black spool-holder denoting an exposed roll. But he hadn't yet taken any film. Then he remembered: it was the film he had shot at Ruth Paget's house four months ago. His thoughts went back to that morning and the thrill of holding his camera after so many years. He had stayed half an hour and photographed Ruth and the children as they played in the garden. She had asked him to send her copies but from the moment he had walked into Walter Blum's office his mind had been over-occupied. He held the black tube in his hand and remembered how tears had appeared in her eyes when she first saw him holding the camera. How beautiful she had looked - and how vulnerable. There had been another look in her eyes but he couldn't define it.

On an impulse he carried the film through into the darkroom. He might as well develop it. At least it would help pass the night.

At first he worked automatically, his fingers quickly remembering the thousands of similar movements. He trimmed the film and loaded it into the feeding reel, his mind occupied with the routine. He flicked on the normal light, mixed the developer and poured it in, then began turning the drum in his hand. He hardly needed to check with the timer - his brain ticked off the seconds. Then out came the developer and in went the stop bath - a gentle shaking - then the stop bath out and the fixer in. He thought of the hundreds of hotel rooms in which he had gone through this exact same sequence. It always held a fascination for him - a sense of anticipation as he waited to see whether his eye and his camera had captured the same image. But in this case he could not clearly remember what his eye had seen. He washed the processed film and clipped it into a collapsible dryer and went out into the sitting room while it dried.

Fifteen minutes later he was back in the bathroom assessing the negatives. It was only a roll of twelve: three of Ruth by herself, three of her with one of the children and six of the other children. He could see that his exposure had been good and also the developing. He transferred the negatives to a contact printing frame and exposed them, using the empty enlarger as a light source. Ten minutes later he was examining the contact prints. There was something about them that he could not fathom and at first he went through a mental trouble-shooting sequence. But he had done everything right and the images were technically very good, with excellent contrast and delineation. There was something else about the tiny prints: something different. He thought perhaps his exhaustion and state of mind had clouded his vision. He picked up a magnifying glass and examined each one carefully for several minutes. Then he straightened up and looked at himself in the mirror as if seeking an answer from his image. He went into the sitting room again and drank another vodka, standing by the window looking out over the half-lit city. After ten minutes he abruptly came to a decision, drained the glass, went back into the darkroom and started working with the enlarger.

At 5 o'clock in the morning he was looking at a row of 8 x 10 prints clipped to a cord above the bath tub. The first six showed children at play. They were unposed and natural. He remembered standing on the patio as they had boisterously raked up the pine cones. After a few minutes they had ignored him and his camera. It was not that they were exceptional snaps that riveted Munger's gaze but that in each case the children were caught in happiness and in such a way that their joy and exhilaration flowed off the paper. They were photographs the like of which he had never taken in his life. The next three showed Ruth bending over, talking to a young boy. Munger even remembered his name - Stavros. She had said he was her problem child. She was holding both his hands in hers. In the first the boy's eyes were downcast, the face sad. In the second the beginning of a smile had started on his lips. In the third the smile had spread across his face. He was transformed from gloom to happiness. It was the first time that Munger had ever photographed a sequence moving in that direction.

Finally his gaze moved to the last three. They were all of Ruth and he had marked the negatives so as to enlarge only her face. They were extraordinary portraits of a beautiful woman and they were more than that. He remembered now how the light had shafted in through the open window. It had shaded the contours of her cheek, caressed her forehead and chin, glinted off her black hair. The composition and light and angles were perfect. But it was the expression which gave them real beauty. Expression emanating from her eyes - the expression of compassion. In two of the portraits the light glistened on tears and yet they created not sadness but a depth to the compassion.

Munger looked at those three photographs for a long time, especially the last one. Finally he unclipped the last photograph and turned again to the enlarger.

When he emerged, light from the rising sun was filling the sitting room. He carried a large print in his hand. He pulled a chair over to the window, sat down and raised the print to the morning light.

It showed only the eyes of Ruth Paget. Just below one eye was a tear drop. Due to the extreme enlargement the print was grainy but that seemed to enhance it, giving an ethereal quality.

Munger held the photograph at arm's length and looked steadily into those eyes and again saw the compassion. He then closed his own eyes, shutting them tight, creating blackness. Into that blackness he conjured up an image. It was easy to do; it was always in his head - the image of the oriental eyes. He saw and felt the pain and despair and, above all, the contempt. He kept his eyes shut, letting the pain and the terror build up and, when his heart began to beat faster with the agony, he opened his eyes and let the light into his brain together with the compassion from the eyes of Ruth Paget.

He did that half a dozen times and each time compassion was the victor. He then carried the photograph through into the bedroom and placed it on the bedside table. He picked up the phone and told the operator he was not to be disturbed. He crossed to the window and closed the curtains tight, then climbed into the bed. As he reached out to turn off the light he looked down at the photograph for a long time, then he flicked the switch and fell back onto the pillow.

He slept for twenty-four hours and he had no nightmares.

CHAPTER ELEVEN

It was early summer again when Walter Blum drove up to Platres. His mood was more sanguine than on the last occasion and he sat next to Spiro in the Mercedes and chatted with him about his family and local politics and the stalled efforts of the United Nations to resolve the Cyprus problem.

As they reached the Troödos foothills, Spiro fell silent as he concentrated on the narrow road. Walter's thoughts turned to his recent trip to Paris. With Efim Zimmerman he had planned the last convoluted steps to stop the French from shipping the Tammuz I reactor.

The Egyptian scientist Yahia el Mashad was to be assassinated on his next visit to France. A Mossad team was already assembled and waiting in Paris. Another team was preparing to plant bombs in the factory at La Seyne-sur-Mer. The two on-site Mossad agents had reported that the construction of the reactor was now slightly ahead of schedule. The optimum time to attack would be in a few months.

Walter knew that under the direction of Efim Zimmerman the activities in France would be successful. He also knew that such success would have a marginal effect and at best delay the project for a few months or a year at most. He remembered a conversation with Zimmerman over dinner: Walter had eaten and listened while Zimmerman had talked. Walter listened carefully and with deep respect for Zimmerman's knowledge of France and the world in general.

In essence Zimmerman believed that in order to halt the project completely it would become necessary for Israel to take 'defensive' military action against the reactor. That meant either a commando raid or a 'take out' bombing strike. Obviously this could not be contemplated on French territory and would have to take place after the reactor had been installed in Iraq. Walter knew that this line of thought was paralleled by General Hofti and the Israeli chiefs of staff.

Zimmerman had gone on to illustrate the vital need for top class intelligence to be available from Iraq. Whether it was to be a commando raid or a bombing strike the planners would need exact and up to date information on the reactor site and, more importantly, when it was due to become radioactive or 'hot'. Obviously it must be destroyed before that moment. El-Tuwaitha was only twelve miles from the centre of Baghdad and if that city of three and a half millions was to be radioactively contaminated, Israel would be universally condemned.

In the intervening months the work of the ORANGE network had become even more vital. With Sadat's visit to Jerusalem at the end of 1977 a new era had begun. Peace could and would be made with Egypt: But such a peace would only intensify the opposition from other Arab states. Iraq's Saddam Hussein would see it as his chance to take over leadership of the Arab world. He would use it as justification for the most extreme measures against Israel, The possession of nuclear weapons would strengthen his hand immensely and serve to raise still further his ambitions. It was unthinkable and he must be stopped.

So Walter had listened and, when he had finished eating, he talked to Zimmerman about Munger. He had only been back in circulation for three months but already his reputation was re-established. He had thrown himself into the work and all his skills had been successfully resurrected. Only that week *Paris Match* had run an in-depth report on the fighting in South Lebanon.

The story had been illustrated with twelve photographs: eight of them had been taken by Munger. Three weeks earlier both *Time* and *Newsweek* had used his snaps to illustrate stories of the South Yemen. Munger had been the only Western photographer to get into that country in over a year. Walter had no idea how he had done it and knew that Misha Wigoda, who was 'running' Munger from his base in Beirut, was unaware of Munger's methods. His latest report to Walter had recounted in awed terms how Munger could cross a closed frontier like other people crossed a street. In a few days he would be making a trip to Kurdish Iran and planned to cross over into North Western Iran to make contact with the Iraqi Kurdish. Contacts that could be useful in the future.

As Walter talked about his new agent, Efim Zimmerman had caught some of his enthusiasm. He remembered the many occasions when Walter's 'feel' and instinct for a man's talents had been well vindicated. However, he felt constrained to ask a few questions: for example, what kind of network was Munger attempting to build up?

Walter was forced to admit that Munger insisted on working alone. That was his nature and that was the way it had to be. He even resented having Wigoda as a 'case' officer. He liked him personally but would have preferred to report directly to Walter on his visits to Cyprus.

On that matter Walter had been insistent. Wigoda was an experienced agent and there could be times when his back-up would be invaluable.

Zimmerman had expressed his concern that the entire ORANGE effort in Iraq was to be contained in one man - no matter how good he might be. At that Walter had shrugged resignedly. At the moment it was the best they could do. In the meantime Mossad headquarters would try to infiltrate a back-up team, to be based in Baghdad. At best it would be a transient unit, probably made up of agents posing as visiting businessmen. They would try to have at least two or three people in the city at any given time.

As Walter watched the countryside turn greener as they drove higher he admitted to himself that the situation was far from perfect. He would be forced to rely on one man and, while that man had extraordinary talents, he also had a flaw. It rankled Walter that he had not been able to understand Munger's nine years of self-imposed exile from society. It was a dark area and until light was shed on it he was going to remain with that edge of doubt.

His thoughts naturally progressed to Ruth. She could have helped resolve that doubt. It was inconceivable to Walter that someone's integrity could be so all-encompassing as to eliminate actions which, while devious, would justify an end. She had left him in no doubt that she would not take part in his machinations. Anyway, he decided that even if she tried it would probably fail. On the back seat lay a box containing a sequined evening dress which he had bought for her in Paris and which he hoped she might wear that night during dinner. He also felt a surge of anxiety for he knew that a week earlier Gideon Galili had visited from Israel. Walter had no illusions about ever possessing more than Ruth's affection but it was disquieting that another man might possess more.

The shadows of his mood evaporated as soon as he walked through the door carrying the box. She had heard the car and come in from the garden. He first saw her framed in the doorway to the patio: she was wearing a short cotton dress and the sunlight from behind outlined the soft contours of her body. Her face lit up at the sight of him. It was such a genuine expression of pleasure that it brought a lump to his throat. She quickly crossed the room, leaned over the box and his protruding stomach and kissed him warmly on both cheeks.

'Is that a present for me?' she asked.

He nodded and held out the box, suddenly shy.

She carried it over to the table, quickly undid the ribbons and lifted the lid. She was mute as she gazed down at the shimmering apparition of smooth silk and sparkling sequins. Very slowly she lifted the dress from the box, held it up and looked at it. Then she laid it against her body and turned to face him.

'It's beautiful,' she breathed. 'You shouldn't have, Walter.'

Before he could say anything she grinned at him and said 'I'm just saying that. Of course you should have! I love it. I haven't worn anything like it for years. Is it the Forest Park for dinner?'

He nodded, feeling like a schoolboy, and she moved towards the bedroom.

'I'll hang this up,' she said, 'and then get you a drink. Make yourself comfortable.'

He walked down the two steps into the lounge, feeling vastly pleased with himself.

He was about to sit down when he saw them: three large framed black-and-white photographs, side by side on a low table. He straightened up and, without taking his eyes from them, shuffled across the floor for a closer look. Two were of Ruth's face, grainy with the enlargement. The third was of Ruth and a young boy. The boy's eyes were looking up at her, his face reflecting happiness and trust. Walter was mesmerised and his great body was still stooped over, his eyes moving between them, when Ruth's voice came quietly from behind him.

'Munger took them. The day he picked up his camera.'

Slowly Walter straightened and turned to face her with an expression of puzzlement.

'Munger . . .?'

She was carrying an ice bucket, from which protruded the neck of an open bottle of wine. She nodded, carried the bucket to a table and fetched two glasses from a sideboard. Walter had turned back to the photographs.

'It's unbelievable . . . Munger . . . You were crying.'

'Yes. I don't know why.'

She brought him a glass and stood next to him, looking at the photograph at the end. The one which showed the glistening tear drop.

'He's never done such work,' Walter muttered. 'If I didn't know you, I'd say you were lying . . . It's the antithesis of Munger's work.'

Ruth moved to the bookcase and lifted down a box and opened it. She showed Walter the other photographs he had taken of the children that day.

He spread them out on the table, shaking his head in wonder. 'They're beautiful. He captures the soul.'

Ruth looked at him in surprise. "That's what Gideon said.'

'Gideon?'

'Yes. He was here last week.' She paused and then said gently, 'We're going to be married, Walter.'

'When?'

'Early next year.' She couldn't detect any change of expression but through the air she could feel his disappointment.

'So you've decided you love him.'

She shrugged. 'I've decided that I don't know what love is. I do know that his feelings for me couldn't be deeper. He will never hurt me. Never lie to me.'

'Is that enough?'

She turned away and walked to the window and stood looking out. Walter wanted to say something, wanted to argue, even to plead. But he couldn't find the words and for once Shakespeare couldn't help him.

So he looked back at the photographs and then asked: 'Can I borrow some of these? Just for a few days?'

She turned. 'Of course. He sent me several copies. Keep a set.'

He picked out four of the photographs.

'When is he coming back?' she asked. Walter looked up enquiringly.

'I mean Munger,' she said. 'He sent me a letter with those. Apologised that they'd been so delayed. He wrote that he'd like to see me when he comes back.'

Walter thought for a moment. 'By now he will be in Northern Iran with the Kurds. After that he's due for a break. He should be here by the end of the month.'

'How is he doing?'

At last Walter could smile. 'He's doing just fine. He's number one again. The best in the business.'

She was relieved at his tone and the lightening of his mood.

It was a happy meal. He had got over his disappointment and besides had reminded himself that a lot could happen in eight months. She was radiant in her new dress and he glowed under her sunlight.

That night, before going to bed, he put the four photographs into an envelope together with a brief note for Professor Chaim Nardi.

Ten days later they were returned, also with a brief note, which gave Walter much pleasure. It read:

'Remarkable. I have recommended to the Dean that on your next visit you receive a degree in psychology. NB: Not honorary!'

Misha Wigoda treated himself to dinner at The Smugglers Inn in Ras Beirut. He did this literally, for he was not the kind of man to cheat on his expense account.

He had a corner table and dined alone, presenting a somewhat forlorn figure: short and dumpy, with his round head and monk's fringe of black hair. It is often the lot of a spy to have to eat alone and Misha's professional limits on social intercourse were compounded by personal shyness. Although he was a highly competent agent his shyness had always limited his career in so far as a successful spy must be gregarious and socially adept. Hence Misha was usually assigned to posts requiring observation or communications.

He was treating himself to an expensive dinner on this night because he was feeling expansive and important. Being made 'case officer' to ORANGE BLUE was a definite promotion and the job was going well. That afternoon he had debriefed Munger after his trip to Kurdistan. The debriefing had taken place in an apartment in the Nabaa district. As a cover, Misha ran an import-export agency and his office building adjoined the apartment building. Like the headquarters of the ORANGE network in Limassol a secret door had been constructed between the office and the apartment. He and Munger had sat there for over three hours while Munger had talked. No notes had been taken, for Misha had the gift of total recall. He had sat still and quiet with his eyes half closed, listing and cataloguing as Munger's voice had droned on. It had been a useful trip. Munger had met many of the Kurdish leaders, both in Iraq and Iran, and he had discovered which of them could be effective and useful. He presented a plan whereby Mossad would channel arms and ammunition to be stockpiled in Kurdistan for the time when the next rebellion would break out. In return the Kurds in Iraq would give Munger support and information. They had many safe houses in Baghdad and other major Iraqi cities. Munger described exactly what weapons the Kurds wanted; how they could be smuggled in through the Kurdish network in Turkey, and where they would be stored.

It was a good plan and Misha had congratulated him and wished him a good holiday, for he was leaving for Cyprus in the morning.

He looked up as the owner, George, approached his table and handed him a menu with his usual smile. Misha only ate in the restaurant about once a month and he enjoyed it because George always made him feel like an important regular.

'How are you, Melim?' George said, addressing him by his cover name and believing him to be a full-blooded Arab. 'But don't look at the menu - I've made Chawarma beef on the upright spit tonight and you'll offend me if you don't try it.'

Misha nodded his head in acceptance and George stayed for a few minutes chatting about politics and the forthcoming festival which he and other traders in the area organised every year. It was named 'Makhoul' after the street and was George's way of thumbing his nose at the civil war and proving that life goes on.

After he departed Misha sat back in his chair, warmed with the contact and contented by the atmosphere. The restaurant and tables were decorated with plants and works of art, for most of the clientele were artists and artisans and George liked to use their work.

There were several local journalists and foreign correspondents among the diners for 'George's place', as it was known, was one of the few good eating places outside the big hotels.

Misha did not know any of them personally but he knew a lot about them for, as a matter of course, Mossad kept extensive files on media personnel. Two tables in particular interested him. At one sat Gordon Frazer with a very beautiful Arab girl. His hand covered hers on the lace table cloth and he was bent forward talking to her earnestly and persuasively. Misha felt a stab of jealousy. Frazer, after all, was at least fifty and by no means handsome, and yet he was very successful with women. Misha, on the other hand, was the eternal wallflower. He tried to remember when he had last taken a beautiful woman out for dinner . . . God, it was months ago, when he was on leave in Jerusalem and she hadn't really been beautiful. She hadn't been very compliant either.

The other table to attract Misha's interest was in the far corner and was occupied by Sami Asaf and Janine Lesage. Two people whose activities took up much of Misha's waking hours. Apart from being Munger's case officer he also still ran the Beirut

ORANGE network and its three other resident agents. He had tried without success to bug Janine's Lesage's apartment and her office.

She was a woman who completely fascinated him, both by her appearance and personality and by her dual professions. She had such beauty, poise and confidence and was the antithesis of his own character. Perhaps due to lack of a complete sex life Misha was prone to frequent sexual fantasies and of late Janine Lesage had been very active in them. Only last night as he lay in bed trying to sleep he had masturbated with her in mind: her flowing hair brushing across his chest and face; her long, slim legs entwined with his and her tongue probing his mouth.

He felt his breath shortening at the memory and he was relieved when the waiter distracted him with the first course - a mixed salad. For a while he concentrated on eating. With Munger's long debriefing he had missed lunch and now he was ravenous. It was fifteen minutes before he looked up again. His gaze naturally travelled to the corner table and the French woman and he was disconcerted to find her gaze travelling back on a reciprocal bearing. She quickly looked away but Misha had the distinct feeling that she had been studying him. He would have been even more disconcerted had he overheard what she next said to Sami Asaf.

'Are you sure, Sami? He looks like an overfed mouse.'

'We're not sure,' Sami replied. 'The PLO came to us with a request to help trace his background. Apparently he claims to have an Iraqi mother.'

'And his father?'

'Lebanese from Batrum. Apparently that checks out, but he's long dead and these days it's difficult to get hard facts in this country.'

She turned again and shot a quick glance across the room. The man was watching her again, but that was not unusual. A lot of men watched her.

'He's been seen too often around sensitive PLO installations,' Sami said, 'and although he operates a genuine and successful business that's no alibi. A lot of Mossad agents do the same. Mossad make sure they're successful.'

'And if he is?'

Sami shrugged. 'I'll try to persuade the PLO to leave him alone for the time being. We'll put a full-time cover watch on him and see where he leads us. One thing is sure: the Mossad effort against us will come from here and so far we're in the dark. Your little mouse could provide a ray of sunshine.'

She smiled, reached out and ran the fingernails of her left hand firmly down his forearm. 'You'll keep me informed, of course?'

He looked down at the four parallel scratch marks, pale against his dark skin.

'Of course, Janine,' he said huskily.

Across the room Misha finished the last of his grilled beef and discreetly burped in satisfaction.

CHAPTER TWELVE

Ruth Paget had spent a satisfying day. In the early morning Gideon had phoned from Tel Aviv. The conversation had contained nothing momentous: he had the weekend off and was staying with his parents and was missing her. So he just called to tell her that he loved her and was literally counting the days until the wedding; His mother was already fussing about the arrangements even though it was months away.

Ruth had lain in bed with the phone cradled between her ear and the pillow and listened to his deep voice and slowly shed the shadows of sleep. It seemed extraordinary to contemplate the details of a wedding reception. In her comatose state she cast her mind back to the reception when she had married Duff. Such hopes, such love. A beautiful young couple with only happiness stretching out before them. She didn't allow her thoughts to sadden her. Gideon's low, vibrant voice in her ear kept her on the edge of contentment.

He had spoken to her for twenty minutes and then she had heard his mother in the background, scolding him like a child about the phone bill. But then she had come on the phone herself for a quick word and chatted on for fifteen minutes. Ruth's own mother had died several years before and, as she listened to Gideon's mother telling her to eat well and keep healthy and be sure to wear a sweater in the cool mountain evenings, Ruth had smiled and felt warm from the maternal contact. It was nice to have plans again; to think solidly about the future; to contemplate finally having a family of her own. During the past ten years it had been the greatest gap in her life. She realised with the merest twinge of conscience that her planned marriage to Gideon was influenced more by her desire for a child than any other factor. Of course, she loved him. He was honest and sincere and handsome. He was also talented and that was important to her. Talent in whatever field gave a man mental stature, even an air of authority. She knew that Gideon was a superbly gifted pilot in the most highly trained and dedicated air force in the world. He was destined one day to be a general, both by his talent and his ambition. Of course she loved him. He would make a wonderful father. His own parents were loving and secure. His lack of doubts, his confidence and his purposefulness were testaments to his upbringing. Of course she loved him.

The rest of the day she had spent at the orphanage. Stavros had finally come out of his mental bunker and was to be picked up by his new foster parents. They were a childless middle-aged couple from Nicosia. Ruth had selected them from a score of couples who had wanted to adopt a war orphan. She had been careful for she knew that the boy needed just the right mixture of authority and love to allow him to develop. Consequently she had insisted that the couple first visit him at the orphanage over a period of months so that confidence could be established. It had worked well and, as she watched him carry his small suitcase to their car and turn to wave goodbye, she had felt pride and satisfaction. Deep down she well knew that it was her patient work that had saved him from spending his life trapped in a mental maze.

In a way he was the last of her worries and when she got home in the evening and poured herself a drink and sat on the patio to watch the sunset, she felt totally at peace with herself. Friends had invited her out for dinner but she had phoned and begged off. She preferred to be alone. To enjoy, by herself, her contentment and both the view in her vision and the prospects in her mind.

So she was slightly irritated when she heard the car in the driveway and the faint knock on the door. It could be any one of the half a dozen friends dropping by. Normally she would offer them a drink but as she walked to the door she decided that on this day she would politely but firmly send them on their way.

A determined expression had already formed on her face as she opened the door and Munger, seeing it, felt a stab of doubt. They stood looking at each other for a startled moment, then he said:

'I'm sorry, but there's no phone at my farmhouse. Are you busy?'

She recovered. 'No, of course not.' Then her gaze dropped and she saw he was holding a bunch of flowers wrapped, in paper. He self-consciously lifted them and showed her the deep hue of red roses. She smiled. 'It's been a very long time since anyone bought me roses.'

He smiled back. 'It's the very first time I've ever bought them - they're to say thank you.'

She took them and held them close to her face and inhaled the fragrance.

Thank me for what?'

'I came here to tell you.'

She realised they were still standing in the doorway. She moved aside and gestured a welcome.

'Come in. Go through to the patio. I'll put these in water and fetch you a drink.'

She got the drink first and, as she arranged the flowers in the lounge, she glanced at him frequently through the French windows. He sat stiffly in a cane chair, looking down at the view. His face was in profile and she remembered back to the day she had first seen him at that party in Hong Kong. How at first his features and demeanour had made no impression on her. How only later she had held his gaze and seen something in those deep blue eyes and caught the spark.

He hadn't changed much, she decided. If anything his lean face was slightly thinner, but he was tanned and looked fit.

As she came out onto the patio she said:

'I have to give my thanks first. For the photographs. They were beautiful - the children loved them.'

He shrugged off her thanks. He now appeared tense, even nervous. She picked up her drink and took a sip and then, to break the silence, told him about Stavros and his new foster parents and how pleased she was that it had worked out so well.

He asked several questions about the boy and she explained his history and his struggle to readjust. He looked out over the view as he listened: it was twilight and the colours on the horizon were deepening and melting. Every few moments he would turn his head to look at her - always directly into her eyes- only for a second but always a look of arresting intensity.

When her voice trailed off there was another silence. It was now quite dark and she could only see the outline of his profile. She could sense the build up of emotion in him and was surprised. Everything she knew about him precluded his showing or even feeling emotion.

'For what do you want to thank me?' she asked.

When he spoke his voice was very low and it carried the emotion as a radio wave carries a message.

'For saving my life.'

She just didn't know what to say. She sat in her chair with her mind in disarray.

'It's like that boy Stavros. I don't know how or why, but like him you saved my mind and in my case that meant saving my life.'

At last she found her composure and her voice.

'Aren't you being melodramatic?'

'No.' The single, flat negative destroyed the practical line she was attempting to formulate.

She plunged back into confusion.

'How? What are you talking about?'

He stood up and walked to the edge of the patio. She could hear his laborious breathing. Over his shoulder he said: 'I'm talking about suicide.'

At last - a word she could understand and get to grips with. Briskly she stood up, walked into the lounge and switched on lights. She glanced at her watch and as she came back out, said:

'You'd better stay for dinner. I've a couple of steaks in the fridge.' She gestured at a barbecue on the edge of the patio. 'There's coke in it. You get a fire started and I'll toss a salad.'

He stood looking at her hesitantly but before he could say anything she turned on her heel and went inside.

He cooked the steaks: his well done, hers very rare. He explained that after half a lifetime of having to eat terrible meat, burning it black had become a habit. He became more relaxed with the activity and, as they sat down to eat, she said:

'Let's not talk seriously until we've finished.'

So they ate mostly in silence but there was a very positive mental communication. It built up slowly like an old steam engine moving away from a platform and gathering speed. She was totally aware of him: his slight frame, his thin face and fair, lank hair. She was in a mental magnetic field and nothing intruded. Not the sound of an owl hooting in nearby pine trees, or the distant crackle of fireworks from a village fiesta, or the occasional car passing on the road behind the house. A sense of expectancy was building within her. She knew that whatever he was going to tell her when the meal ended would have a profound effect:

certainly on him, in the telling; probably on her. So the expectancy was tinged with trepidation. Her sanguine mood of an hour ago had already been cracked. She wondered if it was about to be shattered.

There was another feeling within her, and that too was growing. It was a simple physical attraction: the magnet was not purely mental. It surprised her and made her deeply uneasy, for it was linked to Walter Blum and what she had refused to do for him. Her unease turned to resolve and when they finished eating she said:

'First, before you tell me anything, there's something I want you to know.'

So she told him in detail how, on the night before Walter had tried to recruit him, he had first tried to recruit her. How he had shown her Professor Nardi's report and then, over dinner at the Forest Park, had explained that the great enigma was the sexual aspect of Munger's trauma. He wanted her to try to solve that enigma even if it meant seducing him. Walter could never truly relax until he knew exactly how Munger ticked - until he himself could regulate the mechanism.

Munger was not surprised by this revelation. By now he knew that Walter would go to any lengths to achieve his aim. He said:

'It's ironic . . . and you're very honest.'

She smiled wanly. 'It's been one of my problems. I'd have had an easier life if I'd learned to lie a bit.'

He was studying her and shaking his head and she felt again the ratchet pull of physical attraction. To try to smother it, she asked:

'So, now, what was that about suicide?'

He pulled out a dark, thin cigar from his top pocket. 'Do you mind?'

She shook her head and watched as he lit the cigar and tasted the smoke and settled back in his chair.

'You're a psychologist. Maybe you'll understand - at least more than I do. I'm going to tell you about a nightmare.'

So he smoked his cigar and talked, and she listened. It took a long time for he told her in detail, from when he first had the nightmare nearly ten years ago until it finally stopped in the hotel in Beirut. He told her how he had looked down at the street below and in his mind had seen the image of his dead body, and how close he had come to making that image a reality. How he had developed the film and seen something in the photographs and worked on them and in the dawn had produced a print that exorcised the nightmare.

She listened intently and when he finally fell silent it was as though he had peeled away a layer of skin to show a different face beneath - the face of a human being - not just a composite of features.

She had long finished her wine but she still held the empty glass in her hand, twirling it mindlessly. Now she reached forward and placed it carefully on the table as though not to make a sound to break the spell. She tried to imagine him in that room, sitting by the window trying to banish a pair of eyes in his head with a pair of eyes on a piece of paper. She tried to formulate a sentence, to say something that would sound remotely sensible. It was impossible. Maybe he sensed her difficulty. He reached into an inside pocket, pulled something out and laid it in front of her. It was the photograph. She looked down at it and her own eyes looked back. Munger had said that he saw compassion. She also saw it - and more. Slowly she lifted her gaze. He was watching her. Finally she found her voice.

'So it's over? No more nightmares?'

He shook his head.

'It's not over, Ruth.' He gestured at the photograph. 'That . . . you, helped me to sublimate it. I don't know how. But it's still in my head. I feel it there like a cancer. The lid's on, but for how long I don't know. That's why I'm here.'

She nodded. The trepidation now had a form.

'You have to go back further David. Back to the cause. You need help. More than I can provide. You know that.'

He leaned forward. There was a pleading now in his eyes and when he spoke it was in his voice.

'Yes, I need help. I know that. But I know it with the certainty that only you can provide it. I'm asking more than I have the right to.'

'You're going to tell me?'

'Yes,' he breathed. 'I'm going to tell you what caused the nightmare and then I'm going to ask you to help me. The story is filthy and the help I need may be impossible.'

He sat back and extracted another cigar and lit it. She knew she was walking straight into a minefield. Part of her mind screamed at her to turn and run. The other part, the part that contains the grey matter which stimulates curiosity, kept her clamped in her chair. Forced her to say:

'So tell me.'

It took an hour. He talked in a low monotone. Sometimes he was lucid, the narrative flowing. At other times having to grope for a word - to find it and drag it out. During that hour she was assaulted by a gamut of emotions that left her mind and her body limp. Once she let the tears flow - a release without which she could not have endured.

He told her of the final patrol.

It was the kind of patrol from which correspondents and photographers were definitely banned.

In Vietnam the Americans had long used special forces, including mercenaries, for certain missions. These included hit-and-run attacks into North Vietnam, Laos and Cambodia;

reconnaissance sorties into solid Vietcong territory, and occasionally punitive raids against pro-Vietcong villages and mountain tribesmen. After the Tet offensive in 1967 and the increasing disintegration of the South Vietnamese army these patrols were being stepped up. To the American field intelligence in Saigon they became a rare source of information in an increasingly disjointed situation.

The individuals who manned these patrols were, in one way or another and for various reasons, on the outer fringes of humanity. There were among them US Special Forces, good units and good men. Good in both the moral and productive use of the word. They fought a hard war in a hard way, but they fought it within reasonable if flexible limits. These men were in the minority and, as the time passed, that minority shrank. By the time Munger went on his patrol many of the original units had been supplemented with mercenaries from a variety of countries. There were Frenchmen and Belgians, South Africans and South Americans, Koreans and Cambodians. They were often joined by Meo tribesmen who hated all Vietnamese, whether they came from the North or the South. Munger's patrol was led by a Captain from the US Special Forces. He had been in Vietnam for seven years and, as he once explained to Munger, he had become hooked on killing like a junkie on heroin. To compound his problem he was also hooked on heroin. It had not always been so. Munger had known him from the beginning of 1962 when he was fresh and eager, patriotic and idealistic. He had arrived with one of the early US Military Aid teams and for the first six months had trained units of the South Vietnamese Army: the ARVN. Later he had gone on operations with them as an advisor. After an extended tour of duty he had returned Stateside to Fort Bragg. He had found it hard to readjust to peacetime soldiering and so had volunteered for another tour in Vietnam, and then another, and then another. Munger knew several like him. The war invaded their brains and pushed everything else out until finally they were nothing but killing machines. Their superiors felt uncomfortable in their presence, although they saw them infrequently and only on the occasions, when they gave them orders or pinned medals on their chests. This Captain was twenty-eight years old with a face that had lived a century.

There were three other US Special Forces men in the patrol. One was a thin, taciturn homosexual who came from a slum in the Bronx. He hardly ever talked, except in obscenities. The other two came from the deep South: one was white, the other black. They were both huge men and were linked, like Siamese twins, in a bond of hatred. The rest of the patrol was made up of two handsome Belgians, who wore dark glasses and talked endlessly of their exploits in a dozen wars; a scar-faced Australian who wore Colt 1911's on each hip and tried to talk like a Texan; a Frenchman whose parents had owned a plantation near Hue and had been painfully killed by the Vietcong; and finally there were two Meo tribesmen who were to act as guides and interrogators in the event that prisoners were taken.

Munger had first heard about the patrol whilst having a drink in a seedy bar in Tu Do Street. A group of Marines had been talking about a recent action in the Delta and how tough it had been and how many casualties their unit had taken. The Special Forces Captain and one of the Belgians had been sitting at a nearby table. The Belgian was drunk and he loudly derided the Marines, telling them they knew nothing of the real war. There would have been a fight but the Marines knew of the Captain and what he was capable of, so they finished their drinks and left. Munger had been sitting at the end of the bar and the Captain had grinned at him and called to him to join them. It turned out that he was to lead a patrol in two days' time to an area North West of Vinh Long. For many months the Vietcong had held sway in the area and the High Command thought that they might be building up for a major action. They wanted hard information.

They drank a lot that night until the Belgian passed out. In the early hours of the morning, long after the bar girls had gone home and the bartender had grown weary with boredom, Munger finally persuaded the Captain to take him along on the patrol. It would be difficult, but not impossible. Both the Captain and Munger had great skills in circumventing authority. He would make his own way to Vinh Long and then the Captain would infiltrate him into the patrol as one of its members. He would have to dress accordingly and conceal his camera. There was one cast-iron condition: the Captain would vet any photographs that Munger took. Drunk as he was, at that moment an icy look came into the Captain's eyes. Munger agreed readily, telling himself that he would cross that bridge when and if he came to it.

So he went on the patrol and from the first day it was a roller coaster ride into the core of hell.

It started with a fight among themselves. They had marched for seven hours, deep into the forested hills, and made their first bivouac on a long, narrow ridge. The Meo tribesmen stood the first watch and, as the rest of them heated their rations, one of the Belgians pulled off a boot, examined a large blister on his heel and cursed. The black Southerner made a remark about soft pretty boys. The Belgian said something in French that included '*cochon noir*'. They were two French words that the negro understood and in an instant he had his huge hands round the Belgian's throat. The other Belgian grabbed his sub-machine gun but as he cocked it the muzzle of the Captain's revolver was in his face. The Belgian lowered his gun and the Captain reached over and, with perfect precision, clipped the negro behind his ear with the heel of the revolver butt. So order was restored. The negro was unconscious for ten minutes and his intended victim had livid red weals around his neck for the rest of the patrol.

That night Munger watched the Captain and the Frenchman shoot up with heroin. The white Southerner sniffed coke and the rest of them smoked joints. Munger began to wonder if he would come out alive.

The next day they moved deeper into the Vietcong stronghold. The Meos scouted ahead; the rest of the patrol moved in a fan formation, each man about fifty metres from the next. They were all vastly experienced and, in spite of their nocturnal intake of drugs, moved quietly, skilfully and confidently. Munger was slightly reassured.

On the evening of the second day the white Southerner sat next to Munger while they ate. He was interested in photography and knew of Munger's reputation. He was a man who talked slowly, even for a Southerner - each word was gradually framed by his thick lips and delivered with a slurring drawl.

He explained that he also took photographs. Would Munger like to see them? Munger noted the curious expression in his eyes and he guessed what was coming. It had happened several times before in Vietnam and other places. He shrugged negatively but the Southerner was already reaching into the pocket of his battledress.

There were six of them, tattered and dog-eared. To Munger they were standard atrocity photographs. Dead and mutilated bodies. A man holding a pair of legs on each shoulder, smiling at the camera. The dismembered corpse at his feet. A row of black-cad Vietcong prisoners, elbows tied behind their backs, staring at the camera, looking at death. The next photograph showing them on the ground, limbs twisted. A Meo tribesman spilling human ears onto a ground sheet from a canvas bag while a sergeant from the Special Forces counted them to calculate the bounty. The last one showed a Vietcong tied to a tree, a bayonet protruding from his throat. The Southerner watched Munger closely to see his reaction, looking for the slightest sign of unease - wishing it.

'How about that?' he had drawled.

Munger had shrugged. 'Next time,' he said, 'when you're shooting in the shade, try using an F4 aperture setting. You'll get better in-depth focus.'

The Captain had been watching and listening and he burst out laughing. After an uncertain pause, so did the Southerner.

After that they didn't bother Munger with their stories or their photos.

By the fourth day they had covered over a hundred miles and just past noon they ambushed a column of six Vietcong who were carrying supplies of rice and vegetables.

Again Munger was surprised by their military precision. The Meo scouts had given plenty of warning. The Vietcong were moving down a trail that skirted a low hill. They were in what they thought to be safe territory and so they took few precautions. The Captain placed the two Southerners above the trail and gave them explicit instructions. The rest of the patrol, including Munger, was to spread in an arc below the trail. The Vietcong moved along in single file. As they passed the Southerners, a short burst of sub-machine gun fife cut down the first four. The two at the rear dropped their bundles and ran straight into the waiting arms of the rest of the patrol. They didn't even have time to cock their Kalashnikovs before they were slammed to the ground and their arms bound behind them. The Captain needed information so he needed prisoners.

Munger only had time to shoot six snaps of the action and then the Captain was hustling them away before other Vietcong homed in on the noise of the gunfire.

For the next five hours the patrol marched rapidly East to get away from the scene. The prisoners stumbled along behind, with nooses round their necks. They knew that if they fell they would be dragged along until they choked. They didn't fall.

That night they were interrogated by the Meos. The rest of the patrol looked on, sometimes laughing and sometimes offering unnecessary suggestions. Munger sat away to the side, his arms clasped around his knees, trying to close his ears. It wasn't so much the sounds the prisoners made - their gags were only taken off at infrequent intervals so they could answer questions - but the noise of the laughter. He tried to cut it out of his head, telling himself that these interrogators were not people, not human beings. They were merely the aberrations that focused humanity.

He got no sleep that night, even when it was over. In the dawn he took snaps of the two mutilated corpses. The white Southerner watched with interest and asked him to make copies for him.

That afternoon they reached the village. During the previous night's torture the prisoners had revealed that it was the home of a certain Dien Phang, a Major in the Vietcong Intelligence. As his unit was operating in the general area the Major occasionally was able to visit his family. He had a wife, a daughter and a young son. It was a small village, nestling in a narrow valley. A stream ran through the centre of it.

The Captain and one of the Belgians reconnoitred it and estimated a population of under thirty. There was no sign of armed men: mostly it was women and children and old men, but they had seen one younger man washing himself in the stream.

The Captain decided to move in right away. Their presence in the area was already known to the enemy and they would by now be mounting a major search. Time was running out. The two Meos were posted on ridges at each end of the valley to keep a lookout. The two Belgians were to approach from one side and the two Southerners from the other. Those four usually worked in pairs. The Frenchman and the homosexual would approach from downstream and the Captain and the Australian from up-stream. They all moved to a ridge above the village and the Captain pointed out the salient features and stressed that the younger man he had seen was to be taken prisoner. If he was Dien Phang, the Captain wanted to deliver him to Saigon. He would get at least another medal and the mercenaries on the patrol would get a cash bonus.

While the Captain talked, Munger was busy photographing the village through a telephoto lens. It was a peaceful, even idyllic, scene. Some of the women and children were working, bent over in vegetable fields. Others were washing clothes in the stream, pounding them on the smooth rocks. Three old men sat in the shade of a leafy tree, talking and smoking long, thin, clay pipes. Munger felt a rising tension. He could guess what was about to hit that village.

They synchronised their watches and then fanned out. They would attack in fifteen minutes. The Captain hunched down with the Australian, next to Munger, and surveyed the village through binoculars.

'By the way,' he said to Munger from the side of his mouth. 'You stay up here.'

Munger took his eye from the viewfinder. 'Why?'

The Captain grinned, 'I don't want none of this recorded for posterity.' He lowered the binoculars, turned to look at Munger and the grin was replaced by a hard look. 'You understand?'

'Sure.'

Munger looked through the viewfinder again. Even with the telephoto lens he wasn't going to get much detail of what happened. He had agreed easily enough, but he was there to take snaps and he would take them, no matter what.

After ten minutes the Captain and the Australian slid down the hill to take up their start position. Three minutes later Munger quietly followed. Again the attack went like clockwork. There was no more than sixty seconds of concerted small arms fire and the patrol was in the village.

Munger crept up to the back of a bamboo hut and watched and photographed the aftermath. There were eight bodies strewn about. The three old men had been cut down in one short burst. They lay beneath the tree with limbs twisted and blood soaking into the smooth dirt. Two women had been killed in the river and the slowly moving water was streaked dark red. A boy of about eight and another around six years old were lying like rag dolls, half inside the door of a hut. An old woman clutching a baby was lying on her back, half her head shot away. The baby was crying in her death grip;

The rest of the villagers had been herded into a group by the two Belgians. Some had terror stamped on their faces, others shock, and others incomprehension. Munger shifted his view and snapped the man being dragged out of a hut by the Australian and the Frenchman. He struggled violently until the Australian smashed the stock of his sub-machine gun against the side of his face. He was not unconscious and blood poured down from a wide gash on his cheek. Then the Captain came out of the same hut. He was carrying a Kalashnikov and a bundle of papers and he was grinning broadly. Munger heard him call out to the Belgians that they had got the right man.

As Munger continued taking snaps he felt a surge of relief. With the success of the mission maybe magnanimity would emerge. Maybe the rest of the villagers would be spared.

It was not to be. Just as the two Southerners appeared in the centre of the village, two women in the group being guarded ran out towards the bound Vietcong: one his wife, the other his daughter. They were screaming and pleading and as all attention focused on them, three other women and a young boy tried to escape. They only got ten metres before the women were slammed off their feet in a burst of gun fire. The boy made it a little further but Munger watched as the black Southerner dropped to one knee, sighted carefully along the top of his sub-machine gun and squeezed the trigger. The boy was blasted ten feet into a clump of bushes. In his horror Munger remembered the story of how a correspondent once asked a mercenary in a bar how he could shoot children. The mercenary had grinned and said 'You just aim a little lower.'

Automatically Munger snapped the boy's legs as they protruded, twitching, from the bushes. Then he was fitting a new film and the firing and screaming had started again. The rest of the guarded villagers had panicked and during the next few seconds were shot down one by one. Only the woman and the girl crouching over the Vietcong escaped the carnage. When it was over, silence and smoke hung over the bodies.

By now Munger's brain was numb but his fingers worked automatically and his camera recorded the scene. His eyes saw it through the viewfinder but his mind no longer registered. He had switched it off. Just like he had switched it off so many times before in his career: in Angola, in Biafra, in Borneo and in this ravaged country. He was a photographer doing his job. That was all.

After that he photographed the rapes of the wife and the daughter. They all took part, laughing and arguing for position. The bound Vietcong was on his side, his bloody cheek in the dirt, his eyes wide open, watching.

The girl was only about fifteen and beautiful and most of the men wanted her. The Australian dragged her mother off to one side and soon her screaming started, but the girl endured in silence on the blood-soaked dirt in the village centre. First the Captain, as though by right. Munger saw the virginal blood trickle down her thighs but she made no sound. Then the two Belgians, then the black Southerner, then the white one, then the Frenchman. The homosexual stood with the others, watching with a frustrated look on his face as the young girl's limbs were twisted and contorted to give each man the entry he preferred. As the Frenchman finished with gasping lunges, one of the Belgians laughed and remarked to the homosexual that it was a pity that they hadn't left a boy alive for him. He didn't answer. He was watching the naked girl lying at the Frenchman's feet as he zipped up his pants. She was lying on her belly, her legs spread behind her, her face cradled in her arms. Her long, black hair spread out like a fan on the dirt. With a bestial grunt the homosexual ran out and pushed the Frenchman away and sank onto his knees beside the girl, groping at his fly.

The others laughed again as he pulled the girl's bottom up and wriggled between her legs and, with one brutal lunge, sodomised her. It was the first and only time she screamed: a thin shriek of agony - and it was then that Munger took his final snap. Her violator had grabbed her hair in his fist and pulled it back, trying to jerk deeper into her body. Her head came up, contorted with pain, and she was looking directly at Munger - directly into the lens.

Into her eyes came the expression that was to fill his nightmares.

She held the look and the Captain noticed it and followed it and saw Munger beside the bamboo hut, his camera at his eye. The Captain was loosely holding his sub-machine gun. In a second it swung up and a spray of bullets arced across, just over Munger's head, chopping the bamboo and spraying it over him as he dropped to his belly.

'Bastard!' the Captain roared. 'I told you - no photographs.'

He ran towards Munger, who had twisted onto his side, his fingers working feverishly.

'Give me that fucking thing!'

The Captain stood over him and Munger looked up into the black muzzle of the gun and the furious eyes above. Very slowly, knowing he was an eye-blink from death, he raised the camera - offering it.

With a grunt the Captain took it and Munger scrambled to his feet.

Still holding his gun, the Captain tried to open the back of the camera, but it was difficult. He thrust it back at Munger and then pointed the gun at his chest.

'Open it.'

Munger opened it.

Take out the film.'

Munger ripped out the film.

'Expose it.'

Munger unrolled the film and let it dangle on its spool. With an angry obscenity the Captain swung the barrel of his gun, catching the film and slinging it yards away into the dust. He gave Munger a mean look.

'One more time and you'll end up like them.'

The muzzle of the gun swung to encompass the score or so of dead bodies. Munger turned and walked away, clutching in his sweaty armpit the roll of film he had extracted and replaced seconds before. From behind him he heard two more single shots that signalled the death and release of the woman and the girl.

CHAPTER THIRTEEN

Ruth made coffee. As soon as Munger had finished his story she got up and, without a word, went to the kitchen, ground some coffee - beans and filled the percolator with water. It was difficult because her fingers were shaking. As she waited for the water to boil she couldn't decide what horrified her more: the story itself or the unemotional way that Munger had told it. Somehow that lack of emotion had made him a participant rather than an observer. There had been a question screaming in her head throughout his monologue. She had made the coffee to give herself time to formulate that question; to put it in precise terms so that he could give a precise answer.

But as she carried the tray but to the patio and placed it on the table she still hadn't found a way to ask it without disguising her disgust.

She poured the coffee and pushed a cup across to him and the question came out in icy tones.

'How, in the name of anything decent, could you stand by and take photographs and not do anything?'

He leaned forward and spooned sugar into his cup and stirred it, then he glanced up at her face.

'At the time it never occurred to me,' he said flatly; and she erupted.

For five minutes she poured scorn on him. Piled it like a mountain over him. Questioned his courage and manhood, even his intelligence. 'Only a moron,' she stated caustically, 'could be so unfeeling.'

He sat back in his chair and imperturbably let the tirade wash over him. When she finished he smiled. A self-mocking smile; and for a blinding moment she wanted to leap across the table and attack him physically. She fought to control herself and then stood up and stiffly suggested that he should leave. Then, for the first time, she felt the full weight of his personality. He also stood and faced her across the table. His blue eyes were narrow and dark and his words lanced across and into her.

'You're a stupid bitch. I came here and talked to you because I thought you could understand. Could look at it, and me, without emotion. Examine and analyse. Offer help and advice. Instead you react like a maudlin poodle. You're supposed to have a trained mind, but at the first exposure to horror it collapses. I told you the story exactly as it happened, and my own reactions. If I tried to embellish it with supposed heroics, how could you hope to understand what followed?'

They stood glaring at each other, but his words had been well aimed and she realised that her first reaction had been simply as one woman identifying with the tragedy of another.

She drew a deep breath and gestured at his chair and they both sat down again. He poured more coffee and then started talking again.

'You've read that professor's file on me. So have I. It was largely accurate. I'd managed to create a shell around myself that was impenetrable. At least I thought it was. There are other things you must know. When you spend ten years at this business your brain builds up a defence mechanism. All right, on that patrol I saw people tortured and raped and killed. Yes, it horrified me; it would horrify anyone except a certified sadist, but because of my nature and my experience I was able to block it off. Put my mind into neutral. I don't make any excuses. Of course, if I'd tried to stop them they would have killed me. Of course, I could claim to have been a crusader - that my snaps were taken to bring them to book: to achieve justice. I make no such claims. I never thought about it. I was doing what I'd always done: taking snaps of one set of human beings abusing another.'

There was a tremor of emotion now in his voice; but she couldn't judge whether it was anger or compassion.

'Thirty or forty people died on that patrol. Died badly. But I tell you they were, for me, a drop of water in a bloody great ocean. I've seen legions of people die. Most of them badly. I've seen thousands of children, with limbs like sticks and bellies like balloons, die of starvation. I've seen them die screaming with their bodies burning from napalm - hundreds of them - whole villages. I've seen them thrown live out of helicopters, and machine-gunned in scores like a row of scythed flowers. I've seen bits of them scattered over ten acres by thousand-pound bombs.'

He bent forward now and his whole body was shaking and she saw that his eyes were wet.

'I've walked through the Valley of Death. Walked through it, camped in it, lived in it, eaten from its fields, drunk from its streams, slept under its trees. It was my home - do you understand!'

Now his cheeks were wet and he could hardly get the words out.

'Finally something snapped. Something broke the shell. I couldn't cope with that. You know what I'm trying to tell you?' He was shouting, it turned me into a human being and I can't handle it. I've been trying for ten years and I can't handle it. I can't handle it.'

The words petered out and he slumped in his chair, his whole body racked with sobs. She came out of her chair and moved around the table and knelt down beside him. She put her arms around him and pulled his head against her breast and her own tears fell down and mingled with his.

She thought of Stavros. She had sent him off a few hours ago to a new life. The man she was holding now was, in a way, younger than Stavros. He was a child who had finally been born and couldn't face the world or the memories of the black womb from which he had come.

After a few minutes he got himself under control. She released him and went back to her own chair. He was embarrassed now, after his breakdown, and found it difficult to look her in the face.

In her eyes he was now a totally different man. From her knowledge of psychology she well understood the immense effort he had made to unlock his mind and to share with her the horrors inside it. His tears had been as much from relief as from sorrow. He was now no longer alone, there was a link between them forged in the hottest fire. It was a link which for her carried responsibility. She had been the catalyst. The surgeon probing with a scalpel into his brain. So be it. She would take it to a conclusion.

'So tell me the rest,' she said softly.

He took a deep breath and plunged back into his story. He had returned to Saigon in the afternoon and the first thing he did was develop his films and blow up a dozen of the prints into 8" x 10" enlargements. He pinned them onto the wall and turned a spotlight on them and looked again at the horror of the patrol. At first he tried to decide which newspaper or magazine could best use them. He had to be careful because once they came out he faced two dangers: one from the Captain and one from the American High Command. They would want to know all about them and how he had connived to get himself on a forbidden assignment. The risk was that he could lose his accreditation, which meant he would never work again in Vietnam. So the snaps had to be printed and published in such a way that only the faces of the victims could be clearly discerned. He studied them carefully, deciding how he would cut and enlarge. When he came to the last one it needed no alteration. It was a close-up of the girl's face at the moment she was being sodomised. At the top of the print was a hand gripping her bunched-up hair, pulling her face up. Munger decided that it was one of the most dramatic snaps he had ever taken. Then he studied her eyes and, like a bolt of lightning, their message stabbed out and into his brain.

He had backed away in confusion. It was, after all, just a square of treated paper. A photograph in monochrome. The pain, despair and contempt that flowed from it was a mere trick of shade and light. He moved forward again, looking closer, and the eyes looked back and burned into his head.

He had gone down to the bar, merely disconcerted. When he came back after midnight and slightly drunk, the spotlight was still on and when he opened the door the first thing he saw was the eyes. He was standing off at an angle and yet they were watching him. When he moved across the room they followed. When he went into the bathroom he could feel them, boring through the closed door and into the back of his head.

As soon as he returned to the bedroom he switched off the spotlight, got into bed and quickly fell asleep. Then he had his first nightmare. Its effect was all the more profound for he was a man who hardly ever dreamed. In spite of all the things he had seen in his young life, he had never found difficulty in sleeping soundly. It was an indication of the thickness of the wall he had built around his psyche.

Three times he woke up that night, all within an hour. After that he didn't try for sleep. He got up and went out to the all-night bar and drank till dawn. Maybe in the light of day the eyes would disappear. Back at the hotel he ate a large breakfast, went up to his room, took the snaps off the wall, put them into a box and then the box into a drawer. He did this while keeping his eyes averted from the one of the girl.

Again he tried to sleep but without success, so he decided literally to face the problem and work it out. He pinned the photograph back on the wall, by itself. He brought the spotlight close, and a chair.

For an hour he sat looking at it. The message was clear. The accusation stark. The eyes were humanity being raped. He was the personification of indifference. In itself it made him more guilty than the rapists. A stiletto had pierced his wall.

He had burned the photograph and the others and all the negatives. It was a futile effort to expunge the image in his brain.

Then after the futile session with Janine Lesage, he had left for Hong Kong. He gave his equipment to Chang and caught the first plane out of Asia.

The change of scene did not help. He had gone to South Africa and taken a series of manual jobs. He worked in factories and as a truck driver. He didn't need the money-he had plenty saved up and well invested. It was simply to keep himself occupied. To try to adjust. At times he thought he was succeeding but then the night-, mare would come again, and with it the guilt. It was a guilt which built up inexorably and encompassed all the horror he had ever seen.

'Why didn't you get help?' Ruth asked. 'You must have known that only a psychiatrist could help you.'

He shook his head vigorously. 'I thought if anyone - anyone at all - started to probe into my brain, I would go completely mad. I knew I had a shred of sanity. I tried to build on it. I began to think of expiating the guilt. I began to think of the men on that patrol.'

She leaned forward. 'That bothered me. I mean that they got away with it - escaped all justice.'

Again he shook his head. 'They didn't. I killed them.'

'You what!'

He wiped a palm over his forehead. The night was cool but the effort of telling his story had raised a sheen of sweat on his face.

'I killed them, Ruth. The more the guilt built up and the more I thought about them it seemed the only way to blot out those eyes. At least in the nightmare I would have a reply.'

She slumped back in her chair, stunned by this fresh revelation. In a small voice she asked:

'All of them? You killed them all?'

'No. Three were dead already. It had been two years since that patrol. Two had been killed in action and the third in a bar fight.'

'How?' she asked. 'How and where did you kill them?'

He gestured negatively, it doesn't matter. It took me two years to track them down. They'd left Vietnam when it became obvious that the Vietcong would win. I had to travel to Europe and the States and Panama. But I found them all and they died knowing why. It was strange: it gave me a purpose for two years. It gave me hope that when it was over I could find my head again. I didn't, of course. The nightmare stayed. I came to Cyprus then and, in a way, came to terms with it. Even, after a long while, tried to lead some kind of a life. Then Walter Blum came along with his sledge hammer and demolished what was left of my wall.' He laughed shortly at the memory.

'In his inimitable way he gave me a real chance. So did you. I've got things barely under control now. And I've got a purpose. It's something.'

She got up and went inside and brewed more coffee. It was almost midnight but she had no thought of sleep. She had watched and listened as a man opened himself up for the first time in his life. It was an experience that would stay with her forever. It was frightening but it was stimulating. She came back onto the patio, poured the coffee and asked:

'What now? You said that only I can help.'

He reached for his cup and sipped appreciatively and then smiled. It was his first natural smile and it took away the tension in his face and in the air.

'You may be able to help, Ruth, by doing what Walter asked you to.'

At first she did not comprehend: just looked at him blankly. Then, as light dawned, she burst out laughing.

'You want me to seduce you?'

He smiled again but it was tentative.

'Seduction is hardly the word. I need my manhood back. Something tells me you're the only woman who can give it to me.'

She started shaking her head in amazement and he held up a hand to stop her speaking.

'Wait. Listen. I've tried over the past few months . . . half a dozen times. It doesn't work. Every time I'm with a woman, every time I get close, I see those eyes again - feel the guilt. It kills it. You stopped the nightmares. Maybe - just maybe - you can do this too. I know, it's a hell of a thing to ask any woman . . . I've no right, but I believe that if it happens just once it will be enough. It's vital to me.

It's entirely mental, I'm sure. It's just a block. Once it's cleared I'll be all right.'

He was pleading with her now and she felt close to hysteria. She stood and walked to the edge of the patio, trying desperately to establish reality. She heard his chair scrape and the scuff of his shoe and she felt his presence behind her and then his breath on her neck and then his lips. The contact sent currents through her body. She drew in her breath sharply,

'Stop, David!'

She turned and faced him and, in a few blunt sentences, told him about Gideon Galili. Told him of her impending marriage. Told him that Duff and Gideon were the only two men she had ever made love to. Told him she was sorry, she couldn't help him.

He backed away, nodding in understanding, blurting out words of apology. He had not known, not realised.

They moved back to the table and sat down and an embarrassed silence developed. On his face was a look of infinite sadness. She had no words to offer him, no solace. Yet she felt responsible. It was ridiculous. He had barged into her life, tormented her emotions, destroyed her equilibrium - and she felt responsible. She started to fight a battle with herself. Was he asking so much? Of course he was. And yet in a way it was so little to give and its effect on his life could be profound. Could she be clinical about it? View it merely as a form of therapy? He was a sick, tormented man. She looked again at his downcast face and felt a surge of pity.

He reached for his cup and her hand stretched out to touch his arm in a gesture of sympathy. He turned his wrist and caught her fingers and held onto them tightly. She looked down and saw his brown fingers twisted into hers. Saw them as though they were gripping the edge of a cliff. Slipping from it. She heard her voice saying words that were coming from someone else's mouth. Saying that she would try. Just this one night. But in his turn he must be careful with her, for in matters of sex she too was enveloped in uncertainty.

Still holding her hand he stood and moved round the table and raised her up and kissed her on the mouth and the currents flowed again through her body. He led her silently into the house and to her bedroom, gently and slowly undressed her and himself, laid her on the bed and ran his hands and lips over her body. At first she was passive, mentally and physically. It was still the other woman whose body began to respond and to arch, whose mouth moaned in pleasure. She forgot his problem, forgot Duff and Gideon Galili, forgot her name. When he entered her it was, for this other woman, the first time. The first ecstasy. She had no sense of time. Her first orgasm could have come in seconds, minutes or hours. The second and third followed in a timeless void. There may have been more but her mind and body were welded together and moved from consciousness to fantasy to sleep. It was the ultimate logic of a night of unreality.

She awoke alone in the bed and lay still for a long time listening to the morning chorus of the birds in the garden and trying to separate fantasy from reality. Eventually she rose, slipped on a robe and went out to the lounge. Through the window she saw him sitting in the same chair on the patio and for a moment thought that he had never moved from there - it had all been merely a dream. But her body still ached sweetly; it had been no dream. She walked out into the sunlight and he raised his head and saw her and smiled wanly. In a second her own feelings were forgotten. For him the night must have been a failure. She sat down facing him while the birds sang in the pine trees. She wanted them to stop. The sounds were like a rock band at a funeral.

'It didn't work for you?'

He shook his head. She now felt acute embarrassment, tainted by the memory of her own passion.

'I'm sorry . . . I don't.'

His voice interjected quietly. 'Please, Ruth. Don't say anything, 'It didn't work, but still it was beautiful. I've never in my life seen anything so lovely as your face last night. I'll never forget it.'

She groped for words. 'I don't know. Maybe if I had more skill . . . It got too much for me . . . '

He smiled, it was beautiful. Forget about skills - you need none.' He shrugged, 'I guess I'll have to try to live with the problem. I owe you a great deal for trying.'

She shook her head, swirling her long hair.

'You owe me nothing . . . It's a waste.' She felt confused and desperate. How could it have been so beautiful for her, and yet failed for him? It was savagely unfair. Abruptly she reached a decision. 'When do you go back? To Beirut?'

'In a couple of weeks.'

'Then we'll try again.'

'Thanks, but you've done more than I deserve. You're going to be married. You have to think of that.'

'I've thought about it, I've been unfaithful to Gideon. That's done; it can't be mended. At least we can try to salvage something.' A thought crossed her mind and she looked up and said 'For God's sake don't think I'm doing it for lust, even though I'll tell you now that I have never experienced anything as intense as I did last night.'

He smiled and shook his head. 'You're too honest for that.'

'All right then. Friends of mine have a beach house near Polis on the West Coast. It's very isolated and quiet. Let's drive down there for a few days . . . Let's not rush it. Try to relax and it might work.'

'I feel like a patient.'

'You are. Imagine that you broke your leg and it was set badly. You've had a limp for years. Now the leg has to be re-broken and set again. It could be painful.'

She studied him closely and saw the corners of his mouth twitch into a smile.

'Will you wear a white coat?'

'No. I'll wear nothing.'

So they went to Polis, driving down twisting dirt roads and through tiny villages until they came to the coast road, then they turned West, seeing fewer cars and people. It was an area not yet developed for tourism. An area of vineyards and forests and a steep, rugged coastline. They stopped for lunch at a taverna in Stroumbi and sat outside and drank too much wine and talked of inconsequential things and laughed a little. It was another hour's drive to Polis. They shopped for provisions at the village store and then took the road North through more forests until they came to the promontory and the bay, where legend has it that Aphrodite used to take her bath. The beach house was just beyond it in another tiny bay. Munger had to drive carefully over a little-used track. The house faced the sea and was hidden by a half circle of poplar trees, still and silent in the hot sun.

No sooner had they parked then Ruth jumped out of the car, stripped off her clothes and ran naked into the water. Munger carried their bags to the full-length verandah and quickly joined her.

Half an hour later they lay on their backs on the sliver of beach, being dried by the late afternoon sun. He was thinking that it was the most tranquil spot he had ever known. She was thinking that she must proceed cautiously. He would be tense and nervous. Perhaps dreading another failure.

He rolled over onto one elbow, looked down at her and reached out a finger to touch a droplet of water that had escaped the sun. It nestled beneath her left breast and he watched the nipple rise.

'Last night,' he whispered, 'there was very little light. I want to see you now. To watch your face.'

She started to say something but he moved his finger to seal her lips. Then he was kissing her nipples and running his hand over her belly and she was already wet, her body still conditioned by their lovemaking a few hours before.

She fought a battle in her mind: one part trying to stay in control, to dictate her movements for his pleasure; the other part drowning in her own sensations. His weight was over her, his mouth on her mouth and his rigid length slid into her. She moved her hands to his buttocks, pulling him deep, moaning in her throat. Then through a thickening mist she heard his voice telling her over and over that he loved her. The mist cleared and she saw his eyes and she murmured something, and moments later he was spurting into her and then they were both laughing and crying at the same time.

They stayed for ten days. They swam and lay in the sun and made love. They cooked each other meals and walked in the hills and made love. They danced on the verandah at night to the music of an old battery-powered record player and they laughed, and they made love. Only on the fourth night while she lay in his arms in the darkness did she repeat the words she had murmured into his ear on the beach.

'David, I love you.'

'Yes. So we have a problem.'

'No. But unfortunately Gideon has.'

He rolled over and switched on the light and pulled himself up in the bed. She remained on her back, looking up at him.

'Doctors are not supposed to fall in love with their patients.' He spoke with mock severity.

'But I never took the Hippocratic Oath.'

'So what about Gideon? You're not in love with him any more?'

She frowned and thought carefully. 'Yes, I am, and I'll tell him so.

I'll also tell him that I love him the same way that Duff loved me - and it's not enough.'

'You won't marry him?'

'No. I'm going to marry you - and I want children.' Her eyes opened wide to watch his reaction but she could read nothing in his face.

'You don't like the idea?'

Now he smiled, 'I was just trying to believe my ears. To make it real . . . when?'

'When we marry, or when we have children?'

'Both.'

Now she sat up. 'Let's make some coffee and plan it.' She saw him glance at his watch.

'I know,' she said. 'It's late, but I won't sleep - or make love again - until it's all settled.'

So they got up and sat on the verandah and planned it. At first he wanted to go straight to Limassol and tell Walter that ORANGE BLUE was retiring, but they both knew that such a course would be self-defeating. He had come back into the world for a purpose. That purpose had been the instrument of his rebirth. Ruth was the midwife who had slapped his bottom and brought forth his first cry. The purpose would be a cornerstone of their lives together. It might be two years or more, he warned her. If Walter's efforts in France failed, he would be needed in Iraq.

She did not mind the wait - or the danger. She had a strange confidence in their joint destiny. They had both come through much to start on this road. They would marry when the mission was over.

For the first time she was profoundly positive about something. The love she had discovered inside her put the rest of her life in perspective, particularly her feelings for Duff and Gideon. She was now aware that love happens on a myriad of levels. Perhaps most people never attained a love as intense as she now experienced. She doubted if it could have happened at a much younger age. Surely their past lives had provided the conditions to allow it to come about. She felt a deep sense of gratitude. She was at last completely without doubts or uncertainties: she had discovered what love meant - an emotion compounded of passion and compassion; of need and gratitude. For a long while she bathed in the light of that discovery, then her mind turned to other things and her happiness was clouded.

When Munger returned to Beirut she would visit Gideon in Israel and break the news. He saw the troubled look on her face.

'He will take it very badly,' he said, 'I know that. I know how I would feel. I'd do anything to keep you.'

She shrugged. 'Yes. But it can't be helped. Anyway, he's strong. He'll get over it.' She tried to smile. 'I don't want to feel sad tonight. Not even while we're here. Let's wait for the dawn and then swim. After that I want to make love on exactly the same spot as that first time. After all, we don't have to wait to make that baby. I don't mind being an unmarried mother-in-waiting.'

BOOK FOUR

CHAPTER FOURTEEN

It was one of the very rare occasions in Walter Blum's life when he felt a trifle humble. He sat in an anteroom outside the Prime Minister's office in Jerusalem and he actually had butterflies in his stomach. In a few minutes he would meet for the first time the Prime Minister of Israel, a man whom he admired and who greatly fascinated him. General Hofti had been ushered through a few minutes before and Walter was expecting the call any moment. To contain his nervousness he opened the folder on his knee and read the report that he and General Hofti had prepared during the night: the report that at this moment the Prime Minister would be reading.

1 OF 3

IRAQI NUCLEAR PROGRAMME
Report No. 43A (P.M.): 3rd May 1981

To: Prime Minister
From: General Yitzhak Hofti
Sources: Mossad
Circulation: Nil

SITUATION TO DATE:
In spite of all efforts both diplomatic, by the Foreign Ministry, and covert, by Mossad, the two nuclear research reactors contracted for by Iraq from France have now been shipped and are currently being installed in the nuclear research establishment at El-Tuwaitha on the outskirts of Baghdad.

(Reports 28A (P.M.) dated 18th July 1980 and 31A (P.M.) dated 12th September 1980 detailed the attempts by Mossad, and in particular its ORANGE network, to sabotage both the equipment and the programme. The result of this activity was that the programme was delayed by 12-14 months.)

However, the reactors are now on site together with 265 French scientists and technicians.

2 OF 3

It is estimated that the main 70 MW reactor will come on stream, i.e. become 'hot', between June and September of this year. In Report No. 41A dated 11th February 1981, various options were put forward. At that time your office ordered a further review of the Iraqi potential to manufacture nuclear weapons from material to be obtained from their new reactors. Report No. 42A dated 2nd March 1981 concluded that not only did the potential still exist but that the intention to do so remains a paramount objective of the Hussein regime, particularly since the onset of hostilities with Iran.

There now remain only two options if a decision is made to destroy the reactors:

a) A bombing strike
b) A commando sabotage raid

In consultation with Military Intelligence we have concluded that option (a) is the more feasible.

3 0F 3

The strike must take place before the reactor becomes 'hot'. El-Tuwaitha lies only twelve and a half miles from the centre of Baghdad and prevailing winds would almost certainly ensure that a massive radiation leak would contaminate a large proportion of the city and its three and a half million inhabitants.

Conclusion:
The decision whether or not to destroy the reactor is, of course, a political one Nevertheless, our Research and Analysis Department has distilled an opinion that may have some bearing on that decision.

In essence, as a result of such a strike, the State of Israel will face condemnation throughout the world. Some of it will be hypocritical, i.e. from Egypt and Iran, but on the whole it will be genuinely felt and vociferously expressed. Certainly we shall face the real threat of United Nations sanctions. There will be two main pillars to this condemnation:

Iraq has signed and, to date, scrupulously observed the Nuclear Non-Proliferation Treaty. Israel has not.

The raid will set a precedence of incalculable dimensions. END IT.

Walter closed the folder and wondered how the Prime Minister would interpret its conclusion. He did not have to wait long to find out. An aide opened the door, gestured and then ushered the perspiring Walter into the Prime Minister's office.

He was sitting with General Hofti at what looked like an ordinary dining room table in a corner of the spacious room. He stood up as Walter approached and waved aside Hofti's introduction. As he held out his hand and smiled he said:

'We have never met, but I feel I know you. In the name of Israel and Jewish people everywhere I thank you for the work you have done and continue to do.'

Walter took the hand and shook it, feeling even more humble. He noted with surprise that the Prime Minister was even smaller than he had supposed. He appeared almost frail, but Walter looked into his eyes behind the thick-lensed spectacles and saw nothing but confidence and determination.

As they sat down the Prime Minister said 'You may smoke if you wish.'

Walter smiled and Hofti looked dumbfounded. He had earlier pleaded with Walter not to light up one of his fat cigars, for in this office smoking was strictly forbidden. Walter reached into an inside pocket of his raw-silk maroon-coloured jacket and extracted a cigar. He unwrapped it, clipped off the end and stuck it between his fat lips. Then, to Hofti's relief, he said. 'I'll just chew on it.'

'As you wish.' The Prime Minister looked down at the file in front of him, picked up a red marker pen and began underlining certain passages. Walter studied him with interest.

Menachem Begin was a man who believed in an eye for an eye and a tooth for a tooth, but if the tooth was Jewish he demanded a whole set of dentures in return. He saw himself as the embodiment of the State of Israel. He was passionate in his belief in the historic and biblical rights of the Jewish people. Sometimes it made him, in other people's eyes, a caricature of contradiction. He would vehemently denounce terrorism but in his youth he had led the Irgun Zvai Leumi terror squad. He would lecture the world on the past evils of Nazi collective punishment and the next day give orders to destroy a Palestinian village from whence a PLO incursion had originated. He would talk eloquently of the rights of Jewish settlements in the Sinai and a month later travel to Camp David and bargain away those rights.

Walter found him fascinating and saw no contradictions. Every single act of Menachem Begin was aimed at a single target: the continued existence and well-being of the State of Israel.

Now he looked up from the report and said to Walter:

'Your efforts in France were very commendable.'

It was a curious adjective, for he was referring to two acts of assassination and an act of sabotage. Professor Yahia el Mashad, the Egyptian head of the Iraqi nuclear programme, had been killed in his Paris hotel room. It had been a messy affair: there was a French prostitute with him who had escaped after seeing his attackers. Mossad agents had to track her down and a week later arranged for her to have a fatal traffic accident. The Professor had been in Paris to arrange for the Iraqis to buy into a consortium called Eurodif, which manufactured enriched uranium. The deal was called off.

A few months earlier, in April 1979, Mossad agents had planted explosives in the factory manufacturing part of the reactor, thereby delaying delivery for over a year.

'Unfortunately,' Walter said, 'we only managed to delay matters.'

Begin gestured dramatically. 'That delay was vital. In the meantime we have made peace with Egypt and two of our enemies - Iraq and Iran - are making war with each other. It means that if we have to take such action as recommended in this report, the timing politically is much better.' He turned to Hofti.

'General, you point out very vividly the international repercussions we will face, but you miss the main point.'

Hofti straightened in his chair and asked 'What is that?'

'The President of the United States of America.' The Prime Minister smiled as he saw the puzzled look that passed between Hofti and Walter, then he stood and began pacing up and down as he talked.

'In a strange way, the single biggest threat to Israel is not the Arab armies, or Russia, or even nuclear weapons. No, it is the potential alienation of a US President who might have no ambitions to be re-elected." He turned to face the table.

'You see, gentlemen, with the United States as a fully committed ally we can face virtually anything. In fact, in my opinion, they are the only ally worth having. The European states, with the honourable exception of Holland, will always ultimately act in their own selfish interests. It is America that arms us, and America that gives us the financial aid we vitally need.'

He started pacing again and the tone of his voice went up half a decibel as he warmed to his theme.

'Of course, much of the assistance they give us comes from the warmth of their hearts. However, politics plays a very large part. It is almost impossible for an American President to be elected without the Jewish vote. The same goes for a large number of Congressmen. When Moshe Dayan last visited America, President Carter begged him not to criticise him to the major Jewish organisations. He practically went down on his knees. Moshe told me it was quite degrading.'

Walter interjected 'But Carter lost the election.'

'Yes, Mr Blum, and the Jewish organisations stayed neutral. It was judged that there was little to choose between the candidates as to their policies towards Israel. Carter was a friend, but a weak one. Reagan may be less of a friend but he will make America strong and that is vital to us.'

He sighed. 'The problem is that right now President Reagan is upset with Israel and with me in particular.' He smiled grimly. 'Well, I'm used to being unpopular - and I don't care. Reagan is mad because of our activities in the Lebanon. He expects us to adopt a conciliatory attitude to the Syrian presence there. To the thousands of Palestinian terrorists who use it as a base to murder our women and children. He sent his ambassador to tell me to behave.' He was breathing deeply now and chopping the air with his hands.

'He treats us like spoiled children who need a spanking!' He rounded on the two men, his face working in anger. Then abruptly he controlled himself and smiled mischievously.

'I reminded the ambassador about the American blockade of Cuba. I pointed out that Central America was developing into their own Lebanon. I asked him what the President would do if the Cubans massed a few armoured divisions on the border between Mexico and Texas. If they sent terrorists to Dallas to kill school children.'

'How did he take that?' Walter asked, intrigued to be privy to the intimate details of high State diplomacy.

Begin smiled. 'I haven't had a reply yet, but I expect he got the message.' He became serious again. 'The problem is that Reagan is tough, and in view of his age may decide not to run for a second term. That would take away all our leverage. He could make things very difficult for Israel. As it is we shall have a battle with him over his plans to sell AWAC surveillance planes to the Saudis. It could be a bitter battle and we might lose.'

He came back to his chair and sat down and tapped the report. 'If we bomb this reactor and President Reagan is not totally convinced that it was necessary, then he will be very angry indeed and he may not veto any UN sanction resolutions. That would be very serious for Israel. He may hold up or even cancel military and financial aid. That would be catastrophic for Israel.'

He looked up, first at General Hofti and then at Walter. 'So you see our dilemma. The decision whether or not to bomb this reactor will be taken by the Cabinet. It will be a very difficult decision unless we know that immediately afterwards we can give undeniable proof to one man that the Iraqis were planning to use it to manufacture nuclear weapons.'

'It is so obvious . . .' Walter began, but the Prime Minister cut him short.

'Obvious to us, yes, and probably to everyone else, including the French. But they and the Iraqis and all the Arabs and Russia will scream bloody murder. I don't care - let them scream. Let everyone scream with the exception of President Reagan. He must know why we had to do it. He won't take our word. We need physical proof.'

He sat back in his chair, looked quizzically at General Hofti and asked 'What exactly is the Mossad situation in Iraq? What chance is there of getting an agent inside their nuclear establishment?'

Hofti shrugged negatively and glanced at Walter, who said flatly 'Almost impossible. The security, both French and Iraqi, is naturally as tight as a vice. As to our situation, it's very thin. We have only one good agent in the country.'

'Only one?'

'Yes sir. Oh, we have half a dozen of what we call "fly catchers". They are second-level agents, good for surveillance and occasional strong-arm stuff, but not of the calibre to penetrate such a target. We also have a well-placed agent inside the Iraqi Mukhabarat, but he gives us only limited information. No, we have only one. He's code-named ORANGE BLUE and he's top class.'

Tell me about him. Is he an Israeli?'

Begin saw Walter look at Hofti and he quietly added 'I don't need details, Mr Blum. Just give me an impression of the man who is so important for our country.'

Walter thought for a moment, then said 'He is not an Israeli. His mother was Jewish and she died for Israel. Now he sees himself as Jewish and totally identifies with the Jewish people. He is a brilliant agent, although he came to it late. He is also very independent - a loner. He worked out his own strategy for getting into Iraq on a very favourable basis. Also, when they invaded

Iran he went immediately to Tehran. He was the man who negotiated the deal with Bani Sadr whereby we would secretly supply the Iranians with ammunition and spare parts and in return they would attempt to bomb the Iraqi nuclear establishment at El-Tuwaitha. It was a brilliant plan but unfortunately the Iranian Air Force botched the job. None of the bombs dropped within two miles of the reactor.'

'Yes, it's a pity,' Begin said. 'At first the CIA intimated that it was the Israeli Air Force in disguise. We pointed out that if it had been, they wouldn't have missed. Where is this man now?'

'He's in Cyprus, waiting for me. He's due to go back to Iraq in a few days.'

Begin looked thoughtful. 'One man,' he mused. 'Well, it has often happened in our history that a single man has had a great effect. Look what Cohen did in Syria. Now tell me, General, how will we know when this reactor is due to be made "hot"?'

'That's no problem,' Hofti said confidently. 'Obviously they'll try to keep it secret, but we've long ago penetrated the International Atomic Energy Agency. They will have to know when it's due to come on stream.' He pointed to the report. 'Present indications are that it will be between June and September of this year.'

Begin frowned. 'It gives us little time.' He stood and again started pacing. A small, energetic man impatient to be confined even to a chair. Suddenly he came to a stop and said triumphantly:

'July!' He turned to face the two men and laughed loudly at their expressions of puzzlement, it will be in July when they activate it. As Intelligence agents you should have seen it. "Tammuz" is the name of a Sumerian shepherd god . . . and it's also Arabic for the month of July!'

'It's pure speculation,' Hofti said, but the Prime Minister shook his head emphatically.

'No, Hofti. Of course, with the delay in shipment the exact timing could be haphazard, but Saddam Hussein is a man who sees things in symbols. Many Arabs do. If it's at all possible he will activate "Tammuz" in the month of its namesake. If we are going to destroy it we must do so before July . . . That gives us little time.' He turned to Walter. 'Your agent ORANGE BLUE must act. I must have that proof. In the meantime I will instruct the Air Force to begin precise exercises.'

Walter pushed back his chair and hauled himself to his feet. 'Then I shall get back to Limassol, Mr Prime Minister. Thank you for receiving me.'

Begin came forward and, with difficulty, embraced him. 'Please pass on to ORANGE BLUE a message: Israel depends on him. Please also give him my personal respects and best wishes.'

Walter nodded solemnly and then rolled his way to the door.

CHAPTER FIFTEEN

'There's no chance at all.'

Munger said it flatly and the dewlap jowls of Walter's face dropped lower.

'I agree,' Misha Wigoda added. 'They're certainly expecting some kind of action from us. So are the French, and with scores of their scientists and technicians on the spot they're making sure that security is perfect at El Tuwaitha. There's no chance.'

'I also agree,' Isaac Shapiro said. 'Even to try would be counterproductive.'

Walter grunted in irritation and looked at the fourth man sitting opposite his desk. It was Efim Zimmerman, who was visiting from Paris and had been co-opted in to this all-important conference.

'Maybe, Walter,' he said, 'you're approaching this thing from the wrong direction.'

Walter grunted again, this time ominously, in his present mood even the venerable Zimmerman was not immune from a tongue lashing. For the past hour they had been examining ways of providing the absolute proof that Menachem Begin demanded. Proof that would convince even the most paranoid of sceptics. They had gone through many permutations, from bribing a high Iraqi official to penetrating the nuclear establishment itself. So far, nothing promising had emerged.

'What direction,' Walter growled, 'would you suggest?' Zimmerman was not at all perturbed by Walter's simmering mood.

'Yellowcake,' he said positively. 'The Iraqis have been trying to buy some for the past three years. They've approached the Portuguese, the Brazilians, even the Australians through a front company. They've been in the market for over a thousand tons. Thanks to our intervention their negotiations came to nothing, but until three months ago their efforts have been unceasing. Then abruptly they dropped out of the market.'

'So they gave up,' Walter said. 'Or, more likely, they've found another way to obtain U235 or PU239. Maybe the Russians gave them some?'

Zimmerman shook his head. 'That's very unlikely. You know how they are. No, Walter.' He leaned forward and, in a schoolmasterish tone, said 'Think, Walter. Use your brains. Why else would the Iraqis drop out of the "yellowcake" market?'

Walter glared at him and an eruption was imminent when Munger said

'Because they've already got some?'

'Exactly. It's an obvious prognosis.' Zimmerman sat back in his chair with a satisfied air. 'And it's not difficult to work out where they got it. We know that Libya has stockpiled over five hundred tons. It's a fair bet that the Colonel has done a deal with his good friend Saddam Hussein.'

Walter was smiling and shaking his head. 'It's very logical, Efim, but you're wrong. Because the ORANGE network is compartmentalised, and because of the "need to know" factor, you didn't know that we've had a cover watch on that stockpile ever since Gaddafi started buying. I can tell you the date of every shipment he's received. So far no yellowcake has been re-exported. It's been one of our most successful covert operations.' He gestured expansively. 'Isaac here has been controlling it.'

Isaac Shapiro looked very unhappy. He asked: 'Mr Blum, didn't you read your "URGENT' file?'

'No. I only got back late last night. So far I've only seen the "IMMEDIATE" file. What is it, man?'

Shapiro's prominent Adam 's apple bobbed up and down as he gulped nervously.

'Four days ago,' he said, 'the Libyans transported one hundred tons of yellowcake from the stockpile at Sarir to the naval base at Tobruk. Right now it's being loaded onto a small freighter-the "SS Elmsland". She's six hundred tons, previously owned by a British company but purchased last month by the Hirah Trading and Shipping Company of Beirut.'

There was a pained silence, finally broken by Misha Wigoda, who said very quietly.

'Hirah is an Iraqi front company. In the past they bought fringe military equipment from the Americans. Computers, electronics et cetera.'

So Walter apologised to Zimmerman and the meeting examined the options.

Isaac Shapiro was already drawing up plans to sabotage and hopefully sink the "SS Elmsland". It would almost certainly unload its cargo in the tiny Gulf port of Fao, which was why the Iraqis had bought such a small vessel. Since the closing of the Shatt al Arab waterway by the war, the main port of Basrah was cut off. Fao was originally used by fishing trawlers and could only take very small vessels.

The ship could pass through the Suez Canal and Shapiro thought that a frogman raid might be feasible, while it waited off Port Said for a convoy. The Egyptians might even co-operate. The thought of Saddam Hussein having a nuclear arsenal would give President Sadat nightmares.

They discussed whether another route might be used. The Iraqis were bringing in a lot of supplies through the Jordanian port of Aqaba, and then trucking them across the desert. They were also covertly using the Saudi port of Jeddah while the authorities turned a Pan-Arabic blind eye.

The consensus though was that because of the nature of the cargo and the distinctive drum containers, the Iraqis would almost certainly bring it direct to Fao. At that point Munger, who hitherto had remained silent, asked a question:

'Exactly what do those drums look like, and how many will there be?'

Shapiro supplied the answer, speaking in a prim, lecturing tone.

'Uranium oxide is the colour of egg yolk and has a texture like coarse sand. Hence the term "yellowcake". The Iraqis cannot use yellowcake to fuel the Tammuz reactor, so they only want it for one reason: to pack round the core and extract PU239. That hundred tons of yellowcake will give them enough of it to make about twenty Hiroshima-size bombs. Because it's radioactive and dangerous to swallow or inhale, it is transported in special yellow-coloured, two hundred litre drums with bright red rubber seals. Each drum weighs approximately a third of a ton and has large black lettering denoting the source of the ore and a serial number. The purpose of this was to give some measure of control to the IAEA - it proved to be of little help. There are exactly three hundred drums in this shipment.'

Munger stood up and walked to a large map which covered most of one wall. It showed the Middle East in minute detail. The others watched his back as he studied it carefully. When he turned he was smiling. He said:

'We'd be fools to sink that ship and its cargo. What better proof can you give to President Reagan than a photograph showing the Iraqis taking delivery of those drums?'

He walked back to the table and sat down as a babble of discussion broke out. Everyone saw the beauty of it. The Iraqis would really be caught with egg on their faces. The only question was whether Munger could do it. And where.

He was strangely complacent. After all, taking snaps of forbidden subjects was his speciality. There would, of course, be massive security at Fao, but it was close to the war zone and he could get into the general area. There was another even more interesting possibility: the Iraqis obviously would not send the yellowcake to El Tuwaitha with its hundreds of French scientists and IAEA inspectors falling over each other. No, they would send it to a secret establishment where it would be prepared and stored until such time as Tammuz I was 'hot' and all foreigners expelled from El Tuwaitha. The opportunity might arise to track the shipment and get some snaps of that secret establishment.

The level of excitement rose and so did the noise as the others offered suggestions and back-up plans. But Munger would have none of it. He would be alone and he would have to improvise. Through his Kurdish connections he already had 'safe houses' in Baghdad and other Iraqi cities. He also had an escape route prepared through Kurdistan to the Turkish port of Mersin in case the operation went wrong. The main thing now was to track the "SS Elmsland" and calculate its estimated time of arrival at Fao. As soon as that was established he would head for Iraq.

So the meeting broke up. Isaac Shapiro and Misha Wigoda went away to plan the surveillance of the ship and Walter told Munger that he would contact him in Platres as soon as they had news.

Munger turned to Zimmerman and said 'Efim. If I don't see you before you leave, have a good trip back to Paris.'

They shook hands and, on impulse, Zimmerman embraced him. 'Go with God.'

As he reached the door, Walter said 'Tell Ruth that I'm very displeased with her. She hasn't come down to have lunch with me for over a month.'

'She's been busy, Walter. We're fixing up and extending my old farmhouse. She complains that you send me away too often and she does most of the work.'

'It's no excuse,' Walter grumbled. Tell her she "hast cleft my heart in twain".'

Munger grinned. 'That's impossible, Walter. You don't have one.' He closed the door quietly behind him and Waiter turned to Zimmerman with a hurt expression.

'That's not true.'

'Of course it's not, Walter.' Zimmerman patted his arm comfortingly. 'But it's hidden among so many folds of flesh it tends to be forgotten. Now I need a drink.'

As Walter poured two large Scotches, Zimmerman said:

'Part of me is very frightened that so much rests on the ability of one man. Another part is very glad that it's such a man as Munger.'

Walter handed him his drink and they moved over to a group of chairs in a corner and sat down.

'He's the perfect agent for this job,' Waiter said. 'But it's his independence that worries me. He hates to be controlled, hates to have someone looking over his shoulder. I like to have a complete grip on an operation. To guide and direct it, but in this case I'm a bystander. We all are.'

Zimmerman sipped his drink and settled back in his chair. He sensed that Walter wanted to talk. Perhaps was seeking a little avuncular advice. It was a rare situation and Zimmerman was enjoying it. To encourage Walter he said 'Tell me more about him.'

So Walter talked for half an hour. He explained about his mental condition and how the cause of it was still a mystery. He talked about Ruth and how he had tried to recruit her to seduce Munger and how she had refused, and yet a few months later they had become lovers. When he spoke of Ruth his voice softened and his affection for her was obvious.

He told of the transformation of Munger. How the man's character had blossomed from the inside. Walter was a great sceptic but the first time he had dined with them in Platres he had been struck by the intensity of their love - the completeness of it. Not that it was demonstrative. They treated each other in a relaxed, almost bantering way but during the meal Walter had seen the glances exchanged and felt the charged link which flowed between them.

At first he was worried that it might affect Munger's work; distract him from his purpose. His doubts were soon dispelled. If anything, Munger's efforts intensified, although he spent more time back in Cyprus. His work in Iran had been brilliant and so had his methods of gaining access to the Iraqi war front.

Walter described how, as soon as the Iranian air strike on El Tuwaitha had failed, Munger had arranged deliberately to get himself expelled from Iran. He was accused of photographing the war in Iraq's favour. He immediately flew to Beirut and talked to Sami Asaf. Now he wanted to report the war from the Iraqi side. He wanted freedom of movement and a multiple entry visa. He knew, of course, that Sami was a senior officer in the Mukhabarat but his approach was logical for he was also a long-standing correspondent for the Middle East News Bureau and would have obvious contacts with the Iraqi Ministry of Information.

Sami Asaf made the arrangement and Munger, with his reputation and his recent conflict with the Iranian authorities, was welcomed with open arms. The only person to object had been Janine Lesage. She now hated Munger with an obsession bordering on hysteria. She even wrote an article in L'Universe criticising Munger's photography and intimating that he only worked in black and white because the technicalities of colour were too much for him. The article had caused much hilarity in media circles.

At that point Zimmerman asked what Walter planned to do about Janine Lesage. She was, after all, a highly-skilled agent and working directly against Israel. Walter shrugged. He would deal with her in the course of time. They knew all about her and that was better than the French sending in a total unknown.

Finally Walter talked of his own dilemma. The old man sitting opposite was the only person to whom he could express such thoughts. In simple terms he faced the problem often experienced by puppeteers who became emotionally involved with their puppets. He had grown very fond of Ruth, and now of Munger. He had witnessed their happiness together, rejoiced at the prospects of their joint future. But in the coming weeks he would have to expose Munger to incredible dangers. How to reconcile his duty to his conscience? What would he do if the two came into direct conflict? He talked all around the subject with a troubled face until finally his words petered out and he looked up at the older man for some words of comfort - of reassurance.

Zimmerman sat hunched down, with his chin resting on his chest, his fingers swirling the almost empty glass in which a last, fast-melting lump of ice chinked rhythmically.

'Walter,' he said. 'You chose your course because you became bored with business. You wanted excitement and intrigue. You also wanted to make a commitment. It was a way to satisfy your ego . . . and your conscience.' He smiled to eliminate offence from his words. 'But in doing it you made a sort of pact with the devil. Sometimes the devil demands his due. You've lost other agents. You may lose this one. You had better accept that possibility now.'

Walter grimaced. He hadn't really been expecting words of comfort. At least Zimmerman was spelling it out.

'So that's all you've got to say?'

Zimmerman shook his head. 'No. The time has come to cut down on your excesses. You've abused your body with over-indulgence for long enough. You're reaching the age when your weight could be fatal to that heart which you're not supposed to have. At least cut back a bit. Also on the drink and cigars. You do everything to excess.'

Walter glared at him and Zimmerman smiled in return and held out his empty glass.

'In my case, though, I'm a paragon of health . . . so get me another drink, young man.'

Ruth and Munger whitewashed the wall together. It was thirty feet long - the outside of a new room that had been added to the old farmhouse. It would contain his studio and darkroom. When the mission was over he was going to make a dramatic shift in his career: no more combat photography. He would instead do portraits and maybe special assignments for news or travel magazines. Assignments on which Ruth could accompany him. He would also begin working in colour and would spend more time in the, darkroom balancing out the artistic side of his work with the technical side of developing and printing.

They had started at each end of the wall and, as they worked slowly towards each other, he told her about the meeting the previous day. He told her everything because they had a clear understanding that there would be no secrets between them. It had worked well. She needed the confidence of knowledge, no matter how frightening. He found that sharing his working problems, talking about his doubts and concerns, made them more bearable.

She laughed when he told her about Walter's message and said that she would go down to Limassol in a week or so. Anyway, she needed to do some shopping. She also had something else to do, but she didn't mention it to Munger.

For eighteen months now, ever since those first days at the beach house, she had been hoping, even praying, that she would conceive a child. As the months passed she became a little desperate, for she was in her middle thirties and had begun to see her child-bearing days slipping away. Her gynaecologist in Limassol had been reassuring: there was no reason why it shouldn't happen. He had worked out a chart with her, based on her menstrual cycle, so that she could judge the times when she would be most fertile. It had been an exercise in frustration because on many of the occasions Munger had been away at his work. Her anxieties had increased as the months passed, but in the last few days her hopes had risen sharply. She was very regular in her cycle but this month her period was five days overdue. She tried to keep a lid on her expectations for fear of disappointment, and she hadn't mentioned anything to Munger. She didn't want him to be distracted by anything during the coming dangerous days in Iraq. She would go down to Limassol next week and have a test and, if it was positive, he would have a nice surprise with which to start his new life.

She concentrated for a while on the wall and the whitewash. She enjoyed the labour; enjoyed watching the place develop under their own hands - a place which held out a vista of future contentment. At first she had been a little reluctant when Munger had suggested that, once married, they would live here. It made more sense for him to move into her own large villa. She recognised the mental implications though. It would always have a slight aura of Duff and, while Munger had never indicated that it would bother him, she thought the possibilities should be avoided.

Her first visit to the farmhouse and the village of Phini had convinced her. They had lunch in the taverna and the respect and friendship shown to Munger by the villagers and, through him, to her, gave her a warm feeling of belonging.

In the evening they had gone to dinner at the Papadopoulos' and Helena had cooked *kleftiko* and told her the story of the fire and how she had used the dish finally to lure Munger into friendship. She had patted Androulla's dog and listened as the girl told her of his cut paw and how frightened she had been of the 'bad foreigner'.

So Ruth had felt at home and had directed her energies to renovating the farmhouse. She came almost every day and artisans came out from the village: masons and carpenters and plumbers, and worked with her at what she knew to be very modest wages. Vassos had helped to develop a vegetable garden behind the kitchen and had rigged up a crude but effective irrigation system from the well.

In a month everything would be ready and, from what she had just heard, the work of ORANGE BLUE would also be finished; If only the tests next week were positive her cup would be brimming over.

Her reverie was interrupted by the slap of a brush close to her shoulder and she turned, startled to see Munger's grin. They had met almost in the centre of the wall.

'You were day dreaming,' he said.

'Yes, it was a good dream. Give me a kiss to end it nicely.'

'When the wall's finished,' he answered sternly.

She dipped her brush into the bucket and began to slap whitewash frantically on the wall, but the kiss was delayed. A black car came bouncing down the track: the same car that always brought messages from Walter.

This time it was a very brief note which read:

' "SS Elmsland" ETA Fao June 1st.'

Munger passed it to her and said I'll have to leave tomorrow.'

She nodded and began to slap more whitewash on the wall.

It was four days later when Joseph Levy and David Burg took a walk in the Bois de Boulogne. Levy was the Paris in-house resident for Mossad and Burg was his London counterpart. They were old friends and had fought together in the Haganah in the battle to create Israel. They would often visit each other for weekends and talk about old times and old battles. .

They had been doing that over lunch in a nearby restaurant and, it being a sunny afternoon, they took a stroll in the park afterwards. They were two senior and veteran Intelligence officers and far too experienced to discuss Mossad business in a restaurant or any other place where their words could be overheard or picked up by a hidden microphone.

But out in the empty space of the park, and talking in the lowest of voices, they felt safe to chat about their work and some of the personalities and minor scandals. Eventually, as they turned and ambled back towards the concrete of the city, the conversation turned more serious. Levy had been intimately involved in the Mossad effort to halt the export from France of the Tammuz I reactor. Burg was curious to know what was to happen now that the reactor was installed and about to become radioactive. Of course, strictly speaking Levy should not have discussed it but, after all, Burg was a Senior Mossad official and an old friend, so Levy told him what we knew, which in itself was not very extensive.

One hundred and fifty metres away, in the back of a dark green van parked opposite the Pavilion Dauphine, a bearded man studied the two Israelis through binoculars. They were walking slowly towards him, bending in slightly as they talked. Close to the watching man's shoulder was the long black tube of an ultra-sensitive directional microphone. He realigned it so that it pointed directly at the sauntering men, then turned to the interior of the van. A short, blond man, dressed in overalls, was sitting at a metal table which contained a battery of tape recorders and amplifiers. He was wearing headphones.

'Try it now.'

'What's the distance?' asked the blonde man.

'About one hundred and fifty metres and closing slowly.'

The blonde shrugged negatively but he reached out and punched a button and the tapes on one of the machines started to rotate slowly. He raised his hands and pressed the ear phones tighter and listened and then shook his head.

The bearded man turned and raised the binoculars and every few seconds adjusted the aim of the microphone as the Israelis came marginally nearer. It was obvious that they would not come closer than eighty metres.

They had almost reached the point when the blonde said: 'I'm getting something. Very faint . . . very faint . . . It's fading . . . It's gone.'

The other man cursed into his beard. 'Fuck! Another ten metres - just another ten metres. What did you get?'

The blonde took off the headphones and said: 'It was inaudible, but the lab might be able to bring something out. Let's go.'

Two hours later, at SDECE headquarters, de Marenches was reading a transcript of what the lab had brought out:

BURG: You mean . . . (inaudible) . . . in Iraq? The whole country?
LEVY: Yes. Incredible but true. Only one top agent. BURG: Do you know him?
LEVY: No. He's . . . (inaudible) . . . named ORANGE BLUE. We expect action any time now.
BURG: But one man, it's . . . (inaudible) . . .

The bearded man was sitting nervously in front of the desk. He said:

'I'm sorry, sir. That's all we could lift off the tapes. The distance was over a hundred metres.'

De Marenches smiled and waved away the apology. 'You did well. Very well. It's rare to catch Mossad with their pants down.'

He pressed a button on his intercom and said: 'I want to send an urgent signal to Janine Lesage.'

CHAPTER SIXTEEN

Ahmed Nassir was an avaricious man and he was a coward. The critical question for Munger was whether the avarice would conquer the cowardice. He was the liaison man and interpreter assigned to Munger by the Iraqi Ministry of Information and an obligatory companion even though Munger spoke passable Arabic. It was inevitable that he would also be a member of the lower echelons of the Mukhabarat. He was a short, plump man in his early thirties and he spoke English with an American accent, for he had spent two years at the American University of Beirut. This was the third occasion that he had been assigned to Munger and it was no accident for, after the first time, Munger had dropped a word to Sami Asaf over lunch at the Sinbad Hotel. He had already recognised the uses that could be made of Ahmed Nassir. The avarice was written on his face and the way he constantly fingered his large gold ring. It was confirmed by the way he fiddled his expenses. Even when Munger paid for a meal in a restaurant - and he usually paid - Nassir would ask for the receipt with a conspiratorial smile.

His cowardice was beyond question. His job was to accompany Munger at all times and that included incursions into the war zone. However, whenever Munger went to a dangerous area, Nassir would invent an excuse to stay behind at the hotel. Either he was sick, or he had to wait for an important phone call or an important official. It suited Munger perfectly. He had quickly built up a good rapport with senior officers in the field. He brought them cigarettes and liquor but, more important, he photographed them and sent them prints and sometimes newspapers and magazines in which their faces appeared. They were also impressed with the courage he showed under fire and the fact that he had been expelled from Iran because of bias in Iraq's favour.

So he moved around the war zone with relative freedom and was the envy of other photographers who were restricted to the occasional stage-managed media excursion.

Right now, though, Munger was up against a problem. He was sitting with Nassir, eating dinner in the restaurant of the El Jamhorya Hotel in Basrah, and as he watched him devour the last shreds of a scrawny chicken he had to decide just how much money would be needed to counterbalance his cowardice.

The problem was that Munger was not going to be able to get any snaps of the 'SS Elmsland' unloading its cargo. That afternoon, after a quick sortie to visit a Brigadier commanding part of the defence garrison at Khorramshahr, Munger had driven down alongside the Shatt al-Arab waterway to Fao. Nassir had stayed at the hotel complaining of a slight tummy upset, a malady which had now obviously corrected itself.

Munger had passed through three roadblocks with ease, his papers and connections working well. But at the fourth roadblock it had been a different story. It was only a mile from the port and was part of a heavy barbed-wire barrier which stretched right across the narrow peninsula. Prominently displayed along its length were skull and crossbones signs indicating a mine field.

The Captain in charge of the roadblock was unimpressed with his papers. This was a totally restricted area. Munger tried dropping the names of a Brigadier and two Colonels, but the Captain had smiled and said that even they were not allowed in.

It was very frustrating. In the distance he could see several ships alongside the single wharf and more lying out to sea waiting their turn. The 'Elmsland' was due in two days and presumably would come straight alongside. Munger's instinct told him that no amount of arguing was going to change the Captain's mind. It could even arouse suspicions. So he chatted pleasantly for a few minutes and watched as two trucks full of labourers were let through the barrier after their papers had been scrutinised. He then gave the Captain a pack of Marlboro cigarettes and headed back to Basrah. It was now vital to find out the final destination of the yellowcake.

Nassir gnawed the last morsel of flesh from the last bone and wiped the oil from his face and fingers with a paper napkin. As he reached for a toothpick Munger said:

'Ahmed, I have a problem. Maybe you can help me.'

'What is it, Mr Munger?'

From his pocket Munger took a small square of folded white paper and passed it over. 'I need to get a valuation on these - quickly.'

Nassir placed the paper on the tablecloth and carefully unfolded it. As soon as he saw the four small diamonds his pudgy hand moved quickly to shield them from any other eyes but his own.

'Diamonds!'

'Yes.' Munger spoke casually. 'Frankly, I don't know much about diamonds. It just happened that they came into my possession.'

'You want me to sell them?' Sweat and greed had broken out of Nassir's face.

'I might. But first I want a valuation.'

Nassir refolded the paper but left it on the table in front of him.

'Maybe I can help you, Mr Munger. I know a man here in Basrah. He is in the gem business and he is a friend of my uncle's.

He is an honest man. If you want to sell, he will give you the best price. I guarantee it.'

'Good. When can you let me know?'

Nassir looked at his watch. 'He will be at his home now. I could go and see him.' A thought struck him. 'It is better that you do not come. A foreigner would make him suspicious and you know that dealing in precious stones is illegal.'

'Of course. Anyway, I have to wait here for an important phone call.' He winked and Nassir smiled a little uncertainly. Then he picked up the diamonds and asked:

'Do you want a receipt?'

Munger shook his head vehemently and laid a finger alongside his nose. Nassir's smile was now confident and he pushed his chair back and stood up. 'I'll come to your room as soon as I get back.'

It was two hours later and Munger was lying on his bed and almost dozing off when he heard the conspiratorial tap on the door.

Nassir came into the room wearing a pimp's expression. He accepted a glass of Scotch and sat on the only chair. Munger sat on the bed, facing him. Immediately Nassir passed him the little square of folded paper.

'I have good news, Mr Munger. These diamonds are very good quality. Not the best, you understand - a little imperfect - but still valuable. They are each slightly under one carat and my friend - my uncle's friend - can offer you $10,000 for each of them . . . each of them, Mr Munger. That's $40,000. It's a very good price. You won't get better anywhere. Not even in Beirut.'

Munger was well pleased. He calculated that Nassir would have to share whatever profit he made with the dealer, so it meant that for around $12,000 he was prepared to risk his position, maybe his life, by committing an illegal act. He kept the pleasure out of his voice as he said coldly:

'Those diamonds each weigh exactly one carat and they are all perfect internally flawless "D" colour. Their wholesale value is at least $16,000 each. At least. You were trying to cheat me.'

Nassir showed no alarm. His eyes narrowed. 'If you knew their value why did you ask me to find out? What are you up to?'

'I'm up to finding out if you will take a big risk for a lot of money.'

The Arab leaned forward. 'How big a risk - and how much money?'

Munger chose not to elaborate on the risk. A good salesman only emphasises the positive. Anyway, Nassir would quickly quantify the risks for himself.

The diamonds, with a total value of $64,000, will be yours, Ahmed, in exchange for some information.'

Nassir smiled but his eyes were cold. 'You're a spy.'

'So are you.'

'Yes, but only in a minor way. I cannot believe that any information I have can be worth so much money.'

'No,' Munger agreed. 'You will have to get it.'

'Ah. And therein lies the risk.'

'Precisely, but it is not so great.'

'Who do you work for? The CIA?'

Munger smiled and spread his hands in a throw-away gesture. Nassir nodded and smiled again.

'I thought so. The British would never pay money like that. What do you want to know?'

There's a ship called the "SS Elmsland". It will arrive in Fao within two or three days. Its cargo will be immediately unloaded and sent by truck to an unknown destination. I want to know that destination.'

'What is the cargo?'

'I don't know.'

Nassir guessed that he was lying. He also guessed that the cargo would be arms and munitions.

'It will be very difficult,' he said. 'Fao is a restricted area. Even for me.'

'I know. But the cargo will have to be unloaded from the ship and. then reloaded onto the trucks. There will be at least four of them. So there will be four drivers in the convoy. Maybe even two to a truck. You could get the information from any one of them. Maybe even from the stevedores at the port. Many of them come from Basrah - surely you can locate some of them.'

'It's possible,' Nassir agreed thoughtfully. 'But it will be expensive.'

'You can buy a lot with $64,000,' Munger said and then threw in the clincher. 'You will have two of the diamonds now and the other two in Baghdad, before I leave the country. That will be in less than a week. If your information is accurate and proves useful I will add a bonus of two more diamonds of the same value.'

In the blink of an eyelid Nassir calculated the total of $96,000, less the the few Dinars he would have to pay some truck driver for the information.

'It's a deal?' Munger asked.

'It's a deal,' came the reply.

Munger stood up and reached for his empty glass:

'Let's have a drink on it.'

Seven hundred miles away in her apartment in Beirut, Janine Lesage was also making a deal and, at 5,000 Lebanese Pounds, it was a lot cheaper than Munger's.

'Colonel' Jamil Mahmoud was not a real colonel, but he did lead one of Beirut's small private armies, and he was discreet. His 'army' of one hundred and fifty assorted thugs normally protected the person and property of a wealthy Lebanese industrialist, but

Mahmoud was in the habit of hiring out sections of it on a random basis to anyone who could pay the price.

Janine Lesage needed a dozen men, under a reliable leader, to kidnap Melim Jaheen, hold him for a day or two while she extricated information, and then dispose of him.

The signal had come in from Paris the night before. In essence it informed her that a top Mossad agent, code-named ORANGE BLUE was operating in Iraq. Her instructions were to liaise with the Iraqi Mukhabarat and locate and nullify this agent. Nullify being a euphemism for eliminate. Her course of action was obvious: she knew that Melim Jaheen was more than likely a Mossad agent. He could well know the identity of ORANGE BLUE. She should, of course, have immediately contacted Sami Asaf in Baghdad and used him to spearhead her actions. She had not done so for several reasons. Firstly, he would almost certainly have used his friends in the PLO to pick up Jaheen and work on him and, from experience, she knew that they would only be concerned with their own interests. Secondly, she wanted to bring off a big coup all by herself, both to impress SDECE headquarters and to cock a snook at Sami Asaf. Of late their relationship had cooled considerably. This was partly due to his spending nearly all his time in Baghdad and partly due to a growing antagonism between them. It had really started with the killing of Duff Paget. Months later there had been an inevitable leak from breakaway elements in the PLO and the Americans had discovered that the Mukhabarat had been behind it. With uncommon zeal the CIA had exacted revenge, killing four Mukhabarat agents in various parts of the Middle East. Sami Asaf had been very unhappy. He was even more unhappy about the assassination of Professor Yahia el Mashad in Paris and the sabotage of parts of the reactor and the subsequent delays. He heaped scorn on the incompetence of SDECE, who were supposed to be guarding against such things and he questioned the effectiveness of their help in Iraq if such things happened on their own doorstep. Finally they had argued bitterly when Sami had used his influence to help Munger cover the war in Iraq. Her hatred for Munger was like a lump of coal, smouldering white, in her belly. She had begged Sami not to help him - in fact pleaded with him to use his influence in the opposite direction. She had been unsuccessful. Sami liked and admired Munger, and later took delight in telling her how effective he was in presenting to the whole world, through his photography, the Iraqi side of the war.

Sami Asaf had not been to Beirut for three months. She had visited him in Baghdad twice, but they had been frustrating meetings and totally devoid of sex. On his territory he was confident, even arrogant, and with a curiously inverted set of morals would not be unfaithful to his wife so close to home.

In fact her sex life had been frustrating all round. She had a brief fling with Gordon Frazer but it was, for her, unsatisfying and she guessed for him merely another notch on his bedpost. Apart from that she had indulged in a few one night stands which had only served to illuminate her frustrations.

So it was a bitter, hate-filled woman who negotiated with 'Colonel' Jamil Mahmoud. She settled the details: he would get half the money now and the balance on completion. She did not tell him that Jaheen was a suspected Mossad agent in case he, or one of his men, leaked the story to the PLO. Consequently, when he proposed merely to go out and pick Jaheen up wherever he was found she had difficulty in dissuading him. She knew all about the competence of Mossad agents. He would certainly be armed and probably within a covert protective screen of his own people. It would be suicidal to try to take him either at his office or his home. She knew of several restaurants and bars where he ate and drank. She would have permanent watches on these places and try to catch him in an exposed position. In the meantime she had arranged a safe house in the Moslem-held port of Damour. He would be taken there for interrogation.

So the deal was done and she handed over 2,500 Lebanese Pounds and suggested that they seal the deal with a Scotch.

'Colonel' Jamil Mahmoud pocketed the money but refused the drink. He was a good Moslem. He suggested instead, eyeing her hungrily, that they consummate the deal in a more pleasurable manner and one that was not against his religion. She politely refused. Although fit and wiry, he was over sixty years old and she guessed that the pleasure would travel down a one-way street.

It was the next night when Ahmed Nassir again tapped on Munger's door and again slid in like a lubricated pimp. He tried to appear calm and casual but his face betrayed his excitement and greed.

'We've been fortunate,' he said as Munger gave him a drink and ushered him to the chair. 'I located a truck driver who has just arrived from Baghdad. He is part of a convoy which will convey the cargo of the "Elmsland" to its destination.' He took a large gulp of his scotch as Munger watched him closely, it was very costly. I had to give him money before he would talk - a great deal.'

'Go on,' Munger urged impatiently. 'What did you find out?'

Nassir paused for effect, then said: 'The ship will arrive the day after tomorrow, in the morning. There are five Volvo F12 trucks already gathered here in Basrah to transport its cargo. Security is very tight. There will be troops in each truck and the convoy will be accompanied by Military Police. The roads will be cleared ahead of it. The driver does not know what the cargo is.' He gave Munger a hard look. 'You don't know?'

'I don't. You know how it is in this business. They tell you only what they need to.'

Nassir nodded in agreement. 'Well, the convoy will go to Kifri. That's a city a hundred miles north of Baghdad. They pass through Kifri and about five miles further on there's a military base. That's where they go. The driver has been there before with other shipments. I can show you exactly where it is on the map.'

Munger tried to keep the relief but of his voice. 'When will they get there?'

'Well, it's four hundred miles from Fao. They usually stop overnight near Al Hillah, which is about half way.'

'Good. So we have four days.'

'We?'

Munger smiled grimly. 'Yes. First thing in the morning we go to Baghdad. I will need a day to arrange papers to visit the northern war zone. Kifri is only forty miles from the Iranian border; it would be natural for me to visit the area.'

Nassir was looking very uncomfortable. 'My part of the deal is finished,' he said. 'I've already taken enough risks.'

Munger took a calculated gamble. 'All right. But in that case you won't get the bonus. I said only if your information proves useful. It will not do so unless I get to Kifri.'

Again Munger watched as avarice and fear waged a war across Nassir's face. Finally he asked:

'How will you get papers? No one is allowed up there.'

'I have friends in Baghdad.'

Nassir studied him carefully then said: 'All right. I'll come with you to Kifri, but no further. From Kifri you're on your own.'

Munger nodded in agreement, then Nassir asked:

'After that you will leave Iraq?'

'Yes.'

'And you will never come back?'

'Never.'

'Good.' Nassir stood and walked over to the bottle of Scotch and said: 'I'll drink to that.'

CHAPTER SEVENTEEN

It is a myth that Intelligence agents, or anyone else, can sense the presence of danger, but it is true that they can become aware of being followed. This is not instinct but training and experience. It is a subconscious monitoring of the immediate environment - a monitoring that sets off a mental alarm bell at the first sign of abnormality: a face seen too often, a figure moving in tandem pace. A man looking at a newspaper but not reading it. A moving car or van that does not conform to the traffic flow. Misha Wigoda was a skilled and experienced agent but his alarm bell did not ring because he was not being followed.

He ate an early lunch at a small restaurant in a narrow cul-de-sac in Beirut's Fayadi Ya district. He came occasionally because, in his experience, it served the best *kebbe* in the Lebanon. It was also one of those places on which Janine Lesage had placed permanent surveillance. Within a minute of Misha Wigoda entering the restaurant a man in a coffee shop across the street was on the telephone informing her that Melim Jaheen was alone and unprotected.

Misha ate hurriedly because in the afternoon he was going to the port of Jounieh to talk to a Phalangist agent about future supplies of small arms. His assistant, Tamar Feder, alias Fuad Tawfir, was to pick him up in his car on the corner of Rue Hassel in an hour.

As he enjoyed the food his mind ranged into the future. When Munger's mission was complete, Misha had been promised three months' leave. Tamar Feder would take over ORANGE 14 in his absence. It would be a well-deserved leave, and the first for many months. Misha had been feeling the strain. It was not just the mounting tension caused by the Iraqi situation, but more the effect of living in a hostile environment for over three years and encasing himself in a false identity. There was never any chance to relax, to get drunk, or to talk easily with friends or even strangers. It was the constant need to be vigilant that stretched the nerves. He was overdue for leave and consequently his senses were strained and their perception dulled. He would travel to Europe and North America on his leave and be a mere tourist and eat a lot and drink a lot and maybe get lucky and attract some women, and simply have a damned good time and charge his batteries.

Munger was never far from his thoughts. Only a few hours ago a courier had arrived from Baghdad with a signal giving the final destination of the yellowcake shipment and the information that Munger would try to get his 'snap' within three days.

The courier system was working well. The ORANGE network now had six of them travelling in and out of Baghdad on a fixed rota. They were genuinely involved in business and they traded at a level which justified their frequent visits. Their role was to pick up and deposit messages at a series of constantly changing 'mail drops'. Munger himself never visited the drops - that was done by his Kurdish friends. The 'cut out' was total.

Misha finished his meal, quickly drank a coffee and, with a nod of appreciation to the fat proprietor, went out into the hot and crowded lane.

Two hundred yards away Tamar Feder pulled into the kerb, mopped the sweat from his face and once again resolved to tackle Misha about getting an air-conditioned car. After an hour's driving in Beirut a man was good for nothing.

Automatically his eyes scanned the bustling street. Fifty yards in front of him two men were unloading crates from the back of a van. Across the street was parked a grey Ford truck. The driver was leaning out of the cab arguing with a shopkeeper, irritated by having his display window obscured. Being lunchtime the traffic was sparse but there were many pedestrians and street hawkers urging them to buy their wares.

He caught sight of Misha's bald pate shining in the sun as he pushed his way through the crowd. Tamar was about to switch on the ignition when it happened. Later he was to remember how slick it had been:

Misha was abreast of the van. The men carrying a crate behind him dropped it, grabbed an arm each and simply slung him into the van and dived in behind him. He had no chance at all. The van's doors closed and it immediately pulled out into the traffic. As Tamar turned the ignition key he heard a car accelerating behind him. He looked up to see a green Mercedes flashing by. There were two occupants. The passenger turned to look at him and he recognised from the file photographs the unmistakable features of Janine Lesage.

He was close behind the Mercedes but he was too late. On the periphery of his vision he saw the truck moving diagonally across the street. The Mercedes passed in front of it but Tamar had no chance: his foot slammed onto the brake pedal and his arms came up to shield his face. It was not a bad crash and, apart from a cut on his chin, he was unhurt.

From that moment his actions followed a predetermined and rigid pattern. He had no thoughts of trying to follow and rescue Misha. The door of his car had popped open with the impact and Tamar dived out and into the stunned crowd and quickly put distance between himself and the accident. Two blocks away he waved down a taxi and fifteen minutes later was in a 'safe house' in the Ain Rummaneh district - a penthouse in a tall block of apartments. Its TV antennae on the roof doubled as a radio aerial and, within thirty minutes of the snatching of Misha Wigoda, Tamar was giving a full report to ORANGE headquarters in Limassol. He was told to remain in the safe house. His priority was to ensure that any messages to and from ORANGE BLUE continued to be transmitted.

He was desperate. He had understudied Misha Wigoda for over a year and had great respect for him. He wanted to comb Beirut for him, no matter what the risk, but his orders were explicit: his priority was ORANGE BLUE. Others would look for Wigoda. Others would close down the ORANGE network in Beirut.

He asked whether he should try to send a message to ORANGE BLUE warning him that Wigoda had been taken. Again he was told that 'others' would handle it. He felt sick.

Ruth was half an hour late but vividly happy. As she swept into the Amathus Restaurant she saw Walter at a corner table. A waiter was just putting a plate of hors d'oeuvres in front of him. He spotted her and pushed himself to his feet and, as she reached the table, said sternly:

'I thought I was going to suffer the final indignity of being stood up.'

She kissed his cheek and apologised and then scolded him for starting without her.

He watched her curiously as she sat down and waved away the menu.

'Can I be very extravagant, Walter?'

'Of course.'

'Then I would like caviar, lobster thermidor and champagne - Dom Pérignon.'

Walter's eyes widened, then he nodded to the hovering Maître d'. 'So what are we celebrating?'

'Oh, nothing special,' she replied nonchalantly. 'I'm just feeling happy. Perhaps because I'm lunching with you. I've missed you.'

Walter grunted sceptically. 'You've managed to hide it well. I haven't seen you for weeks.'

'I've been terribly busy. Now, you go ahead and eat. I don't want you keeling over from starvation. But first, is there any news of David?'

Walter popped an olive into his mouth and nodded. He was still puzzled. 'Yes. Things are going well. I hope he'll be finished and out in four or five days.'

She gave him a dazzling smile. 'You'll let me know immediately?'

'Of course.' He studied her again and then said abruptly, 'You're pregnant!'

Her look of surprise was comical. 'How on earth . . .?'

Walter was smiling complacently. 'It's obvious and logical. You're radiant and happy when you should be tense and nervous. Only one thing could cause that. I'm very happy for you and David.' He stood up ponderously, moved round the table and kissed her on both cheeks. She was suddenly demure and embarrassed.

Back in his chair Walter asked:

'When did you find out?'

She grinned. 'Just now. That's why I was late. The doctor had some emergency and I had to wait an hour.'

'So you are totally forgiven. Are you surprised?'

'In a way. We've been hoping for months.' She shook a finger at him. 'It's all your fault, sending him away at the wrong times.'

The waiter brought the caviar and the champagne and Walter solemnly proposed a toast to the forthcoming baby and stole some of the caviar.

'When will you marry?'

'As soon as possible. It takes a couple of weeks to get the licences.'

For a moment a look of sadness crossed her face.

'What is it?' he asked.

'Gideon. It will make him very unhappy.'

'He still writes?'

'Yes, on the first day of every month, and always the same.'

It was not the first time she had discussed the problem with Walter. Gideon Galili had not accepted the break-up of their engagement the way she had hoped. At first he had been stunned and then relentlessly determined. He had never broken down into self pity or despair but had calmly, almost icily, attempted to win her back. She had told him that she would not be marrying Munger for many months. She could not tell him why. He saw this as an opportunity. In the beginning, during her brief visit to Israel to break the news, he had debated with her logically, pointing out that one marriage to a combat photographer had never really worked. Why should a second be any different? She talked about love and he answered that his love for her was so strong, so all-encompassing that in the course of time it would attract, like a magnet, a reciprocal love from her. He was quietly positive about it and she could not shake that belief. She tried to get angry, telling him it was irretrievably finished. He was young and handsome and successful. A Major already at thirty-one. There would be other women - younger women. He would fall in love again. In her desperation to make him understand she had screamed at him, trying to shake his stoical attitude. Her anger had washed over him like waves over a rock. He was determined. He would not accept his loss of her.

A month later he visited Cyprus while Munger was away on assignment. For three days he stayed at the Forest Peak Hotel. They were the unhappiest days of Ruth's life. He was at the same time both determined and pathetic. His background and rigid military training together with success in his career had made him a man incapable of accepting failure and the loss of Ruth to another man represented the ultimate in failure. On the other hand his obsessive love for her reduced him at times to a maudlin boy. During the first two days they must have talked for over ten hours. Several times he was in tears; literally pleading with her. Seeing his torment and being unable to help him almost broke her heart. She reminded him of the old clichés: 'Time is a great healer' and 'Out of sight, out of mind'. Then she saw his determination. He insisted that he would never forget her, never give up hope, never accept the loss of her. He had planned to stay at Platres for two weeks, but after the second day she could not face him. She took her phone off the hook and locked the gates of the driveway. He spent the entire day standing outside the gates. He did not call out or do anything. He just stood there. She could see him from the bedroom window. A tall, ramrod-straight figure, his dark, handsome face a study in melancholy.

That night in desperation she phoned Walter for advice. After hearing the story he told her to go to sleep and not to worry. He would do something about it. She begged him not to make it hard for Gideon and he gently reassured her. He, above all, had an inkling of what the young Israeli was going through. After breaking the connection she felt a little easier but she still could not sleep throughout the night. At eight in the morning she rang the hotel and the receptionist told her that Gideon had checked out two hours before and taken a taxi to the airport. She immediately rang Walter and he told her that sometime during the night Gideon would have received a phone call from his squadron commander ordering his immediate return for a specific mission. Gideon would suspect nothing, and, with the current situation in the Lebanon, a mission would certainly be arranged. Even the squadron commander would not know the background of the sudden recall.

Ruth thanked him warmly and hung up praising God that Walter had such powerful connections. Half an hour later a taxi delivered a dozen long-stemmed red roses and a letter. It was from Gideon explaining his urgent recall and how he had tried in vain to phone her. Also that he would write to her every month until she was married.

The letters were always the same. They arrived during the first week of the month and they stated that he remained unattached and was waiting.

'Perhaps he thinks that something might happen to Munger,' Walter suggested. 'A lot of combat photographers get killed.'

She shrugged, 'It may be in his mind. I just get the impression he thinks that one day I'll come to my senses.'

'He's obsessed,' Walter remarked, it's not unusual - you know that from your experience in psychology.'

She nodded glumly. 'A few months ago I wouldn't have believed that love could run so deep.' She looked up and smiled. 'But with David I've found out that there is no limit.' She brightened up. 'After we're married, Gideon will accept the situation. It will break his obsession.'

The waiter arrived with the lobster and a two inch thick porterhouse steak for Walter. He had just savoured the first mouthful when the Maître d' approached and informed him that there was an urgent phone call from his office. He grunted in irritation, gave instructions for his steak to be kept hot arid told Ruth that it would only take a minute.

But it was twenty minutes and she had finished her lobster before he returned. As he sat down she looked at his face and went cold.

'It's trouble?'

'Yes.'

'David?'

'Not directly.'

'Tell me, Walter.'

Walter sighed and then waved away the plate that the waiter was attempting to put in front of him. That single action spelled out exactly, the gravity of his news.

'Misha Wigoda has been kidnapped in Beirut.' He had no hesitation in mentioning names. He knew that Munger told her everything. It worried him but he had to accept it.

'When?'

Walter glanced at his watch. 'Just under an hour ago.'

'Was it the PLO?'

Walter sighed. 'We're not sure, but we do know that SDECE is involved. Janine Lesage was on the scene.'

'Oh God.' Ruth slumped back in her chair. She now knew all about Janine Lesage and how she had been somehow involved in Duffs death. She had even met her once, many years before, at a party in Hong Kong. Munger had told her that one day he or Walter would even the score. Now Walter said with a heavy voice:

'I shouldn't have waited. I should have taken care of her. She's an evil, malignant woman.'

'You've warned David?'

He looked up. 'We're doing that now. We think he's between Basrah and Baghdad.' He saw the panic in her face.

'She'll make Wigoda talk, Walter. You know that. You have to find David and get him out!'

He leaned over and patted her arm reassuringly. 'Don't worry, we'll find him. There's time. Wigoda is a highly-trained agent. Yes, he'll talk, but it will take time. Maybe days, even weeks.'

She was crying now. She took a handkerchief from her bag and dabbed at her eyes.

'But you can't be sure. It could be only hours. God knows what they'll do to him. They're animals. David could walk into their arms. You've got to warn him.'

'Don't worry,' he repeated. 'We've contacted our people in Baghdad. As soon as David gets to his hotel he'll be told. He'll know what to do.'

'When, Walter? When will he get to his hotel?'

Walter shrugged. 'We can't be sure. We know that he checked out of the El Jamhorya Hotel in Basrah. He may have gone to the war front on his Way to Baghdad. We're trying to find out.'

She dried her eyes and composed herself. 'I'll go home now. You'll let me know if there's any news? Any news, Walter? Good or bad. I'll stay at home.'

'Of course.'

Outside he offered to have Spiro drive her to Platres. Her own car could be sent with another driver. She thanked him but refused. She was all right. He stood by his Mercedes and watched as she backed her Renault out. Before she drove away she called out: 'Thank you for the lunch. Please call me the instant you have news.'

'I will.'

With an expression of sadness and something else he watched the back of her car as it pulled away. She glanced in her rear view mirror and caught the expression.

It took her an hour to reach Platres. The first thing she did was to make herself a cup of coffee. She kept seeing in her mind the expression that she had glimpsed in Walter's face: sadness and something else. As she raised the cup to her lips it came to her and she froze at the implication: the something else was guilt. The cup dropped from her fingers and shattered on the tiles and she screamed as the hot coffee scalded her legs.

Walter was not going to warn him. He was hoping that Wigoda would hold out long enough for Munger to complete his assignment. Walter Blum had weighed in the balance his duty and the life of his friend, and he had come down on the side of duty.

She rushed to the phone and had already dialled the first digits of the Walen Trading number when the realisation struck her that it would be no good. Walter would lie to her. He had decided on his course. He would reassure her and make promises, but he would do nothing. Slowly she cradled the phone and forced herself to think rationally. She went back to the kitchen and swept up the broken cup and made herself more coffee while her mind ranged over the possibilities. She could try to get a phone call through to Baghdad; she knew he always stayed at the Sinbad Hotel. She could call the American Embassy in Nicosia. The CIA man who had told her of Duffs death was still there. Maybe he could help. Finally though she accepted that any such moves could be dangerous. Baghdad was seething with suspicion and deceit. By a precipitous move she herself could put Munger in peril.

There was only one way. She would warn him herself. She would fly to Baghdad and find him. The only question was the flight schedules. She knew there was no direct flight. He always went in through Amman. The visa was no problem: months ago, using her contacts in the US Embassy in Nicosia, she had obtained visas for as many Middle East countries as possible. She had always had the fear of Munger being wounded while working. If it happened she wanted no delays in getting to him. Of course, for some countries such as Iran and South Yemen, it was impossible, but she had valid, visas for the Lebanon, Jordan, Syria and Iraq.

She ran back to the phone and called the airport at Larnaca and, after a frustrating delay, discovered there was a flight at 7 pm to Beirut. From there she could connect with a Jordanian Airways flight JD 407 to Baghdad via Amman. It was a two-hour drive to Larnaca so she just had time.

She went to the bedroom and threw clothes into a bag small enough to carry onto the plane. Then she opened a bedside drawer and took out a small 8mm semi-automatic Beretta. Duff had given it to her years ago because of the time she had to spend alone. She knew how to use it. She also knew all about the security checks at airports but, living for years with combat photographers, she was aware of the methods they used to smuggle rolls of film.

In the kitchen she found a square tin box an inch deep and six inches across. She went to the study and fetched several sheets of carbon paper. She wrapped these around the Beretta, so disguising its shape. Then she put it into the tin box and filled up the corners with a cigarette lighter several lipsticks and some coins - all metal. The tin box was then packed at the bottom of her vanity case. She was confident that the airport X-ray checks would indicate no ominous shape.

At 4.30 pm she was in the Renault and racing down the mountain towards Larnaca.

Janine Lesage arrived at the house on the outskirts of Damour fifteen minutes after the van. It had taken her longer to negotiate the PLO and Leftist roadblocks. Jamil Mahmoud was waiting for her in the dusty courtyard. His men had formed a protective screen around the house. She climbed out of the Mercedes, wearing black slacks and a black short-sleeved blouse. She carried a small black bag. She smiled at him.

'Well done. It went like clockwork.'

He grinned back, 'I have done as you instructed. He is prepared. You want me to torture him now? I'm an expert.' His eyes gleamed, as he said it.

She shook her head. 'Maybe later; if it's necessary. If he's what I think he is, he could resist physical abuse for days. I don't have much time.'

'So?'

She held up the black bag. 'I'll use a truth serum. With luck it will unlock his tongue very quickly.'

Jamil nodded sagely. 'Ah, yes. I've heard about it-sodium penta . . . something.'

She smiled and shook her head. 'That's old-fashioned. Nowadays we use pure valium.'

'Valium!' He was astonished. 'My wife takes that to calm her down.' He grinned. 'She takes a lot of calming.'

'I can imagine. But this will be a far greater dose -20 milligrams straight into the vein.' She turned to her bodyguard-driver who was standing by the Mercedes.

'Wait here. Keep an eye on things.' To Jamil she said: 'Let's go.'

Misha Wigoda was lying naked on his back on a wooden table. His legs and arms were splayed and bound tightly, the cords already biting into his wrists and ankles and making them swell. There was nothing in the room except the table he lay on and a single unshaded light bulb hanging on a cord from the ceiling.

He turned his head at the sound of the door opening and saw Janine Lesage and Jamil Mahmoud behind her. He kept his face expressionless as she moved up to the table and put a black bag beside him. Jamil took up position near his feet and looked on with interest.

Janine first checked the cords binding him down and nodded in satisfaction. Then she reached down and lifted his penis and smiled. It was circumcised. She dug a long, red-painted finger nail into its exposed head and his back arched in agony but he made no sound. She smiled again and said in Arabic:

'Melim Jaheen. You are not an Arab. You are a Jew and you work for Mossad. I want some answers and you will provide them. You know that, don't you? One way or another you will provide them. Talk now and save yourself untold pain.' She looked into his eyes. Unblinking, they looked back.

She nodded as if to confirm a prognosis, then she opened her bag and took out a syringe and a rubber-capped phial containing a colourless liquid. Jamil watched in fascination as she pushed the needle through the rubber top and drew out the liquid. As Misha saw the syringe his head straightened. He looked up at the ceiling, his eyes narrowed in concentration. She knew he was remembering his training; trying to compartmentalise his mind. Isolate and hide those things about which he must not talk,

Quickly she leaned over and gripped his arm just below the elbow, pressing hard with her thumb to bring up the vein. He was plump and twice she missed the vein and curbed. She was hurrying too much. She took a deep breath and concentrated and, on the third attempt, the needle found its mark and she carefully depressed the plunger, watching the graduations on the syringe until she had pumped in exactly 20 milligrams. She then took a roll of tape from her bag and carefully bound the syringe to his arm so that the needle remained in the vein.

For the next few minutes she watched his eyes closely. She was waiting for him to enter a state of ptosis when involuntarily the eyelids would half closes and his mind would lose all its natural inhibitions. He would be awake and aware but his subconscious would be exposed and the shackles of his thinking, logical mind would be cast off.

It took just under five minutes. He kept his gaze fixed on a spot on the ceiling but suddenly the eyelids flickered and dropped. She reached forward and, with her thumb, lifted one of them. The eye was glazed, the pupil dilated. He was ready.

She asked him questions first in Arabic and then English. He remained silent and she knew that the tiny portion of his mind that was still lucid was fighting a battle with the mists that engulfed it. The first words he said were in English - a mumbled phrase that she had to bend over him to hear. She had asked what day it was and he replied: 'Never on Sunday.'

She laughed. All kinds of things could come out of the subconscious. Today was Tuesday.

For the next hour she moved through the maze. Twice she had to inject more valium to keep him in a state of ptosis. She was impatient but forced herself to go slowly. She only wanted one answer. As the minutes passed her frustration grew. He would ramble about his childhood, old school friends, his mother, a long-ago car accident, a woman. Whenever she skirted close to his work he became incoherent, the pressure in his brain contorting his face. He had been trained and conditioned for just such a moment and she knew that she could not extract any detailed information about his work. But she did not want to - she only wanted one answer: one name.

She leaned over him and whispered 'ORANGE BLUE. Who is ORANGE BLUE?'

His face immediately twisted and a surge of excitement passed through her. His reaction proved that he knew something. His subconscious was in conflict with his training. For five minutes she kept repeating 'ORANGE BLUE - who is he? What is he?'

At one point she paused to inject more valium. Her fingers were shaking and she had to be careful. Too much and he would sink into a coma-perhaps for hours.

'ORANGE BLUE,' she kept repeating. 'Who is he? What is he?'

She began to think she would lose and she became frantic, leaning over him, one hand on his chest, the other on his belly, her lips close to his ear. Then for the first time Jamil spoke. In awed tones he said: 'Look. Look at it!'

She turned her head and was looking at Misha Wigoda's erect penis. It was ludicrous and she started to laugh hysterically, but then she remembered and got control of herself.

'Yes. It can happen. Valium in that dosage takes away every inhibition. It's even a kind of aphrodisiac.'

'Who would believe it?' Jamil breathed. 'Such a tree from so small a root.'

She smiled and then something occurred to her. Maybe it was her touch that had caused it. Maybe that could be used to advantage.

She reached out and gripped the erection and moved her hand slowly up and down. The bound man moaned and writhed on the table. Jamil began to breathe deeply. She leaned close and licked Wigoda's face. He was moaning constantly now, and his tongue came out, searching for her, and his back arched pushing his erection up into her hand.

Abruptly she released him and stood back. 'ORANGE BLUE,' she said. 'Who is he? What is he?'

He was gasping in frustration and she played on it. Half a dozen times she toyed with his erection and then withdrew until the drugged man was in a frenzy. Then she said:

'Tell me. ORANGE BLUE. Tell me and I will give it to you.'

In the kaleidoscope of his brain something snapped. His voice came out as a croak.

'Munger.'

At first she didn't comprehend, but he was repeating it, pleading.

'Munger . . . ORANGE BLUE . . . Munger.'

She backed away from the table, her face at first showing shock but then becoming suffused with wild pleasure. It was the crowning moment of her life. Jamil was watching her curiously. He had not understood her or Wigoda but he had never seen a woman so thrilled by a mere word.

'What is it?' he asked. 'Did you get what you wanted?'

'Oh yes,' she breathed. 'More than I wanted. Much more.'

She was savouring the moment. Savouring the thought of Sami Asaf getting the news. Learning that the man he had helped get into Iraq and work there and travel the country was a Mossad spy. She was savouring the thought of Munger being arrested and taken away to God knows what. She hated him from the soles of her feet to the tips of her hair - the hair that he had so scorned.

She would not signal Baghdad. She wanted to be there, to see their faces. To laugh in their faces. She would catch the first plane to Baghdad. A few more hours would not matter; they would be hours of pleasurable anticipation. Jamil's voice broke into her reverie.

'Do I kill him now?' he asked eagerly. 'Are you finished with him?'

She looked at Wigoda. He was still writhing and straining against the cords, his erection huge in relation to the size of his body.

'No,' she said.' Leave us. I'll call you.'

Jamil moved towards the door, watching her curiously. He started to say something but she snarled at him to get out. He went into the corridor outside and banged the door behind him but he did not quite close it. It was slightly ajar-just enough for him to see into the room.

He watched as she reached up and pulled the pin from her hair and shook it free. She unbuttoned her black blouse and slacks and kicked off her shoes. His breath drew in at the sight of her long, naked body.

She climbed onto the table and straddled Wigoda. Her lips were drawn back from her teeth, her eyes were mere slits, the inside of her thighs already wet from anticipation. Inch by inch she impaled herself, grunting with pleasure.

Wigoda's eyes were wide open now, staring up at her as his hips bucked. It could not last long. Her buttocks pounded up and down to a rising crescendo. Suddenly as she reached her orgasm, she gripped his ears, pushed back his head and sank her teeth deep into his exposed neck - into the jugular.

'Colonel' Jamil Mahmoud turned away and vomited onto the stone floor.

CHAPTER EIGHTEEN

It is standard practice among Intelligence agencies to obtain passenger manifests from airports in sensitive areas. These manifests are then fed into computers so programmed that certain names produce a reaction.

It was natural that the ORANGE network had such an arrangement at Larnaca Airport. It was simplicity itself. Walen Trading was the major shareholder in an air freight forwarding company with offices in the terminal building. For a small monthly stipend a junior officer in the airport administration would drop off, within fifteen minutes, the passenger manifest of all arriving and departing flights. For departures he didn't even bring a typewritten list - merely the punched telex tape that had been used to send the manifest to the airport of destination. This was fed into the telex machine and appeared simultaneously on the telex machine at the ORANGE network headquarters in Limassol.

So it was that only twenty minutes after the departure of Cyprus Airways flight 502 for Beirut the ORANGE duty officer cast his eye down the passenger list and saw the name: Mrs R. Paget.

He knew that Walter would still be in his office next door so he punched a button on his intercom and passed on the information. It took Walter two minutes to discover that there was a Jordanian Airways flight to Baghdad from Beirut at 9.00 pm.

The flight time from Larnaca to Beirut is only twenty-five minutes but even as Ruth was nervously checking through Beirut immigration, Tamar Feder was receiving an urgent wireless message in his 'safe house'. He was to drop everything and rush out to the airport and, by whatever means possible, ensure that a Mrs Ruth Paget, in-coming passenger from Larnaca, did not get on the Jordanian Airways flight to Baghdad. A detailed description of her followed. Two minutes later he was in his car and cursing the rush hour traffic.

Ruth breathed more easily as the Customs man merely glanced at the array of lotion bottles and compacts on top of her vanity case and waved her through. Very often a beautiful woman would have problems at Customs: the officers like to keep them a long time and sometimes maul through their underwear.

She passed out into the main hall and headed for the departure area and the Jordanian Airways counter to pick up her ticket. Due to the civil war the once bustling airport had become more like a mausoleum. To the left a few passengers were at the check-in counter. She glanced up at the departure board. Her flight was the only one for the next two hours. She bought her ticket and the man behind the counter confirmed that the flight was on time. She was halfway to the check-in when she saw her, standing at the back of the short queue. She had been dominating her thoughts and she recognised her instantly - Janine Lesage.

Ruth turned away in confusion. She carried her bag and vanity case to a row of seats and sat down. She forced herself to think rationally. If Janine Lesage was going to Baghdad she must have already finished with Misha Wigoda. He must have talked. Ruth tried to work out why Janine Lesage herself was going to Baghdad. Surely she could signal the information? But Ruth had no idea what the communications might be like. Maybe she was taking the information herself? It would fit her character - and her ego. She would want to be on hand - she hated Munger.

With total certainty Ruth knew that Janine Lesage must not get on that plane. She started to formulate plans to stop her, but they were confused. She was in Beirut. She knew no one. She could not go to the police.

It quickly became obvious: she would have to stop Janine Lesage herself. But how? Shoot her? Where? It could be either here in the terminal building or on the plane. But that was dangerous. She might recognise her. It had been a long time but she would remember Duff Paget's wife.

Ruth watched as she reached the front of the queue and passed over her single suitcase and smiled winningly at the check-in clerk. Ruth had to make a decision. Time was running out. Then the French woman was turning away holding her boarding pass. She walked diagonally across the hall and through a door which had a black plastic sticker showing the outline of a woman - she had gone to the toilet.

Ruth knew it was her best chance. She picked up her vanity case and moved purposefully across the hall.

Through the door was a long room. Six cubicles lined one side and five wash basins and a wide mirror the other. Janine Lesage was standing at the middle basin. Her handbag was open and she was carefully making up her face. She glanced sideways as Ruth came through the door and then went back to applying her lipstick.

Ruth put her vanity case beside a basin and fumbled with the lock. It was the combination type and for one heart-stopping moment she forgot the numbers. She took a deep breath to calm herself and then remembered and spun the wheels. She was icily determined now. She lifted the top tray out of the case and rummaged through to the bottom. She eased open the tin, lifted out the Beretta, unwrapped it from the carbon paper and slipped off the safety catch. The gun felt good in her hand, which was no longer shaking. She was standing only four feet from her target and she would not miss. She glanced sideways at the mirror. Janine Lesage was now working on her eyebrows, leaning over close to the mirror. Ruth picked her spot, just under the left breast. She started to lift the gun and, at that moment, a toilet flushed loudly behind her. Startled, she plunged the gun back into the case. Her hand was shaking again. A cubicle door opened and an old Arab woman came out. She shuffled to the basin between the two Europeans, reached for the soap and began to wash her bony hands. Ruth slowly regained her composure and determination. It was a race now between the old woman's ablutions and Janine Lesage's vanity.

At first Ruth thought she would have to do it in front of the old woman. Her target had finished her eyebrows and was patting face powder onto her checks. Perversely Ruth thought 'You're getting old, you bitch. The lines are showing.' Then she saw the woman's eyes watching her in the mirror, curiously, and she began rummaging about in her case, keeping her face averted.

At last the old Arab was rinsing her hands and looking around for a towel, not seeing one, and mumbling under her breath. Then she was heading for the door, shaking water onto the floor. The door closed and once again Ruth had the gun in her hand, but now Janine Lesage was staring at her with recognition in her eyes.

'You're ... '

The gun came clear as Ruth turned to face her.

'Yes, you bitch, I'm Ruth Paget.'

Maybe having to spit out the words slowed her, maybe it was just inexperience. In one reflexive, feline movement Janine Lesage dived and her right hand chopped down. The gun was only half raised when it was slammed out of Ruth's fingers. It bounded on the tiled-floor and skidded under the door of a cubicle.

Janine's shoulder crashed into Ruth and both women tumbled to the floor, scrabbling to get a grip on each other. It should have been an uneven fight: Janine Lesage had been trained in such matters, but Ruth had greater motivation and a great rage. The inhuman strength of a mother protecting the life inside her. As they wrestled across the slippery floor she had mental flashes of Duff, whom this woman had killed; of Munger, whom she wanted to kill; and, above all, the embryonic foetus forming in her belly. Janine Lesage fought with strength and skill. Ruth fought with ferocity.

It was the distilled ferocity of a wildcat fighting for her young and for her mate. She was hissing through her teeth as she fought to get her hands round the other woman's neck. Janine broke the hold easily, aimed a kick with her heel at Ruth's knee and at the same time stabbed the spread fingers of her right hand at Ruth's eyes. The fingers missed as Ruth jerked her head back but the heel connected. As Ruth grunted in pain Janine rolled away trying to give herself room to get to her feet. She almost made it, but Ruth twisted after her, managed to clutch an ankle and brought her tumbling down. She tried to cushion the fall with her left hand and fell heavily onto it. There was a crack of wrist bone and Janine squealed in pain and then Ruth was on her again. She fought without form or plan, only instinct; smashing her fists into Janine's face and body unaware of the pain in her knee or her knuckles as they connected with Janine's teeth and angular bones. Janine scrabbled back and struck out wildly with her feet, catching Ruth low in the belly. It slowed her down and Janine was able to scuttle into a corner and with her good hand push herself to a crouch. Ruth was on her knees gasping in pain, her hands clutching her belly. They looked at each other. Janine's left arm hung limply. Her face was battered, both lips split and bleeding and her nose broken and bent. Her blouse had been ripped open and her breasts were red and scratched. In her eyes was a mixture of rage and fear. In Ruth's eyes there was only rage. Slowly she rose to her feet, took her hands from her belly and started to move forward. As her weight came onto her left leg she winced with pain and almost collapsed. A look of triumph came into Janine's narrowed eyes: her adversary was at least partially crippled. She looked beyond Ruth to the door of the toilet under which the gun had slid, then with her right hand she reached up and pulled out the long silver pin holding up her hair. As the blonde tresses tumbled to her shoulders, she held the pin out pointing it at Ruth. Through her bloody lips she said:

'You're going to die. Just like your husband died and just like that bastard Munger is going to die.'

Hatred flowed between them like strands of poison. Keeping her weight on her right leg, Ruth edged forward. Janine waited with her back to the corner, the pin held like a dagger. Then abruptly she sprang forward, lunging with the pin at Ruth's face - at her left eye.

It almost found its mark but Ruth spun away and the pin went deep into her upper cheek under the bone. She screamed and jerked her head tearing the pin from Janine's fingers and spinning it tinkling into a wash basin. But it had served its purpose and Janine was past her and rushing for the toilet door and the gun. Only one thing saved Ruth's life. In her frenzied rush Janine wasted a precious second trying to pull open a door that she should have pushed. That, and the position of the gun, gave Ruth vital time. As Janine knelt over scrabbling behind the toilet bowl for it with her one good hand, Ruth dropped on her back with all her weight. Janine's forehead smashed against the cistern and she momentarily blacked out. In that moment Ruth grabbed a handful of the yard-long hair and wound it twice round Janine's neck. With her left hand she held the Frenchwoman's head hard down into the bowl. Slowly and with savage strength she began to pull and tighten the thick coils around the long elegant neck. The toilet bowl amplified the sounds of choking.

Tamar Feder parked right in front of the terminal entrance, leapt out of his car and bounded up the steps. He went straight to the check-in counter and asked if Mrs Ruth Paget had checked in.

The clerk consulted his list and shook his head. She would have to hurry, he remarked, or she would miss her flight. Tamar's gaze swept the almost empty hall. There was no one who answered the description of a tall, beautiful brunette. He walked slowly down the hail, beginning to think that the people in ORANGE headquarters were losing their sanity. He still hadn't decided how he could stop the woman boarding the flight. His options ranged from gentle persuasion to slugging her over the head. He stopped and looked around again and then, twenty yards away, the door of the women's toilet opened and she staggered out, holding a blood-stained handkerchief to her face, her hair and clothes dishevelled. He was next to her in a moment, his body shielding her from view.

'I'm from the ORANGE network. What happened?'

She looked at him uncomprehendingly, eyes glazed. Gently he held her by the shoulders and said:

'Mrs Paget, I'm Tamar Feder from the ORANGE network.'

Her eyes cleared and she muttered: 'Janine Lessage.'

'Where?' He shook her. He couldn't help himself. 'Where? Mrs Paget?'

She pointed with her thumb to the toilet.

'Sit over there.' He gestured at a row of seats and as soon as she started moving he slipped his hand under his jacket to the butt of his gun and pushed through the door.

When he came out thirty seconds later she was standing by the chairs. A few people were looking at her curiously, at the blood on her white blouse and handkerchief. He moved casually but fast, putting his left arm around her, his right hand still under his jacket. As they reached the entrance the loudspeaker called her name. She should check in immediately.

She started to mutter something about having to get to Baghdad but his arm was firm about her. As he propelled her down the steps to the car he said:

'You're going back to Cyprus.'

CHAPTER NINETEEN

'Why the hell do you want to go up there?'

'My nose tells me something is going to happen,' Munger replied.

Sami Asaf smiled, but not in disbelief. Munger's nose had a reputation for smelling a conflict before it happened.

They were sitting in a corner of the bar of the Sinbad Hotel. Sami was drinking orange juice and Munger his usual vodka. Most of the other occupants of the room were western businessmen relaxing after a hard day negotiating with Iraqi Government officials. Munger recognised one of them but they did not acknowledge each other. He was a Belgian arms dealer called Pierre Renard and only a year ago had acted as a broker between Iran and Israel in the arms transactions that Munger had initiated. He had done a good, discreet job and Munger liked him and had subsequently recommended him to Walter Blum. It was an indication of the amoral nature of the arms business that he was now in Baghdad selling to the Iraqis. There is no better formula for profit than supplying both sides in a protracted war. He also had another role: he was now a courier for the ORANGE network and that too was profitable. Munger had not expected to see him in Baghdad. Obviously Walter was stacking the deck.

'I'd better have a word with the Army Command,' Sami said with a grin. 'The northern front has been quiet for months - hardly a skirmish; but if you're going up there with your camera maybe that's going to change. How long will you be there?'

'A few days. Maybe a week. I'd like to leave in the morning.'

'No problem,' Sami said. 'I'll make a phone call tonight. You can pick up your papers at the Ministry first thing in the morning. Nassir is going with you?'

'Of course. You know he has to. I don't mind – he's a good man.'

Sami leaned forward and said very sternly, 'That's not true and you know it. I know exactly why you want Nassir.'

Munger felt a moment of panic but then Sami was smiling.

'He's lazy and useless. You like him because he doesn't hang around your neck like some of the others would.'

Munger grinned and quickly changed the subject. 'When are you off to Beirut again?'

Sami's face turned serious. 'Not for a while. You heard about Janine Lesage?'

'No. I only got in from Basrah an hour ago. What happened?'

'She's dead.'

'Oh?'

Sami took a sip of his orange juice. He looked very sombre. 'Yes. She was killed in the women's toilet at Beirut airport yesterday.'

'She had a lot of enemies, Sami, and apart from you, few friends.'

'Yes. It was very brutal. They strangled her to death with her own hair.'

There was a long silence, then Munger said: 'I told her she needed a haircut.'

Walter Blum was camping out in his office. That is to say, his secretary had been evicted and her office turned into a temporary but very comfortable bedroom. The next few days would see the culmination of years of work and he was determined that nothing should go wrong at the eleventh hour. He was also receiving constant signals from General Hofti. A Cabinet meeting would take place in three days and a final decision had to be taken. The election campaign was turning into one of the most bitter in the history of Israel: Shimom Peres, Leader of the Opposition, had been briefed on the possibility of an air strike on the Tammuz I reactor and he was firmly against it. He suspected that Begin's motives for such a raid would be largely political. So, to obtain the absolute proof of Iraq's illegal intentions had become even more critical.

But as Walter sat in his office late at night he did not consider those factors. His thoughts were on Ruth Paget. He had received a signal earlier in the evening that Tamar Feder was going to smuggle her out of the Lebanon from the Christian held port of Jounieh sometime during the night. Within twenty-four hours she would be in Limassol. Walter dreaded the coming meeting. At best she would be coldly disdainful; at worst, violent. He shook his head with awe at the thoughts of her killing Janine Lesage and the method of it. What a woman. What incredible effects love could have. She had almost certainly saved Munger's life. If Janine Lesage had sent a message before her death he would have been arrested already, but only an hour ago Walter had received word that he had arrived at the Sinbad Hotel in Baghdad and had already met with Sami Asaf.

Immediately after Misha Wigoda's kidnapping Walter had drafted more agents into Baghdad. They were little more than 'fly catchers' and they would not be able to stay long without arousing suspicion, but for the next few days he would have a twenty-four hour cover watch on the Sinbad Hotel and the various 'mail drops' near it. A wireless link had been established with one of the Baghdad 'safe houses' so Walter would receive up to the minute reports.

As he reviewed the overall situation Walter, in spite of his mounting tension, felt a touch of complacency. His agent was in place and about to collect the proof that was needed. The Mukhabarat had no suspicion of him and in fact, through the good offices of Sami Asaf, were even helping. Meanwhile in Israel the Air Force's top squadron was prepared and waiting to destroy the reactor.

Everything looked good to Walter, except for his impending meeting with Ruth.

To Munger it looked like an old airfield and Nassir confirmed it.

'The British built it in the nineteen-twenties. It was during the time they tried to police rebellious areas with their new Air Force - dropping bombs on the peasants. It worked in the flat desert areas but not up here. There was too much cover.'

Munger studied it through powerful binoculars. It was late afternoon and the light was good. He was sitting in the car parked beside the road to Kalar on a high knoll above the barbed-wire perimeter about two miles away. To the east the mountains rose steeply towards the Iranian border.

The bonnet of the car had been raised and Nassir was standing beside it with a dirty rag in his hand. Anyone passing would assume that the car had overheated - a common event on the mountain roads in the summer.

Through his binoculars Munger could just make out the rectangular shape of the old runway. It had long since become overgrown but, from his raised view, he could see the smudged outline. It was obvious why the airfield had ceased to function as such: it was situated along a ridge of the foothills and its length was restricted by the topography. Only light, propeller-driven aircraft could ever have used it. To one side of the old runway was a row of Nissen huts; some were derelict and some had been repaired. As he watched, three men in uniform came out of one and walked towards a larger brick building further down the runway. He surmised that it would be the old officers' mess and might be serving a similar purpose today. On the other side of the runway was the new installation: two adjoining buildings forming an elongated 'T'. The upright was long, low and windowless with floor-to-ceiling sliding doors in the middle. The cross piece was two-storied and had many windows. Munger assumed that it was the administration block. These two buildings were circled and cut off from the rest of the installation by a heavy, wire-mesh fence. On top of it he could just make out the rows of distinctive white supports which carried another wire. He had seen such fences before. It was electrified. There was only one gate with a guardhouse beside it and several soldiers holding what looked to be sub-machine guns. That fence represented the second and innermost barrier for, around the entire installation, there were thick coils of barbed wire. It was new; Munger could see the lowering sun glinting on it. At a distance of about fifty yards inside this barrier a single wire ran along the tops of foot-high stakes, and facing outwards were a series of poles holding the skull and crossbones signs denoting a mine field. There was only one route through it from the outer gate, which also had a guardhouse and armed sentries.

'How long will you be?' Nassir called nervously.

'A few minutes. Keep quiet. Fiddle with the bloody engine.'

Slowly Munger traversed the binoculars and measured approximate distances. From beyond the outer fence he would not be able to guarantee clearly defined photographs, even using his most powerful telephoto lens. Also the Nissen huts would obstruct his view of the sliding doors where the yellowcake would surely be unloaded.

However, from the Nissen huts and using a 500mm mirror lens he would be able to get excellent detail, even through the mesh fence. The problem was to get to the Nissen huts. He did not relish the thought of tiptoeing through a minefield in broad daylight, let alone darkness.

He saw a score or so of men emerging from the administration block. Presumably work was over for the day. He watched as they walked through the gate and then across the old airstrip towards the Nissen huts. Some of them stopped and began to kick a football about. He could see where piles of stones had been laid to represent goal posts. He watched them for a while but then Nassir started whining again and he moved his gaze back to the minefield. It was going to be a real problem.

For the next few minutes he wrestled with it. He knew the gates would be guarded day and night. He had already seen one car go through and the soldiers had searched it thoroughly, even running a wheeled mirror under the chassis. He was beginning to feel desperate when a movement caught his eye. One of the footballers had shot for goal and sliced the ball wildly. It bounced across the sun-baked ground, rolled under the single strand of wire and came to rest in the middle of the minefield. Munger was astonished to see one of the players casually hurdle the wire run across the minefield and retrieve it. He started to laugh. The skull and crossbones signs were a decoy - like a scarecrow to frighten away birds. The authorities were saving money by digging a facade. The minefield was only in the mind.

He swung the binoculars and studied the road which ran outside the barbed wire. There were deep, overgrown storm culverts along both sides. They would give him good cover. He swept his field of vision back to the Nissen huts. Just behind them was a narrow ruined building, the jagged walls jutting up three or four feet. He guessed that fifty years ago it had housed a row of latrines. It too would provide good cover.

He put down the binoculars, picked up a notebook and pencil and drew a rough plan of the installation, marking off the distances. Nassir's face showed great relief when he finally told him to close the bonnet.

It was short-lived relief. As they drove back towards Kifri Munger explained what Nassir had to do. First he was to find and purchase a pair of wire cutters, then, in a few hours, drive Munger back to a precise point on the road. He would drive slowly and, coming into a bend, Munger would tumble out so that the car would not be seen to stop.

The yellowcake shipment was due to arrive in the early afternoon of the next day. One hour after sunset Nassir was to drive back to the same spot and pick him up.

Nassir was very unhappy. He did not want to do it but Munger pointed out the facts of life: he was already involved; there was great profit in it. Besides, if Munger were caught he would be tortured and eventually would confess about Nassir's involvement. He really had no choice. Nassir grumbled all the way to Kifri, but it was true. He had no choice.

It went well. At 10 o'clock that night there was little traffic on the road. Munger sat in the passenger seat dressed all in black, including a skull cap and scarf. He carried a canvas bag which held his camera and lenses, the wire cutters, khaki camouflage jacket and trousers, A thermos flask full of hot coffee and another of iced water, a packet of chicken sandwiches, a tube of dexedrine tablets and a can of mosquito repellent. He carried no weapons for, if he was spotted, he would have needed a Panzer division to get him out.

Nassir was quivering with fear but he managed to keep the car at around ten miles an hour as they approached the bend.

'Your only chance,' Munger told him, 'is to collect me tomorrow night. Once I'm out of Baghdad you can relax.'

'I would never have done it,' Nassir moaned. 'Not if I'd known.'

'Think of the money,' Munger said, and opened the car door and, clutching the bag, rolled out.

He did not even lose his footing. For a few paces his momentum carried him down the road after the car, then he slowed and veered away to the side and dropped into the culvert. He watched the red tail-lights disappear round the bend and, in spite of his contempt for Nassir, felt a moment of loneliness.

There was a sliver of moon, just enough to delineate form a few yards ahead. For ten minutes he waited and listened. There were lights in the mess building and he could hear the faint sound of music. He was about to approach the barbed wire when he heard the low-geared noise of engines on the road. He ducked and stayed down for five minutes while a military convoy passed by a few yards away. He had to control a moment of hysterical amusement: had Sami Asaf really taken him seriously? Were the High Command reinforcing the northern front?

Then it was quiet again and Munger pulled himself out of the culvert, wound the black scarf around his lower face and carefully approached the barbed wire.

It took him an hour to cut his way through because he had to arranged the strands behind him so that his passage could not be casually detected in daylight. As he crept across the dummy minefield he still felt trepidation. They might after all have planted a couple of mines. But he reached the single strand of wire and carefully stepped over and then, keeping his body low and using the lights of the mess building as a reference point, scuttled across the open space to the ruined latrines. He found a dark corner where the outer walls rose almost five feet and an inner wall six feet away hid him from the opposite side. First he stripped off his black clothing and sprayed his naked body with the mosquito repellent, then he put on the camouflage clothing, poured coffee into the cover of the thermos flask and washed down a Dexedrine tablet. Then, using his black clothes as a cushion, he wedged himself into the corner.

It would be a long night but, although she was far away, he had Ruth to keep him company. She was in his mind, his heart and his soul and she kept him warm as the night turned cold. He imagined her up in Platres waiting for him. She would be in bed by now. She told him she always slept early when he was away. He pictured her black hair on the white pillow, her knees pulled up into her soft belly, her hands and arms clutching a pillow to her breast. It was something she always did when he was away. She called that pillow her surrogate Munger. He had joked that at least it never snored and she had smiled ruefully and replied that it did nothing else either.

So he sat and sipped his coffee and waited out the night, with Ruth in his mind.

Ruth's hair was not spread over a white pillow, neither was she clutching one to her bosom. She was sitting on the other side of Walter Blum's desk, listening as he talked of his duty and his dilemma. She was very composed and he was amazed at it. Apart from a plaster on her cheek and scratch marks on her neck she could have just returned from a weekend excursion. Only when he looked into her eyes did he see the strain.

He talked about Israel and the future, about Israel and the past. About the sacrifices that had been made, and must be made in the future. He candidly admitted that he had been prepared to sacrifice Munger for that future. She might not believe him but he was prepared to make the same sacrifice himself.

She did believe him and told him so, but it was now irrelevant. She had killed for her man and the only thing she cared about was to get him back. She had a baby forming in her belly and she wanted it to have a live father.

He brought her up to date. Munger had gone north to get his snaps. It was only a matter of a day or two and he would be out. Walter was in constant communication with Baghdad and he would know as soon as the mission was complete. He would call her in Platres immediately.

She shook her head. She would stay in Limassol. When her man was out, she would go to Larnaca immediately to meet him. Walter was all solicitous understanding. He would book her a suite in the Amathus Hotel.

Shaking her head she stood up, limped to the door of the secretary's office, opened it and surveyed Waiter's temporary and sumptuous sleeping arrangements.

'I'll sleep in there,' she said and then gestured at the narrow settee next to his desk. 'You can sleep there.'

Walter's mouth dropped open.

'Or go to the Amathus,' she said, with a hint of a smile.

He shrugged in acceptance. 'Try to get a good night's rest. I'm sure he'll be all right.'

'You're not sure, Walter. You're just hoping. So am I. Just do one thing for me. Don't quote from Hamlet - or I'll strangle you,' She went through the door and closed it behind her.

The night had been cold but within two hours of sunrise Munger was hot. He squatted on his haunches and bounced up and down, exercising his cramped leg muscles. Then he opened the other thermos flask and drank a little cold water. He repeated that action every hour on the hour. Just a few sips to wet his mouth and throat. Not once did he look over the low wall. He knew the sound of a Volvo F12 truck and he was not going to risk being randomly spotted by peering over the wall until he had to. He heard several other vehicles during the morning - in fact a surprising amount. Obviously the arrival of the yellowcake was to be a red-letter day at this establishment. Several times he checked the Nikon and the long, fat, telephoto lens until finally he scolded himself. He was acting like a novice. If he kept it up he'd forget to take off the lens cover.

It was just after 2 o'clock when he heard them: a deep-throated rumble from five, 300 horsepower engines. He picked up the camera and, with an inward chuckle, unsnapped the lens cover.

Very slowly he raised his head and did a quick three hundred and sixty degree scan. Then he felt sick.

The five trucks were moving through the inner gate, preceded and followed by army jeeps. However, sitting with their backs to the wall of a Nissen hut fifty yards away, were three soldiers playing cards and smoking cigarettes. It was the same hut that he hoped to hide behind while he took his snaps. He dropped back on his haunches and cursed every soldier who had ever skived off. The question was: how long they would stay there? He could not leave his ruin without them spotting him. Surely to God, with such a shipment arriving, they would be going about their duties?

He heard distant shouts of command and the hissing of hydraulic brakes being applied, then the metallic grating as the sliding doors were rolled back. He risked another look over the wall. Hallelujah! The three soldiers were getting up and brushing the dust from their backsides and picking up their sub-machine guns. But hell! One of them was walking towards him. Munger ducked down. Had he been seen?

He waited with nerves on edge: heard the scuff of a shoe, then the footfalls getting closer. He held his breath, willing his limbs to stay inert. The soldier was very close. There was a rattle of a stone kicked aside, a short grunting cough - then silence, apart from the sound of breathing.

In those seconds Munger was aware of how much noise a human body generates: the thumping of his heart, even the beating of his pulse, the squelch as he gulped. Then there came another noise - a hissing and splashing. Moments later he smelt it. The bastard was taking a piss! He had a wild urge to laugh. Remembered as a child how he used to try to piss in as high an arc as possible. It had been a game at school. He had once pissed right through a latrine window six feet above the toilet. If this soldier tried it Munger would get wet. He heard the man sigh in relief and the few last splashing squirts against the bricks behind him. Then the footsteps moved away.

Munger waited another minute and then took another peek over the wall. His way was clear. The trucks were obscured by the Nissen huts but there was a lot of noise from that direction: shouting voices, the clanging of metal against metal.

He picked up his camera, took a look behind him and then put his right hand on top of the wall and vaulted over it. He ran in a crouch to the Nissen hut, edged to the end of it and very slowly peered around. The five Volvos were lined up with their rears to the open doors. He was looking from an angle of about sixty degrees and could see two fork-lift trucks as they manoeuvred to take off the cargo. There were dozens of soldiers: some inside the trucks, manhandling the drums, others just standing around. There were also several officers standing in a group watching. Also in the group were two men in white coats - the sort of coats worn by doctors and scientists. As the first two drums were lifted down by the prongs of the fork-lift these two men moved forward to inspect them.

Munger raised his camera, through the view-finder he could see the black lettering on the yellow drums and the bright red seals.

The two men in white coats leaned over and inspected the seals. They were in a jovial mood; he could clearly see their smiles. One of them patted the drum affectionately as Munger took his snap.

It was the only one he got. He heard a sound to his left and his head jerked round. Two men were coming out of the mess building a hundred yards away. He was in full view.

Only his camouflage saved him. He had the sense not to move. He was a chameleon, matching colour to habitat. He was in view for less than ten seconds before they passed in front of the Nissen hut. During that minute Munger came to understand the impact of the theory of relativity - it had felt like an hour. He cursed himself. He had got his angles wrong. By his estimation he should have been out of sight of the mess building. He had also been lucky, but he now had to make a decision. He was exposed. Others might come out at any moment. He only had one snap. Was it enough? It had to be. He was a professional - the image was on the film.

He turned and scuttled back to the ruin and dived over the wall, rolling onto his back and cushioning the camera to his belly.

There was only one more anxious moment that day: sitting in the culvert wondering whether Ahmed Nassir would pick him up. Wondering whether his cowardice would finally overcome his avarice.

A dozen times he checked his watch and then he heard the car. It came slowly around the bend with the passenger door open. He leapt out of the culvert and ran along beside it for a few yards and then jumped in, bumping into Nassir's shoulder and causing him to steer dangerously across the road. He laughed at Nassir's squeal of panic and pulled the door closed behind him.

'It's done?' Nassir asked as he stepped on the accelerator.

'It's done,' Munger answered.

'It's all finished?'

'Yes, it's all finished.'

Nassir grinned with relief. 'So I get the other diamonds?'

'Yes,' Munger said as he twisted and struggled to pull off the camouflaged shirt. 'First you drive to Baghdad - to the Sinbad. Then I do an hour's work and then you get the diamonds.'

'And you leave Baghdad . . . forever.'

'For sure.' Munger looked at his watch. 'We won't get to Baghdad before 9 o'clock, so I'll miss the last flight. I'll catch the Jordanian Airways in the morning. What you do, my friend, is drop me at the hotel and then come back an hour later and pick up your diamonds. And listen - don't be stupid. Don't start living in a lavish style. That's how crooks get caught.'

'I'm not a crook, Mr Munger,' Nassir said. 'I've stolen nothing; just rendered a service. If you want to know, I don't support this regime. I go along with it because I have to. Oh, you can say I commit treason but then so do you. An Englishman working for the CIA - for the Americans. It's no different.'

'You're right,' Munger said placatingly. 'Now please watch the road. Let's get to Baghdad in one piece.'

Nassir concentrated and drove well and they arrived outside the Sinbad Hotel just before 9 o'clock. Munger reached behind to the back seat for his bag, opened the door and said:

'Come up to my room at 10 o'clock then.'

'Why not now?'

Munger shook his head. 'I have something to do first.' He could not explain that first he had to develop the negative and make sure that the snap was clear. If not, dread the thought, he would have to go back and try again and he would need Nassir. He could see the struggle on the Arab's face, and the suspicion.

'Relax, Ahmed. I won't leave the room. Come up at 10 o'clock. Go and see your wife. Show her a good husband - a rich husband.'

Nassir smiled sheepishly. He knew there were no flights out till the morning.

'10 o'clock then,' he said.

Munger slapped him on the shoulder and watched him drive away. Then he went into the lobby, picked up his key from reception and checked for messages. There were none. He turned and walked across to the lifts and saw Pierre Renard about to enter one. He quickened his pace and Renard politely held back the door and ushered him in. As the lift started to move Munger asked very quietly:

'Room number?'

'302.'

Those were the only words. At the third floor Renard walked out without a backward glance and Munger went on to the fifth floor and his own room.

Two minutes later he was in the bathroom developing the negative. Half an hour later two contact prints were hanging up to dry. He studied one through a magnifying glass. It was perfect; the delineation crystal clear. He could read the black numbers and letters on the yellow drums. One of the white-coated men was in the act of patting a drum as though it were a pet poodle. The other was beaming at his colleague. Munger wondered who they were. Both were middle-aged and wore spectacles. They looked Arabic and they looked like scientists. Then again, they looked like doctors - it was the white coats.

As soon as the prints were dry Munger wrapped one in cellophane together with the negative and slid it into a slit in the bottom of his shaving bag. By the next afternoon it would be on Walter Blum's desk and his job would be over. However, he was going to give himself insurance. He had planned to put the other print in one of the 'mail drops' but decided that Pierre Renard was a safer bet. He put the print into an envelope and wrote on the front:

'ORANGE ONE. FASTEST'

He took the stairs instead of the lift, located 302 and slipped the envelope under the door.

Back in his room he stripped off his shirt, unbuckled the money belt and extracted a folded square of paper containing Ahmed Nassir's diamond bonus. Then he dropped the money belt into a drawer, poured himself a large vodka and soda and looked at his watch. It was 9.40.

He was desperately tired and his eyes and head ached from the Dexedrine tablets he had taken to stay awake the night before. He went to the phone and rang Jordanian Airways and booked a seat out on the 8 o'clock flight. Then he rang reception and booked an alarm call for 6 o'clock. The only thing left now was to pay off Nassir. Again he looked at his watch: 9.50.

The tap on the door came five minutes later and Munger smiled. Nassir was impatient. He picked up the square of paper and went over to the door. He would get it over with quickly. No drinks, no celebration.

He opened the door with a smile and found himself looking at Sami Asaf. On each side of him were two men holding sub-machine guns. Behind them were four other men.

Sami's face was bleak. 'Ahmed Nassir sends his regrets,' he said. 'He was unavoidably detained.' His gaze moved to the square of paper and he reached put and took it from Munger's nerveless fingers. Then he prodded him in the chest, pushing him back into the room.

With eight people in it there was not much space. Sami told Munger to sit on the bed and he told the two gunmen to shoot him in - the legs if he moved. Then he went to the bathroom door, looked inside and sniffed. Even from the bed Munger could smell the developing chemicals. As he turned another man came into the room and reported that according to the doorman Munger had not left the hotel after his arrival at 9 o'clock.

'So they are here,' Sami said, and gave instructions to the four men and the new arrival. They were looking for either negatives or prints, or both.

They were experts and they were methodical. They literally shredded everything in the room and the bathroom. While they worked Sami pulled up a chair opposite Munger and went through the contents of the money belt, placing the cash and the diamonds on the bed beside Munger. The two gunmen found it difficult to keep their eyes away from the fortune.

'You were unlucky,' Sami said conversationally. 'This afternoon a Lebanese was arrested at the airport just as he was about to leave. Our people had been watching him for months on suspicion that he was a courier for illegal currency dealers. He made frequent visits to Baghdad. Well, we were right. A great deal of money was found on him and also two diamonds.' He gestured at the glittering pile next to Munger. 'Exactly like those. After strenuous questioning the courier admitted that he had got them from a certain dealer in Al Azamiya, and that dealer admitted, again after strenuous questioning, that he had bought them two days ago from a certain Ahmed Nassir. That was when I was called in - just an hour ago. We went straight to his house. As you well know, he's a coward. It only took half an hour and he was talking - and what a story, the famous photographer David Munger is a CIA spy!' He laughed unpleasantly.

'There's a good precedent for that. Remember Duff Paget. He was a CIA spy. Incidentally, I saw a report this afternoon from the Beirut police about the death of Janine Lesage. Apparently a prime suspect is Paget's widow.'

For the first time he saw an expression in Munger's eyes and he laughed again.

'Yes, the beautiful Ruth Paget. She was at the scene. In fact she was booked on the same flight to Baghdad. Neither of them caught the plane. Ruth Paget was seen being helped out of the airport by a man. She was bleeding.'

Munger was looking at him intently. He started to say something but was interrupted by an exclamation from one of the men in the bathroom. He came out holding the shaving bag in one hand and the little square of cellophane in the other.

Sami unwrapped the negative and print, took them directly under the light and studied them. He nodded in satisfaction.

'Only one? That's all you took?'

Munger shrugged and said nothing.

'You will talk, Munger, believe me. I'm personally going to conduct the interrogation. I'm going to enjoy it. I don't like people who betray me. I helped you and you made a fool of me.' He was standing next to Munger, towering over him, his eyes narrowed in anger. Munger looked up and said:

'It wasn't difficult.'

Sami's arm swung and his fist caught Munger full in the face, slamming him onto his back on the bed. He came up in an instant, his hands reaching for Sami's throat. But the two barrels of the sub-machine guns came up to cover him as Sami jumped back and laughed.

'That's just the beginning, Munger. You're going to Kasr al Nihaya . . . Being a spy, you will have heard about it. They call it "the Palace of the end".'

CHAPTER TWENTY

The Cabinet meeting took place during the morning of June 5th and was predictably stormy. Major-General David Ivri, Commander of the Israeli Air Force, waited in an anteroom. If the decision was taken to strike, the raid would take place on the 7th, which was a Sunday, and when hopefully most of the French scientists and technicians would be off the site.

The Cabinet had divided itself and for half an hour the hawks and the doves had been shouting at each other. By their natures the hawks were a little louder.

Menachem Begin let them rant on. In a few minutes he would call the meeting to order and the decision would have to be taken and the consequences faced. There were no doubts in Begin's mind: the reactor bad to be bombed. But as he listened to the hubbub around him he knew that the Country would be just as divided as his Cabinet. If anything, the raid would help the coalition's chances at the coming election but for the rest of his life he would be accused of acting for political reasons. He sighed and pounded the table with his hand.

The noise had just died down when an aide opened the door, crossed to Begin and gave him a note. They all saw his eyes light up as he read it.

'General Hofti is outside,' he said. 'It seems that he has something interesting to show us.' To the aide he said 'Ask him to come in.'

The aide bent down and whispered something in his ear and Begin nodded and said 'Yes, him too.'

A moment later General Hofti and Walter Blum entered the room. Hofti was holding a large manila envelope. Begin was immediately struck by how much Walter Blum appeared, to have aged in the intervening days since he had first met him. His face was pale and the flesh seemed to droop from his bones. For a moment Begin thought that the news might be bad but then he saw the excitement in Hofti's eyes and was reassured.

Chairs were found for them and Begin said 'You all know General Hofti.' He indicated Walter. This is Mr Blum. Some of you will know that he has served our country well.'

Walter nodded at the rows of faces.

'What do you have for us, General?' Begin asked.

Hofti opened the envelope and took out a dozen copies of a large photograph. They were passed around the table. Some of the Ministers had to share a copy. There was total silence as they ail studied the photograph, then Begin said 'Please interpret it for us, General.'

Hofti cleared his throat, it was taken by one of our agents in Iraq two days ago at a secret establishment in the north-east of the country. The drums contain uranium oxide - yellowcake. They are part of a shipment of one hundred tons supplied by Colonel Gaddafi. The numbers and lettering have been checked and are on file with the IAEA in Vienna. As you know, the Iraqis cannot use yellowcake as fuel for their new reactor. They can, however, extract enough Pu239 from that shipment to manufacture about twenty Hiroshima-sized nuclear bombs.'

They were all watching him intently. He cleared his throat again and said: 'The two men in the picture are Professor Jabar Mohammed and Professor Saddam Azzawi. They are two of Iraq's top nuclear scientists. Two years ago they were officially reported to have been executed for treason. That was obviously a smoke screen to hide the setting-up of a secret research centre away from the prying eyes of the French and the IAEA inspectors.'

He sat back in his chair and Ariel Sharon laughed quietly and said: 'Is there any more argument?'

There was a general shaking of heads and Begin said 'Then we can give David Ivri his orders.' He turned to Hofti. 'Well done, and to you Mr Blum. It was a magnificent job. Please convey our congratulations and thanks to the man who risked so much to get this proof.'

There were murmurs of agreement around the table and then Walter said flatly:

'I cannot. They caught him.'

Begin's face fell. 'Oh God. When?'

'Only hours after he took that photograph. He managed to get a copy out with a courier.'

Ariel Sharon, always the man of action, asked: 'Do we know where they're holding him? Is there any chance of getting him out?'

'They're holding him in the "Palace of the end".'

'Oh.' Sharon looked glum. He knew all about the "Palace of the end".

'There is a chance,' Hofti said, turning to Begin, it's a very slim one and it's why I brought Mr Blum with me here. But to attempt it will need a Cabinet decision.'

'Explain,' Begin said and Hofti outlined the plan. It centred on the fact that Mossad had an agent, Hammad Shihab, inside the Palace. Up to now he had been passive but this time he would have to be made active, even if it took a threat of exposure to do it. He had already reported that very morning that the agent was being interrogated. So far he had said nothing and the Mukhabarat still believed that he worked for the CIA. In Shihab's opinion the agent could not last more than a week.

Mossad had long had detailed plans of the Palace and, through Shihab, even the exact location of the agent's cell. It was at the end of a corridor. On the other side of the corridor and through a heavy metal door was a courtyard surrounded by stone walls fifty feet high and eight feet thick. Shihab could obtain the key to the door.

'A commando raid?' Sharon asked.

Hofti shook his head.

'Impossible. The Palace is well inside the city. No, we have to breach that wall at a given time. The only way it can be done is by a bomb dropped by an aircraft - a low-flying aircraft. We would like the Air Force to detach one of their planes from the reactor raid and attempt it. The target area is only eight metres by ten.'

'And if the wall is breached,' Begin asked, 'what then?'

Walter supplied the answer. 'One hundred and fifty metres away across the square is the "souk". We believe that in the confusion of the bombing our agent, together with Shihab, could reach it. There will be people waiting for them. It will not be difficult to disappear in the souk. Then they will make their way to a Kurdish safe house. Shihab's wife and two children will be there already. After that the Kurds will get them out through Kurdistan and Turkey. The escape route is arranged.'

Begin asked: 'Have you talked to David Ivri?'

'Yes,' Hofti answered. 'We had a brief chat before we came in here. We showed him the plans of the Palace and the location. He made two points: firstly, that the chances of success given the size of the target and the difficult approach are very slim. Secondly, that because of distance and the need for stealth and deception only eight F16's are to be used on the raid, covered by six F15's in fighter role. He pointed out that five or six bombs will be needed on target to destroy the reactor, so with eight possibilities the margin for error is already very low. That's why he would need a Cabinet decision.'

'We can't send an extra plane?' someone asked.

Mordechai Zipori supplied the answer. 'No. Fourteen in total is the absolute maximum and they have to be exactly co-ordinated. They've been practising for two weeks. The raid is two days away. You can't throw in another plane.' He looked around the table and added grimly 'The choice is stark and simple. For a very slim chance to rescue this agent we must significantly reduce the margin of error in the reactor strike.'

There was a heavy silence, then Hofti said 'Before you take that decision I would like to point something out. We in Mossad have always gone to any lengths to save our agents. It's one of our great strengths and it stems from, the principles on which this country was founded.'

Walter leaned forward, 'I too would like to say something. This agent is not an Israeli, but he is Jewish through his mother, who herself died for Israel here in Jerusalem in 1948. He is a man of great courage who already in his life has been to hell and come back. He is now in hell again. He was to be married after this mission. His wife-to-be is expecting a child.' He pointed to the photograph in front of Begin. 'She too risked her life in order for that photograph to be taken. She collapsed in my office when she heard yesterday that her man had been taken. She's now in hospital under sedation.' He sat back and slowly looked in turn into the eyes of all sixteen Ministers.

'Well,' Begin said. 'We'd better take our decision.' He called out very formally: 'All those in favour of detaching one aircraft from the reactor strike?'

Immediately and in unison sixteen hands were raised.

Two hours later Walter was in another meeting. He had flown with Major-General David Ivri to the Air Force base at Etzion in the Sinai Desert and was standing beside a huge table in the briefing room, watching Colonel Daniel Rener play with a toy aeroplane. The Israeli Air Force has scale models of every major city in the Middle East and at this moment Baghdad in miniature was covering twenty square metres of the table. A small red plastic flag was stuck on top of the inch-high "Palace of the end". Colonel Rener, the mission leader, was leaning over the table holding a tiny F16 in his hand and demonstrating to Walter the difficulties of a low-level bombing run over a built-up area. On the other side of the table Major-General David Ivri was watching and nodding his head in agreement at the points Rener was making.

'The pilot will have the target in sight for only five seconds before releasing his bomb, and he will be coming out of a very tight turn, so the "G" load will be high. If he's ten metres too far left, he misses the corner of the wall. Ten metres to the right and his bomb goes right into your agent's cell.'

'That would be better than missing to the left,' Walter said grimly.

Rener nodded in understanding and went on: 'The pilot only has one pass.' He pointed with his finger to several black circles on the model. 'Surface-to-air missile sites - very nasty. So after release he has to make a sharp banking climb through here. If he gets it wrong by as little as two or three degrees he gets zapped.'

Walter sighed. 'I never thought it would be easy, Colonel.'

"There's another factor,' Rener said. 'Normally for such a mission a pilot would train for many days. The on-board computers would be specially programmed.' He waved at the model. 'OK. A film of this goes into the flight simulator and he has some practice. Also we mock-up and film the building and the wall and that goes into the simulator; but the raid is Sunday. It's not enough time.'

'But it is possible?'

Rener shrugged. 'Anything is possible. I'm just pointing out the chances. I want you to understand. It's about one in three.'

'It's better than nothing,' Walter muttered. 'You'll use your best pilot . . . apart from yourself, I mean.'

'Mr Blum, all my pilots are top rate. They're the best in the best Air Force in the world.'

Walter inclined his head in acknowledgement. 'Let me put it another way. If you yourself were in that place and about now being tortured - who would you want in the pilot's seat?'

Rener slid a look at General Ivri who smiled and said: 'Answer the man, Daniel.'

Rener shrugged. 'It would have to be Major Gideon Galili.'

Waiter smiled grimly. 'Somehow, from the tips of my toes, I thought you would say that.'

CHAPTER TWENTY-ONE

Munger heard the voice through a mist of pain. It was a whispering, insistent voice and it infuriated him. They had kept him awake for seventy-two hours. Counting the night before he was arrested he had gone without sleep for four days and nights. Now, when it last, in spite of the pain, he had finally slipped into unconsciousness, this probing voice was jerking him back to reality and pain. Slowly he opened his eyes, expecting to see the cruel, vengeful face of Sami Asaf. It took a while to realise that the features above him were not contorted with rage, the eyes not filled with hate. They were filled with impatience, but they were kind eyes.

'Munger, can you hear me?'

He managed an affirmative croak.

'My name is Hammad Shihab. I'm a friend. I can only stay a few minutes. It is dangerous. Please listen. The Israelis will attempt to rescue you tomorrow in the afternoon at exactly 5.30. We have to cross the square outside - cross it fast.'

Munger's head rolled on the bunk's wooden slats, 'Never . . . I'll never make it.'

'You can. I'll be with you. I'll help you. It's less than twenty-four hours.'

'But I'll be worse than I am now.'

'No. You will not be tortured again. Sami Asaf has gone to Kifri to find out why their security was so bad. He won't be back until tomorrow night. He gave orders that only he is to interrogate you. That is why they let you sleep. Try to keep your strength. Just one more day.'

'But how? How will we get out?' He was feeling better now. There was a glimmer of hope in the recesses of his brain.

'They will blow up the wall in the courtyard. I don't know how.'

The glimmer became brighter. Munger had an inkling of how they would do it.

'There is a message,' Shihab said. 'From ORANGE ONE. He says to keep faith.'

A slight smile twitched on Munger's lips. 'Yeah, he would . . . Why are you doing this?'

Shihab shrugged. 'ORANGE ONE gave me little choice. Anyway, it's time I left this place before I go insane.'

Munger grimaced. 'I agree with the sentiments.'

'I must go,' Shihab said. 'Try to sleep now.' He reached down and gently squeezed Munger's shoulder and then quickly withdrew his hand and apologised as Munger winced in pain.

After Shihab left Munger tried to decide whether he had been hallucinating or dreaming but the pain in his shoulder even from the gentle pressure had been real enough. He closed his eyes. Time would tell. He would keep faith. He began to slide into sleep again and the face of Ruth drifted out of the mists. It was real. She was with him. Just as she had been, all the time, making the nightmare bearable. Even as they beat him with rubber hoses, as they clamped the electric leads to his body, as they laughed and joked as he twisted in agony. She was always there - a lifeline to his sanity.

On Sunday morning at 10 am Baghdad time the Iraqi Ministry of Information called a press conference and, amid much indignation and propaganda, announced to the world that the Security Forces had arrested a CIA spy. He was the famous photographer David Munger, caught trying to smuggle classified war information out of Iraq after attempting to bribe Iraqi officials.

At 11 am Walter Blum was sitting in Daniel Rener's office listening to him say:

'It's totally out of the question. Galili has already spent eight hours in the simulator. There's no time for another pilot to get practice. God, man, we take off in just over five hours. Why the hell didn't you tell me all this earlier?'

'I didn't expect it,' Walter said unhappily, it was a complete surprise. I can only imagine that the Iraqis are trying to embarrass the Americans for reasons of their own. At least it shows that Munger is holding out.'

'You're sure that Galili will connect it?'

'Of course,' Walter said. 'The moment he hears the news . . . I don't suppose there's a chance of isolating him before take-off?'

Rener shook his head. 'No way.' He glanced at his watch. 'Right now he's in the simulator. He'll be finished in half an hour. Then the crews have a light lunch together and take a rest for a couple of hours before final briefing. Some of them will have already heard it on the radio. It'll be a big talking point.'

Walter sighed and Rener said in awe: 'I've heard of love triangles but nothing like this. Sure, Gideon's been very quiet and withdrawn the past year or so. I had no idea what caused it.'

'He's a man obsessed,' Walter said glumly.

Rener shook his head as if to clear it. 'Mr Blum. You're worrying too much. I've known Gideon Galili since he was a trainee pilot twelve years ago. He's a fine man, and a fine Israeli. He was thrilled when he got this assignment. Thrilled to have a chance to save this man.'

'He didn't know who he was.'

'It makes no difference,' Rener said firmly. 'He's a professional and a patriot. He'll do his best.' His eyes narrowed. 'You'd better believe that. You know the odds. If he misses it won't be for want of trying.'

Walter sighed again and Rener asked: 'Do you want me to talk to him?'

'No, I'll do it.' Walter got to his feet. 'I'll catch him as he comes out of the simulator.'

Half an hour later Rener looked through his office window and saw them walking together outside the briefing room. They presented an odd contrast: the tall, slim pilot and the fat, garish civilian. Galili was bending his head to catch Walter's words. For a moment they stopped and turned and watched as a formation of F15's lifted off the distant runway and screamed into the sky. Then they were walking again and the pilot was talking and putting his hand on Walter's shoulder.

At 3.00 pm Spiro parked the Mercedes outside the main doors of the Saint Barnabas Hospital in Limassol. He saw Ruth hobbling down the steps and quickly went up to take her small suitcase.

As they drove up towards Platres he kept glancing at her in the rear view mirror. She was lovely and she was sad.

She had received a phone call from Walter an hour before. He was keeping a promise. His voice was faint and he said nothing indiscreet. Just that action was being taken before 6 o'clock. There was only a slim chance. He would let her know as soon as he had positive news - one way or the other. He asked her how she was and she told him much better. She would go home to Platres. She would wait for news there. He was pleased. He told her he would get in touch with the office. Spiro would collect her.

As they passed through the village of Kalini she saw the little Greek Orthodox church on the square. On an impulse she pressed a button and lowered the glass partition and asked Spiro to stop.

Being Sunday the villagers were dressed in their best clothes. They sat on chairs and benches at their front doors and outside the taverna, gossiping and fanning themselves in the sultry heat.

They watched her curiously as she limped across the square and went up the steps into the church.

An old, bearded priest dressed in black and with a high, flat-topped hat greeted her at the door arid told her that the service was over. Then he noted with curiosity the small gold Star of David at her throat. She looked past him into the dark, cool interior and at the high altar with its icons and long, ivory candles with flickering flames.

'Is it possible,' she asked, 'for me to stay here for an hour or two?'

He looked down at her and caught the sadness in her face and nodded. 'You are welcome.'

She turned and went back to the car and asked Spiro if he would wait for her. He smiled and gestured at the taverna and told her to be as long as she wanted.

In the church she sat at a pew near the back. She was not a religious woman. She could not remember when she had last consciously prayed. She was in a church, alien to her own, but it made no difference. She entertained no thoughts of a divine intervention. In this place, this house of God, she would compose herself.

It was an hour later when the priest came back from his afternoon siesta. He looked in through the door and saw her on her knees.

CHAPTER TWENTY-TWO

At 3.45 pm the transports took the pilots out to the aircraft.

Dressed in their anti-G suits and torso harnesses and carrying their helmets and oxygen masks they looked like astronauts about to invade outer space. They did not talk much. There was no false jocularity or words of bravado. Each was a finely-tuned amalgamation of natural talent and endless hours of competitive training. They represented the elite of the world's pilots.

Gideon Galili's five-man ground crew watched him climb out of the transport and, as it moved away, stand and for over a minute gaze at his aircraft. It was something he always did.

The F16 gleamed and glistened in the sunlight, the long slug of the bomb bulging under its sleek belly. There was an impatience about it as though it was irked to be shackled to the earth. The ground crew did not see it that way. For them it was a machine that needed hours of pampering care. A machine with miles of wires, thousands of moving parts and a host of temperamental electronics. It took thousands of man-hours a month to keep it operational. But when it flew it was the finest weapon in the skies.

Gideon nodded at the crew and moved forward to do his walk around check, intoning to himself:

'Intake-orifice covers and plugs removed . . . Ground locks out . . . Panels secured . . . Bomb secured . . . Fusing lanyard connected.'

The crew watched impassively. It was routine. They knew, and he knew, that everything was perfect. Like him, they were the best.

He reached the metal steps, handed his helmet and oxygen mask to his fitter, clambered up and leaned into the cockpit.

'Brakes on . . . Armament switches safe . . . Ejection seat safe . . . Parachute and drogue lines correct . . .'

Around the airfield inside thirteen other widely dispersed blast shelters thirteen other pilots were going through exactly the same checks. On this day and for this mission not one of them would find the merest fault.

Gideon Galili climbed into the cockpit, settled himself into the reclined seat and his fitter leaned over and helped to connect him up.

'Survival pack to torso harness . . . Lap belt tight . . . Parachute harness to torso harness . . . Helmet on . . . Oxygen and R/T lead connected . . . Oxygen flow OK . . . Ejection seat safety pins out . . . Firing handles live...'

The fitter climbed down, removed the ladder and went to the front of the aircraft to wait for start-up. Gideon ran through the pre-start-up checks. Then, when they were complete, he waved a raised thumb in front of his visor. The fitter had slipped on ear plugs and a throat mike. A wire snaked up to a socket under the F16's jaw.

It was 4.15 pm and, from the other side of the airfield, they heard the first engine roar into life.

In the cockpit Gideon's thumb was about to press the starter button when the decision finally erupted like an exploding star shell in his brain. He was stunned by it. Stunned by the certainty. He was going to miss! He was going to miss to the right!

He lay there with his thumb poised on the starter button. He was in a state of sublime exultation. He was as one with the bomb three feet below him. With all his talent, all his training and all his will, he would guide it ten metres to the right of the target. It would have a new target. What had they told him? Better to miss to the right than the left . . . Better he dies than be left to the mercy of the Mukhabarat. Gideon Galili would give him that release.

Suddenly the fitter's voice was in his ears. He shook himself and brought his mind back. Took in the anxious words.

'Is everything all right sir? All the others have started up.'

'Sure. All checks OK.' His thumb stabbed out. He heard the engine wind up, the igniters crackle and a moment later felt and heard the dull roar as the F16 came to life.

At 4.30 the aircraft began to taxi out. Walter stood in the control tower next to General Ivri and watched them emerge from their shelters and converge on the end of the runway, each slotting into position as if in a formal choreographed dance. There was no R/T communication between the aircraft and the tower or between themselves. They would not risk even the slightest chance of a freak radio wave being picked up by enemy ears. They were moving into pairs now; the F16's in front and the F15's following.

'Galili is on the left in the third pair,' Ivri murmured and then he added, 'Colonel Rener told me of the connection between him and the agent. It's amazing . . . But you can set your mind at rest. Gideon Galili will do his job, and do it well.'

'I know,' Walter answered, 'I talked to him for half an hour.

'Afterwards I felt embarrassed about my doubts.'

There came a crescendo of noise and the seven pairs of aircraft were gathering speed down the long, black runway. The first pair lifted off in front of the tower, raising their noses and climbing steeply. The second pair became airborne but stayed low to avoid the slipstream of the first pair. The third pair completed the pattern by lifting high.

Walter was watching the left-hand plane in the third pair. He could just make out the visored head under the canopy. He felt a surge of confidence. The whole spectacle had been one of graceful perfection.

'Now the waiting starts,' Ivri said. 'Thank God this time it won't be too long. Just an hour.'

'This time?'

'Yes. The last similar occasion was the Entebbe raid. I wasn't in command of the Air Force but I was on the planning - and the waiting. I aged ten years in one day.'

He took Walter's arm. 'Come on. Let's go to the Command Room.'

Gideon flew the plane like an automaton, but he flew it well. His right hand resting lightly on the stick at his side, his feet gentle on the rudder bars, his eyes scanning the instruments and the changing pattern of the windscreen's head-up-display which was on navigation mode. The radars were at standby with blank screens so as to avoid the possibility of enemy signal detection.

The F16's were flying in loose tactical formation and though most of Gideon's brain was not functioning he kept his position instinctively as they crossed the Gulf of Aqaba and then banked slightly onto a new course over the coast of Saudi Arabia. The working part of his brain was occupied with thoughts of Munger and Ruth and Walter Blum. They were not rational thoughts, but scattered and random. Listening to Walter Blum: 'She loves him. You must understand that. She collapsed when she heard the news. Couldn't take it. Whatever happens I believe that she'll never love anyone else . . . never.'

His own words: 'Be calm, Mr Blum. I'll do my best. It has nothing to do with Ruth or anything else. I know why he's in there. What they're doing to him. It's tricky but I'll do my best. Have no doubts.'

He thought of those first hours when Colonel Rener told him he had been selected to attempt the roof-top skimming bombing run to release a man who had risked so much for Israel. He remembered the pride he felt. He remembered the hours strapped into the simulator, seeing for the first time the impossibility of what they were asking him to do. Then working at it, applying all his skills, making one simulated 500 knot run after another, always missing the target as he tried, all within fleeting seconds, to acquire the target, line up with the HUD symbol and trigger the computer to unleash the bomb at the release point. Time after time he had fluffed it, acquiring the target too late and missing. Then, during the third session, as the simulator crew had watched with growing admiration, he had begun to get it together; flying smoothly and accurately, acquiring the target earlier and earlier, shrinking the diameter of the bomb impact points. By the last session over sixty per cent of his attacks were on target. When he climbed out of the simulator for the last time the crew gathered around and shook his hand and shook their heads in awe. But it was the motive that had driven him. The motive that concentrated all his faculties.

Then waiting for him outside was Walter Blum and he had dropped his bomb - right on target. The hero at the other end was Munger. It was a name like a cancer in Gideon's mind. Munger - the man who had taken Ruth. Munger, the demon who had destroyed his future. So something had snapped. It was a schizoid cleaving of his brain. The large part was paralysed; the tiny part still functioning had taken the decision and now flew the aircraft. The F16 was in the hands of a mentally ill man.

There were sounds in his ears again. It was Colonel Rener talking to the controller at the Ma'an base. Gideon only half listened to the carefully rehearsed Arabic patter. A few minutes later the fingers of his left hand worked over the navigation computer console and his eyes watched the symbols of the HUD display flicker and change as the formation banked onto a new course-East-North-East towards Baghdad.

In the Etzion Command Room General Ivri pointed to a spot on a wall map and said to Walter:

'He'll leave the formation here, just south of Ar Ramādī. Then, three minutes later, he'll be over Baghdad on his bombing run.' He turned to look at a wall clock.

'About fifteen minutes from now.'

Walter nodded and looked around the room. There were banks of computer screens watched by calm operators, a girl passing out plastic cups of coffee. The base Commander and a group of officers clustered in a group, talking quietly. Occasionally one of them would glance up at the black loudspeaker in the top corner of the room. It would carry the voice-relays when the pilots broke radio silence to report success or failure of their bombing runs. He felt he could sink his fingers into the tension. His own heart was racing.

They crossed the Iraqi border at 200 feet. Occasionally the planes would rise and fall gently like drifting seagulls on a breeze as the pilots hugged the contours of the rolling desert below.

At 5.20 pm a symbol flashed on Gideon's HUD and the operating portion of his brain clicked into gear. He peeled his F16 out of the formation and headed due east. His left hand reached out and flicked on the missile warning receiver. He crossed the flat water of the Lake of Habbaniyan and a minute later screamed over the first outer suburbs of Baghdad. There were three pictures now in his brain, flashing intermittently one after the other: what he could see through the windscreen, superimposed on recollections from the simulator runs; the symbols of the HUD display and, finally, the grey stone wall of the "Palace of the end".

There were higher buildings now. The F16 banked first to the left and then to the right, weaving a path to take it clear of missile emplacements. He started his final run in and in his mental vision was the model of the wall. He was looking at a point ten metres to the right - a point above a wide buttress. That was the point on which he would place his HUD target symbol in a few seconds. That was the point behind which Munger lay waiting.

Now he saw reality through his canopy. A curving row of buildings, a different darker colour than those on the simulator - but the same. He was banking sharply, forced back into his seat by the G-force. He knew that beyond those buildings was a broad avenue and then the square and facing him across that the "Palace of the end" and the wall. In his mind's eye he saw again the point above the buttress covered by the HUD symbol. Every second was being split into milliseconds. He saw everything perfectly. Buildings flashing past his wing-tip only metres away. The avenue opening as the F16, straightened up. There was the square. There was the wall - and the buttress. The attack symbol slid above it. His fingers moved to the computer trigger.

Then . . . a voice in his ears - calm, flat. The voice of Colonel Daniel Rener.

'Red Leader to base. Bomb gone - on target.'

It was the voice of a pilot - an Israeli pilot completing a perfect mission and in an instant it slammed into Gideon's brain like a bolt of lightning and healed its sickness. In the next millisecond his right hand shifted the stick while his left foot nudged the rudder bar. The HUD target symbol swung a fraction across the looming wall and his fingers triggered the computer.

Three seconds later the F16 jumped as it shed 1000 lbs and rose, bouncing away into the sky. The bomb had a delayed fuse of half a second. It slammed into the grey wall, paused and then blew it apart. Up in the sky Gideon Galili was sobbing behind his visor, his whole body quivering with the shock of how close he had come. How close to negating every principle, every element of his beliefs and his training. He pulled the F16 into a climbing turn to the west down a predetermined missile-free track. He turned and saw the explosion and the debris punched into the sky and across the wide square. He heard the other pilots reporting their successes at El-Tuwaitha and he flicked on his microphone and, in a shaking voice, said:

'Red Three to base. Bomb gone - on target.'

Then he was levelling the aircraft out and turning back. He was going to take a look. He knew his fuel limitations and he knew about the missile danger. He did not care. He had been dead and now he was alive - resurrected. He eased forward the stick and cut the power and speed right back and slanted down to the dust-filled square.

He thought he saw them. They were two-thirds across. Two men. One was hobbling, the other helping him, arms around him, half dragging the limp torso. They were moving painfully slowly. There was no other movement in the square. They would surely make it to the 'souk'.

Then from out of the dust around the "Palace of the end" a group of men dressed in khaki uniforms appeared, running towards the fugitives.

He cursed. If only the F16 had not been stripped of its cannon. No matter. He poured on the power, felt the punch as the plane leapt forward out of its glide and lined up on the pursuing men. An F16 afterburner screaming twenty feet above a man's head is akin to a lifetime in hell distilled into two heartbeats. As Gideon pulled up he turned and saw the men scattering, their hands over their ears. Three of them were lying huddled on the ground. He laughed out loud. It was a fair bet that they all had brown trousers. There was no sign of Munger and his helper. They had made it. Gideon's laugh died. He had a mental picture of Ruth waiting for her lover - her future husband. So be it. He would live with the pain.

He looked at the HUD and had started to compute his course out when there came a high-pitched shriek and his eyes flicked to the missile warning receiver. His heart went cold when he realised that missiles were locked onto him. His last dive and pull-out had taken him close to the Palace housing the Government offices and close to the banks of missiles guarding it. He knew they would be SAMs and probably two salvos of two. He pulled round in a tight left-hand turn, momentarily blacked out from the G-force and then automatically he hit the electronic countermeasure button. He knew the distances exactly. If a SAM got within two hundred metres it would lock on and his countermeasures would be useless. At one hundred feet, its radio proximity fuse would detonate and metal rods would explode at hypersonic speed into his line of flight. From his missile warning receiver he could tell that one had broken lock. The other was coming in from left. He could not outpace it so he dived and turned hard towards it, hoping that his G's would cause the missile to overshoot.

He almost made it. Surely it was a matter of only a yard or two. But the shriek continued and he knew he would die in a second. He actually saw a silver shape from the corner of his eye. His last thought was: 'I gave him to you'.

There was a flash of fire in front of him and Gideon Galili and his F16 disintegrated in a ball of flame.

CHAPTER TWENTY-THREE

As news of the Israeli air strike on El-Tuwaitha spread across the world, condemnation bounced back in a mighty echo. While officers of dozens of the world's air forces quietly applauded the planning and precision of the raid, the politicians and statesmen of those countries loudly and publicly proclaimed their horror. Orchestrated by France and Iraq they waxed eloquent about the unbridled aggression of the Jewish state and they endorsed the statement of the Secretary General of the IAEA that all the evidence at the disposal of his agency showed that Iraq's nuclear programme was designed only for peaceful purposes.

President Reagan issued a statement which was later described as couched in the strongest language ever directed by an American President at its long-time ally.

In the halls and corridors of the United Nations delegates began drafting a resolution demanding mandatory sanctions against Israel. The American delegation, was confused and silent. It was rumoured that the State Department was advising the President to teach Israel a lesson by drastically reducing US military and financial aid. A White House 'leak' reported that Reagan considered Menachem Begin akin to a dangerous lunatic.

Three days later in the early morning of June 10th, General Yitzhak Hofti arrived in Washington aboard a transport plane of the Israeli Air Force. He went straight to Langley and spent two hours with William J. Casey, the Director of the CIA. In the afternoon a meeting took place in the Oval Office of the White House. It comprised President Reagan, Alexander Haig, General Yitzhak Hofti and William J. Casey.

From his briefcase General Hofti took a slim file and a large photograph. Together the President and Secretary of State read the file and studied the photograph. Then they looked up at William J Casey. He nodded and said:

'Our analysts confirm that it's authentic.'

There was a long silence and then Reagan said to Hofti:

'The Secretary of State will issue a statement indicating that although our Government feels that Israel acted precipitously, there are grounds to believe that there was justification.' He paused, glanced at Haig, and then added:

'Of course, there will be no cuts in aid. Any sanctions resolution at the UN will be vetoed by our Government.' A slight smile appeared on Hofti's lips, 'Thank you sir.' Reagan glanced down at his desk. 'Tell me, General. How was this photograph obtained?'

'With great courage and sacrifice, Mr President.'

EPILOGUE

It was a decade later. A decade that had seen Israel slowly and painfully make peace with its neighbours. It was a peace sometimes strained, and often suspicious; but it was peace and the people of Israel gradually adjusted and spent their energies arguing with each other, which is what they enjoyed most.

On a late summer afternoon Walter Blum drove to Ben-Gurion Airport to greet a visitor. Since his retirement he had lived in Jerusalem and rarely travelled abroad, preferring instead for his friends to come to him.

He was an old man now, and not in the best of health. Two slight heart attacks the year before had caused much concern. He was told to cut back on his over-indulgent habits, but his philosophy was such that a life without indulgences was no life at all. He was quite resigned to meeting his maker and arguing the point.

He had many visitors from all over the world but he was especially looking forward to greeting this one. He was a ten-year-old boy and he would stay with Walter for two weeks. His parents were away in the West Indies on an assignment for a magazine and concurrently celebrating their tenth wedding anniversary. During the coming two weeks Walter was to show the boy something of Israel and, at the same time, explain a few things about his antecedents. His parents thought that he had reached an age when he could understand, and that Walter was the ideal person to explain.

The boy came out through Customs, spotted Walter immediately, ran over and threw his arms around his neck. Walter beamed and held him at arms' length and studied him. He had grown a lot since last year. He was tall for his age, and slim, with dark hair and very blue eyes and an open, enquiring face.

So they toured the country, visiting the old battlefields in the deserts and the mountains, the archaeological sites and the historic monuments and buildings, the kibbutzim and the cities. All the time Walter talked and the boy listened; sometimes he grew a little bored as any ten-year-old would, but he never showed it, for he loved and respected the old man.

On the last day they went to Mount Herzl in Jerusalem, to the burial ground of the men and women who had helped create Israel; the soldiers and statesmen, the workers and thinkers.

In spite of the proximity of the city it was strangely quiet among the endless rows of flat, white gravestones. Walter led the boy to one of them and translated the Hebrew inscription and told him about his grandmother. The boy asked a lot of questions and listened to the answers solemnly. Later they walked to the Memorial of the Unknown Soldier. This is surrounded by the graves of men and women who had been killed in the many wars and never been identified. It also contains graves for those whose bodies have never been recovered. The gravestones are all alike.

The boy noticed a few small pebbles on several of the graves. He asked about them and Walter explained that the custom went back thousands of years to when the Jews lived in the desert. Stones were piled over graves to protect them from scavenging animals. Somehow the custom had survived as a symbolic gesture of protection for the dead.

They reached a grave close to the Memorial and Walter took the boy's arm and translated the inscription and told him of a man who had died on the 7th June, 1981. When he finished talking the boy stood looking at the gravestone for a long time. Then he reached down and picked up two small pebbles from the path and laid them on the white marble.

The name of the boy was Gideon Munger.

The name on the gravestone: Gideon Galili.

Printed in Dunstable, United Kingdom

70487872R00188